full ride

Also by Margaret Peterson Haddix

The Missing Series
Found
Sent
Sabotaged
Torn
Caught
Risked

The Shadow Children Series
Among the Hidden
Among the Impostors
Among the Betrayed
Among the Barons
Among the Brave
Among the Enemy
Among the Free

The Girl with 500 Middle Names
Because of Anya
Say What?
Dexter the Tough
Running Out of Time
Game Changer
The Always War
Claim to Fame
Palace of Mirrors
Uprising
Double Identity
The House on the Gulf
Escape from Memory
Takeoffs and Landings
Turnabout
Just Ella
Leaving Fishers
Don't You Dare Read This, Mrs. Dunphrey

SIMON & SCHUSTER BOOKS FOR YOUNG READERS

An imprint of Simon & Schuster Children's Publishing Division

1230 Avenue of the Americas, New York, New York 10020

SIMON & SCHUSTER BFYR is a trademark of Simon & Schuster, Inc.

For information about special discounts for bulk purchases,
please contact Simon & Schuster Special Sales at 1-866-506-1949
or business@simonandschuster.com.

The Simon & Schuster Speakers Bureau can bring authors to your live event.
For more information or to book an event, contact the Simon & Schuster Speakers Bureau at
1-866-248-3049 or visit our website at www.simonspeakers.com.

Book design by Krista Vossen

The text for this book is set in Apollo.

Manufactured in the United States of America

2 4 6 8 10 9 7 5 3 1

Library of Congress Cataloging-in-Publication Data

Haddix, Margaret Peterson.

Full ride / Margaret Peterson Haddix. — 1st ed.

p. cm.

Summary: After her father is convicted of embezzlement, Becca Jones, fourteen, and her
mother flee Georgia for small-town Ohio but three years later she learns that his misdeeds
may have jeopardized not just her future but also her life.

ISBN 978-1-4424-4278-8 (hardcover)

ISBN 978-1-4424-4280-1 (eBook)

[1. Secrets—Fiction. 2. High schools—Fiction. 3. Schools—Fiction. 4. Mothers and
daughters—Fiction. 5. Criminals—Fiction. 6. Ohio—Fiction.] I. Title.

PZ7.H1164Ful 2013

[Fic]—dc23

2012038146

FIRST EDITION

MARGARET
HAD[...]

full rid[e]

SIMON & SCHUSTER BFYR

NEW YORK LONDON TORONTO SYDNEY NEW DELHI

For three true friends: Christy, Kathy, and Patti

Then

My mother and I ran away after the trial.

We'd gone back to the house and it felt completely wrong: too big, too empty, too booby-trapped with memories.

I used to sit there by the front window when I was a little kid, waiting for Daddy to come home from work. . . . He won't be coming home now.

We always put our Christmas tree in that corner. Why would we bother putting up a Christmas tree ever again? What would we have to celebrate?

I wandered through the living room, the dining room, the kitchen. Mom had sold off all the furniture that was worth anything, so only the mismatched and the broken and the pathetic remained behind: chairs too spindly to actually sit on, lamps that would have been yard-sale rejects, things we'd put down in the basement to fix or give away and then, in happier times, simply forgotten. We'd been eating our meals the past few months at a card table with a bad leg, so I'd gotten into the habit of holding onto my dishes as I ate, for fear that the table would suddenly plunge to the floor and all would be lost. But now even that card table looked like an ancient artifact, a remnant of a more hopeful life.

Because hadn't the plunge I was most afraid of just happened? Wasn't everything lost now? Why had I been foolish enough to think I could save anything by holding on?

Like the furniture, I was just some pathetic broken thing left behind. I'd been powerless to stop anything.

In the kitchen, I bumped into the back wall. I felt so ghostlike and hollow that I was almost baffled at not being able to just walk on through it. Maybe I was more like a different kind of monster: one of those zombies that got trapped in a corner and could never turn around, and so just kept walking endlessly in place, going nowhere.

I made a sound deep in my throat that might have been the start of a chuckle if it'd come from somebody else's throat, at some other time.

Or the start of hysterics, coming from my throat, then.

"Oh," Mom said from behind me. "The calendar. That. When . . ."

I'd forgotten about Mom being there. Which was weird, because we'd practically been joined at the hip during the trial: hustled together past the waiting cameras into the federal courthouse each day; sitting side by side in the courtroom's churchlike wooden pews throughout the testimony, even taking bathroom breaks together because it was easier for the paralegal to sneak us in and out all at once.

I turned around—*see, I can do that much! I'm not actually a zombie, after all!* But any small burst of triumph I felt disappeared at the sight of Mom.

She was still wearing the conservative gray suit she'd had on in court. The lawyer had given strict instructions about what Mom and I were supposed to wear: Everything had to be bland, dull colored, unprovocative. Who actually owns clothes like that? On our budget—on what had become of our budget—this meant shopping in secondhand stores in hopes of finding something left over from the 1950s. Hopefully, previously owned by a nun.

"No teenager should have a whole section of her closet devoted to going-to-court clothes," Mom had said once, standing in the doorway of my room.

But I did.

At fourteen, I was still small boned and flat chested and scrawny. The best I could hope for in those courtroom clothes was that they might make me look Amish. And so that was one of the thoughts that had gotten me through the hours of testimony.

I am not going to get upset about the awful things people are saying about my father. I will just pretend I am a simple Amish girl with nothing on my mind except milking cows and churning butter. And God. Wouldn't a simple Amish girl think about God? Wouldn't she be praying with all her simple heart that her father would be cleared of all the charges against him?

She would have, and I did too.

But the jury found my father guilty.

I was still staring at Mom. I realized I was trying to get my eyes to see her differently: in a floral sundress, maybe, her honey-colored hair sculpted perfectly around her smiling face, a pitcher of lemonade and a tray of sugar cookies in her hands as she headed outside to host a pool party or a garden party or yet another of my famous birthday parties. . . . That was my real mother. That was how she was supposed to look, how she was supposed to act.

Except our pool was drained and covered now. We hadn't used it all summer. We'd stopped the yard service, and the garden was being taken over by kudzu. And my birthday . . . my birthday had happened during the trial. Mom had tried to celebrate, as much as she could. She'd suggested a special breakfast before court: maybe something from Starbucks, a forbidden luxury now. Or maybe a late dinner after court with a few friends, not the usual huge pack but the really special ones, the ones who had stayed by me.

"No," I said. And Mom was kind: She let it go. She didn't make me spell out my reasons.

This birthday could never be anything but awful, and pretending to celebrate would only make things worse. And, anyhow, what makes you think I have any *friends who stayed by me?*

I didn't receive a single happy birthday e-mail, card, or call. The closest thing I got to a gift was a lie I allowed myself about why all my friends had ignored my birthday:

That's just not how teenagers do things. If I still had a cell phone, my friends would be texting me birthday wishes like crazy. If the lawyer hadn't told me to take down my Facebook page, I'd see a thousand "Happy Birthdays" there. Everybody says happy birthday on Facebook, no matter what. No matter who you're related to.

Actually, one other person besides Mom did remember: Daddy. He turned around in his defendant's seat, even though he wasn't supposed to, and he gave me a big thumbs-up and mouthed the words, *Fourteen today! My grown-up girl!*

There was more that he expected me to lip read—probably something about how he'd throw me a really huge party after this whole mess was over, after he'd proved he was innocent and he'd won a multimillion-dollar lawsuit for being prosecuted unfairly. But I'd looked away, drilling my gaze into the official United States court seal on the wall. Above the words "Northern District of Georgia," the arrows in the eagle's claw looked mercilessly sharp.

"It's next week," Mom said, bringing me back to our own

kitchen, to the postverdict world, to a real life that simply could not be mine.

"Huh?" I said. I put together everything Mom had said: *Oh, the calendar. That. When . . . It's next week.* I couldn't tell if the problem was that she wasn't making sense, or that I was incapable of finding sense in anything anymore.

Mom lifted one shaking hand and pointed at a single square on the calendar on the wall: Tuesday, August 4. Way back at the beginning of the year, Mom had drawn a lacy border around that date and written in her frothy, exuberant script: "Becca's first day of high school! Hurray!"

Tuesday, August 4, was next week.

Even though I'd completely forgotten about it, high school was one week—no, five days—away.

I backed away from the calendar.

"Mom, I can't," I said, my voice clotted with shame. "I can't do it. Everybody will know."

She looked at me, looked deep. And I think she had to have seen the truth in what I was saying, or at least my rock-solid conviction: I really couldn't. I couldn't climb the stairs of Belpre High School. I couldn't walk those marbled hallways that had seemed so shiny and exciting and promise filled back during eighth-grade visit day, back before my father was arrested. I couldn't fold my body into those gleaming wooden desks and sit there and learn anything about English or science or math while I was assaulted with stares and whispers and behind-my-back gossip: "Don't you know who that is? Don't you know what her father did?" I couldn't go to cheerleading tryouts or football games or homecoming dances. With all the crimes that the jury had convicted my father of, they'd actually left one out: He also stole high school from me.

And Mom knew this. I could see it in her eyes, as she was seeing it in mine.

"Then . . . don't," Mom said, as if she were just now figuring this out. As if it were easy. "You don't have to go to Belpre. You can go somewhere else. Somewhere nobody knows about your daddy."

I let out a bitter laugh, twisted and mean.

"Mom, it was on the news," I said. "Everybody knows everywhere."

I got a sick feeling in the pit of my stomach—it was like I could feel the news spreading, right that moment. The news of the verdict would be on TV newscasts and radio talk shows and Internet websites. I could practically hear the words whispering past me, the invisible waves streaming through me, a poison, an epidemic, a plague. It would be on Facebook already, that mix of gloating disguised as sympathy *(Did y'all hear Becca's daddy's going to prison? Can you imagine what it'd be like to be her?)* and the comments that were nothing but pure meanness *(They should have the death penalty for people like him. . . . And what about Becca? Don't you think she and her mom knew all along what he was doing?)*.

"I don't mean around here," Mom said. She was starting to get a wild look in her eye. She ran her hand over her head, knocking against the severe barrette that had clenched her hair back into its prim court-appropriate bun. The barrette hung half-in, half-out. "We could move. We could go far away, where nobody knows anything about us. We could start fresh."

"Mom, it was on the *national* news, remember?" I reminded her. "It was on CNN. It was in *The New York Times*. There's nowhere we can go to get away from this." I looked down at my sacklike dress. "Unless you want to go live with the Amish. Or in Antarctica."

Mom yanked out a kitchen drawer and pulled out the tray of silverware. It was like she was preparing to pack already.

"Mom?" I said doubtfully.

Mom pulled out the next drawer and added a stack of dish towels on top of the silverware. She *was* getting ready to pack.

"Everybody's heard about your father and what he did," she said. "Everybody saw pictures of him. But not pictures of us. Not so much. Not as many. That's *why* we always hid our faces, going in and out of court."

She started to laugh, a little manically.

"Really, who's going to remember your name? Or mine?" She flailed her arms wildly. "Our last name is Jones! Jones! There are a million Joneses! Even the IRS can't keep track of them all!"

This had been a major factor in Daddy's trial, because some other Roger Jones's tax records had gotten mixed up with his. The lawyer had thought it would be a way for Daddy to get off scot-free. He'd been wrong, but Mom seemed to have forgotten this.

She moved on to yanking open the cabinet where we kept our plates.

"It's perfect!" she cried. "Why didn't I think of this sooner? We don't have to get fake, new, anonymous-sounding names to go into hiding because we already have anonymous-sounding names. We'll just go where nobody knows us, and we'll be fine!"

She pulled down a stack of plates and began counting mugs. If I didn't do something soon, she'd have the whole kitchen in boxes.

"Mom, what about . . . ," I began. I really wanted to say, "What about our friends? How could we leave them?" But I couldn't force the words out. Not after nobody had wished me happy birthday. Not after all the casseroles and the drop-by visitors had stopped showing up on our doorstep about the time it became clear that this wasn't just "one huge awful governmental mistake," as everyone had wanted to believe.

"What about your job?" I asked instead. "You said you were going to get a job."

Mom stopped her counting and looked me right in the face.

"Who was ever going to hire a notorious criminal's wife?" she asked.

I heard an echo in her words, something she would never say but I knew was there: *And who would ever give a criminal's daughter a fair shake in high school? Who would ever pick her as a cheerleader, who would ever give her the lead in the school play, who would even save her a seat in the school cafeteria?*

Mom put her arm around my shoulder and hugged me close.

"But everything will be fine, as long as nobody knows who we are," she said. "It'll be like . . . like our own private witness protection program."

"Witness" sounded like such a pure, innocent word. Like some poor unsuspecting bystander who had just accidentally ended up in the wrong place at the wrong time. Someone who deserved protection, who deserved to be kept safe from crimes and criminals and everything else that was ugly and evil in this world.

I was standing there in my stripped-bare house, having just spent the past three weeks hearing that everything I thought I knew about my father and my family and my safe, happy, cozy childhood was wrong. It was like my life had been picked over by vultures—my memories of the past were ruined and my dreams for the future were ruined and everyone and everything I'd ever cared about was ruined. I was standing there in a baglike dress that might as well have been sackcloth and ashes.

And Mom was saying we could walk away from all that. We could start over again, clean and fresh and new.

And maybe she could. But the purity, the innocence of that word "witness" hovered just out of reach for me. I couldn't claim it for myself.

How could I, when I'd been the reason for my father's crimes?

Still Then

We decided to head north. This seemed right to me. Everybody always moved south—to Georgia, to Florida, to the Carolinas—for the sunshine, the warmth, the easy living. Mom and Daddy had moved south when they'd gotten married. It made sense that Mom and I would reverse that, buck the trend, go backward to start new.

And, anyhow, it didn't seem like we deserved sunshine or warmth or ease anymore. Things froze in the north, in the wintertime. I was looking forward to ice and numbness.

But in the meantime it was August in Georgia. It was 106 degrees as we packed the car, the day after Daddy's sentencing. We couldn't get everything to fit, so we had to rent a U-Haul trailer to hitch onto the back. The guy at the rental place wasn't sure Mom could handle it.

"Don't worry; I grew up around trucks," she told him. "My daddy was a mechanic. I was always the one who helped him with busted axles."

Just the way she said those two words—"busted axles"—made him look at her hard. She was back to wearing what I thought of as normal clothes: khaki slacks, a classy, understated-but-still-sexy Ann Taylor blouse. And even though we were moving and it was hot, she'd put some effort into her hair, so it framed her face in its usual honey-colored waves. But "busted axles" made it sound like she was some completely different person underneath those clothes and that hair. It was almost like she'd peeled back that tailored blouse to reveal a tangle of tattoos across her skin.

We got back in the car, the trailer hitched on tight, and I was unaccountably furious.

"Mom, why . . ." I couldn't even put a name to the reason for my fury. I settled for, "Why'd you have to dress like that here? Why didn't you just wear jeans and a T-shirt? That's what any normal person would wear to move!"

Mom spun the steering wheel, backing out before she answered.

"I had to look like my credit card wouldn't get rejected," she said. "Like they wouldn't even have to check."

That silenced me. Were we in danger of having our credit card rejected? Had we become that kind of people?

Of course we had. The government had confiscated almost everything we owned. Mom was allowed to keep the house, but it hadn't sold yet. And she'd been allowed to keep her Lexus, but she'd traded it in for an eight-year-old Ford. She'd used the leftover money to pay some of the legal fees and other debts.

Was there any money left after the debts?

I sat there, almost panting in the heat, and I knew I had to offer Mom some sort of consolation, some comfort. Some guarantee that *I* wouldn't turn against her.

"At least the rental guy didn't know who we are," I said. "He didn't know *why* we don't have any money anymore."

Beside me, my mother started crying.

• • •

We drove through Tennessee, where Daddy had grown up, and Kentucky, where Mom had grown up, and we didn't stop to see anyone. I put in my earbuds so Mom would think I was listening to my iPod, but really, I couldn't. Happy music made me sad, and sad music made me sadder, and any music that I remembered hearing from before—even at the most meaningless moments of my past, walking through the mall or listening to Pandora or flipping through TV channels—even those songs brought such intense pain that I might as well have been pressing ground glass into my ears.

So I hung my head out the window—because the Ford's air-conditioning didn't work—and listened to nothing but the wind whipping through my long brown hair.

We were barely out of the Atlanta area when I started playing a game. I'd pick a house I saw from the highway—sometimes a grand one, sometimes a run-down one, sometimes just one that stood out because it looked completely alone—and I'd tell myself firmly, *The people who live in that house don't know a thing about Daddy. They haven't seen the news. They don't care. I could go knock on their door and they'd answer it. They'd say, "Yes?" and even if I told them my name—even if I told them Daddy's name!— they'd still look at me like I was no different from anyone else.*

Sometimes I could make myself believe it. But usually I'd catch a glimpse of something that flipped my arguments upside down just as the house passed out of sight. I'd see a huge satellite dish in the backyard that all but shouted, *Are you kidding? These people spent more on their TV than they did on their house! They don't do anything* but *watch TV! Of course they saw the CNN specials!* Or I'd see a cop car in the driveway, parked in a way that made me think the police officer lived there. Or I'd see the silvery glow of a computer screen reflected in a window, and I'd know, no matter how far out in the middle of nowhere these people lived, they were still linked to the rest of society—and they, like everyone else, had judged and condemned my daddy.

Or—even worse—they might have been some of his victims.

"Daddy didn't kill anybody," I whispered to myself, whispered into the wind.

And wasn't that awful, that that was the best thing I could come up with for comfort? If he had killed somebody, would I have been saying, *He only killed one person. It's not like he killed two or three. It's not like my father's a serial killer or anything.*

My daddy didn't kill anyone. He just lied and tricked people and stole millions of dollars.

Oh—and computers. He also stole laptop computers.

That was how it started. At least, the way he tells it. Or sort of tells it. He had to do some work near Emory University one day, and it made him mad to see that all those rich college students just left their laptops lying around. They'd leave their laptops behind to hold a table at Starbucks, or to hold a study carrel at the library, and then they might get busy talking to a friend and take forty-five minutes or an hour to get back to it.

So one day, just to teach some kid a lesson, he took one of those laptops.

That, by the way, was the only crime Daddy ever admitted to, even to Mom or me. He couldn't very well not admit to it, considering that J. Cooper Eddington III's MacBook Pro was found in Daddy's car.

The thing is, J. Cooper Eddington III's grandparents, J. Cooper Eddington I (naturally) and his wife, Mary Lou, also got a call at three a.m. on the first Friday night that J. Cooper Eddington III (known as "Coop") spent at college. Mary Lou picked up the phone, and someone she thought was Coop was sobbing hysterically (and possibly drunkenly) on the other end of the line: "Grammy! You've got to help me! They're going to charge me with DUI if I don't pay for all this damage right now! Mom and Dad are going to kill me if they ever find out!"

And Mary Lou, who had always secretly considered Coop her favorite grandchild, jumped up out of bed and drove to an all-night drugstore and wired $7,500 to the number "Coop" gave her.

Later, on the witness stand, Mary Lou Eddington blinked back tears from behind her magnifying-glass-size frames and said in her whispery old-lady voice, "I'm not stupid. I know there are scams. But the man on the phone knew that I drove a Cadillac, and he knew that I call my car Josie, and he knew that I once backed into a trash can myself, one time after I had a little too much merlot at bridge club. . . . How could I not think it was Coop? How could I not help my Coopie?"

Is it wrong that, sitting in the courtroom, I almost hated tiny, ancient Mary Lou Eddington for not thinking clearly when awakened from a sound sleep at three o'clock in the morning? For not remembering that she herself had posted a picture on Facebook of her new Cadillac, affectionately nicknamed Josie? For not thinking that her own daughter-in-law might have e-mailed her grandson, newly away at college, "Grammy had a little fender bender last week. Nothing serious, just hitting some trash cans, but Dad and I wonder if we need to start talking about taking her keys away. When you were there visiting, did it seem like Grammy's glasses were strong enough?"

The federal prosecutors said Daddy stole cell phones, too, and hacked into people's voice mail. He wasn't the first person who ever ran a computer or phone scam preying on grandparents wanting to protect their college-age grandkids. But, as *Time* magazine put it, he was "the most thorough researcher, the most convincing liar, the best at covering his tracks."

And, as far as the law enforcement officials could tell, he made the most money at it. And then he evolved the most, from being a small, two-bit scam artist to being a millionaire criminal entrepreneur. He started a company to make it look like he'd earned the money legitimately, and the company's supposed purpose was—wait for it—computer security. And then he used those connections for more crimes, scamming people who'd hired him to protect them against scams. He laundered money for other criminals; he began taking investments and used new investors' money just to pay the old investors. And even after he moved on to more complicated, more sophisticated, more lucrative crimes, he kept doing the cruel, heart-rending ones: calling up people in the middle of the night and telling them their loved ones were in trouble—send money now.

Until he got caught.

Even then maybe he could have stayed just an ordinary criminal. Richer than most, but still ordinary. Maybe nobody outside Mom and me and the people we knew—and, okay, the people he tricked and stole from—would have known or cared about his case.

But even as he wasn't confessing, wasn't cooperating with the investigation, and wasn't agreeing to a plea agreement, he was also commenting on how crazy people were to put their whole lives out there on social media and then be surprised when criminals used it.

He made people hate him. He made them *love* to hate him.

And then, while still not confessing or cooperating or agreeing to anything, he speculated about why someone who'd started out poor like him would feel justified running computer and phone scams against foolish rich people: for the sake of their own kids.

"How else would someone like me ever be able to send his own kid to college?" he asked. And this was caught on camera, so it was played over and over again, and quoted and requoted and YouTubed and Facebooked and tweeted so many times that I was sure everyone on the planet knew about it.

"Daddy, were you trying to make me hate you too?" I whispered into the wind whipping over and around our car.

I felt Mom's hand on my arm, and for a horrible moment I was afraid she'd heard me. Her grip tightened like a vise, her fingernails digging into my skin. I jerked away, popped the earbuds out of my ears, and started to protest, "Mom—"

She took her hand off my arm to put it over my mouth. Then she pointed at the car radio.

I reached over and turned it up, so the announcer seemed to be shouting over the thundering sound of air rushing in my window: "—speculation about why Jones's wife and daughter didn't show up for his sentencing—"

"You said the lawyer said we shouldn't, because then it'd be harder to hide," I complained to Mom. "Now they're going to criticize that, too?"

Mom shook her head warningly and put her finger over her lips.

"Now sources tell us Jones's family has abandoned their multimillion-dollar mansion," the radio announcer continued. "Neighbors reported seeing a U-Haul in their driveway early this morning. . . ."

I burned with hatred for our neighbors. For a moment I was too mad to hear anything, and when I started paying attention again, a second radio announcer was wisecracking, "Oh, so now the Joneses have to move the same low-class way as the rest of us? Renting a U-Haul? Anybody know where they're going?"

I flashed back to the U-Haul rental guy. I'd been so sure he hadn't recognized us. But what if he had? What if, the whole time he'd been talking to us, he was secretly calculating what he could get for selling us out?

The first radio announcer chuckled.

"Of course we know where the wife and daughter are going," he said. "Do you doubt our crack news-gathering team?"

"Mom!" I cried out in panic.

The color drained from Mom's face. She jerked the steering wheel to the right and slammed the brake. I lurched forward, the seat belt locking and cutting into my shoulder. Then we were stopped by the side of the highway, practically in the ditch. Without the sound of the rushing air through the windows, the radio announcer's voice boomed out so loudly it seemed like everybody in the world should be able to hear it.

"The Joneses did a one-way rental," the announcer said. "They paid with a credit card. Don't they know these things are traceable?"

I closed my eyes. It was useless. We couldn't hide. *Everything* was traceable.

"Roger Jones's wife and daughter are moving to . . ." The announcer hesitated dramatically. In his radio studio, wherever he was broadcasting from, he began tapping his fingers in a cheesy drumroll. "Bradenton, Florida!"

My eyes flew open. I let out a great gulp of air I hadn't realized I'd been holding in. I laughed.

"He's wrong!" I said. "They don't know anything! They're just joking around!"

Relief made me giddy. What had I been worried about? This was some stupid radio show, not a team of hard-hitting investigative reporters.

Then I looked over at Mom. I wouldn't have said it was possible, but her face was even paler now. Her lips looked gray. No, there was a thin line of bright red, too, where she was biting down so hard, she'd drawn blood. But she didn't seem to notice.

"Mom?" I said doubtfully. I reached over and flicked off the radio. The sudden silence felt painful in my ears. Then a semi zoomed past, making the whole car shake. I jumped, all my fear returning.

"Mom, what's wrong?" I asked. "Didn't you hear—they *don't* know where we're going."

But my voice sounded uncertain.

"I thought he was overreacting," Mom mumbled. She seemed to be in shock.

"What are you talking about?" I asked.

Mom turned to face me.

"The lawyer," she said. "Mr. Trumbull. He insisted on renting a second trailer. So we could switch. Overnight, when it was dark, while you were asleep . . . I did tell the U-Haul guy I'd be returning my trailer in Bradenton, Florida. Mr. Trumbull's having someone else do that for us. To throw everyone off our trail. And Mr. Trumbull used a fake name, he paid in cash, so the trailer we're actually using can't be traced. . . ."

I squinted at Mom, my brain working at a snail's pace. Daddy's defense attorney, Mr. Trumbull, had known the U-Haul guy would recognize us. Mr. Trumbull had known the U-Haul guy would tell the media. Mr. Trumbull had saved us from being exposed before we even got to our new home.

"Why didn't you tell me before?" I protested.

Mom winced.

"I didn't want to scare you," she whispered. "I didn't think . . ." She glanced toward the radio I'd silenced. "I didn't think it would matter."

Another truck zipped past us, and this time Mom scrunched down in her seat as if she was trying to hide.

"What good is that going to do?" I snapped.

Mom didn't answer. She just hit the accelerator, spun the steering wheel, and sped back onto the highway. She pulled out too close to a green minivan, and the driver blared his horn.

"Mom—watch out!" I screeched.

Mom sped up, struggling to keep control of the car.

"I should have done everything Mr. Trumbull suggested, right from the start," she muttered. She hunched over the steering wheel and turned her face to the side, away from the minivan swerving past us. An exit appeared to our right, and Mom veered toward it. She barely managed to stop at the bottom of the ramp. She sat there clutching the steering wheel and gasping.

"We'll take back roads from now on," she said.

Miles later we came to a Walmart on the outskirts of a pathetically tiny town. Mom made me wait in the car while she ran in— her head down, her hair hidden by a raincoat hood, even though it wasn't actually raining. Then we both sneaked into the filthy restroom of an ancient-looking gas station next door. Mom pulled out a box of Clairol Nice 'n Easy.

"What color is that?" I asked. "Dried mud?"

"It's something that won't look too weird when it grows out," Mom said. "So I won't have to keep buying hair dye."

Did she mean this was her natural hair color?

I reached for the Walmart bag.

"What'd you get for me?" I asked.

The bag was empty. Mom frowned apologetically.

"Mr. Trumbull said there were at least a dozen pictures of me floating around out there with the news articles about your daddy," she said. "Remember—in *Vanity Fair*, in *Time*, all those online stories. . . . But they just kept using the same one of you over and over again. And—Becca? You don't really look like that anymore, anyhow."

I knew the picture she was talking about—I'd seen it with the news stories and spread all over the Internet and on TV, too.

It was one that I'd kept as my Facebook profile picture for more than a year because I'd liked it so much. My friends and I had all gotten our hair cut and styled and then we'd gone for professional photos. The stylist had told me if I went supershort, I'd look like one of those perky, pixie-cute gymnasts in the Olympics. I'd look like a model. Everyone would want to look like me.

I glanced at myself in the hideous gas-station mirror with its scratched-off splotches and painted-over graffiti. Mom was right: I didn't look perky or pixie cute anymore. My hair had grown out into a shapeless, untrimmed mass that hung down below my shoulders. In the fluorescent light, my skin was greenish, the unsightly color relieved only by the dark circles under my eyes.

Even I didn't recognize myself anymore.

"But, Mom," I protested. "Shouldn't I dye my hair, too, just in case?"

Mom winced.

"We can only afford one box of hair coloring, okay?" she said. "We can't use the credit card anymore. Gas is three cents more a gallon here than in the last town we went through, and we're going to have to fill up at least once more. . . ."

She was serious. A cheap little box of hair coloring, three cents—things like that could ruin us. Without the credit card, we were that close to being penniless.

I turned my face toward the wall.

"Becca?" Mom said. "We're going to be fine. There are thousands and thousands of Susan Joneses out there, probably almost that many Becca Joneses. Mr. Trumbull told me everything I need to do. I change my appearance a little; no one's going to know who we really are. It's true that we're not going to have much money. But we can handle that."

I made a sound that could have been a snort, could have been a gasp. Mom sighed.

"I needed to have this talk with you, anyhow," she said. "Without a credit card, we won't ever be able to buy anything unless we have the cash in hand. I know it's not what you're used to, economizing, but . . . I remember how it works. It's how I grew up. And I survived."

Mom's stories about her childhood—about her entire life before she met my father—were about things like eating squirrel stew and being grateful for it, or about getting blisters on her feet from outgrowing her shoes, but not wanting to tell her parents because they couldn't afford new ones.

I started to complain, "Mom, you were miserable growing up."

Then I looked at her.

She had such a death grip on the Nice 'n Easy box that the sides were caving in. And her expression was resolute but hollow—her clenched jaw, pursed lips, and narrowed eyes might as well have been a mask. I could tell: All her determination was paper thin. If I said one thing wrong, just the sound of my voice could pierce her mask and her resolve and everything holding her together.

What if there's nothing underneath? I wondered. *What if there's actually nothing holding her together except the mask?*

"You survived," I said, parroting Mom.

Mom rewarded me with one curt nod.

"We will too," she said. "We'll be poor but honest. Nothing wrong with that."

Poor but honest . . .

The words struck me as strange somehow. No, worse than that—wrong. It was the "but." "Poor" and "honest" seemed to go together fine. Of course, if you were honest, you'd end up poor. It was rich people whose honesty would be surprising. Most people couldn't be rich if they wanted to be honest; most people couldn't be honest if they wanted to be rich.

Oh . . .

Oh . . .

Oh no.

I was thinking the way Daddy thought, the way he'd taught me to think.

I was so horrified to find Daddy's thoughts in my mind—practically his voice in my brain, doing my thinking for me—that I reeled to the side, hitting my head against the wall.

"Becca?" Mom said, panic in her voice, the mask slipping.

"I can be honest," I said, as if clutching for a mask of my own. I might as well have been trying to hide behind tissue paper. I gulped. "But how can we keep Daddy a secret if we're being honest?"

"We won't *lie*," Mom said. "I guess we just won't talk much. Except to each other. We can say anything we want to each other."

I was fourteen, remember? Maybe all mothers of fourteen-year-old girls want to believe their daughters can tell them anything. Maybe Mom wasn't as blind as she seemed, huddled in a filthy bathroom, about to dye her hair the color of mud on our way to a new city and a new life where she thought we could start fresh, the past left behind and forgotten, our futures rosy, both of us bursting with joy at the thought of being poor but honest.

But maybe most mothers had always been their daughters' favorite parent. Maybe most fourteen-year-olds and their mothers had used all those years to build up to the deep, important teenage confidences.

Me? I'd always been closer to Daddy.

Still Then

We crossed over into bland, boring Ohio on a one-lane, out-of-the-way bridge. I kept sneaking glances at Mom with her newly mud-colored hair. She'd also hacked a lot of it off. Considering she'd styled it using nail scissors in a gas-station bathroom, she didn't look as bad as you might expect. But she didn't look like herself. She just looked . . . wrong.

It felt wrong to be in Ohio, too. Back in fifth grade when we had to memorize the states and know how to find them on a map, Ohio was one of those states I always forgot.

But now I would be living there. That was where Mom had found a job.

It was late in the day when we arrived in Deskins, Ohio. It looked like it'd been built about five minutes before we got there. Everything in the downtown looked new, and many of the housing developments we passed were still just half-finished. In the dim light of dusk, it looked like the new houses were marching across the fields, taking over.

Nobody has any history here, I thought, and smiled.

"There's the hospital," Mom said, pointing at a shining glass building set far back from the street.

I squinted out the window. The concrete sidewalks around the hospital didn't look dry yet; trees with their roots in burlap lay on the bare ground nearby, just a promise of eventual land-scaping. The side of the hospital was still framed by scaffolding.

"Is it even open yet?" I asked.

"Last week," Mom said. "But they're doing a gradual start-up, so it will be a while before they're at full capacity. That's why they're still hiring nurses."

"Your job's a sure thing, though, isn't it?" I asked, suddenly anxious. "It's not like they'll suddenly decide you need another interview, only in person this time, or that you need to take some test, or—"

"Becca," Mom said, and her voice was steely now. "All I have to do is fill out paperwork. I have good experience. They were eager to hire me."

Mom had worked as a nurse until a few years earlier. Then she and Daddy had decided she didn't need to work anymore, because his company was making so much money.

Of course, now we knew where all that extra cash really had come from.

The full meaning of Mom's explanation sank in.

"Wait, Mom—your experience—you had to tell them where you worked before?" I asked. "So they know where you're from? And—"

"Relax, Becca, they don't know anything," Mom said, waving my concerns away.

I grabbed her arm, my anxiety escalating.

"How can you be so sure? How—"

Mom pulled up to a stoplight. It had just turned red, so she had plenty of time to turn her head and look me right in the eye. But she didn't. She kept staring straight ahead.

"Mr. Trumbull helped with that, too," Mom said. "He said there are ways to deal with this, that women use when they're trying to escape abusive relationships, and—"

"*Abusive?*" I shrieked. "Mom, Daddy never beat you! Or me! Anyway, it's not like he could hurt us now even if he wanted to. He's going to be in prison for the next . . ."

Ten years. That was all I needed to say to finish the sentence, but it was all too new and fresh, like a wound that hadn't scabbed over yet. I couldn't force the words out.

I wish I had. I wish I had said "ten years" in such a cold, clinical voice that Mom decided to treat me like an adult. Maybe she would have told me everything right then.

Instead, Mom reached over and patted me on the shoulder. She finally turned and looked me in the eye, but her expression was guarded. This time she was wearing a mask of concern and pity. When she spoke, she sounded like she was speaking to a toddler.

"Becca, we're safe here. I promise," she said. "You don't have to worry about anything."

Maybe that tone had worked on me when I was young, happy and secure and certain that, no matter what, Mommy and Daddy and everybody else would always love me. But I was fourteen and my whole world had just fallen apart, and I wasn't certain of anything anymore.

How could I not worry? How could I ever feel safe again?

The new student orientation at Deskins High School was the next afternoon. We were lucky school started later in Ohio than in Georgia. Still, Mom and I barely had time to unload everything into our tiny new apartment, return the U-Haul trailer, and squeeze in quick showers before it was time to go.

"Mom, hurry up!" I yelled, banging on the bathroom door.

The door was flimsier than our doors back home. My third knock was too much for the latch, and the door swung wide open.

Mom was standing on the throw rug before the sink, having just stepped out of the shower. She was completely naked.

"I'm sorry! I'm sorry!" I cried, yanking on the door handle to pull it shut again, even as Mom grabbed a towel. "I didn't mean to do that!"

"Becca, just wait! I'll be out in a minute!" Mom called.

I leaned against the wall—also flimsy—and grimaced. Somehow it didn't seem so horrifying that I'd seen her naked body, as that I'd seen her naked face. Freed (she thought) of the need to keep up appearances for me, she'd been leaning toward the mirror. And in the one unguarded moment before she saw me watching, I could have sworn that she'd been whispering to herself: "I can't do this. I can't . . ."

Mom came out of the bathroom, fully clothed in a classy dress with a light-blue sweater. I was wearing my favorite Abercrombie & Fitch shirt and my favorite jeans—I figured Abercrombie & Fitch and jeans were a safe bet anywhere. It hadn't really been worth it to sell our clothes, the way we'd sold our furniture, so at least we could both still *look* good. Even her hair looked okay.

I decided I'd probably been wrong about what Mom was saying to the mirror.

"The school's right across the street, so how long do you really think it will take to get there?" she teased.

If she wasn't going to say anything about what she'd been whispering in the bathroom, I wasn't going to either.

I dodged stacks of boxes and bounded toward the front door. Mom was still rifling through papers in her purse, so I stood in the doorway for a moment, looking out. We were in the last unit of the Whispering Pines apartment building, then there was the wide street called Chargers Way (Was the school mascot maybe the Chargers?), then there was an immense green yard, and then, at the top of a hill, Deskins High School loomed above us. The building was red brick and imposing, with a three-story portion in the center and two-story wings jutting out on either side.

Everything will be fine there, I told myself. *I don't know anybody and nobody knows me and that's* good. *I'll make a good first impression. I always make a good first impression. As long as it's just me people are judging.*

"Okay," Mom said, catching up to me. "Let's go."

I glanced toward a paper sticking out of her purse. STUDENT INFORMATION FORM, it said at the top.

"What's that?" I asked.

"Nothing," Mom said. "Paperwork. If they ask you to fill out any other forms, just let me take care of it. I don't think they will. They made a big deal on the website about how that was the parents' responsibility, and—"

She stopped talking because I reached over and yanked the paper away from her.

The form looked a lot like the ones I'd handed in every August in elementary and early middle school, back home in Georgia. After that, the school had gone to having everything online, but I guess Deskins High School still liked old-fashioned paper. After the basic information about me, Mom had filled in her own name as "Teresa Jones," as if she went by her middle name. That was weird, though I could understand why she'd done it. But then . . .

On the line labeled "Father's name," she'd written "N/A."

"N-A?" I said, puzzled.

"Not . . . ," Mom began. She gulped and finished in a faint voice: "Not applicable."

I stopped in my tracks.

"Not applicable?" I repeated. "Like . . . like I don't even have a father? Like he doesn't exist? Like I never had one?"

"Becca," Mom said. "You don't want anyone to know who your father is. Or *where* he is. Right? What do you want me to put on that line? And on the 'Father's Address' line right below?"

I gaped at her. I wanted to turn around and run away, not to have to deal with any of this.

No, wait. We already did that.

This was what we'd run *to*. This was our fresh new start where nobody knew us, and if I turned and ran or did anything else strange, I'd ruin everything. Especially since I could already see kids arriving at the high school across the street. And they could already see me.

"I don't know," I muttered.

"Look," Mom said. "Lots of kids don't have fathers. The school will be sensitive about it. They won't ask questions."

I gritted my teeth. I wanted to yell at Mom, "I thought you said we weren't going to lie!" But, really, this wasn't a lie. The school wanted both my parents' names, so they'd know who to call if I started throwing up in biology class or broke my arm in gym class or some such thing. And Dad would never be available for any of that.

He really didn't matter.

Do I believe that? Do I want to believe that?

I didn't want to think about it. Not now, not when I needed to be plastering a calm, easygoing look on my face, not when I needed to act the same way I always did back home that made people like me, and made me have friends without even trying.

Before Daddy was arrested, anyway.

"Fine," I snarled at Mom. I wasn't calm yet, but I told myself

I was getting the last of the anxiety out of my system. I shoved the form back into her purse.

"Becca," Mom said pleadingly, reaching for my arm. But I'd already stepped past her, rushing forward again.

"Let's get this over with," I said.

We didn't talk the rest of the way to the school, which gave me time to look over the kids streaming through the wide front doors of Deskins High School. I saw several Abercrombie & Fitch shirts and a few girls with the same kind of jeans I was wearing, so that was okay. One thing that was different from back home was that a lot of the kids with darker skin didn't look African American—some of them were Indian, I guessed, others, maybe Arabic. And there was a sprinkling of Chinese- or Japanese- or Korean-looking kids too. If I'd stayed in Georgia and gone to Belpre High School, pretty much everyone would have just been black or white. Or a mix of the two.

What's going on? Are people from all over the world running away and ending up in Deskins, Ohio? I wondered.

The thought made me smile. If there were a lot of different people here—and different types of people—then nothing would seem strange about me.

But how would I know how to fit in?

I stayed close to Mom as we stepped through the doors and moved toward a table where three women sat before laptops.

"My daughter's enrolling as a new student. She's a freshman. Becca Jones," Mom said to the woman in the middle, behind the J–N sign.

The woman kept her gaze on the computer screen. I could see her starting to type, "J-O-N-E—"

"I didn't fill out anything online. Everything's right here," Mom said, pulling the student information form out of her purse. She dug deeper in her purse and added a few other papers. "Here's her transfer information too."

The woman frowned, as if annoyed at having to deal with paper. I was annoyed too—why hadn't Mom filled out everything online ahead of time? She was no computer expert like Daddy, but this was *basic*.

The woman pulled the papers closer and stared flipping through them.

"Okay, but we need *all* her records from her old school," she said.

"Her homeschooling equivalency scores are there," Mom said. "That should take care of everything."

Probably I was the only one who heard the tiny tremor in Mom's voice. The woman was still looking down at the papers, so I'm sure she didn't see me whip my head toward Mom. I barely managed to keep from crying out, *What? Homeschooling? What are you talking about?*

I'd never been homeschooled. I'd gone to Apple Valley Elementary School and McCormick Middle School. And back at Belpre High School, back in Georgia, there was a thick file on me, with school pictures from kindergarten on and all my standardized test scores and my report cards and everything else the school system thought was important enough to keep. I knew it was there, because when we'd gone for eighth-grade visitation day, one of the guidance counselors had made a big deal about how your permanent record followed you, and how the records were sent to the high school right after school ended in May, and so all of us should keep our noses clean in eighth grade if we didn't want to start high school with a bad image right away.

I hadn't done anything to mess up my eighth-grade record. But did schools write down things like, "Becca's father was arrested/Becca's father was deemed a flight risk so he had to go to prison even before the trial/Becca's father was convicted and sentenced and will be in prison so long she'll have time to graduate from high school and college and maybe even grad school, too, before he gets out"? If they did, I didn't want my permanent record following me. If they did, Mom was doing the right thing.

But if all my previous years of school were replaced by made-up numbers on a thin sheet of paper, then who was I?

Mom's eyes were begging me not to make a scene. She leaned in close and whispered, so softly only I could hear, "I'm sorry. I was going to tell you but . . . the time never seemed right. I thought I could handle it while you were signing up for classes, and we could talk about it later."

I opened my mouth, though I wasn't sure whether I wanted to thank her or yell. Mom leaned toward me a second time.

"I didn't say you were homeschooled, just that we're using those scores to get you in," she whispered directly into my ear. "And they match your real scores, so it's accurate. They'll put you in the right classes."

The woman, ignoring us, was typing in my information. I was still standing there openmouthed. Behind me a loudspeaker crackled to life, and a man's voice called out, "All new freshmen and sophomores, please report to room one-oh-six, by the guidance office. Juniors and seniors, go to room one-oh-two. Parents, please report to the cafeteria."

I took a step back from Mom. Mom started to ask the woman at the computer, "Um, where—"

"Mom, it's okay. We can just follow everyone else," I interrupted.

I didn't wait for her answer. I just turned and walked away. I saw where Room 106 was, but I purposely walked past it. I went to a drinking fountain outside Room 112 and bent over and pretended to drink while I pulled myself together.

Mom's just watching out for you, I told myself, leaning my head against the wall. *She's just making 100 percent sure nobody knows we're related to Daddy. So I can just be myself here. Isn't that what I wanted? Isn't that why we moved?*

I straightened up and went back to Room 106. I made my stride casual and carefree; I smiled at the few kids coming from the other way. But I was the last one to step into the room. Only two seats were left: one beside a girl with red hair; the other beside a girl wearing a head scarf. I guessed she was Muslim.

Oh, I want a head scarf to hide behind! I thought. *One of those full-body thingies would be even better—a burkah? Why didn't Mom and I wear those in court?*

I reminded myself nobody knew I'd spent so much of the summer in court. Nobody knew Daddy was in prison. And Mom had made sure nobody in Deskins ever would.

I eased into the seat beside the redhead.

"Hi," I said, trying to sound just as cheerful and likable as the Becca Jones I'd been before Daddy was arrested.

Redhead turned reluctantly toward me. I realized I'd interrupted her flirting with the guy on the other side of her. He was a muscular hottie—either he was some big athlete or he worked out all the time or he was on steroids. Or maybe all three.

Redhead saw me checking out Muscle Boy. She started to narrow her eyes like I was competition. I made my eyes all wide and innocent and raised my eyebrows a little, hoping she'd get the message, *No, no, I can tell you saw him first. He's all yours. Good for you! I can play wingman—wing-woman—to help out. What do you want me to do?*

This was the kind of thing that worked back in middle school in Georgia. I hoped the rules for getting people to like you wouldn't be that different in high school in Ohio.

Redhead's expression relaxed.

"Hi, I'm Shannon," she said. She flipped her hair over her

shoulder as if trying to attract the entire room's attention: *Are you watching this? See how everyone wants to talk to me?* She elbowed Muscle Boy. "This is Brent."

I lifted my eyebrows a little higher and thought at Shannon, *See? I gave you an excuse to touch his arm!*

"I'm Becca," I said.

"I moved here from Marysville, and Brent's transferring from Grove City so he can play football—did you hear about those schools canceling sports?" Shannon asked, loud enough to be heard two rows away. She was definitely trying to turn every kid in the room into her audience.

I concentrated on looking as horrified as she wanted me to and congratulated myself for figuring out Brent was an athlete.

But I should have braced for Shannon's next question.

"Where are you from, Becca?" she asked.

I stared at her.

"I—" I began, and stopped.

Stupid! Didn't you know if you talked to people, they'd ask that? Why didn't you have an answer ready? Just make up something! Er, no, what if you name someplace that Shannon knows all about and she starts asking tons of questions and then she can tell you're lying? Just say, "The South." No—then she'll say, "Where in the South?" and you're right back in it. What if she knows all about Daddy, what if she remembers he was from Georgia, what if just saying "Georgia," makes her know who I am, no matter how hard Mom worked to hide it. . . .

It was starting to look really weird that I hadn't said anything after "I." I could tell by Shannon's expression that she was on the verge of switching her opinion of me from "friend potential" to "definite social liability." And she'd been so loud—was every kid in the room waiting for my answer? Just to buy myself time, I started fake-coughing. I made the coughs sound deep and resonant and troubling, and I gestured at my throat and then out toward the hall.

"Got—to—drink—" I sputtered between coughs. And then I bolted from the room.

I hoped I was judging Shannon correctly, and she wasn't the kind of girl who'd leave her seat beside a hot, muscular football player just because some other girl she didn't even know was practically choking to death.

Out in the hall I found I couldn't stop coughing, so I really did walk back to the water fountain I'd stopped at before. I gulped in the lukewarm water, which tasted like it'd been sitting in a rusty pipe all summer. The water made me cough more. I stood there, hunched over the fountain, coughing and gulping and thinking, *You can't even pretend you're the same Becca Jones you used to be. You can't be popular here. You have to make it so nobody notices you, nobody wants to ask you questions, nobody cares who you are . . .*

I felt a hand on my back and heard a voice say, "Are you all right?"

I whirled around. It wasn't Shannon behind me. It was the girl in the head scarf.

We stared at each other for a moment, and then she said, "I think I scared the coughing away."

She had a faint accent, but I couldn't place it, and I wasn't about to ask where she was from. But it would be weird if I didn't say anything, so I agreed. "You cured me! Thanks, um—"

"Jala," she said, vaguely pointing at herself, as if she thought I might need that to understand.

"Becca," I said, making the same gesture.

She didn't seem to know what to say after that. I was stricken by a fear that she would settle on the same question Shannon had chosen—"Where are you from?"—and I didn't have a safe answer yet.

Head off a question with another question, I told myself, and so I blurted out the first one that came to my mind: "Does it help? The head scarf, I mean?"

Something in her expression closed down, and I remembered she was a new kid too. She probably didn't know anybody at Deskins High School, either.

"It's called a hijab," she said flatly. For a minute I thought that was all she was going to say, but then she went on, "Do you mean, does it make people stare more than they would otherwise? Does it make them say mean things, and act like they think I can't hear them through the cloth?"

I was suddenly frantic at how completely she'd misunderstood.

"No, I mean, does it help you remember who you are—who you're supposed to be, what you believe—even though you're in a strange place, among strangers?" I asked.

She tilted her head, considering this seriously.

"It *should*," she conceded. "The fact that it doesn't—that's probably my fault. I shouldn't worry so much about everyone staring. But at my old school back in Michigan, there were a lot more Muslims. I'm not used to being the only one in a classroom."

Jala was just from Michigan? Her accent was just Michigan-ish—Michiganian? Michigander? I guess it sounded exotic to me because I was used to the way people talked in the South.

Jala didn't seem angry at me anymore, but I wasn't going to let talking about her old school lead to questions about my old school. I saw that she had a piece of paper in her hand labeled "Class Schedule Requests."

"What are you signing up for?" I asked.

Jala handed me her paper. I could tell she was a freshman like me because she'd listed Phys Ed I. Other than that, all her classes started with the words "honors" or "advanced."

If Daddy hadn't been arrested and convicted and sent to prison, and Mom and I hadn't run away, I would have moved naturally from McCormick Middle School to Belpre High School without so much as a hiccup in my life. I would have hung out with people like Shannon, not like Jala, and not just because there probably wasn't a single Muslim at Belpre High. I would have chosen my friends based on who was popular and good-looking, and whether they could make me seem popular and look good too. I would have picked my classes based on what I could glide through with the least effort, so I had time for hours of texting and exchanging gossip on Facebook and planning parties and hanging out.

But I couldn't be around people who lived for gossip anymore, because, if I wasn't careful, the gossip at Deskins High School would be about me. I needed to be around people who were quiet and trustworthy and kind—and maybe studying too hard to care about gossip or nosy questions. And if the Jalas of Deskins High School were all in the advanced and honors classes, then those were the classes I would take too.

I handed Jala's class schedule request sheet back to her.

"That's almost exactly what I'm signing up for," I said. "Except for that one."

I pointed to the last course title she'd filled in: Honors Computer Programming I.

"You don't like computers?" Jala asked.

"No, not at all," I said, shaking my head for emphasis. "I hate everything about them. I'm horrible with computers."

And that was the first lie I told at Deskins High School.

Between Then and Now

I became a normal kid again, with a normal life.

Well, sort of. As much as possible. As long as nobody looked too close.

And believe me, I didn't let anybody look too close.

Now—

Three Years Later
The Beginning of Senior Year

I slip into an aisle seat in the school auditorium. Three rows behind me, Jason Sprunger and Martin Lee are pounding their fists on the seat backs and chanting, "Sen-iors! Sen-iors! Sen-iors!" Three rows ahead of me Shannon Daily—the redheaded girl I met at new student orientation and have barely spoken to since—is holding court with her usual crowd, the self-proclaimed "popular girls." Pretty much everyone else refers to them as the mean girls, but they're mostly just cannibalistic, constantly fighting among themselves about who's queen bee and who's second tier and who's kicked out of the group. They consider the rest of us beneath their notice, which is fine with me.

"You know, my mother was homecoming queen at her high school, and my grandmother was homecoming queen at her school, so it's almost like a family tradition," Shannon is saying, a little too loudly. "I wouldn't want to let them down."

I bend my head down so I can roll my eyes without anyone seeing. Poor Shannon is so good at clawing her way to the top of the mean-girl clique, but she's totally inept at staying there. The power always goes to her head. She'll probably be out as queen bee by the end of this assembly. Maybe temporarily out of the group entirely. Sometimes I've considered sidling up to her and giving advice—as a secret power behind the throne, perhaps— but I don't want to make myself a target of the other mean girls. A few would be devious enough to find out the secrets in my past—and evil enough to use them against me. Helping Shannon isn't worth the risk.

"Borderline personality disorder," my friend Rosa Alvarez mutters beside me.

"Are you diagnosing Shannon or just doing your AP psych homework?" I ask.

Rosa grins at me from beneath her unfashionably heavy bangs.

"Both," she says. "This is going to be a tough year. I'm all about the multitasking."

Rosa is the only one of my friends who will join me in keeping track of the machinations of the in crowd. She says it reminds her of the telenovelas she watched back home in Mexico. Since Mom sold our TV the first winter we spent in Deskins, I'm similarly starved for entertainment.

But I wouldn't want to be in the middle of all that drama, I tell myself. *Who needs it? Even if it weren't for Daddy, I'd be happier flying under the radar.*

I've taken to automatically labeling many of my thoughts "truth" or "lie," and I'm not sure about that one.

"People, people, quiet down," our principal, Mr. Gordon, says from the stage. "You don't want to disturb the underclassmen, do you?"

The "Sen-iors! Sen-iors!" chant behind me dissolves into sarcastic comebacks: "Why not?" and "Who cares?" and "We're seniors! We can disturb anyone we want!"

"Jala had the right idea graduating early, if this is how everyone's going to act all year long," Rosa mutters beside me.

I nod distractedly. I've learned it isn't wise to dwell on who or what you've lost, and Jala is the closest thing I had to a best friend for the past three years. That's weird to say when neither one of us has even been to the other person's home—Jala has six younger brothers and sisters who make her house, as she put it, "chaos to the nth degree," and I've always used the excuse that my mother worked nights and I didn't want to bother her when she was sleeping during the day. But Jala was a good school friend, and school doesn't seem right without her.

Really, all I have now are school friends: the kind of people you partner with in chemistry lab or sit with at lunch or shoot the breeze with walking to class. I don't have the kind of friends you'd tell deep, dark secrets to.

In the past three years I haven't told a single soul about my father.

And nobody has figured it out.

And it isn't like Daddy's in the news anymore. So what do I have to worry about?

Mr. Gordon pounds his hand against the podium, a signal that he's getting mad.

"Let me remind you gentlemen in the back that you are still subject to my authority until graduation day, and I personally can determine whether you graduate or not," he threatens.

To my surprise, the rowdies behind us actually quiet down.

"Thank you," Mr. Gordon says with exaggerated patience. "Now, seniors, this assembly is for your benefit. If statistics hold, some ninety-five percent of you are planning to further your education after high school, which is a really good idea if you intend to make more than minimum wage. So hopefully you all picked up the handouts in the back—"

"Wait!" someone cries out. It's Ms. Stela, my guidance counselor, who's running down the far aisle waving a stack of papers.

"The copier broke this morning, and I just printed the last one and . . . here! Pass them down!"

She starts thrusting papers at the kids at the end of each row.

"Couldn't she have printed those handouts before today?" Rosa mutters disgustedly beside me.

"That's Ms. Stela for you," I mutter back.

Ms. Stela's maybe twenty-eight, and always frantic. She said to me once, "I'm so glad there are kids like you who don't have problems, so I have time to deal with the ones who do."

I think that comment alone should disqualify her from her job—shouldn't guidance counselors be more observant? But it's not like I'm going to turn her in.

The handouts flow down the row toward me. When Rosa hands me the stack, I take one and stand up and walk across the aisle to pass the rest on. I've grown four inches since moving to Deskins, and it's a little amazing to me how quickly I can move now that I have long legs. Still, by the time I get back to my seat, Rosa has already flipped through the whole packet and is ready to rattle off all the ways it's objectionable.

"Like we don't already know that grades and course selection and extracurriculars really matter for getting into the college of our dreams?" she asks scornfully. "Didn't they tell us that a million times freshman year alone?"

"Oh, who remembers freshman year?" I murmur back, shrugging.

If I hadn't put that as a question, it would count as an immense lie. Because I remember everything from freshman year. I remember how cold our apartment felt when I sat in it alone after Mom left for work each night. I remember how I cried when Mom told me Daddy was being transferred to a federal prison in California, of all places, and there was no way we could afford to visit him any time soon. I remember how, most of the time, I couldn't decide if I was more angry than I was sad, or more sad than I was angry—when I did see Daddy again, would I want to hug him or slug him? If I ever wrote him a letter, would I curse him out or try to comfort him?

I didn't write any letters. I sat staring at blank sheets of paper for hours on end and then put the paper away, still blank. I let Mom tell him whatever she wanted about us and our new lives in Deskins. To keep anyone from knowing our connection to Daddy, all her letters—and Daddy's, back to us—had to be sent in care of his attorney. I told myself that was what made it impossible to write. And, because phone calls are so easy to trace, the attorney said we shouldn't talk to Daddy by phone, either.

What did I feel the strongest: relief at not having to communicate? Or just more of that battle between sorrow and fury?

Not much has changed in three years. I'm still angry and sad, but I've buried all those emotions deep down inside me. When our junior-year AP language teacher made us write character studies of each other, Jala described me as "the most even-keeled person I know."

So I've fooled even my best friend. I deserve an acting Oscar.

Rosa is still ranting about Ms. Stela's handouts.

"And this sheet," she says, turning to the last page. "Are they trying to convince us that we can afford college or that we should just give up because we can't?"

She shakes the packet at me, so I have to dart my eyes back and forth to see what she's talking about. That last page is a reprint from some magazine, and the headline says, "What If the Middle Class Really Can't Afford to Send Their Kids to College Anymore?"

And below that headline, there's a picture of my father.

Now

"Gaa," I croak.

Rosa looks at me strangely, because there are rules to responding to her sarcasm, and one of them is, you never take anything too seriously. And in addition to making weird, incoherent sounds, I'm sure I look seriously disturbed. I can feel the blood draining from my face—my skin is normally about two shades paler than Rosa's, but now it's probably more like fifty. And I can't seem to regain control. My eyes refuse to stop bugging out; my jaw just keeps hanging.

Rosa pounds me on the back—evidently she thinks I'm choking.

"Relax! Calm down! You'll get tons of scholarships. It's the C students who really have to worry," Rosa says.

Even though her voice seems to come from a million miles away, I understand: She thinks I'm just worried about paying for college.

What a relief.

I shake my head, throwing myself into full acting mode.

"Sorry," I mutter. "Panic attack. College just never seemed real before, you know?"

Rosa is still regarding me with the same kind of curiosity she usually reserves for the daily ups and downs of the popular crowd.

"My sister warned me everyone freaks out about college senior year, but I didn't think you'd be the first victim," she says.

I'm saved from having to answer because Mr. Gordon bangs on the podium again.

"Okay, people, *now* you have the handouts, so look at the first page," he orders.

Rosa obeys. I pretend to forget the difference between "first" and "last," and flip my packet open to the article with my father's picture. I just intend to glance quickly, to make sure I wasn't imagining it was him and panicking over nothing. But I can't help skimming the opening of the article:

> Infamous scammer Roger Jones, who bilked innocent victims out of millions, tried to justify his crimes with the excuse, "How else could someone like me be able to afford to send his own kid to college?"
> Obviously that was the wrong approach, as Jones is now serving time in prison. But other parents, faced with college costs that escalate at a pace far beyond inflation, might be tempted to turn to similarly desperate measures. The reality is . . .

As far as I can tell from reading quickly, that's the only mention of my father in the whole article. Why did they even use his name or show his picture? My gaze drifts to the offending image.

Daddy . . .

I'm pretty sure this picture was taken the day of the verdict, as he was being taken in to court. It's a fuzzy reproduction, so I can just barely see the handcuffs glinting around his wrists. He's holding his head high, a cocky expression on his face. It looks like he was thinking, *You people do not have the goods on me! You may have caught me, but you don't really have enough proof now, do you?* Or maybe he was just thinking, *I have to look like I'm confident I'm going to get off. Act cocky!* Maybe inside he was terrified.

Oh, Daddy . . .

Probably millions of people have seen this picture in the past three years, and probably practically every one of them thought, *What a jerk! That guy deserves to be punished! It's a shame they didn't catch him sooner!* But I see the man who pushed me on my backyard swing set again and again and again when I was a preschooler; I see the man who introduced me to rocky road ice cream; I see the man who bought me practically anything I ever asked for . . .

With other people's money.

Rosa jabs her elbow in my side.

"Do not go all *loca* on me about paying for college!" she whispers. "You know Clarice and Stuart and Lakshmi are going to be psycho all year long about whether or not they're going to get into Harvard—I've got to have someone sane around me!"

I shrug apologetically and try to keep my hands from shaking as I flip the packet back to the first page. But that page might as well have been covered in random squiggles, for all I read of it. I don't hear Mr. Gordon's droning voice, either.

What if, when we get to that last page, and Mr. Gordon has everyone staring at that picture of Daddy . . . what if someone says, "Hey! Doesn't this guy look like Becca? And his last name is Jones, too! What do you bet they're related?"

I do look a lot like Daddy. We have the same chestnut-brown hair, which he always wore a little bit too long for a typical suburban dad. And mine streams most of the way down my back now. That's mostly just because haircuts cost money—I stopped thinking of my long hair as a disguise a long time ago. But now . . .

So what if we have the same hair color? That's a black-and-white picture! No one's going to be able to tell what color hair Daddy has!

But Daddy and I also have the same wide-set eyes, the same high checkbones, the same slightly arched nose. We even have the same teeth. The only feature I inherited from my mom was my heart-shaped chin.

Stop it! Think of a good comeback! How about, "Yeah, of course two people named Jones would have to be related. Because Jones isn't a common name at all." Deliver that with the right tone, and you'll be fine.

In the past three years, ever since my freeze-up at new-student orientation, I've perfected all sorts of comebacks. If anyone asks where I lived before Deskins, I say, "Oh, here and there. I've moved around. Nowhere that really stuck with me."

If anyone asks, "Hey, don't you kind of have a Southern accent?"—though I've done my best to get rid of it—I shrug and say, "You know, I pick up accents so easily! I always sound like the last person I talked to! I talk to Rosa for five minutes, and you'd swear I was born south of the Rio Grande!"

If anybody asks, "What's your father do?" I say, "Enh, he's not really in the picture. It's just me and my mom."

The trick is to sound so bored with my answer that nobody wants to ask anything else.

I'm just not sure I can pull that off right now, after looking at the picture of Daddy, after reading those words. After feeling, once again, that everything was my fault.

Rosa elbows me again.

"Wh-what?" I ask, jarred.

"You liked this assembly so much, you're going to sit here

until they do it again for next year's seniors?" she asks.

I look at her blankly.

"It's over! We've been released from the torture *del día,*" she says. "It's time for lunch."

I realize I'm the last senior still seated. Everybody else is fleeing. Shannon Daily walks by with her head down, her face red. She looks like she's holding back tears.

I was right. The queen bee has been deposed, I think.

Being right doesn't make me happy.

Rosa and I have the same lunch period as three of our other friends: Stuart, Oscar, and Clarice. As Rosa drops her brown-paper lunch sack onto the table, she begins surveying the crowd: "Everybody feeling okay? How's your blood pressure? Your pulse? Nobody's stressed out yet, are you?"

"Of course I'm stressed out!" Stuart snaps. "I've got eighteen college application essays to write between now and January first—six of them before November first, if I do early action at Chicago and Georgetown and Yale. And AP calc is going to ruin my GPA, but I can't drop it, because that will look like I'm just being lazy. And the band director says when we get close to contests, we're going to have to practice an extra hour every night, which I don't have time for, but I can't drop that, because then I won't have the marching band president position to put on my college applications, and—"

"Stuart," Oscar says. "Shut up."

Rosa shoots me a triumphant look.

"It's starting," she sings. I think she's trying for the same eerie effect as a narrator in a horror movie.

"Guys," Clarice says earnestly. "Promise me we are not going to be mean to each other over this. My brother said some kids in his class stopped speaking to each other for a while over who got into which schools and who got which scholarships and . . . we're not doing that, okay?"

"Dream on," Stuart snorts, even as he reaches out and tries to smash Oscar's head into his french fries and ketchup. But Oscar sees him coming and dodges the shove. Stuart ends up with ketchup on his hand.

I signed up for honors and advanced classes freshman year because I thought smart kids would be nice. And this is what I got?

Honestly, at first it seemed like they really were nicer. I was just a timid mouse who sat at the back of every room—no threat to anyone. But even Stuart, who was a total stranger to me then, kindly patted me on the back when he saw I got a 79 on my first writing assignment in honors freshman English. "You'll do better next time," he said. He got a 98.5—he could afford to be magnanimous. (And condescending. He's always been very good at condescending.)

But then a funny thing happened. Did you know that if you can't afford a cell phone and you don't have a Facebook page and you're scared to let even your closest friends know too much about you—and you can't even try to be popular—then that really doesn't leave much for you to do except homework?

And, surprisingly enough, homework is actually kind of important in high school?

On my second writing assignment in honors freshman English, I got a 96.

Stuart got an 89.

When he saw my grades, he shoved his face near mine and yelled, "I hate you!"

This struck me as so ridiculous that I started laughing.

"Next time, Jones," he threatened, actually shaking his fist at me. "Next time we'll see who dominates!"

I kept laughing. It didn't even occur to me that he might be serious until he'd left the room, and Clarice and Lakshmi crowded around me, speaking to me for the very first time.

"Are you all right?" Lakshmi asked, as skittish as a bird. She kept darting her gaze around, as if she feared Stuart would come back and she wanted to be ready to fly away if he did.

"That boy is just nasty!" Clarice declared, shaking her head. "But—is it true? Did you get an A? The only A in the class?"

And I saw something I hadn't known before: There were other things to want in high school besides popularity. The kids who were chasing high GPAs and top class ranks could be just as cutthroat as the Shannon Daily mean-girls crowd. But the proof of their success was more . . . absolute. I'd learned in eighth grade that you could go from being the most popular girl in school to being a total pariah in nothing flat if, say, oh, I don't know. Maybe your father got arrested? Maybe his picture was all over the news and people called you up pretending to care when they really just wanted ammunition for making fun of you? Maybe you swore and double-swore and triple-swore and quadruple-swore—even on a stack of Bibles, even though you felt kind of wrong about it—that he really was innocent, just wait, everyone would see?

Only, he wasn't?

Meanwhile, an A on your report card—nobody could take that away from you.

You might think having Stuart yell, "I hate you!" would have scared me away. But it didn't. It made me want in, all the way. It made me want to beat him again.

And it made us friends, to the extent that you could say anyone at Deskins High School was my friend, when nobody knew a thing about me.

Oh, and when I brought home my first high school report

card, covered in nothing but A's? Mom burst into tears of joy.

"Then—you're going to be okay," she exclaimed, simultaneously crying and laughing into my hair as she hugged me a little too tightly. "This proves it. You're not going to start doing drugs, or dressing all in black, or cutting yourself, or—"

I shoved her away.

"You thought I would do any of that stuff?" I demanded. "Really, Mom?"

"I-I was joking," Mom stammered, still reaching out, her arms hugging nothing but empty air. "I was working up to 'holding up liquor stores,' and, um, I don't know, 'cheating on your taxes . . .'"

Both of us froze, and she let the words dribble away. Cheating on his taxes was one of the things Daddy did.

And I could see it in her face, the shock exposing her like a camera's flash: She really had been afraid for me. Of course. My father was in prison. I was being raised in a single-parent home. I was "at risk." All those things that hadn't even occurred to me were the things she'd been terrified I would do, the person she was afraid I'd become.

Or worse.

Was it because she thought I was too much like Daddy?

"Oh, thanks, Mom. Thanks a lot," I exploded. I was shaking. My words slurred together, self-propelled. I wanted to hurt her as badly as she'd hurt me, just by the way she'd looked at me. Just because of what she'd feared for me. "What else are you going to accuse me of? Are you saying I must have cheated to get these grades? At least *Daddy* always thought I was smart!"

That was the nuclear weapon of comebacks.

And in my memory, it was nuclear winter in our apartment for weeks after that, both of us like survivors picking their way through radioactive wreckage, each of us too alone in her own misery to reach a charred hand to the other person. We said nothing deeper than, "Are we out of cereal?" and "Which days are you working next week?" and "Where's the remote?"

Let me translate: What we were really saying, either one of us, anytime we spoke—or even when we didn't—was, "You huuurrt me. I'm in paaaain." And, "I'm sorry. I'm so, so sorry."

Mom started going to church again.

I refused. And, to my surprise, she didn't force me.

Mom started apologizing all the time: for having to sell the TV, for keeping the heat in our apartment set barely above freezing, for serving macaroni and cheese several days in a row, for "everything else."

The second or third time she apologized for "everything else," I said, "Okay! I heard you! Just forget about it, all right?"

And that's how we left it.

But before, in that cold, dark, ashen place that was my life freshman year, I thought about all the things I could do just to serve Mom right—to serve both my parents right. Anybody who spent more than five minutes at Deskins High School could tell who the drug dealers were; even in the honors and advanced classes I heard about parties where kids stayed drunk all weekend long. I heard about kids who went joyriding in stolen cars, kids who hooked up with anybody they could find, kids who walked away from school and just never bothered coming back.

I did none of those things. I made geometry my drug of choice; I drowned my sorrows in *Rebecca* and *The Great Gatsby* and *Things Fall Apart,* in the League of Nations charter and the laws of thermodynamics. I piled up golden A's around me like I was building a fort.

Did I really have to work that hard just to prove Mom wrong? (Or . . . right? Which was it?)

Now again

(Really. I'm staying in "now." I worked too hard to get away from "then." Why go back?)

So, anyhow. It's the start of my senior year, and I'm sitting atop three years of those shiny, hard-earned A's. I'm number four in my class. I will be number three if Stuart really does drop or flunk AP calc, but I know he's not going to do either of those things. And I'm sitting at a tableful of my fellow high-ranked seniors, and everyone's eating and laughing and talking. And even though Stuart still has ketchup on his hand, I'm sure that anyone watching from afar—say, a timid, insecure freshman who doesn't know anyone yet, the person I used to be—would think we act like we rule the universe. The people I'm with have that confidence built into their marrow, that air of assurance that everything's going to go their way. It's like they're genetically engineered to succeed.

And I'm good at faking it.

Clarice taps my arm and asks, "What about you, Becca?"

"Huh?" I say, ever so eloquently.

Rosa playfully jostles against me.

"Earth to Becca! Earth to Becca! What is wrong with you today?" She appeals to the rest of the table. "She was zoned out the whole time we were in that assembly, too."

"I think that's a sign of advanced intelligence," Oscar says, and I blow him a kiss.

There is nothing romantic going on between me and Oscar. We just goof around like that all the time.

"Focus, people!" Stuart scolds us. He trains his green eyes on me. Really, Stuart isn't bad looking—until he opens his mouth. Then he's so obnoxious you forget what he looks like.

Unfortunately, Stuart talks a lot.

"The question on the table, *Becca*," he asks, smirking a little, "is what would you do, if you had to, to go to your dream college? What laws would you break? What moral dictates would you toss aside?"

And, yes, he really does say "moral dictates."

"Would you sell your soul?" Clarice asks.

"Would you sleep with Mr. Dingleheimer?" Oscar asks.

Mr. Dingleheimer is one of the physics teachers, and he weighs four hundred pounds. I'm guessing Mrs. Dingleheimer probably doesn't even sleep with him.

"Would you pay someone to take the SAT for you if they could guarantee perfect scores?" Rosa asks. "Would you rob a bank? Would you sell state secrets to the Chinese?"

"Hey!" Oscar says. His family came to the United States from China, like, three generations ago, but sometimes he acts like it was yesterday.

"Would you hack in to Harvard's admissions system and sabotage your competition?" Stuart asks.

I am still a little off today. It isn't until I hear the word "hack," that I realize what started this whole guessing game.

That article about Daddy and what he did, I think. *They're just laughing at it.*

I can feel my legs and my hands start to tremble. I slide my hands under the table and hold on to my knees.

Fake it fake it fake it fake it . . .

I put on my sweetest smile.

"I would practically kill myself to get an A in AP chem," I say. "I would spend four Friday nights in a row taking SAT practice tests. Oh, wait. I already did those things last year! I'm all set!"

I turn toward Oscar, because I'm sure he's going to put his hand out for me to high-five—he's so nerdy and predictable like that. But he's just sitting there, gazing at me sadly. He shakes his head a little.

I look back at the rest of the group, and they're all wearing the same pitying expression.

Do they know something? I wonder. *Did one of them figure something out?*

"Oh, Becca," Stuart says, appointing himself spokesperson for the group. "Becca Becca Bec."

"What?" I say. Or screech, actually.

"What did you do all summer—hide under a rock?" Stuart asks. "Didn't you work on college stuff at all?"

"I worked at Riggoli's," I say. "You know—making money for college? Do the math: Every minute I spent shredding mozzarella or slicing pepperoni earned me point-oh-eight seconds in a college classroom."

I know this group: They won't let a ridiculous statement like that stand unexamined. I didn't actually do the math myself, but Rosa will. She'll pull out her calculator. She'll ask how much I make, and then she'll figure it all out: How much time my summer of pizza making would earn me at a private school, a public school, a community college . . .

I'll have them distracted in nothing flat.

But all of them are still staring at me.

"You'll never earn enough for college working at Riggoli's," Stuart says flatly. "That's if you even manage to get in anywhere good. Grades and test scores aren't enough. Do you know, there are people with almost-perfect SAT scores who still don't get into Georgetown? Georgetown! It's not even the Ivy League!"

"Stuart, you have got to stop looking at collegedata dot com," Clarice says. "It's making you crazy."

"And stop texting me about it!" Rosa adds, waving her peanut butter sandwich at him for emphasis. She sees me looking confused and seems to remember that I don't have a cell phone, so I haven't gotten any texts. "Collegedata's this website that tells you your chances of getting in at any school."

"And where kids like you got in last year, and what kind of aid they got," Stuart adds. "Though everyone says this year's going to be even tougher. . . ."

He does look a little wild-eyed. Maybe this conversation hasn't exactly been a joke. But then, Stuart's the kind of person who walks out of an exam moaning about how this time he's sure he's failed, he's ruined his life forever, he'll be lucky someday just to get a job emptying Porta-Johns. And then it will turn out that he only missed one question, and with the curve, he's got 100 percent.

"You'll be fine," I tell him. "You've got a million extracurriculars. Marching band president, remember? Aren't you senior class president, too?"

Stuart shakes his head violently.

"That's not enough," he says. "There's a senior class president at every high school in America. Do you know how many spaces there are in Harvard's freshman class? One thousand, six hundred and fifty-seven. A certain percentage of those are legacies; a certain percentage has to be international students—you break it down far enough, I'm probably competing with ten thousand other kids for just five spots!"

"You like competition," I say.

"But how is that fair, when the odds are so stacked against me?" Stuart asks. He stabs his fork a little too hard against his cafeteria tray. "It used to be, if you were a decent student, you did okay on the ACT or SAT, you could go anywhere you wanted."

"If you were a white male," Rosa mutters. "And rich."

Stuart ignores her.

"But now it's like, if you haven't already discovered the cure for cancer as a high school student, forget it," Stuart says. "You don't have a prayer."

"So discover the cure for cancer, already," I say. "You've got a couple months."

I look around—surely Oscar will high-five me for that zinger. But he and both the girls are slumped down. Stuart has them all stressed out now, worrying about college. He's discovered something, all right: insta-depression. He could market it to people with bipolar disorder, bring them down from their moments of euphoric mania just by talking.

"Or, I know," I say. "You could take your gloom-and-doom act on the road. Go around telling high school seniors everywhere just how screwed they are. You'll be famous, and that's what will get you into Harvard. Then ten thousand senior class presidents will murder you because they don't appreciate the irony."

"Very funny," Stuart says.

Then, to my horror, he picks up a stack of papers from beside his tray—the packet Ms. Stela passed out in the assembly. Stuart flips it over to the last page, to the picture of Daddy.

"This guy," he says, and he puts his finger right on Daddy's face. "He stole millions of dollars, right? You don't actually need that much to pay tuition. I bet he was going to buy his kid's way into Harvard. That's what I would do, if I had that kind of money. That's what lots of people do. It's like, nowadays, you have to cheat to come out on top."

I'm standing before I even realize I've moved. Now everyone is staring at me again. Kids at neighboring tables are staring at me too.

I've made a huge mistake. I need to turn this into a joke, make it seem like I planned it and I'm just setting up another punch line. But there's not a single funny thought in my mind right now. Every cell in my body has switched over to "dead serious" mode.

The setting right before "And now we cry."

I have to say something before that happens.

"I'm not going to let you ruin my senior year," I fling at Stuart. *Not bad,* I congratulate myself. Except my voice sounds like somebody else's, like it belongs to some robot I may or may not be able to control. And I'm still talking. "You want to know what happens to cheaters? Cheaters get *caught.* They go to prison. They *lose* in the end."

I barely stop myself from saying, "Like that guy did. Like Daddy."

Bring it back to Stuart, I tell myself frantically. *Stop talking about Daddy.*

"So . . . if you're going to be a cheater . . ." My voice wobbles, but I have to go on. "Or if you're just going to be all negative and nasty all the time . . . then . . . then . . . I'll eat somewhere else."

Okay, that was acceptable, I tell myself. *Nothing that Oscar and Rosa and Clarice wouldn't have wanted to say too.*

I turn around and walk away, feeling oddly triumphant. I've abandoned my unopened lunch sack and I left my gov book behind, but someone else will get them for me. I just need to make it to the girls' bathroom and calm down.

I'm halfway there when I hear Stuart calling after me.

"I'm only telling the truth, Becca," he says. "You can't run away from the truth."

I just finished a summer reading list of the classics. I bet I'm the only person in AP lit who actually read the whole of *Moby Dick*, instead of just skimming the SparkNotes online. But even with all that supposedly great literature sloshing around in my brain, somehow the only words I can think of are from a children's story:

> *Run, run, as fast as you can*
> *You can't catch me, I'm the Gingerbread Man.*

The words in my head are in Daddy's voice. The way he always told that story, nobody ever caught the Gingerbread Man. He didn't fall for anyone's tricks; the fox didn't gobble him down. He never met his deserved end. He just kept running and running and running, the happiest Gingerbread Man around. He could run away from anything.

How am I supposed to handle any truth? My head was filled with lies from the very start.

Now

(Still not "then."
But maybe some "if . . . then . . .")

I pretend I don't hear Stuart. I keep walking. I shove my way into the girls' bathroom, and it is blessedly empty. God still loves me, after all.

Debatable, I think.

I can't bear to consider *that* issue right now. And I can't count on the bathroom staying empty. I enter the stall at the far end and bolt the door, guaranteeing myself eight square feet of privacy. I lean against the concrete block wall, which is probably exactly like the concrete block walls imprisoning my father.

Vanderbilt, I think. *Vanderbilt University.*

If my father really had stolen all that money for me, it wouldn't have been Harvard he'd try to buy or bribe my way into. It would have been Vanderbilt.

If.

He wasn't actually stealing all that money for you, I tell myself.

But it's too late. I'm plunged into some alternate-world fantasy based on another "if": *If Daddy hadn't been caught . . .*

If Daddy hadn't been caught, I would still live in Georgia. He and Mom and I would have spent the summer visiting various college campuses, maybe with groups of my giggling friends, all of us imagining glorious futures for ourselves of frat parties and sorority formals and midnight pizza runs. . . .

We would have saved the trip to Vanderbilt for a special day. Maybe it would have been just the three of us; maybe I would have picked some truly beloved friend to marvel with me at Daddy's tales of *his* days as a student at Vanderbilt.

"I lived in that dorm freshman year," he'd say, pointing at Tolman Hall. "My roommate and I were always playing pranks on each other. . . . One time I answered the phone and he'd put shaving cream all over the earpiece."

And:

"Those are the gates we all walked through, starting out as freshmen," he'd narrate as we'd stroll around. We wouldn't even need the official campus tour, because we'd have Daddy. "Founders Walk, it was called. And then my whole class marched through them again, all together, after graduation. . . ."

I know my father's Vanderbilt stories by heart.

The thing is, after he was arrested, it came out that he'd never actually gone to Vanderbilt. Not as a student, anyway. He'd worked in the dining hall washing the real students' dishes. He'd put in again and again for a job in the computer lab instead, but it had never come through.

People swore to this version of my father's past in court. That Vanderbilt dish-washing job must have been the last one he'd gotten without a lie. After that, in job interviews, he'd talked about his Vanderbilt degree, his years of computer experience. He made it all up. And then he got big, important jobs; he got those years of experience; he started his own company.

All because of the Vanderbilt lie.

I know my daddy lied. I know he lied to me and Mom and pretty much everyone else he ever met—including all those people whose money he stole. I know the truth about my daddy.

But there's still some dumb, hopeful voice whispering in the back of my mind, *I want to go to Vanderbilt like my daddy. No—I want to go for real.*

I don't cry. I can do this sometimes: hold back the tears until it's safe to let them out. I tell myself I'll wait until tonight, after Mom's left for work and I have the apartment to myself. But maybe I won't cry even then. Maybe I'll fill out college applications instead.

The sixth-period bell rings and I step out of the bathroom like I'm perfectly fine.

Rosa drops my lunch sack and my gov book on my desk when I get to AP lit.

"Aren't you starving?" she asks. "I bet Ms. Darien would let you eat in here if you explain what happened."

I frown and shake my head.

"I can wait until after school," I tell her. "Besides, what's there to explain?"

Rosa smirks at me.

"Stuart's in Ms. Darien's third-period class," she says. "I bet if you said, 'Stuart Collins was acting like a jerk and made me miss lunch,' she would totally get it."

I shrug to let Rosa know I don't need to do that. And I don't need to talk about this anymore. But Rosa continues leaning toward me.

"Just a warning," she says, lowering her voice conspiratorially. "The trending topic in DHS gossip is that you and Stuart secretly dated over the summer, but your relationship couldn't take the strain of being back at school. So that's why you were screaming at each other at lunch."

I must have a completely blank look on my face, because she adds, "People think you were breaking up."

I jerk back, away from Rosa.

"Who would think that?" I ask. I make a face. "Me and *Stuart*? Why would *anyone* date *him*?"

I decide not to let Rosa answer that one. I have a tiny suspicion that, for all her complaints about Stuart, Rosa might actually have a crush on him herself.

"Besides," I say, "nobody ever gossips about me. Who cares?"

I am a nonentity as far as the DHS gossip machine is concerned. I've worked very hard to try to stay that way.

"It's a slow news day," Rosa says. "And after three years of the Shannon Daily crowd holding center stage, that whole scene's getting a little boring. You're fresh meat."

Lovely, I think.

I buy myself some time by pulling a blank sheet of paper out of my lit folder, carefully centering it on my desk, getting ready for Ms. Darien to start class. I look back at Rosa.

"You can fix this, can't you?" I ask. "Can't you send out some texts, tell people nothing happened, it's all a bunch of lies?"

Rosa looks around, so I do too. We're surrounded. Someone is sitting in every seat nearby, and Josie Wu, Tamela Evans, and Dustin Dubowski are standing at the very edge of my desk. Rosa leans in so close she can whisper in my ear.

"Which is better?" she asks. "To let people believe the lies or have them know the truth?"

I freeze.

She knows she knows she knows she knows she . . .

I close my eyes. I clench my teeth.

"Please," I whisper. "Please don't. . . ."

But Rosa is still talking.

"Don't you know I'm poor too?" she whispers. "Don't you think I understand?"

Poor? I think.

I pull back from Rosa so I can stare her right in the face. Probably my eyes are burning with all those unshed tears from the bathroom, and my face is flushed with the shame of what I thought Rosa was going to reveal.

But her eyes are burning too.

She tugs on my arm, pulling me close again to whisper some more.

"People like Stuart don't know what it's like," she says. "He complains all the time about not having enough money, but really . . . Remember how his family took that vacation to Aruba last spring break? Remember—"

"Rosa," I say, twisting away, trying to break her grip on my arm. "I don't care how much money Stuart Collins has."

She doesn't let go. She is unrelenting. She is acting like this is a problem that God himself has ordained that Rosa Alvarez must solve. Like it's AP calc or something.

"For college, *it doesn't matter,*" Rosa hisses into my ear. "My sister said, when it comes to financial aid, it's actually better to be flat broke. They see you can't pay a dime, they don't expect you to. So don't worry about it."

Rosa thinks this is all about money. She thinks I'm ashamed. She thinks I would rather have people think I secretly dated Stuart Collins than know I can't afford college.

She thinks that is all I have to be ashamed of.

I look her full in the face again.

"Rosa," I say, "you're a good friend."

What else can I tell her?

Now

The school day ends, and I walk across the street to home. I am, as usual, the only person walking. Even the other kids who live in my apartment complex drive, or get friends with cars to drive them. Or, if they have neither cars nor car-owning friends, probably they are loitering at school so no one will see them leave.

I did that freshman year. I actually joined the cross-country team just so I didn't have to walk past all the other kids roaring out of the school parking lot in their Mustangs or Jeeps or even the practical Civics and Corollas and hand-me-down minivans from their moms. No heavy-duty symbolism there: I ran away every day that fall. At the end of the season the coach, who still hadn't learned my name, said, "Kid, you've got stamina. You and that Muslim girl—the two of you came in last or second to last every single race. But you've got staying power; I'll give you that much."

Jala ran with me. I would have quit without her. But it was always the two of us bringing up the rear of the pack; it felt like I owed it to her to keep showing up. It would have been too lonely for either of us to be the only one losing. And then it was natural, in November when the cross-country season ended, to follow her into math club and Spanish club and service club and other activities that, it turned out, I was actually good at.

It is mostly thanks to Jala that I have any extracurriculars to put on my college apps.

Does Jala think of me as poor, like Rosa does? Do Oscar and Clarice and Lakshmi and Stuart and . . .

I stop myself before I end up listing everybody in my class, every single person I've met in Deskins.

I know, because my sociology teacher made a big deal about it last year, that Deskins High School is very "economically diverse." Some people (like Stuart Collins) live in mansions; some people (like me) live in the apartments. People in Deskins call our complex just "the apartments," not "Whispering Pines Apartments" because, as it turns out, these are the only apartments in town. But, thanks to the bad economy, lots of people who live in actual houses are poor too. Mr. Stoddard, the sociology teacher, said the factor everyone looks at is how many kids get free or reduced lunches courtesy of the government. At DHS, it's 20 percent of the student body.

I am not in that 20 percent, even though I am pretty sure that I qualify. This is one of Mom's quirks, that every single year she refuses to fill out the paperwork. I think this is her way of doing penance: It's like she thinks that if Daddy is eating free government food in prison, we don't deserve to sign up for me to get free government food at school.

Not that she's actually said that.

I am clinical and detached as I think about this all the way across the street. I make my strides long and carefree. I am just pondering government statistics and sociology class and paperwork—nothing that actually *matters*. Then I reach the front door of our apartment. Open it, shut it behind me, lean against it like I leaned against the concrete block wall in the bathroom during lunch. I drop my backpack and let myself remember the expression on Rosa's face in lit class, the tone in her voice. I let myself identify the emotion behind that expression, that tone:

Pity.

No, no, I tell myself. *You can't call it pity when she says she's poor too. That makes it empathy, compassion. She thinks she knows how you feel. She thinks you're both alike.*

She thinks.

It's not the same. We're not poor for the same reasons.

And if she did know the truth about me? Would the pity/empathy/compassion turn into disgust? Revulsion? Hatred?

It doesn't matter, because Rosa is never going to know. No one is.

I kick my backpack to the side just because—well, it was on the floor. It was just asking to be kicked. My stomach growls, and I remember I never ate lunch. Sheepishly, I pull my backpack back to me and take out the lunch sack. It's flattened, much less appealing for having been carried around for an entire day instead of just the first half. And for being kicked and rolling under my gov book.

I open the sack and find that my potato chips are crumbs, my carrot sticks are dried out and streaked with white splotches, my turkey sandwich is pancake thin and starting to reek. Four years ago I would have thought nothing of throwing away such an unappetizing meal. I might have even whined to Mom, "I'm starving! Can't you take me to Panera or the Corner Bakery to get some real food?"

Now I just start eating.

Is this proof that I am poor? Or that, like Mom, I am still trying to do penance for Daddy's sins?

I accidentally rip the lunch sack, and there's a corresponding sound from the back of the apartment: a creak of mattress springs.

Oh, crap. I woke up Mom.

The groaning mattress springs turn into other sounds: the floor creaks, the toilet flushes, water flows in the bathroom sink. I walk down the hall and knock at the bathroom door.

"Go back to sleep," I say. "You're working tonight, right? I promise I'll be quiet."

The door opens anyway, and Mom blinks at me, her eyes adjusting to the light.

"That's okay," she says. "I'm not that tired. I want to hear about your day."

This is awful and shallow and petty of me, but I don't like looking at my mom anymore. I do better talking to her through doors. Every time I see Mom I think of *The Picture of Dorian Gray*, which we read sophomore year in honors English: It's like Mom is the cursed picture. Daddy did the crimes, but Mom is the one who aged and sagged and developed gaunt hollows in her cheeks.

I try to tell myself she just looks different because once she stopped coloring her hair, it grew in gray. But that's not all that changed.

Looking older isn't the same as being cursed, I tell myself. *And, anyhow, how do you know Daddy's looks haven't changed just as much? You haven't seen him in three years. It's not like he sends pictures with his letters.*

I have this argument with myself practically every time I look my mother in the eye. It's exhausting.

"How was school?" Mom asks.

"Oh, you know. School," I say.

I am not going to tell her about Ms. Stela handing out the packet of papers with Daddy's picture. I am not going to tell her about Stuart saying you have to cheat to come out on top. I am not going to tell her about Rosa accusing me of being poor.

Or about that moment when I thought Rosa knew everything about me.

"I remember senior year," Mom says wistfully. "We had so much fun."

Mom went to some dinky school in Middle-of-Nowhere, Kentucky. Everybody was poor there, but they didn't know it. They just thought it was normal to make their own clothes, to cut the flowers for school dances out of their own gardens.

It is funny how Mom's stories about her childhood have changed over the past three years. Before Daddy went to prison, they were all, "We had nothing! We were miserable!" Now it's, "We had so much fun!"

I do not want to get her started on the thrill of hanging out on a Friday night at the town's one and only root-beer stand.

"Yeah?" I say. "Now senior year is all about the stress of getting into college. And figuring out how to pay for it."

It is not so funny that, even now, there is some little part of me that wants to punish Mom. (For what? Marrying Daddy? Not being able to stop him from becoming a criminal? Not being able to hide his crimes from the entire world? Not being able to give me all the luxuries on her legal salary that Daddy gave us with his illegal funds? Not completely giving up, which would have given me permission to completely give up too?) Mom flinches at the way I say, "And figuring out how to pay for it."

That was exactly what I wanted.

Still, she pastes on a tired smile and pats my arm.

"You have excellent grades and test scores," she says. "I'm so proud of you. I'm sure you'll get in anywhere you want. And you'll have dozens of scholarship offers."

"I'm fourth in my class," I say. "There are three people ahead of me to scoop up the big-time acceptances and scholarships. Not to mention thousands of kids at other schools."

Maybe I absorbed more of Stuart's stress and panic than I thought.

"Don't worry," Mom says. "Things will work out."

This is ridiculous advice from someone whose husband is in prison. Someone who's been living like a cross between a mole and a hermit for the past three years. Someone who, with each passing year, seems to fret more and more about keeping our connection to Daddy secret.

I remember the fear I saw on her face that day we were driving to Ohio, when we heard the radio report about our faked U-Haul destination. It's like that fear has settled into her face, into her bones, into her soul. It never leaves her.

That's what changed about Mom over the past three years.

Mostly I try to ignore it, and I don't talk about Daddy even with Mom. But today there's something I have to ask.

"Mom," I say. I start fiddling with the loopy chain of my necklace. It's one my father gave me, but I didn't remember that when I put it on this morning. I was just thinking it's one of the few things I brought from Georgia that doesn't look too childish now. One of the few things I didn't outgrow. "Are you sure there isn't some . . . college fund Daddy tucked away anywhere? Something else we were allowed to keep when they took away all Daddy's money?"

I dare to look straight at Mom, but she's not looking at me. Instead, she's staring down toward the floor, as if the hallway baseboard has suddenly become fascinating.

She's also shaking her head no.

"I should have been a better businesswoman, selling the house," Mom says. She looks back up and offers me a pained smile. "I guess there are a lot of things I should have done differently."

Not marry Daddy, I think. *Stopped him from becoming a criminal. Become fabulously wealthy with a legitimate job so it didn't matter to lose all Daddy's illegal money.*

But I say dutifully, "No, Mom, you did the best you could. It's not your fault we owed more on the house than it was worth."

I kind of think it was her fault. Why wasn't she paying more attention before Daddy was arrested?

Then she would have known too much. The government would have seen her as a coconspirator, and she would have gone to prison too.

No matter what, I lose.

I put on the same kind of grim smile Mom's giving me. Or maybe it's more of a grimace.

"Anyhow, Rosa says it's good to be flat broke when you're applying for financial aid," I tell her. As if my grimace isn't enough, I go for some black humor. "The joke's on the government—they took all Daddy's money, they're going to get stuck paying for my college. It is the government that gives all that financial aid, right?"

Mom's smile freezes.

"Mom?" I say. "There won't be any problem with me getting financial aid, will there?"

It suddenly hits me that college financial aid, like free or reduced lunch in high school, would require a stack of paperwork, lots of lines to fill out and boxes to check. Maybe the forms are even online, leaving a digital trail that could link me to Daddy and his crimes forever.

If the government or some college or university—Vanderbilt?—is going to give me thousands and thousands of dollars, they're probably not going to be satisfied with a "not applicable" answer to such a basic question as "father's name."

So what? I think. *Surely all that information is kept private. Who cares if some clerk in some office somewhere knows the truth? I won't have to see or talk to them.*

And I am stunned at myself. Have I actually changed that much from three years ago? Strayed so far from Mom's constant fear? Freshman year, the thought of *anyone* knowing about my connection to Daddy was enough to make me cower under the covers. It was enough to make me turn in my cell phone and shut down my Facebook page without a peep.

It was enough to make Mom and me move five hundred and fifty miles away from home and cut off ties with all the people we cared about. It was enough to make us deny my father's existence and abandon my academic records and build a new life that hid the truth from everyone.

I think about how I felt this morning, seeing that picture of Daddy and knowing that every single one of my fellow Deskins High School seniors was holding the same picture. Or this afternoon, talking to Rosa, during that one moment when I thought she'd found out the truth.

I'm not any less ashamed than I used to be, I think. *But—maybe I want something else so much that I'm willing to let my guard down just a little?*

I am like Stuart, after all. He wants Harvard enough to cheat; I want Vanderbilt enough to . . . well, to tell the whole truth. Just once. It would be worth it to get into Vanderbilt or someplace like it. Someplace that will be a reward for all my golden A's, someplace that says to the world, "This girl is quality. She's not a liar like her father. She's not an ignorant, terrified dupe like her mother."

All this is breaking over me, and thanks to all my advanced-level English classes, I know exactly how to label it: I have had an epiphany.

Meanwhile, Mom's frozen smile is cracking. Not in a good way.

"I—I have to check with the lawyer," she says. She catches a glimpse of my face, and maybe she kind of understands. Because she adds, "I'll call Mr. Trumbull right now."

She goes back in her bedroom and closes her door. And I don't exactly try to eavesdrop, but it doesn't seem reasonable to walk all the way out to the living room when she's just going to come back out in a few minutes. She keeps her voice low—and seems to be listening more than she talks—but I hear her say, "Should be able to apply for financial aid" and then, "Why? Why can't she even have that?" And then there's a mumbled reference I don't catch until the third time she repeats the same words: "Unique circumstances . . ."

"Unique circumstances"? I think. *She's talking to Daddy's defense attorney! He hangs out with criminals and their families all the time! In his eyes, we're not the least bit unique!*

Mom steps back out of the bedroom, and she looks worse than ever. Her face has a clammy sheen and she keeps gulping hard, like she's trying to hold back tears. Talking to the attorney always sets her off.

I really can't look at her now.

"Let's hold off on anything like that," she says, and it's painful to hear how hard she's trying to sound normal for me, how hard she's trying to make this an ordinary-mom answer to an ordinary-teenager question. "It's not a definite no, but . . . for now you can't apply for financial aid. It's not due anytime soon, is it? Probably you'll get so many scholarship offers, it's not going to matter. *I* have faith in you."

I can't let myself think about why she's so distraught—or about how likely it is that "for now you can't" will eventually turn into "you won't be able to, ever." That's how these things work. Instead, my brain skitters off in a rebellious direction: *Is "I have faith in you" the kind of thing she said to Daddy when they were newly married? Before he'd done anything worse than stretch the truth about his educational background? Before he'd turned to crime as the only way to give her everything she had faith in?*

Now

(Why, oh, why aren't I in a different now?)

Ever since that awful winter of my freshman year, the rules of my relationship with Mom are that I don't argue with her. No matter what she says, or what Mr. Trumbull tells her we have to do. Even now—especially now, when I have all those furious and unfair charges flashing through my brain—all I can do is look away and mumble, "Okay."

I am a terrible person. It is unforgivable that I can blame Mom for any of this. Everything is Daddy's fault.

Why can't I believe that?

Mom has her hand stretched out to me, like she wants to draw me into a hug. But I pull back.

"I need to get started on my AP physics homework," I say.

Mom opens her mouth like she wants to say something else. But she doesn't.

"Maybe you should just lie back down," I tell her. "This will be quiet homework. I'll mute my calculator."

Mom touches my cheek, moving quickly enough that she actually makes contact for an instant.

"You're a good kid," she says. "You deserve—"

"Yeah, yeah," I interrupt, before she can tell me what I should get, but won't. "Who ever gets what they deserve?"

And then the answer is huge between us: *Daddy. Daddy got what he deserved. Only, we got punished too.*

Neither of us says it.

"Good night," Mom says, yawning. "Er, afternoon."

She goes back into her bedroom and shuts the door. I head into my own room, but I don't drag the physics homework with me. I fire up my laptop—the same laptop that was confiscated three and a half years ago with all of Daddy's computers, the day he was arrested. I was so mad that day, so indignant: "*How* could anyone *do* this to me? How am I going to check Facebook? How am I going to get into my iTunes account?"

Then I found out they were taking Daddy away too.

I remember him bending down to my level and looking me straight in the eye right before they took him away. He kissed me on the forehead and said in his calmest, most soothing voice: "Honey, this is all a mistake. You know I didn't do anything wrong. We'll get it all straightened out and you'll get your computer back and everything will be fine."

But it turned out that my father had done some of his crimes on my computer—mine! So it was evidence, and I didn't get it back until after the trial. Daddy's attorney had to mail it to us after we moved.

At least it still works, I tell myself, though sometimes that's a little iffy, too.

I go to the Vanderbilt University website and learn that 60 percent of its undergraduate students get financial aid. I learn that 89 percent of first-year students were in the top 10 percent of their class.

I learn that I got a better SAT score than most of those students.

So, maybe . . . I think.

I switch over to the website Stuart and Rosa were talking about at lunch, collegedata.com. Right in the center of the home page, it says, "Will you get in? Find out! Estimate your admission chances at any college, and see how to improve your odds." But when I click on the strip that says "Calculate your chances!" it turns out that the site wants all sorts of information from me first: name, birthdate, address . . . I put my finger on the B key for "Becca," but I don't press down. I am remembering.

There was a no-man's-land of time after the verdict but before the sentencing, after Mom and I decided to move but before we left Georgia. It was like our old life had ended but nothing else had replaced it. My most vivid memory from that time was an afternoon Mom and I spent in Mr. Trumbull's office. He was talking to Mom, but looking at me: "You two, of all people, should realize that you'll have to be very, very careful about what you do online. You log in somewhere to get some, I don't know, free iTunes download or something, and the next thing you know, anyone on the planet can find your new address."

This is why I never opened a new Facebook account.

This is why I barely use my computer except for homework.

This is why, when I look at my laptop, I don't see it as an innocent companion, a fun way to pass the time. Even with my old sixth-grade Hello Kitty sticker peeling from its case, I see the computer now as a grenade ready to blow up in my face, a ticking time bomb that might explode at any minute.

Collegedata.com has reassuring letters in green at the top of its page: "https," meaning it should be a secure site. And I am not looking for anything as frivolous as a free iTunes download. I am looking for my future. I am looking for permission to be a high school senior like Stuart and Rosa and Oscar and Clarice, people who think they can plan their futures.

But I take my hands off the keyboard. I reach for the mouse and shut everything down.

I barely sleep that night. In the morning I am waiting outside the guidance office when Ms. Stela arrives.

She's juggling a Starbucks cup and a briefcase and such a huge sheaf of computer printouts that it might be the records of every student in the school. Or maybe, everyone who *ever* attended the school.

"Please don't tell me your schedule's messed up too," she says, somehow finding a spare hand to push back a strand of her long hair before it snakes down into the coffee. But she's off-balance now; I grab the coffee cup to keep her from spilling all over the computer printouts.

"Thanks," she says, using the briefcase to motion me to follow her through the waiting room into her office, which she unlocks with a key hanging from a lanyard around her neck.

She drops the printouts and briefcase on a chair, searches for a pen and a Post-it note, and then says, "Now, Becca. Which class do you want into or out of?"

"This isn't about scheduling," I say. "I need to find out about applying for scholarships."

Ms. Stela puts down her pen.

"I told Mr. Gordon we had that assembly yesterday too early in the year," she mutters. She seems to realize she shouldn't criticize the principal in front of a student and puts on a comforting smile. "Look, you don't have to worry about scholarships yet. Those deadlines are later. Right now you should just think about where you want to apply, do any remaining college visits, and work on your essays. Remember, if you go to the guidance website, there are links to help. And, of course, you need to focus on keeping your grades up, so when you send out your first semester grades to colleges, they'll see . . ."

She seems to be shifting into some guidance-counselor spiel that she gives so often, she doesn't even have to think. She's glancing toward the printouts as if she's already mentally sent me on my way.

"I *do* need to start thinking about scholarships now," I interrupt, with an edge to my voice that I don't usually have with grown-ups. Or with anyone, really, except Stuart yesterday. That was dangerous—I lost control. But I have to make Ms. Stela see how important this is.

I try again.

"I . . . might have a problem applying for financial aid," I say. "I may not be able to do that. So I'll *have* to get scholarships. I need to know what's possible."

Ms. Stela stops gazing toward the computer printouts. She studies my face in a way that makes me think she may be a more observant guidance counselor than I ever suspected.

It makes me nervous.

"Why, Becca Jones," she says, emphasizing my last name oddly. She looks puzzled. "Are you an illegal immigrant? I mean, an undocumented alien?" She jerks her hands up like a traffic cop signaling "Stop!" Or, as if she's trying to take back her own words. "No, no, don't answer that. I don't need to know."

"I'm not an illegal immigrant!" I say. Though a split second later I wish I'd let Ms. Stela believe that. It would be easier. "There are just some . . . issues with my family's finances."

"Right," Ms. Stela says, nodding sagely. "Lots of families have . . . issues."

I don't like the way she says that. Or the fact that she steps past me to pull her door shut, making our conversation private. If any of the guidance secretaries were listening outside, this probably convinces them that I am an illegal immigrant.

From where? I think. *From the land of kids with imprisoned parents?*

I tell myself I'm being paranoid, and push on.

"Anyhow, that's why scholarships are so important," I say. "And why I need to know how much scholarship money I'll get so I'll know if I need to . . . to fill out the financial aid forms or not. You know."

What I really mean is, *Will I need to fight with Mom and Mr. Trumbull to get to fill out financial aid forms? Is that a fight I can run away from, like everything else? Or is my choice fight that fight or don't have a future?*

Ms. Stela turns into some version of a deeply concerned guidance counselor I've never seen before. She clears off the stack of paper from her least cluttered visitor's chair and gestures for me to sit down. She waits until I obey. Then she eases into her own desk chair.

"Becca," she says gently, and I imagine her using that same tone of voice with girls with unplanned pregnancies. Or maybe with actual illegal immigrants. "The timing isn't on your side for deadlines and announcement dates. For pretty much any college application you'd turn in, you need to check a box about whether you're applying for financial aid. Those applications are almost all going to be due by the end of December. The FAFSA—the federal financial aid form—that's due in mid February. Depending on where you apply, you may not know about certain school-related merit aid until well after that. And the local scholarships, the ones that are for Deskins students only—the ones that are easiest to get— we don't announce those until the senior awards assembly in May."

I knew that last part. As a National Honor Society member, I'd handed out the programs to proud parents at the senior awards assembly last May. I'd glanced at the lineup of scholarships and prizes during lulls between families coming in.

The information just hadn't seemed so devastating last May.

"So you're saying, if I don't fill out the FAFSA, I may not even be able to go to college?" I nearly wail to Ms. Stela.

I must look and sound thoroughly shell-shocked. Ms. Stela starts patting my knee.

"No, no, that is *not* what I'm saying," she assures me, shaking her head for emphasis. "But if you really can't fill out the financial aid forms—and your family doesn't have the money to pay full freight, which, who does these days?—then you're going to have to be strategic about where you apply. You're a good student. The University of Toledo has really started offering a lot of merit aid to attract top students. So has the University of Kentucky. Depending on what you want to study, there are other schools, too, which may not be terribly well known or prestigious, but you would be pretty much guaranteed—"

"I don't want to go to Kentucky or Toledo or some school nobody's ever heard of," I say. "I want to go to Vanderbilt."

I sound like a spoiled toddler about to cry because she doesn't want the small, plain-vanilla ice cream cone; she wants three scoops of rainbow sherbet in the chocolate-dipped waffle cone with the fudge sauce and sprinkles on top. And I must have waved my arms almost like a tantrum-throwing toddler, because suddenly coffee is sloshing from the cup I'd forgotten I was still holding for Ms. Stela.

She takes the coffee cup from me and puts it on one of the few uncluttered spaces on her desk, right at the edge.

"I'm not saying give up your dreams," she says, and her voice is as cautious as someone trying to reason with a small, irrational child. "I'm not saying, don't even try. But you need to have a backup plan. Just in case. The rules have changed recently so more people can get financial aid, but if you really don't think you can, you'll need to apply widely to lots of colleges and—oh!"

She jumps as if she's just thought of something amazing. But at the same time she jolts her knee against the desk, which sends her coffee cup tumbling off the edge. The cup hits the floor and the lid bursts off, sending liquid gushing across the carpet. I grab Kleenexes from a box on her desk and dive down to try to soak it up. Ms. Stela scrambles after me.

"This is why the custodians hate me," she says.

I realize there are already several rings of coffee stains on the off-white carpet.

"I don't know," I say. "I think it's kind of an improvement on the original design."

Ms. Stela laughs and says, "Remind me to give you the comedy-writing scholarship application come January."

She stands up and walks to a filing cabinet.

"This is what I just remembered," she says, pulling out the drawer. "This is what I know you'll want to see . . . now, where is it?"

She's rifling through folders. She sounds so excited, I stand up and walk over close enough to see the labels on some of the folders: "The Scott Prescott Memorial Scholarship," "The Amanda DeVries Memorial Swim Scholarship," "The Ronald Higgins Memorial Technology Scholarship . . ."

"Are all scholarships named for dead people?" I ask.

"On the local level, yeah, most of them are," Ms. Stela says. "It's a way for parents who lose children to make sure that their kid's memory lives on and that something positive comes out of what might otherwise seem like a senseless death."

She sounds so clinical that I'm surprised when she sniffs and swipes a hand at her eyes.

"Sorry," she says. "One of my best friends was killed in a car crash my junior year. Her parents set up a scholarship fund, and we had all sorts of fundraisers for it . . . and then I ended up getting one of those scholarships. Still not the same as having my friend around, you know?"

"That's too bad," I say. But Ms. Stela has already moved on. She's at the back of the drawer now, pulling out a folder labeled "Whitney Court Scholarship." It figures she wouldn't have the files in alphabetical order. And that she'd leave out a vital word like "Memorial."

"Okay, this is what I was looking for," Ms. Stela says, opening the folder and holding it out for me to see. "This is a fairly new scholarship, and its deadlines are earlier than the other local ones. I have it marked on my Google calendar to send out this information to all the seniors next week, but that's so close, I'll give this to you now and bump it up for everyone else, too."

I bend down and read the first lines of the paper on the top of the folder:

> Whitney Court spent her entire childhood in Deskins and graduated from Deskins High School fourteen years ago. . . .

"This is last year's handout," Ms. Stela says, reaching around me with a pen to cross out the "fourteen" and make it "fifteen." "I'll have to update it before I hand it out to all the seniors. Let's see, are there any other changes?"

She reads over my shoulder as I go on:

> Whitney was very involved in DHS activities and thoroughly enjoyed her time here. It would not be an exaggeration to say that she loved each and every one of her classmates, and they loved her. In her honor, her family has begun awarding a scholarship each year to one graduating DHS senior. Scholarship amounts vary but can be for up to a full-ride scholarship at a private university, renewable for up to four years . . .

I have to back up, make myself reread the magical words a second time.

"Full ride?" I say. My voice squeaks with amazement. "This is for a full ride?"

"It's *up to* a full ride," Ms. Stela corrects.

I barely notice.

"So, if I get this, it could pay for everything at Vanderbilt, or some other school like that . . . any school, really." I laugh, almost giddy with the news.

"Well, maybe. *If* you get it, and *if* they give the full amount," Ms. Stela reminds me. "But the deadlines are good for you too, since the application is due in mid-October and they announce the winner by the end of December. It's totally weird but, hey, if someone wants to donate money to DHS students, they can set it up practically any way they want."

"This is exactly what I need," I say. "I'll do anything to get this."

I remember Stuart's questions from yesterday: "What would you do, if you had to, to go to your dream college? What laws would you break? What moral dictates would you toss aside?" Then I push that out of my mind. Some scholarship administered through the school is not going to require breaking the law.

Ms. Stela shakes her head and rolls her eyes at the reverence in my voice. But she's grinning, too.

"The requirements for this are unusual," she says. "Not as strange as some of the scholarships you'll find online, where kids can win money for playing marbles or making prom clothes out of duct tape or taking tests about fire sprinklers. But, still. Most scholarships require a personal essay—about volunteer work or your plans for the future or what DHS has meant to you . . . stuff like that. The Court scholarship requires an essay about some student who graduated in Whitney's class."

I do a double take.

"You mean, *any* student who graduated then?" I say. "I could just pick somebody at random? And then write about what they've done since high school?"

I'm just as glad not to have to write about myself. But this seems cruel, like Whitney's parents are gluttons for punishment. The little summary of her life doesn't say anything about her death, but she must have died late enough in senior year that she still got a diploma. Or maybe right after graduation. She couldn't have lived long after that, if they're still so fixated on her high school years. So why would her family want to hear again and again about all the glorious accomplishments her classmates went on to achieve without her?

"You can pick anyone from that class at random, yes," Ms. Stela says. "But you don't write about their lives since high school. You write about their high school years."

This I understand. If I'd lost Daddy simply because he'd died, I'd probably want to dwell constantly on our happy memories. I would have welcomed people reminiscing with me. That's pretty much what the Court family is doing, right?

"I get it," I say. "This is great."

I beam. Ms. Stela's office is still coffee stained and cluttered. But it suddenly feels like a holy site for me. I feel as though a ray of sunlight has broken through three years' worth of clouds around me. I feel as though there might as well be an angelic choir in the filing cabinet belting out the Hallelujah Chorus. I feel . . . hope.

"Becca?" Ms. Stela says, an edge of worry to her voice. "Remember, this isn't guaranteed—"

"I know," I say.

But I want so much to believe that it is.

Now—

finally, a happy now. Sort of

I sit through my morning classes in a daze. At lunchtime I don't go to the cafeteria. I go to the yearbook office. It's too early in the year for anyone to be hard at work on it yet, so the office is deserted except for Mrs. Iverson, the advisor, straightening her desk after her last class.

"Can I look through some old yearbooks?" I ask. "I won't take them out of the room."

She glances up, jolted.

"Oh, is *that* starting already?" she asks. "For the Whitney Court Scholarship?"

I nod, and she sighs. She points toward a row of books lined up against the wall.

"Over in the corner. Her senior year is the purple one," she tells me. "And if anyone else comes in, you have to share, all right? I am *not* spending my lunch period policing this."

I guess my idea of looking through old yearbooks to find out about Whitney's class isn't as original as I thought. I guess seniors do it every year. But thanks to Ms. Stela, at least I have a head start. If I'm lucky, she'll forget to give the information to the other seniors until the last minute, and I'll have a huge advantage.

But would that be fair? I wonder. *Or is that like Stuart-style cheating?*

I push the questions aside. I'm just glad that, once Mrs. Iverson leaves for lunch, I have the room to myself.

I pull out the yearbooks from fifteen, sixteen, seventeen, and eighteen years ago and sit down with them at a long table. I'm actually a little surprised that there *was* a Deskins High School so long ago, since everything in Deskins seems new. But I open the book from Whitney's senior year and find that I'm staring at a picture of a completely different building: a small, plain, brick structure. It's labeled, "Deskins Junior-Senior High School, Grades 7–12."

They had six grades in one building back then? I marvel. *And it's still such a small building—and such a small yearbook?*

I feel a little like I've just discovered that Deskins, like me, has a secret history.

Then I turn the page and forget about Deskins. Now I'm staring at a picture of Whitney Court.

She's a pretty blond girl in a DHS cheerleader's uniform. The camera has caught her midjump, so the pleats of her white skirt are flared out; her ponytail bounces behind her. Her smile is a mile wide, and she's clearly so full of joy and vigor and, well, *life*, that even though I don't know the girl, tears actually spring to my eyes at the thought that, probably not too long after this picture was taken, she died.

Sitting at her feet in the picture is a cluster of younger girls, also in cheerleading uniforms. They're maybe sixth or seventh graders. Some of them are sitting awkwardly, their clothes too baggy or too tight—you can see that they're not quite comfortable in their own skins. But it's clear from their upturned, reverent faces that they *adore* Whitney. They want to be exactly like her. She's apparently just showed them how to do a handspring or a cartwheel or a cheer—or maybe just how to be happy.

I almost feel like whispering, "Oh, please. Show me too!"

And I know that this is Whitney because some long-ago yearbook writer evidently thought it was clever to label the picture, "Whitney Court, holding court."

The yearbook must have been finished before she died, I think. *Because otherwise there'd be some mention of her death here. This would be a tribute page.*

I feel a pang, not just for poor, dead Whitney, but also for those worshipful girls at her feet. They'd be, what, nearly thirty now? Can they stand to look at this picture knowing Whitney died? Maybe it would be like me looking at pictures of my life before Daddy was arrested. I know Mom has old photo albums stashed at the back of our hall closet, but I haven't looked at them once in the past three years. It would hurt too much.

Stop it, I tell myself. *It's not the same. You didn't even know Whitney Court. She's nothing to you but a chance for money.*

It's harsh, but I have to think that way to get myself to turn the page.

Whitney's there too. In this picture, she's wearing chemistry-lab goggles and making a comical face as a short, pudgy guy beside her prepares to combine two liquids in a beaker. He's laughing, too, and holding his nose. Behind them four or five other kids are cowering, their hands over their ears, their mouths open as they scream or shriek or call out warnings. I can almost hear them crying, "It's going to blow!" or "Duck!" or "Watch out!"

Evidently Whitney even had fun in chemistry class.

I keep going. Whitney is everywhere in this yearbook: in the musical, on the tennis team, on the science fair committee and the homecoming parade float committee and the teacher appreciation committee . . . She's in a lot of the candid shots, too. Here she is hugging her fellow cheerleaders at their last football game together; here she is in a pile of kids crammed into a Volkswagen Beetle like so many circus clowns; here she is, her arm looped casually around the waist of one of the basketball players. She and that same basketball player, Corey Wisner, reappear together on the prom page wearing, respectively, a ball gown and a tux, and matching crowns: They're prom king and queen.

I turn a couple more pages and there Whitney is again, wearing a white cap and gown, speaking at a podium: She's one of the three valedictorians.

On top of everything else, she was smart? I think. *A cheerleader, an athlete, prom queen, a girlfriend, and valedictorian, too?*

Now I have to remind myself that Whitney died, that something tragic and awful and unbearable was waiting for her soon after the last page of this yearbook. Because otherwise I would be so jealous of Whitney Court.

She had everything, I think. *She was so happy in high school.*

I glance toward the newest yearbooks in the lineup against the wall. I've been at Deskins High School for the past three years, of course, but you could search the books from my freshman, sophomore, or junior years and not find a single shred of evidence that I ever stepped foot in the place. I'm not in any of the club pictures or the candids. I'm not in the cross-country team shot from freshman year. I'm not even in the class-by-class rows of pictures that should show every kid in every grade. Right before picture day my freshman year, Mom read a newspaper article that freaked her out, about how some yearbook company's records were hacked, and the hackers got access to the names and personal information of every single kid pictured in more than eight hundred high school yearbooks.

"If even one TV station tracked you down through the year-book . . . ," Mom said.

She didn't have to finish the sentence. She and I filled out all sorts of privacy paperwork with the school. Just as she'd made Dad's name "not applicable," on my school forms, she turned me invisible in the yearbook. The few times anybody noticed me missing—Jala did, looking at the freshman yearbook; Oscar did last year—I just shrugged and said, "I guess there was a mistake."

But looking at what was essentially the Whitney Court memorial yearbook makes me regret all that. What if I actually do want some of my classmates to remember me?

Reality check here, I chide myself. *There would not be fifty kazillion pictures of you like there are of Whitney. It'd be two or three fuzzy, forgettable shots, and that's not worth getting upset about. Focus. Which of Whitney's classmates are you going to write about? Who's going to win your scholarship for you?*

I know the answer instantly. Only one student who graduated from DHS fifteen years ago drew my eye again and again as I turned the pages of the yearbook. Only one student seems worth researching and studying and writing about.

My essay is going to be about Whitney herself.

When the bell rings for sixth period, I put the yearbooks away and stumble out into the hallway. My head is still full of the DHS of Whitney's era—a place with cornfields behind the school building and a Future Farmers of America chapter and a quaint tradition where the entire senior class worked together to serve their parents breakfast on the last day of school. It looks like Deskins itself was just a small rural town then, not an extension of greater metropolitan Columbus, not the glitzy new suburb that looks like it sprang out of the cornfields five minutes before

Mom and I arrived. Deskins evidently used to be the kind of place where everybody knew everybody, where people minded one another's business, for better or for worse. It was more like where Mom grew up.

Old Deskins wouldn't have been a good place for Mom and me to hide.

I'm so intent thinking about all that, and Whitney's life, and however it was that she died, that when I get to AP lit, it takes me a few seconds to realize that Rosa is giving me the sad-puppy-dog look.

"*Chica,*" she says mournfully as soon as I sit down. "Don't make me do this."

"Huh? Do what?" I ask.

"You know how I hate getting people to make up," she says, drumming her fingers on her desk. She turns to face me. "You want to teach Stuart a lesson? Fine, teach him a lesson. But don't take it out on the rest of us."

"Teach Stuart a . . . ," I repeat blankly before I realize what she's talking about. "Oh, you think I skipped lunch because I'm still mad at Stuart? That's not the reason. I just had something I had to do."

"Don't we *all* have things we have to do?" she asks, frowning. "We only get one senior year of high school. It'll be over before we know it. Do you really want to spend the whole year just working and studying? Never having any fun with your friends?"

I blink. Has Rosa taken up mind reading? I could have shrugged off that argument without a second thought yesterday. But not today. Not after spending my entire lunch period looking at pictures of a girl whose life ended right after her senior year.

I put up my hands like I'm surrendering.

"Okay, okay, I promise. I'll be at lunch tomorrow," I say. "I'll be *fun*. I'll even sit beside Stuart, if that makes you happy. But I'm bringing duct tape, so I can cover his mouth if he starts getting annoying again."

"Now, that would be fun," she says, nodding approvingly. "Even Stuart might like it, since it would give him some 'suffering' to write about in his college essays. He'll turn it into, 'How I overcame having friends who tortured and abused me . . .'"

I groan.

"Can I take back my promise?" I ask. "Did Stuart spend the whole lunch today talking about how kids like him are at a huge disadvantage because they've never had anything bad happen to them?"

He'd been on that kick for a while last year, because someone had decided that junior English classes needed to work on preliminary drafts of college essays. Stuart maintained that, to have the right material for a good college essay, you had to have overcome something like cancer or incest or rape or, at the very least, parental divorce.

And the whole time I sat there thinking, *I am not writing about Daddy being in prison. I will never write about that.*

"Stuart talked about other things, too," Rosa says. "He invited all of us to go on a college-visit road trip with him when we have that three-day weekend in October."

I snort.

"Hasn't he already visited every top school in the country?" I ask. Starting last September, Stuart and his parents began jetting all over the place, and he'd come back to regale the rest of us with so many pompous stories that even the teachers made fun of him. "What was it this weekend?" our AP lang teacher would ask him on Monday mornings. "The glory that was Stanford? The grandeur that was Yale?"

"He says he still wants to see a few more," Rosa says. She has a hint of wistfulness in her voice. "In the South. He says his parents will pay for gas, so it won't even be an expensive trip."

Vanderbilt? I think. *Is Vanderbilt on his list?*

I'm almost ashamed at the way my heart leaps at this thought. Could it be? What if this is just one of those days when everything goes my way?

It's about time, I think.

Before I can ask Rosa for more details, Ms. Darien taps her desk to get the class's attention.

"Listen up," she demands. "You're going to want to hear this."

She starts passing papers down the aisles as she talks. I'm at the back of my row, so by the time I get a sheet, kids are already gasping in the seats ahead of me.

Ms. Darien has just handed out the Whitney Court Scholarship information to the entire class. I can turn my head to the right and see the same papers flowing down the rows in Mr. Techman's gov class across the hall. Ms. Stela was apparently more organized than I thought: All seniors must be getting this now.

"This is that scholarship I was telling you about," someone hisses on the other side of the room. "They *are* doing it again."

I look around—most kids in the class are wearing the same *Yeah, I knew that* expression they always keep on their faces in advanced classes, whether they understand what's going on or not.

But in this case . . . other kids would have known about this if they have older brothers and sisters. Or if they have friends who graduated already, I think.

At least I'm not the only one who was clueless.

"Am I reading this right?" Tyler Marco asks, making a big show of holding his paper closer and then farther from his eyes.

What can I say—he's in drama club. "Does this really say the scholarship's a full ride?"

"I would hope, by the time you're a senior, you would be capable of reading those two one-syllable words," Ms. Darien says drily. "If not, the Deskins school system has failed you. But I would hope that you could also read the three words before 'full ride.'"

Tyler immediately begins acting like a kindergartner struggling to learn to read: "Uh-uh-uh-ppp! T-t-t-o uh. . . ."

"Aw, fifty cents would count as being 'up to' a full ride," Shaquon James complains, throwing his paper down on his desk in disgust. "Why do you have to fool us like that? Has anybody ever gotten a full ride out of this?"

"Not that I know of, but this is only my second year at DHS," Ms. Darien says. "I do know Emily Riviera got ten thousand dollars last year. Not a full ride, but nothing to sneeze at. Ten thousand dollars a year—forty thousand dollars total—that would have put a serious dent in *my* student loans."

For a moment an awed hush falls over the class, which is impressive. Normally, Tyler and Shaquon never shut up.

"As you can see if you read this, the way to apply for this scholarship is by writing an essay about some DHS student who graduated fifteen years ago," Ms. Darien says. "Want to brainstorm a little about how you might gather information for that essay?"

Nobody speaks. But the silence is different now—not awed, but anxious. Suddenly it's like we've all turned into that miser from *Silas Marner,* jealously guarding his gold. No one wants to share any brilliant idea that might help the competition.

I'm certainly not saying anything about yearbooks.

Ms. Darien laughs.

"Funny, that's how this conversation went last year," she says.

"Okay, if you need any help, you're welcome to come see me privately. Let's move on to *Moby Dick*. . . ."

I glance over at Rosa, and she's clutching the scholarship paper to her chest. She has an older sister; she probably knew about this a long time ago. Maybe she and my other friends have talked about it at lunches that I've skipped, or in the texts and Facebook posts that I always miss.

She still looks as awestruck as I feel.

"This is exactly what I need," she mutters. "If it's four years of a full-ride scholarship, I wouldn't have to start racking up student loans until law school . . . I've got to win this."

I can see how it's a glittering dream for her, the same as it is for me. I feel guilty that I got a five-period head start and had an entire lunch period of looking at old yearbooks by myself.

"*One* of us has to win it," I say, and I think I'm being incredibly generous, acknowledging that we both want this.

She looks at me, blinks a few times, and then nods. "Oh, sure. One of us."

But I know both of us are thinking, *Me, me, oh, please, let it be me.* . . .

Still now

(Must fight against then . . . must resist . . .)

I have what seems like a hundred pages of homework to do that night, and I'm scheduled to work at Riggoli's from five to nine. But when I get home that afternoon, the first thing I do is fire up my laptop and look for Whitney Court online. A simple Google search doesn't pull up anything useful—unless you think it's helpful to find out that that's evidently a popular street name.

Daddy told me there are ways to search the deep Web, to find stuff that never shows up on Google, I think. *That's how he got a lot of the information for his scams.*

I do not want to win this scholarship by thinking like Daddy.

I sit still for a moment, my fingers motionless on the keyboard. Then, very deliberately, I type: f-a-c-e-b-o-o-k-.-c-o-m.

I start to gag. I fight back nausea.

You're okay, I tell myself. *It's all right. You can do this. Everybody uses Facebook, not just criminals like Daddy.*

We learned in AP psych about aversion therapy—how psychiatrists might try to get patients to have a negative association with behavior they're trying to stop, like smoking or drinking or doing drugs. Sometimes this works naturally, as with an allergy:

If you break out in hives and your throat swells and you have trouble breathing every time you eat shellfish, you're really not going to be rushing to all-you-can-eat shrimp buffets. Feeling like you're going to die has a way of making you rethink your behavior.

Facebook is not going to kill you, I tell myself.

But I still don't hit enter.

My treacherous memory has rewound three and a half years, to the time after Daddy was arrested but before anybody else knew.

At least, that's what I thought.

I was supposed to go over to my friend Annemarie's house that Saturday afternoon, and even though my parents had fallen into some rabbit-hole world of police and lawyers and computers being taken away, it seemed like everything could still be normal if I just acted normal. I texted Annemarie and asked if her mom could pick me up because "something came up" for my mom.

I sat on the leather seats of Mrs. Fenn's BMW, and Annemarie and I giggled about which of our friends had a crush on which boy. We talked about the dresses we were going to buy for the end-of-eighth-grade dance, and how we'd have to get our moms to take us shopping together. Annemarie asked if I'd seen the pictures she'd just posted on Facebook.

"There's something wrong with my computer," I said, not quite lying. "I'm going to go into Facebook withdrawal if Daddy doesn't fix it right away."

I pretended to quiver, like an alcoholic or a drug addict desperate for the next fix.

Maybe I wasn't entirely pretending. Maybe I would have started quivering anyhow.

Annemarie giggled and patted my shoulder.

"Poor baby," she said, sticking out her lower lip, looking for a moment just like she had in kindergarten. Even in eighth grade, Annemarie was still baby faced and a little childish; she didn't have any sharp edges yet. "You can check Facebook on my computer when we get home."

We pulled into the Fenns' three-car garage, and then it was two flights up to Annemarie's pink palace of a bedroom. Annemarie and I made a game of rushing up there. She tugged on my arm as we scrambled up the steps; she called out, "Come on! You can make it! We're almost there!" And I played the addict-in-withdrawal role to the hilt, tripping and reeling back and forth and moaning, "Must . . . have . . . Facebook. . . . Must . . . have . . . Facebook. . . ."

I really did feel a little desperate for Facebook. It wasn't enough to have Annemarie right there, all apple-cheeked and giggly and normal. I needed to dip into the love and adoration that only Facebook could give me, with hundreds of friends to buoy me up, their every post on my wall carrying the underlying message, *People like you, Becca! I like you! You're popular!*

I needed every single one of my friends right then.

Annemarie's laptop was sitting open and ready on her desk, but we dragged it over to her bed and sprawled on our stomachs across the puffy pink comforter. Annemarie generously shoved the computer toward me and said, "Go ahead. Check your page."

I logged in, and Annemarie said, "Wow, you're even making it look like your hands are shaking. You're such a good actress, Becca."

I hadn't noticed that my hands were shaking. I wasn't doing it on purpose.

My Facebook page came up, and I breathed a sigh of relief. Except there, right at the top, was a post from a girl named Sadie Everly who went to my school. She'd written: "OMG! I heard your dad just got arrested and taken to jail! Is that true?"

She hadn't even done that as a private message. She'd put it on my wall.

I really fast clicked on the mouse to refresh the page. I wanted a do-over, a new version of my page and my day and my life that didn't include my father being arrested.

"Why don't you just delete that and block Sadie?" Annemarie asked. "You know she makes up lies like that all the time."

But my refresh brought in an explosion of other comments and questions: "Why were all those cop cars in front of your house this morning?" . . . "I just heard about your dad on the radio in the car—did he really do all those things?" . . . "All that money my dad invested in your daddy's company—your daddy stole it?!?!?!? I hate you!" There was even a message from a reporter, of all things: "Becca, my niece Hannah goes to your school. I know this is a difficult time for you and your family, but I would really like to be able to talk to you and your mom, to get your side of the story . . ."

I slammed the laptop shut, so hard it could have broken. Then I made the mistake of turning and looking Annemarie right in the face. I still thought I could make something up, convince gullible Annemarie that nothing she'd seen on Facebook was true.

But it was like, in that one instant, Annemarie had gone from being a bunny rabbit to a wolf. The angles of her face seemed plenty sharp now. Her jaw was set, rock hard and judgmental.

"Why . . . why didn't you tell me?" she asked, as if I'd betrayed her.

That was the last time I ever went on Facebook, except when I took my whole page down a few days later.

I didn't go back to school the following Monday, either. I finished out eighth grade with some weird, too-easy online school that I think was actually designed for truants and juvenile delinquents and kids who had been suspended. I had to do it on Mom's computer, since mine was "evidence." I didn't go to the eighth-grade dance. I became my mother's shadow, spending hours rubbing furniture polish into tables and chairs and armoires and bookshelves that she had to sell, just for there to be enough money for us to live on.

None of that was Facebook's fault, I tell myself firmly. I force myself to press down my pinky, my weakest finger, on the enter key.

I'm back on Facebook.

It's not the friendly place I knew before Daddy's arrest, but neither is it the horrid, nightmarish land of people virtual-shouting at me, "Your daddy's a crook!" There's nothing personal about it: Facebook doesn't remember me. It's just a nearly blank page asking me to log in or, if I don't have an account, to start one. But of course that requires giving a name and an e-mail address, just like the collegedata.com site last night.

What if I can't win this scholarship without going on Facebook? I wonder.

Technically, I know no one is supposed to use fake identities on Facebook. But of course it's possible. Even easy. I trade my own bland last name for an even blander one—Smith—and create a nondescript Yahoo e-mail. I pick "Sarah" for a first name, because it's the most common girl's name I can think of. I make up a birth month and day at random, but use my correct birth year.

My stomach is roiling as I click on "Sign Up."

Right before I see the screen welcoming me to my new Facebook page—or, rather, welcoming "Sarah Smith"—I blink and get one last glimpse of the information I entered. That random date I just made up? Not so random.

I used Daddy's birthday.

Daddy made up all sorts of fake identities on Facebook, I think. *He used them to trick people into giving him money. Having a fake identity was, like, the gateway drug for his crimes.*

The only reason I know that fake identities are prohibited on Facebook is because the lawyers talked about it in Daddy's trial. The only reason I know how easy it is to get around the rules is because Daddy did it all the time. He dodged little rules like "Don't pretend to be somebody else on Facebook," and he dodged big rules like, "Don't steal millions of dollars."

And Daddy got caught. Daddy *deserved* to get caught.

I am almost retching as I *x* out of "Sarah Smith's" brand-new Facebook page. I can't do it. I can't be this much like Daddy.

But what if there's an RIP page on Facebook for Whitney Court? I wonder. *I know she must have died a long time ago, but people leave those things up forever. And everybody loved her. There would be tons of comments on there I could use for my essay. And lots of names of people to contact . . .*

I can't use my real name. Even if reporters have given up on searching for Mom and me, I can't risk someone I knew in Georgia finding me and posting anything that would tell everyone I know in Ohio exactly who I am. Outing me, as it were.

I sit for a moment, staring at my blank computer screen. Then I reach for our apartment phone and dial one of the few numbers I know by heart in Ohio.

Jala picks up on the first ring.

"Becca? It's really you, Becca? I'm so glad you called!"

She sounds so delighted that I feel guilty. We haven't talked since June, when school ended. We just never had that kind of friendship, where we called each other all the time or got together a lot outside of school. I was always too afraid to allow myself that.

"How's college?" I ask.

"Okay," she says, but her voice is guarded now. "Ohio State is very big. I don't really know anybody yet besides the other kids from DHS. And the few times I've run into any of them, they say, 'Wait, Jala, weren't you just a junior last year? What are you doing here?' Yesterday I got brave and went up and talked to this other girl I saw wearing a hijab—and it turned out that she just got here last week from Yemen and she doesn't really speak English yet. She's not even in school; she's just married to a grad student. Married!"

"She must have been happy to have somebody else to speak Arabic to," I say.

"She told me my accent was terrible," Jala said. "She was kind of mean."

Even over the phone I can hear the loneliness in her voice. I feel even guiltier. Jala is still living at home, not on campus. We really could get together sometime in Deskins. I could do that without revealing too much.

As soon as I finish this scholarship essay, I tell myself.

"Well, you're not missing anything in high school," I tell Jala, trying to sound cheerful. "Stuart is freaking out even more about getting into college. And everyone is getting cutthroat about this scholarship we found out about today."

Quickly I tell her about it.

"I remember that one," Jala says. "I didn't apply because I hadn't decided yet last fall that I was going to college early. Or— my *parents* hadn't decided."

I don't know the whole story, but it kind of seems like Jala's parents forced her to graduate early.

"Yeah?" I say. "Well . . . remember how my mom's so strict she won't let me have a Facebook account?" Jala and I have talked a lot over the years about having restrictive parents. Only, most of my complaints are half lies, placing the blame on the wrong parent. "I think I need to go on Facebook to look up stuff for this essay. . . . Would you mind if I logged on to your account? I wouldn't look at any of your messages or anything, and of course I wouldn't post anything. . . ."

"Sure," Jala says, so fast that it almost seems she's excited to be asked. Like she wants to go back to that mean Yemeni girl and tell her, "See? See? I have friends! This is proof!"

Jala tells me her password, and I assure her I'll only use her Facebook once. Then she can change her password.

"Don't worry about it," Jala says. "I trust you. Let me know what you find out!"

That is definitely an invitation to call her again.

We both say good-bye and I log into Jala's account. It's like just talking to Jala cured me of my stupid psychological reactions to Facebook. My stomach is perfectly calm. I am still using a fake identity, but I have permission. I am not breaking any rules, even silly ones.

Jala's page comes up.

Jala has posted very little about herself: a profile picture that mostly just shows the side of her head, harmless comments like, "I'm starting at Ohio State tomorrow!" That was her most recent post. But of course she's friends with Rosa and Stuart and Oscar and all our other mutual friends, and their posts are all over the place. Suddenly I really want to see the selves my friends present to the online world beyond Jala's wall; I want to go to all their profile pages and study them in-depth. Are they the same people online as the ones I know in real life? Would I like them more or less? Would I know them better? Would I want to?

I know Jala wouldn't mind me checking anybody else's profile, and if I actually had a Facebook page of my own, of course all my DHS friends would friend me. But I don't let myself sneak a peek at anyone. I'm only here to look for Whitney Court.

I type her name into the search engine.

Nothing comes up. There's not even a wrong-person Whitney Court out there anywhere.

Are you serious? After all my effort . . .

I remember—belatedly—that if there'd been a Whitney Court RIP page, it would have shown up in the Google search. And, anyhow, even though I don't know exactly when Whitney died, it must have been before Facebook. Facebook hasn't been around that long. It just seems like it has.

It's like you don't even remember what Facebook's like, I scold myself. *Did you think Whitney's family or friends would have set up an RIP page ten or twelve years after she died?*

This reminds me to at least look for some of her friends and classmates. I start with Corey Wisner, Whitney's fellow prom royalty and possible boyfriend. He shows up instantly, and I know it's him because his profile says that he's on his class's fifteen-year Deskins High School reunion committee. And there's a Facebook page set up for that.

Now we're getting somewhere, I think.

I click over to that page, thinking I'll send messages to anyone whose name I recognize from being in pictures with Whitney. I'll have to say that they should send their replies to my e-mail address, not Jala's Facebook, but . . .

There's a lengthy post at the top of the reunion page:

> To all current DHS seniors seeking information for the Whitney Court Scholarship: While we want to support our fellow Chargers, we all have jobs, families, etc., and really don't have time to answer questions from three hundred different people in the course of a few weeks. So we've settled on a policy. I will answer questions from anyone writing specifically about me; Samantha Shreves

will answer questions from anyone writing specifically
about her; etc. But that's all. We will have to ignore
all other requests, no matter how witty, desperate,
profound, or profane you make them. Good luck! (P.S.
We are so glad college wasn't as expensive back in our
day! But some of us are getting kind of close to having to
pay tuition for our own kids. . . . So you all can laugh at
us in another five to ten years!)

It's written by Corey Wisner. Evidently some of my classmates got to this page even before me. Corey's answering them
and everyone else, preemptively.

Great policy, I think. *What am I supposed to do, since Whitney
is dead? Am I going to have to change the person I write about?*

I really don't want to. It just seems like an essay about Whitney
Court would automatically be the best one, the most poignant.
Anyway, won't the scholarship judges be impressed if I manage to
succeed at the hardest assignment?

Now I just have to succeed.

Now and now and now

I work crazy-hard over the next few weeks. My AP physics teacher seems to think we should be able to solve even the problems that perplexed Albert Einstein himself, and the homework loads are challenging and huge in all my other classes too. One of my coworkers at Riggoli's quits, and I pick up a lot of the extra shifts.

But what I work on the most is finding out about Whitney Court.

I go back to the yearbooks—now having to elbow my way into the room beside dozens of other seniors—and I look up the teachers at DHS back then. Two of them, Mr. Trencher and Mrs. Huggins, are still on staff, and I'm lucky enough to talk to both of them before they each post a sign on their classroom doors saying they've reached their quota of the maximum number of Court scholarship interviews they're willing to do. Mr. Trencher's sign includes a drawing of an earthworm and the words SEE? IT'S TRUE THAT THE EARLY BIRD GETS THE WORM! Mrs. Huggins's sign includes a PS: MAYBE THIS WILL TEACH YOU NOT TO PROCRASTINATE THE NEXT TIME!

Both signs make Stuart furious. He missed out on interviewing either teacher.

"I bet there isn't even a real scholarship attached to this," he rants at lunch the day those signs go up. "I bet this is some psychology experiment, or a secret plot all the teachers are in on, trying to teach us we're going to be competing for everything the rest of our lives."

"It's no different from teachers saying they can only write so many college recommendations every year," Clarice points out. "Teachers only have so much time. They work hard. They have to draw the line somewhere."

Clarice takes being a teacher's pet to new heights. She forgets she's allowed to turn it off at lunch.

"Ms. Stela told me lots of scholarships are strange," I offer. "You can win money for making clothes out of duct tape or—"

"Don't bother googling 'weird scholarships,'" Stuart advises. "You can only get, like, a thousand dollars or so for any of those. This Whitney Court thing *pretends* to be about serious money, but it's probably not."

I'm debating whether to admit, "A thousand dollars sounds like serious money to me," when Rosa leans into the conversation.

"Emily Riviera got a ten-thousand-dollar renewable scholarship from the Courts last year," she says calmly. "It meant she was able to go to the University of Chicago. David Lin got a twelve-thousand-dollar scholarship the year before. He's at Case Western."

We all stare at her.

"What?" she says. "I checked around. And then I messaged both of them on Facebook to ask their strategies for winning."

Stuart grabs her arm.

"So, spill," he says. "Share everything. Help your friends."

Rosa jerks her arm away, almost knocking over her milk.

"Oh, no," she says. "Only one of us can win this thing. I'm not doing your work for you."

Stuart slumps in exaggerated despair over his chicken nuggets.

"But I've got so much else I have to do . . . ," he moans.

I decide to take pity on him. At least a little.

"If it makes you feel any better, my interviews with Mr. Trencher and Mrs. Huggins didn't help much," I say. "Mr. Trencher told me Whitney was really good at biology. Mrs. Huggins said she was really good at English."

"Aha!" Stuart says, stroking his chin like some Sherlock Holmes in training. "So you chose Whitney Court herself as your essay subject?"

I hadn't meant to reveal that.

"So?" I challenge.

Stuart continues massaging his chin. He just needs a pipe and one of those houndstooth-checked hats for the complete impression.

"It's a little risky, don't you think, choosing the dead girl?" he asks.

"If anyone can carry it off, Becca can," Oscar says loyally.

I flash him a grateful look, then challenge Stuart. "Do you even know how she died?"

"No. Do you?" He challenges right back.

I shrug in a way that's supposed to be mysterious. But the truth is, I don't. I don't even know when she died. I should have asked Mr. Trencher or Mrs. Huggins, but there was something a little . . . off . . . about both those conversations. It was like there was something they didn't want to tell me, something they were afraid they might let slip by accident. Both of them seemed to put their guard up the minute I told them who I was writing about. I thought mentioning her death would just make everything worse.

How can I find out if anybody else is writing about Whitney, and if they're doing any better than I am?

"Okay, let's be fair," Rosa says. "Becca just told who she's doing. Everyone else, confess."

I love having Rosa around.

It turns out that my idea to write about Whitney wasn't obvious to anyone else. Oscar is writing about Brian Klontz, who was the president of the DHS computer club. Rosa is writing about Tanya Dodson, who organized a protest of military recruiting at the school. (Only two other people joined her.) Clarice is writing about Lacey Rice, who started four different service clubs. Stuart is writing about Cameron Craig, one of the other valedictorians with Whitney.

I start laughing.

"What's so funny?" Clarice asks suspiciously.

"It's like you're all writing about yourselves!" I snort. "Or the person you would have been in Whitney's class. . . ."

"*You* aren't doing that," Oscar points out. "You're not a cheerleader."

"Rah, rah, team! Goooo, Chargers!" I say mockingly, pumping my arms up and down and making goofy rolling motions with my fists.

I am covering.

Did I pick Whitney because she had the high school experience I wanted, the one I would have had if Daddy hadn't gone to prison? I think. *Not that I would have been a cheerleader necessarily, but . . . involved. At the center of everything.*

A darker possibility occurs to me.

Or did I pick her because, if I don't get this scholarship, my future could be doomed too?

• • •

I double down, work harder. After a ridiculous amount of cross-checking names and addresses and phone numbers, I find three retired teachers to talk to. One is in the process of moving to Florida and says the only thing she has time to tell me is, "Whitney was such a delightful girl in high school. She was a pleasure to teach, a spark plug in every class."

There's a moment of silence on the other end of the phone, and then she adds, "Really, that's the only thing I'd have to say about Whitney, anyway. Good luck!"

And then she mutters something about the movers scratching her priceless antique cabinet, and hangs up.

The other two conversations are virtual repeats of my talks with Mrs. Huggins and Mr. Trencher. I now know that Whitney was also good at geometry and Spanish.

I still have the sense that the teachers I talked to were tiptoeing around something. Of course, I'm tiptoeing around something too.

Ask when and how she died, my brain commands me. *Ask!*

But I've messed myself up, linking Whitney's post-high-school tragedy with my own future. I know she was still alive on graduation day, so her death wasn't part of senior year. That means I won't have to write about it. I don't have to deal with it at all—do I?

The day after my last teacher interview, Rosa comes into sixth period and slaps two sets of stapled-together papers down on my desk.

"I don't want to be depressed alone," she says. "Read."

I flip the papers over. They're essays, one titled, "Julie Hanover," by Emily Riviera, the other, "Mike Sellings," by David Lin. I shoot Rosa a quizzical look.

"Yeah, they're the winning essays from the Whitney Court Scholarship for last year and the year before," Rosa tells me.

"What can I say, I can be *very* persuasive on Facebook. I thought it would help. Not make me want to slit my wrists."

"Because . . . ," I begin.

Rosa points at the pages, and I obediently dip my head down and begin reading.

Julie Hanover and Mike Sellings aren't even names I remember from the yearbooks—I never would have considered picking either one of them. But during her senior year Julie evidently had to deal with her five-year-old sister needing a heart transplant, and Emily Riviera's writing makes me feel like I'm sitting right there in the hospital room, crying right along with the Hanover family. The essay about Mike Sellings is totally different—he apparently didn't care about anything but cars, and the only way the teachers got him to pass senior year was by making everything automobile related: English essays, history papers, even math problems. He met his final science requirements with a special project on "Internal Combustion Engines I Have Known." The essay is hilarious, but touching, too; it's really a tribute to how much Mike's teachers cared.

I look up.

"I feel like I now know Julie Hanover and Mike Sellings better than anyone in *our* class," I tell Rosa. "Even the kids I've had practically every class with for the past three years. Even *you*."

Rosa nods grimly.

"I know," she groans. "I'll never be able to write that well. I mean, Tanya Dodson was amazing, and I have some really great stuff, but when I write it down, it doesn't go anywhere. And I just start thinking, *I'm going to lose. I'm going to lose. I'm going to lose.*"

Rosa is writing already? She's done with all her research? I feel my panic level ratchet higher.

"Maybe Ms. Darien can help you," I say. "She offered, remember? At least you *have* good information. The best thing I have is, 'Whitney Court was a pleasure to teach.'" I make my voice wooden and dull, as lifeless as Whitney Court herself. "I can't even find out where the Court family *lived* when she was in high school. Isn't that ridiculous? And there's no record of any Courts living around here now."

"What, did the whole family leave Deskins after Whitney died?" Rosa asks. "Can you blame them?"

I shrug. Ms. Darien starts class before I can say anything else. But a few minutes later Rosa slips a piece of paper onto my desk with her familiar scrawl:

Whitney Court lived on Seldom Seen Road.

I give her a wide-eyed look, and she writes some more:

Tanya Dodson talked about going to parties out there.

I pull the paper toward me and start writing back:

Thank you!!!!! But—I thought you weren't going to help anyone else?!?

Rosa writes back:

Us poor kids have to stick together.

Two hours later, I have an interview set up with Joann Congreves, a woman who, according to online property records, bought her house on Seldom Seen Road in 1982. She would have been the Courts' neighbor the whole time they lived there, the whole time Whitney was growing up. And the best thing?

She's promised to tell me everything.

A relieved now. And then . . .

"Whitney was always such a sweet girl," Mrs. Congreves says. "Such a sweet, sweet girl."

We're sitting on her screened-in porch, overlooking what she's already told me used to be the hill where all of Old Deskins' kids (including Whitney!) would go sledding whenever there was snow. Sometimes it didn't even take that—sometimes they just rode saucers and sleds downhill on frozen mud.

"Deskins wasn't so stuck-up back then," Mrs. Congreves says. She gestures toward the window and makes a face. "It wasn't like *that*."

"That" is an invading army of McMansions, row after row of oversize houses that have taken over the entire view. They dwarf whatever slope would have made the area a good sledding hill. Or maybe the developers flattened the hill when they built the whole neighborhood practically in Mrs. Congreves's backyard. Really, none of the houses are any larger or showier than the one Mom and I left behind in Georgia, but three years of living in a tiny apartment has changed my perspective. Why would so many people need such enormous houses? I can see why Mrs.

Congreves preferred looking out on a field full of laughing, playing children as they sledded in the wintertime, flew kites in the spring, set up bike-race courses in the summertime, or held pumpkin-rolling contests in the fall.

"If it hadn't been for all those kids coming around, Seldom Seen Road really would have been seldom seen back then," Mrs. Congreves says, even though she's already told me that on the phone and when she greeted me at the door. I have a feeling it's a line she uses a lot.

"Fifteen years ago it was just your house and the Courts out here, right?" I say. If I crane my neck a little, I can just barely see the corner of the sprawling ranch house where Whitney Court grew up. It's about as big as some of the McMansions, but it looks homier, more comfortable. Less pretentious. Mrs. Congreves has already told me how Whitney used to stand out on the back patio practicing cheers and tennis serves, and I can almost picture it. But I don't need to peer out the window watching for her family now: I've also learned that Whitney's parents sold the place and moved to Cincinnati ten years ago.

"Oh, yes," Mrs. Congreves says. "This whole area had a different feel to it back then. . . . It's hard to imagine being so isolated now, isn't it?"

She casts one last resentful glance out the window and stirs another spoonful of sugar into her glass of the iced tea she insisted on pouring for both of us. Mrs. Congreves seems to have a lot of nervous energy. She's rocking her wicker chair pretty ferociously for someone who announced that she had her seventieth birthday last week.

She's also told me her husband was an engineer, but he died of a heart attack four years ago; her daughters were six and eight years younger than Whitney, and they both went to Ohio State and now live in Dayton and Indianapolis; Mrs. Congreves herself has been getting over a bout of bronchitis and pneumonia, even though, yes, it is a bit strange to have those ailments this time of the year . . .

When she promised to tell me everything, I thought she meant everything about Whitney, not everything about everything.

I decide I need to take control of the conversation.

"So when all those kids would come over here to sled—were they Whitney's friends?" I ask. "Was that still going on when she was in high school?"

"Oh, sure, Whitney's friends, then my girls' friends later on. . . . Yeah, the high school kids loved sledding out here," she says. She rocks a little harder and starts a long, convoluted tale about three high school boys having a dramatic crash at the bottom of the hill, and one of them breaking his leg so terribly that everyone on the hill could hear it, and some of the girls started screaming because the blood looked so extreme, dripping in the snow . . .

I am taking notes furiously until I think to ask, "And where was Whitney when that happened?"

Mrs. Congreves looks startled.

"Oh, she wasn't here then," she says. "Those were friends of my Rachel. That was long after Whitney graduated and . . . well, you know."

I decide not to follow up on the "you know." Not yet, anyway. I want to keep Mrs. Congreves talking about happy times.

"What's your favorite memory of Whitney?" I ask.

"Oh, probably all those times she'd come over and watch Rachel and Tiffany for me," Mrs. Congreves says. "She was the best babysitter! She'd get down on the floor and really play with them. She had all these games she made up for them, make-believe worlds where animals could talk and zebras had pink and purple stripes. . . . Dan and I would get home and the girls would say,

'No, no, Mommy and Daddy! Go away! We want to keep playing with Whitney!'"

This is good stuff. I am writing as fast as I can.

"Tell me more about those games and the make-believe worlds," I say.

"Oh, I don't remember it all," Mrs. Congreves says. "There was something about a cat—or was it a pig?—that could speak Spanish . . . or French. Yeah, it was French, because I can remember Tiffy running around saying, 'Par-lay voo fran-say?' It was the cutest thing. Or, wait a minute, did she pick that up at preschool?"

I clench my teeth.

"Do you think maybe I could talk to your girls about what they remember?" I ask.

"Oh, sure," Mrs. Congreves says. "I'll give you their phone numbers. Rachel's is five-one-three . . . oh, let me go check for the exact number—I never dial it anymore, I just type in 'Rachel . . .'"

She gets up and goes into the next room.

I take a sip of my iced tea, which is way too sweet, and tilt my head so I can see the Courts' old house a little better. Now that I'm sure that really was where Whitney lived, I'll slow down driving past on the way home. Maybe I'll even knock at the door, ask if I can see Whitney's old room. Or would that seem too stalker-ish?

Mrs. Congreves comes back and hands me a paper with numbers written down for each of her daughters.

"I remember something else," she says. "Looking out the kitchen window reminded me. When Whitney would play with Rachel and Tif, she'd always say they lived in the Land of the Two Seas. Get it? Because 'Court' and 'Congreves' both started with C's? They'd pretend that there was an ocean on either side of our house."

I like that one a lot. I write down "Land of the Two Seas—C's" and grin at Mrs. Congreves as she settles back into her wicker rocker. I can already see that description playing a big role in my essay.

"That's so great," I say. "Like, poetic even. I love it that she was so good with your girls when she was so much older, in high school and all."

Mrs. Congreves frowns.

"Actually, I'm thinking that was more when Whitney was in middle school," she said. "Seventh, eighth grade, you know? Once Whitney was in high school, she was busy with so many school activities, it got so it was hardly worth my time to call over there and see if she was available. I had to start calling other babysitters instead—Sandra Stivers, for example, or Lana Graham, or—"

"But Whitney still babysat for you some during high school, right?" I interrupt a little desperately.

Mrs. Congreves's frown deepens.

"Oh, I'm sure, some," she says doubtfully. "At least once or twice."

This gives me permission to still use the stories about the Land of the Two Seas and the pig/cat who spoke Spanish or French, but those tales seem less valuable now. Mr. and Mrs. Court might be involved in judging the scholarship contest, as well as sponsoring it. What if they specifically remember that Whitney stopped babysitting for Rachel and Tiffany Congreves after eighth grade? What if that prejudices them against my entire essay? If somebody's kid dies right after high school, wouldn't the parents remember the high school years that much more, because they don't have newer memories of their kid?

"Tell me what else you remember about Whitney in *high school*," I say, perhaps emphasizing the "high school" part too hard.

"Oh, that girl was always on the go," Mrs. Congreves says. "She'd leave for school at seven in the morning, and then we wouldn't see her car coming back down the road until ten or eleven at night, she had so many afterschool activities. My husband and I would joke, 'Was that trail of dust Whitney going by?'"

Meaning, you really didn't see her at all when she was in high school, I think with a sinking heart.

I lead Mrs. Congreves through more questions: "Did you ever go to the football or basketball games and watch Whitney cheer?" "Did you see her in the musical, playing Maria in *The Sound of Music*?" "Did you see her school plays?" "Do you remember her being prom queen?" "Did you ever just see her hanging out with her friends?" But everything is vague and distant; there's nothing more along the lines of the Land of the Two Seas. It's clear that Mrs. Congreves and her family were on the sidelines of Whitney's life by her high school years. Mrs. Congreves seems to want to help, I'll give her that, but it's like I'm asking her to dig up the old, dried-out bones of someone she didn't even know that well to begin with.

Ugh, why did I have to come up with a corpse analogy? I scold myself.

For every lively, interesting memory I try to push Mrs. Congreves to give me about Whitney, she keeps veering off into tales she knows better about other people. I feel like I've now heard everything about Rachel and Tiffany Congreves's high school years, as well Joann and Dan Congreves's high school years more than fifty years ago. And the high school experiences of various friends and relatives of Mrs. Congreves who might have graduated from Deskins High School anytime over the past century.

"But, about Whitney," I say, interrupting a long, rambling story about why Tiffany Congreves lost out on becoming prom queen *her* senior year.

Mrs. Congreves squints at me, as if she doesn't understand why I'd stop her in the middle of such a fascinating tale.

"About Whitney," I repeat. "Tell me . . ." I am desperate. I can't make a whole essay out of the Land of the Two Seas. I have to get something else that's at least that vivid. "Tell me about her funeral," I blurt out. "Surely you went. What did people say about Whitney then? Why was everyone so sad when Whitney died? Why did they say she *mattered* so much?"

I wince at my own words. They're too blunt. Too heartless. I wouldn't be surprised if Mrs. Congreves told me I was being rude.

She doesn't do that. Instead, she tilts her head. Her squint deepens, and she blinks several times.

"You thought Whitney was *dead*?" she asks. "*Dead*? Whitney Court didn't *die*. She . . ."

And then Mrs. Congreves, who's been talking practically non-stop for more than an hour, clamps her mouth shut and shakes her head like she's refusing to say another word.

Now—

totally confused

"She what?" I demand. I half rise out of my wicker chair. "What you do mean, Whitney Court isn't dead?"

Mrs. Congreves just looks at me.

"If Whitney Court isn't dead, then why is there a memorial scholarship named for her?" I ask, baffled.

Mrs. Congreves is still pressing her lips together like she's trying to keep herself from talking. But she opens her mouth enough to say faintly, "I don't think it's called a *memorial* scholarship, exactly."

Is she right? I remember that it was listed only as "The Whitney Court Scholarship" on both the information sheet that Ms. Stela put directly in my hand and the one I got from Ms. Darien, along with everyone else in AP lit class. There was no "memorial" in the official name. But I thought that was just another of Ms. Stela's careless mistakes.

Didn't the description of the scholarship say it was "in memory of" Whitney? I wonder.

Or was the wording more like, "in honor of Whitney Court"?

I can't remember. I start shaking my head, just like Mrs. Congreves.

"Okay, I am totally confused," I admit. "If Whitney Court didn't die, then why's there a scholarship in her name, whether it's in her memory or her honor or whatever? Why didn't anything about her current life show up on the Internet when I looked her up? What happened to her?"

Mrs. Congreves has her lips pressed together so tightly now that it seems like it'd take a crowbar to get her to open her mouth again.

"I thought you knew," she finally mumbles. "I thought you were just being . . . tactful."

"Tactful? About what?" I wail. "Why are you acting so mysterious? What *did* happen to Whitney Court?"

Mrs. Congreves goes back to shaking her head, more emphatically than ever.

"It's not really . . . my place . . . to tell you that," she says.

"Then whose place is it?" I'm almost begging now.

Mrs. Congreves keeps shaking her head. All the warmth has gone out of her eyes.

"You would have to talk to the Courts about that," she says. "It's really for the family to decide who they tell and who they don't."

She glances at her watch.

"Oh, dear, how did it get so late?" she asks, in a totally different voice than she's been using with me all along. It's like she's not even trying to keep it from sounding fake. "I'm sorry, young lady, but I think we're going to have to end this. I do have other obligations."

This from the woman who assured me over the phone when I said I had a lot of questions, "Oh, that's no problem! I've got nothing on my schedule this afternoon."

"Please," I say to her. "Please *explain*."

"I really can't," Mrs. Congreves says, and it's so odd: For

someone who clearly loves to talk, it sounds like she's relieved not to have to tell me anything else. It's like a magician's trick: She may still be sitting right in front of me, but she's vanished from the conversation.

"Can I show you to the door?" she asks.

She stands up so abruptly, her wicker chair slams against the wall.

I am on autopilot now. I have a moment of flashing back to how I behaved during Daddy's trial: Stand when someone tells you to stand; walk when someone tells you to walk. Your head may be spinning, but somehow your body can do what it's supposed to.

Without quite realizing it, I propel myself out of my chair and stumble across the floor. Mrs. Congreves grabs my arm to help me—or, maybe, to make sure I keep moving.

My mind is stuck on repeat: *But . . . But . . . But . . .*

We reach the front door, and I resist the temptation to brace my feet against the doorframe and refuse to go. What good would that do?

"Good luck with your essay," Mrs. Congreves says.

And then she gives me a little shove. I stumble out onto the front porch.

She immediately shuts the door behind me.

An even more confused now

I stand numbly on Mrs. Congreves's porch.

What was that all about? I wonder.

I half expect the door to spring back open, Mrs. Congreves to come bursting back out: *Oh, all right. I'll tell you the rest of Whitney's story.*

That doesn't happen. The door stays firmly shut.

Out of the corner of my eye, I see the blinds of Mrs. Congreves's front window twitch slightly: She's checking to see if I've left yet.

She might call the cops, I think. *The cops could look up my records; they might even tap into some database that shows the connection to Daddy . . . then they'd treat me like a felon's daughter . . . my secret would spread . . .*

I'm extrapolating way too much—thinking too much like Mom—but at least I understand the problem of being related to Daddy. I can't understand anything about Whitney. I stumble on out to Mom's car, which I've borrowed for this expedition. I put the key in the ignition, turn it, drive slowly down Mrs. Congreves's driveway. Barely thinking, I veer into the next driveway over, the one leading to Whitney Court's old house.

I pull to the edge of the driveway and stop the car. A wind chime dangling by the patio sends out an eerie tinkle. Was that wind chime there fifteen years ago, when Whitney lived here?

Why would it have been? I think. *No Court has lived here in a decade. They probably couldn't stand to stay after Whitney . . . what? If she didn't die, was she maybe kidnapped? Is that what happened? Is that what destroyed her?*

I tell myself that's a ridiculous theory. If she'd been kidnapped, everybody would know. There would have been all sorts of references online, and people would still talk about it. The Courts would have spent their money trying to find her, not giving out scholarships.

I take the car out of park and let it inch forward slightly. Two of my tires are on the grass, digging into the Courts' former lawn. There are no other cars in the driveway, but I think I see a flicker of movement through one of the back windows of the house. It could have been a dog or a cat or a shadow or just my imagination, but I still hit the brake.

It feels like many eyes might be watching me: from Mrs. Congreves's house, from the Courts' old house, from the dozens and dozens of McMansions stretching toward the horizon. I am behaving suspiciously, and for what? Even if someone is home at the Courts' old house, there's no reason anyone there would know Whitney.

I put the car in reverse and back up to the road. It's a public road; there's nothing suspicious about me driving here. I make myself accelerate to a normal speed and drive home. But I'm still dazed.

I can tell the apartment is empty as soon as I step inside. Mom has left a note on the table:

Bec,

*They called me in early b/c 3 day-shift nurses got sick.
Kelly's picking me up and will bring me home tomorrow.
So you've got the car all night. (Be careful!)*

Love,

Mom

*P.S. If I keep getting overtime—or a second job?—
maybe it won't matter if you can't apply for financial
aid. We'll pay for everything on our own.*

I crumple the note in my hand. Has Mom gone totally nuts?
Does she have any clue what college actually costs? She can talk
all she wants about being poor but honest and paying our own
way, but financial aid is going to be the only route for me, unless
I really do get a full-ride scholarship.

And that brings me back to Whitney Court.

Maybe Mrs. Congreves is just senile and confused? I tell myself.
And she just doesn't remember that Whitney died?

Mrs. Congreves didn't *seem* senile—it's hardly a sign of
dementia that she couldn't remember whether an imaginary animal from fifteen or twenty years ago was a pig or a cat. But I
decide to try calling the Congreves daughters.

"Hello, you've reached Tiffany Congreves at Imagitechnics.
Please leave a message."

"Hi, Tiffany here, or, actually, not here . . . You know what to
do if you want me to call back."

"You've reached the offices of Dillman Incorporated. If you are calling after hours . . ."

"Rachel's not available right now, so . . ."

I've run through all their numbers, work and home and cell. I don't leave any messages. I want to know what happened to Whitney Court right *now*, not whenever Mrs. Congreves's daughters feel like calling back some stranger who thinks their mother might be senile.

I glance at the clock. It's five forty-five p.m., a time when normal adults like the Congreves girls—er, women—would be driving home from work or maybe starting to fix dinner or hanging out with their boyfriend/significant others. (Mrs. Congreves said they each have one.) They probably won't answer their phones for an unidentified number anytime soon.

I think of looking up the Courts' new number in Cincinnati and calling them—Mrs. Congreves did say they were the ones to talk to about whatever happened to Whitney.

Yeah, right, I think. *That would make a great impression: "So if your kid's not dead, what happened to her?" I bet that would make them blackball me from the scholarship, right there.*

I want to talk to *somebody* about this. I think of Rosa's "Us poor kids have to stick together," but I don't want to admit to anyone I'm competing against that I'm so woefully confused.

Jala, I think. *She's not competing for this scholarship.*

I dial her number. I get her voice mail too, her musical voice saying she's sorry she can't answer in person.

I clear my throat and start rambling: "Hi, uh, I was hoping you could talk . . . I just had the weirdest conversation about that scholarship and I thought maybe you could help me figure something out . . . Anyhow, call me when you can. And, uh, hope everything's going okay at OSU . . ."

A beep cuts me off before I'm done talking.

I sit there, staring down at the phone. Who else do I want to call?

Daddy, I think.

I drop the phone. I ball up my hands into fists and pound them against my forehead: *No, no, no!*

I do not want to talk to Daddy. Even if I did, it's not like I could call the prison in California and they'd casually bring him to the phone, at my whim.

But Daddy would know how to find out about Whitney, I tell myself. *He knew how to find out anything about anybody online. You could just pretend you were talking to him. You could just do what you know he would tell you to do.*

I am so tempted.

The computer knowledge itself didn't make Daddy a criminal, I remind myself. *It was how he used it.*

I sit down at the table and open my laptop.

"I'm not breaking any laws," I say out loud as I turn it on. "I'm not doing anything an ordinary person couldn't do, if they knew how."

The computer fires up, and I type in the words "social security death records." This takes me to a genealogy website that promises access to eighty-nine million records, from all fifty states.

How old was I when I first saw Daddy playing around with this site? I wonder. *Eight? Nine? Ten?*

I can remember sneaking up on him in his office as a prank; I was young enough to be amused by the panic that raced across his face. I thought that meant my prank was a good one, not that he was afraid I'd be smart enough to figure out he was doing something wrong.

I wasn't that smart. Not then. And he covered quickly.

"Oh, here I am acting like such an old man, looking up relatives who have been dead for years," he said with a rueful laugh.

I knew to look respectfully sad. All of Daddy's closest relatives were dead. Or at least that's what he'd told us.

"Let's turn this into a game an old man can play with his daughter," Daddy said, teasingly ruffling my hair. Now I'm suspicious: Was he just doing that so his arm would block my view of the screen while he closed down whatever else he had open? Was it something I might have asked questions about?

Regardless, we began competing to come up with the most boring names we could think of. We got points for both dullness and the number of people who had died in the United States bearing that name. I won with "Joe Gray," which had been carried by more than eight thousand dead people.

"And it's boring and colorless, almost by definition!" Daddy said. "Gray—perfect! I could never beat that!"

Later, after Daddy was arrested, I found out that "Joe Gray" was one of the most common fake identities he used in his scams. He used it for years.

Was I supposed to feel honored that Daddy valued my suggestion that much? As he looked at the death records that day, was he thinking, *Wow, Becca is really good at this. I'll definitely have to bring her into the family business when she gets a little older?*

Did anybody besides Daddy and me ever know that "Joe Gray" was my idea?

I realize I am pressing down on the keyboard so hard that it hurts. I'm making an incoherent row of *k*'s and *d*'s and *f*'s.

I take my hands off the keys and clench them together.

"You're not doing anything wrong," I tell myself once again.

I erase my mistakes and type in the name "Whitney Elaine Court"—I know her middle name from the yearbooks. I don't know her exact birthdate, but I know she turned eighteen in

May of her senior year—they had a birthday cake for her during the cast party for the musical. So I can put in the month and the year.

No death records come up. Does that mean Mrs. Congreves was right and Whitney is still alive?

Maybe Whitney got married, I tell myself. *Maybe that's why nothing's showing up, because she had a different name when she died.*

The same genealogy website brags about having marriage records from all fifty states, so I try Whitney's name and birth month and year on that search form instead.

Nothing.

I sit back, staring at the screen.

Maybe she died overseas? I wonder. *Maybe she studied abroad during college and something awful happened to her? Maybe she was on some sort of volunteer trip to some dangerous part of the world?*

I'm pretty sure that would still show up in the social security records. But maybe there was some mistake.

Wouldn't there be newspaper articles about that? I think. *Wouldn't I have found an obituary, if nothing else?*

Not on the regular Web. Not from thirteen, fourteen, fifteen years ago.

That's why you go to the deep Web if you really want an answer. . . . On the deep Web, pretty much anything that's ever been on the Internet is still there . . .

I can hear Daddy saying that. It's like he's infested my mind tonight. Reinfested. Whatever.

But he gave that advice when I was a fifth grader doing homework, I think. *He wouldn't have told me to do anything illegal when I was just a little kid!*

How else am I supposed to find out anything about Whitney?

She's not dead, not married, not on Facebook, not on LinkedIn, not employed in any job that shows up online . . .

If I didn't know better, I'd think Whitney didn't even exist!

I start the deep Web searches.

There's nothing about anyone named Whitney Court dying overseas. But I unearth two old articles from a newspaper in tiny Gambier, Ohio. One is just a listing of police reports. After accounts of stolen wallets and a gym bag taken from an unlocked car, there's this:

> A 20-year-old female was reported to the Gambier police
> for erratic behavior and suspected drug use. Subject was
> identified as Kenyon student Whitney Court. She was
> taken to the police station and then released.

The other article is also brief, only two paragraphs. But it's notable enough to have its own headline: KENYON STUDENT ARRESTED FOR DUI, REFUSES BREATHALYZER.

So, three paragraphs total, and I think that gives me Whitney's entire story. She must have become a drug addict, an alcoholic. That's why there's nothing about her online after these articles. For all her golden-girl promise in high school, she's probably spent the last fifteen years in and out of rehab. The pressure of living up to all her high school success was too much for her. Or maybe she was already abusing drugs and alcohol in high school, and all those glowing yearbook photos were cover-ups and lies.

And now her parents think she deserves a scholarship in her honor?

I shove the computer away from me. It slides across the table, the top part wobbling dangerously. It's fragile, on the verge of falling apart. It skids to a stop at the other edge of the table, perilously close to falling over. If I'd shoved just a little bit harder, it would have crashed to the floor. It would have shattered.

There's a part of me that wishes it had. I want to destroy *something*.

I jerk back from the table, knocking over my chair. I stalk away and kick a pillow that has fallen from the couch to the floor. It flops over, landing a mere foot away. I kick it again, harder.

I am so, so mad.

You had everything! I want to scream at Whitney Court.

I have all those golden-girl images of yearbook-Whitney swirling in my mind. Whatever she was doing in the background then, she was still so smart, so talented, so beloved. . . . And she had two parents who were so successful and so eager to pay for college that they'll pay tuition for total strangers.

Why'd you have to throw it all away? I imagine asking Whitney. *Why, when there are people like me who have nothing, who would give almost anything to have what you had?*

Maybe I say that out loud. Maybe I scream it.

I am as judgmental as a DARE officer: *That first swallow of beer, that first puff of marijuana, you are just pouring your life down the drain. You are just asking for your life to go up in smoke.*

Kids always make fun of DARE, but the DARE people were right about Whitney Court. She did throw her life away.

It's like Daddy, I think. *He was so smart, so talented, so handsome. If he'd just stuck to the right side of the law, maybe he wouldn't have made quite so much money, but he could have stayed out of prison. He could have been successful without everyone hating him, without everyone hating me and Mom. . . .*

I sink into the couch. I didn't mean to uncage that beast, my fury with my own father. Now it's like an animal pinning me in place, threatening to devour me.

I dodge it. I think about Whitney's parents instead. I pound my fists against the couch: I'm mad at them, too.

And you two! So magnanimous, so praiseworthy, giving money to poor kids like me. . . . All we have to do is 'honor' your daughter, who's really some loser who threw away the kind of life most of us can only dream about. It's ridiculous! It's hypocritical!

I stop in the middle of my mental screed. I back up and sort through the same thoughts at a snail's pace this time around.

The Whitney Court Scholarship is ridiculous and hypocritical. More than that, it's . . .

Unlikely, I think.

I freeze on that word. I'm completely still now. I'm done shoving and kicking and pounding things. I furrow my brow, thinking harder: I'm as deliberate as someone inching along the edge of a cliff.

Isn't it unlikely? If the Courts really want to hold up their daughter as some saintly creature everyone should revere, why set up scholarship requirements that send kids digging into the past? I wonder.

Sure, none of my friends picked Whitney to focus on, but I bet every year there's at least one person like me who goes looking for Whitney's story. I'm not such a research genius that I'm the only one who could ever dig up the truth about Whitney.

What if that's part of the point?

I examine this theory.

If the Courts wanted to use Whitney as a cautionary tale, they would have made her story public from the very beginning, I think.

Her descent into drug and alcohol abuse would have been right there in the scholarship info; the message would have been, "Don't do what our daughter did. Use our money to fulfill your glorious potential." And the essays required for the scholarship would have been like DARE sermons: "Why Not to Do Drugs." "Why Drinking Is Bad."

Why didn't the Courts set up the scholarship that way?

The answer comes to me in a flash. It's an answer I am uniquely capable of seeing:

The Whitney Court Scholarship is ridiculous and unlikely because it actually isn't real. What it *really* is, is a scam worthy of my own father.

And I'm pretty sure Daddy was the one who set it up.

Now—

stunned, stunned, stunned

I'm gasping with the force of my suspicions, my revelation. I'm so flabbergasted that for a moment, my mind goes blank. I realize I've started whimpering, "No, please no, not this . . ."

I try to force myself to be cold and analytical, to sort through my evidence.

Fact: There is something odd at the heart of the Whitney Court Scholarship. Even odder than scholarships that celebrate fire sprinklers or duct-tape prom clothes.

I remember Stuart complaining that the whole thing seemed like a setup. I remember not just Mrs. Congreves dodging questions, but the teachers and Whitney's classmates, too. I remember something Ms. Stela said about the scholarship: "It's totally weird, but, hey, if someone wants to donate money to DHS students, they can set it up practically any way they want."

This is money being given away, not stolen. Of course no one's going to look too closely at a few oddities.

When Ms. Stela called the scholarship weird, she was talking about the deadlines and announcement dates being earlier than for any other local scholarship. And those deadlines are terribly inconvenient for most high school seniors, since this is when we're supposed to be visiting college campuses and writing essays for our college applications and keeping our grades up because they still count. Stuart has complained about the overlapping deadlines all along.

But the deadline and announcement dates are perfect for someone like me, who wants to know about scholarship money before she has to decide about filling out financial aid forms. I remember how I felt standing in Ms. Stela's office when she told me about the Court scholarship—it seemed like a gift, almost as if it were designed especially for me.

Maybe it was, I think.

I dig my hands into the cracks between the couch cushions and squeeze. I'm not sure if I am just trying to hold on or if I am trying to destroy the couch. This could be one of those crazy folk sayings: You can't get blood from a turnip; you can't make a purse from a sow's ear; you can't squeeze truth from foam rubber and ancient upholstery.

Don't jump to conclusions, I tell myself.

Still, I bring out more evidence: the thought I'd had only moments ago, before my deep Web search. *If I didn't know better, I'd think Whitney didn't even exist!*

My head spins trying to think of how much someone—Daddy?—would have had to invent and plant to make it seem as though a girl named Whitney Court graduated from Deskins High School fifteen years ago if there was no such person.

Two small-town newspaper articles that could be accessed only on the deep Web? That would be nothing for Daddy or someone like him to make up and hide online.

But yearbooks that purport to be from fifteen years ago? Teachers who would lie and talk about a student they never had? A former neighbor who would make up stories at length? An entire graduating class of kids/now grown-ups so united that, at the very least, none of them would step forward and proclaim, "The emperor has no clothes! There never was a Whitney!" This would require bribe upon bribe upon bribe.

Even with bribes, no graduating class could be that united, I think.

And, anyhow, even though of course Mom has told Daddy that we're in Deskins and I'm going to graduate from Deskins High, no one knew to expect that fifteen years ago. A hoax like what I'm imagining would have required years of prep work.

So scratch that theory, I tell myself. *Whitney really did exist. Whitney, the high school golden girl who evidently became the college druggie. . . .*

I remember something the federal prosecutor told the jury about Daddy's scams: *The hoaxes Roger Jones carried off were full of misrepresentations, yes, but they were utterly believable to their victims. Because every single one of them was wrapped in a solid veneer of truth.*

It would be entirely like Daddy to pick someone like Whitney for his veneer of truth. He often looked for someone who had a secret shame, an unknown vice. Whitney threw her life away on drugs and drinking; her parents apparently slunk out of town in shame a decade ago. They probably cut off ties with everyone in Deskins as thoroughly as Mom and I cut off ties with everyone outside it. They'd never know if someone else gave away money in Whitney's name.

Whitney Court and her family were ripe for this kind of scam. Deskins was too—Deskins, where most of my classmates were new within the past three or four years; Deskins, where fifteen years ago might as well be ancient history.

And Daddy would have loved setting this whole thing up— tricking the prison officials somehow into giving him computer access, erasing all traces of his searches and communications afterward, fooling not just a single victim but an entire school. An entire community, really.

This isn't that different from scams I know Daddy did, I think. *It's like his old scams flipped inside out—giving away money instead of stealing it, sure, but still tricking people to send money where it's not supposed to go.*

I am strangling the couch cushion beneath me. I let go. The cushion refuses to reinflate. I slide over onto the next one, a fresh victim.

Fact: Even after Daddy got caught, even after they confiscated his business records and his personal records and his computers, everyone was always convinced he'd gotten away with huge sums of money. The media was full of speculation about how he had to have set up an escape fund in the Cayman Islands or some other offshore haven where the American legal system couldn't reach it.

I remember hearing Alice Gladstone, one of our neighbors back in Georgia, ask Mom about this supposed Cayman fund.

It was in the early days after Daddy was arrested, when we were still answering our door to people we knew. Mrs. Gladstone had come over with a fresh-baked peach pie. I could smell it from upstairs, and I'd tiptoed over to the top of the stairs where I could hear without being seen.

I'd already learned that the best way to find out anything was to stay out of sight.

"Oh, you poor thing," Mrs. Gladstone declared loudly, as if she wanted everyone on our street to witness her charity and kindness to the new neighborhood outcasts. Or maybe it was for the sake of TV cameras.

There was a pause, probably while Mrs. Gladstone gathered Mom into one of her overly perfumed hugs. I heard the door being shut.

I noticed that Mom did not invite Mrs. Gladstone out of the entryway into the living room to sit down. Mom did not say anything.

Maybe she was crying.

"How much?" Mrs. Gladstone stage-whispered. Her voice was softer than usual, but still loud enough that I could hear her from upstairs. "I'm sure he put aside something for you and the girl—do you have to wait until after the trial or the plea agreement before you go to the Caymans to claim it? How many millions is it? You'll still be perfectly comfortable, won't you?"

"Get out," Mom said, her voice as hard as steel.

The door opened. I heard Mrs. Gladstone gasp—evidently Mom was pushing her back outside. Mrs. Gladstone was starve-yourself-thin and prone to wearing teetery high heels; I'm sure Mom overpowered her easily. Next, I heard a shattering sound that might have been a pie-filled baking dish smashing against our brick porch. I wanted to know: Had Mrs. Gladstone dropped the pie, or had Mom thrown it after her?

I didn't ask. I didn't ask anyone about the Cayman Islands fund, either. But in the early days after Daddy was arrested— before I heard his victims testify, before I knew everything he'd done—I liked thinking about it. I'd tell myself, *Just get through this. Get through this, and then you'll be on the beach in the Cayman Islands, not a care in the world* . . .

Instead, I ended up poor and friendless and studious in Deskins, Ohio. I stopped believing in the Cayman Islands fund.

But maybe, I think. *Maybe, maybe, maybe* . . .

I lean over onto the third couch cushion, too overcome to keep sitting up. I'm stretched across the whole couch now.

Fact: Daddy really did love me. He really does.

I sniff. I am a high school senior with good grades. I do well in subjects requiring logic. So I know I can't classify that as a fact.

It's only an opinion, a theory, a belief. A belief that was sorely tested three and a half years ago.

It is a fact, I think stubbornly. *It's true.*

I can assemble all my evidence now, build my case.

If Daddy has some huge sum of money stowed away somewhere . . . If Daddy really loves me . . . then of course. Wouldn't he do anything he could to make sure I have money to go to college? And since he's in prison and he stole all his money, he couldn't just mail me a check. So, duh, of course he'd set up some sort of hoax to funnel the money to me.

Hadn't Daddy pretty much told the whole world he stole his money just to be able to send me to college?

Wasn't it his dream as much as mine that someday I'd go to Vanderbilt? That I could have that glorious, prestigious college education he only pretended to have?

A fake full-ride scholarship contest would be *easy* for Daddy to pull off. Though, maybe from prison he would have had to use an outside accomplice. Maybe he'd paid a big bribe to get help from someone he used to work with, someone he'd never cheated, someone who got as big an adrenaline rush as Daddy did from fooling people. Maybe that person told Deskins High School he was Whitney Court's father and he wanted to set up a scholarship in her name. Then Daddy and/or his accomplice just had to conduct the whole contest online and—ta-da!— eventually announce that a certain Becca Jones would win this year's award.

Just for insurance, to throw off any suspicions, they would have set up the scholarship a few years early, thrown out token amounts of money to other kids in earlier classes.

Wouldn't Daddy think like that? Doesn't that last part about setting up the scholarship early have Daddy's fingerprints all over it?

I put my hands over my face and discover my cheeks are wet: Tears are streaming down, rolling across the bridge of my nose, soaking into the couch. I have started sobbing and I didn't even know it.

And I don't quite know *why* I'm sobbing. Is it because I have proof now (well, almost proof) that Daddy loves me after all, that he didn't go off to prison and leave me and Mom with nothing? Is it because I'm sure now (almost sure) that I will be able to afford an expensive college education, even with my father in prison?

Or is it because I'm angrier than ever with my father? How dare he! How dare he try to make me his accomplice, knowingly taking his stolen money. That would taint my entire college education. That would ruin everything. That would make me a criminal too.

Didn't he think I was smart enough to figure this out?

The door is locked and the blinds are drawn and there's no one else in the apartment, but I still feel too exposed, sobbing so openly on the couch in the living room. I stumble to my feet and careen into the bathroom. The next thing I know, I'm crouched on the floor, vomiting into the toilet.

Am I trying to throw up the part of me that's furious with Daddy—or the part that desperately wants all of this to be true?

Still now—

for some reason, time doesn't stop. It just keeps moving on

The phone rings while I am still huddled on the bathroom floor. I have stopped throwing up, but I haven't been able to force myself to get up. The phone motivates me.

Maybe it's Mom, I think. *Mommy . . .*

If it's Mom, I will tell her everything. She will come home right away and put a cool hand on my forehead and smooth back my hair, just like she did when I was a little kid. And she'll tell me, "Don't worry. Mommy will fix everything."

I want to believe that. I want to believe she *could* fix everything: She'd protect me from Daddy's schemes and his tainting college for me, and somehow she'd magically (and legally!) come up with the money I need for Vanderbilt . . . I want to believe that she, at least, would act sane and sensible and courageous and save me from everything bad.

As if Mom has ever seemed sane or sensible or courageous at any point the past three years.

I also want to believe in Santa Claus and the Easter Bunny and the Tooth Fairy. But it's been more than a decade since I believed in any of those things—since I found out they were just my parents pretending to be all-knowing and all-wise and all-giving.

I trip walking toward the phone. But I keep walking.

Maybe it's Daddy, I think.

And this truly is magical thinking, because Daddy couldn't just call me up at the drop of a hat. There are designated calling times in prison, I think, and this probably isn't one of them. And we all agreed three years ago that phone calls were off limits. And, anyhow, how would Daddy know that he needed to call, that this is the exact moment when I found out everything?

Still, I'm thinking about what to say to him.

I would say thank you, I think. *Thank you for the scholarship. Thank you for taking care of me. Thank you for remembering me.*

But could I say that? Or would that be like reporting Daddy's latest crime, since the prison phones are probably tapped?

Do I *want* to report him?

I pick up the phone without looking at the caller ID.

It's not Mom or Daddy. It's Jala.

"What do you need help figuring out?" she asks breathlessly.

I actually pull the phone back from my ear and peer at it in bafflement. *Oh, right. Jala's calling me back. I called her after I talked to Mrs. Congreves, but before I knew what really happened to Whitney.*

I put the phone back against my cheek.

"Oh, I don't need help anymore," I say. "Sorry. I just figured out everything on my own."

I can hear the distance in my own voice—my tone comes with its own KEEP OUT signs.

But Jala is intrepid.

"What was the problem?" she asks. "What'd you figure out?"

"It's . . . complicated," I say. I'm hiding behind Facebook-speak. But I can't tell Jala what I learned about Whitney. Everything's too fresh. I can't trust myself not to slip and also tell her about Daddy.

"That's okay," Jala says. "I like complicated. And it'd be nice to hear about *somebody* having a problem solved, instead of all the ones that seem unsolvable, like in my calculus and chemistry classes."

"No, really, it's too long a story," I say. "And I've got tons of homework tonight—probably you do too. You say your calc and chem classes are really hard?"

If in doubt, change the subject.

"Not *that* hard," Jala says. "It's just . . . maybe OSU isn't the right place for me? Maybe I'd do better at a smaller school? Oh, never mind." She gives a halfhearted laugh. "I guess I just had a bad day. I'm sure I'll be fine tomorrow."

There's an undercurrent to Jala's words. No matter what she actually said, it's like she's begging me, *Ask why OSU might not be the right place. Ask why I want a smaller school. Ask what's wrong that I need help with.*

But my face is stiff with dried tears, and my mouth still tastes like vomit. I have no room in my head for anybody else's problems.

I pretend I don't hear any hidden message in Jala's words.

"Sure, you'll be fine tomorrow," I echo. "Anyway . . ."

All I have to do is mention my homework load again, promise to call her back sometime, and hang up. But somehow I can't do it. Somehow I still need the comfort of holding the phone to my ear, of knowing that Jala is still at the other end of the line.

Even if I can't tell her anything, she's there.

Except now there's just silence between us. Silence and dead air.

"Well," Jala finally says. "Are you . . . are you going on that trip Stuart's planning for fall break? To look at colleges in the South? Vanderbilt and Emory, right?"

"I don't know," I say, and it's like my voice is coming from somebody else's mouth—somebody standing a million miles away.

So that's ruined for me too? I think. *My chance for a visit to Vanderbilt, taken away because Stuart wants to go to Emory, too?*

Emory is in Atlanta. No way could I ever go back to the Atlanta area. What if I ran into somebody I used to know?

"Jala, I have to go," I say, because suddenly I'm terrified that I'm going to start crying again.

"Are you okay?" she asks.

"Yeah, sure. Bye," I say.

I stab at the button on the phone that turns it off. I stand there panting for a moment. I've won my race against the tears, because I'm not crying yet, not crying yet, not . . .

The phone rings in my hand. I drop it to the table. The ringing stops, and I imagine the voice mail Jala is leaving, the hurt tone undoubtedly underlying whatever trumped-up excuse she's come up with for calling back.

Jala is a nice person and a good friend. It's horrible that I hurt her.

Something else to blame Daddy for, I think.

Now I am crying again.

And then I'm mad that I'm crying, mad that I hurt Jala, mad that Daddy forced me into this position. My anger is like one of those fireballs you see in movies: There's a spark and a flash and suddenly the whole room is engulfed in flame.

My whole body—my whole soul, my entire *being*—is engulfed in fury.

A fireball is always looking for the next thing to burn, and I'm like that too. I want Daddy to know how mad I am. I've got a phone, but I can't call him. I've got car keys and a car, but I can't drive to see him in prison.

The irony? I don't even have enough money to make it to California, I think.

My fury burns hotter. I grab my laptop from the table

because it's something Daddy gave me. He gave me the Hello Kitty sticker on it too. He probably gave it to me because he wanted me to stay as cute and cuddly and adorably clueless as Hello Kitty.

And as silent as Hello Kitty, I think. *Why didn't I ever see how creepy it is that poor Hello Kitty doesn't even have a mouth?*

That does it. I was kind of planning to hurl the laptop to the floor, to delight in its destruction. Instead, I slam the computer back onto the table and begin typing:

"I hate you, Daddy."

This feels *good.* I will not be silent. I will not be voiceless. I will write down everything and let Daddy know just how much I hate him.

I will make him feel as bad as I do.

I put my hands back on the keyboard, to keep writing. I realize that I've accidentally typed my words into a search engine, and the computer is offering me choices: Do I want "I hate you, Daddy" the poem? The song lyrics? The YouTube video?

I don't want any of that. I want my own version. I open a blank Word document and start over.

I hate you, Daddy. How stupid do you think I am?
Didn't you know I would figure out the whole
scholarship is a hoax? And how did you think I was
going to feel when I figured all that out? Did you
want to turn me into a criminal like you? Is that
what horrible people like you dream about for their
children? You're like some drug dealer trying to get
some new customer hooked. "Here, here, just take this
full-ride scholarship . . . It's free! I made it up just for
you!" And then I'm hooked. Then I'm obligated. Then
I'm just as evil as you.

I write and write and write. I write about how mad I am at Whitney for ruining her life, how mad I am at Daddy for ruining his, how devastated I am to think that he wants me to ruin mine, too. It feels like I am sobbing onto the page, like I am bleeding onto the page. I can't stop.

> Did you think, after everything that happened, that I'm still the little girl who worships you? Did you think that I'd just do what you want for me—that I'd march off to Vanderbilt like a good little student because it's *your* dream school?

"Oh, God," I whisper. "*Is* that what I'm doing?"
I'm not sure if I'm praying or cursing.
I keep writing.

> How did you even know, back when you set this whole thing up, that I would make the grades and have the test scores to get in to Vanderbilt? Did you think I was just some wind-up doll you could program like a computer, like you customized my operating system, you could make me the person you wanted me to be?

I stare at those words, at the cursor blinking on the screen. My heart pounds. How true is that?
I remember orientation freshman year, when I decided to take hard classes.
Because of Jala! I remind myself. *Because she was nice to me, and I thought I needed to be around nice people, not gossipy ones!*
I remember how hard I've always worked in my high school classes, how I've always wanted the top grades.
Because I didn't have anything better to do than study! Because

Stuart was crazy-competitive way back in freshman honors English, and that made me want to beat him and . . .

I am so confused. I don't understand. I've had such tight control over myself all through high school, I've barely let myself think about my father. But now I find myself remembering what he told me every time I brought home a report card in middle school: "This is fine, honey, for sixth grade (for seventh grade . . . for eighth grade . . .). But you're really going to have to step up your game once you get to high school. That's when it really counts."

And I had good grades in middle school. They just weren't perfect.

After everything that happened, am I still just trying to please my father? Trying to be what he wants me to be?

Why?

Just like that, the anger goes out of me. As I furiously typed away, I kind of thought that I would print this whole mess, put it in an envelope, and drive it to the post office right away. I typed up whole paragraphs imagining the pleasure I would get from dropping this letter into a government-certified mailbox, making it irretrievable, even if I calmed down later on.

But now I just scroll the cursor up to the top corner of the page, to the red-boxed *X*. I click.

Close.

My computer, ever cautious, offers me a chance to reconsider. Do I want to save this file? Not save it? Cancel?

I let the cursor hover between the three choices. Do I want to keep such a toxic document? Hold on to so much poison? Why?

To remember how mad you were, I think. *Even if you never send this to Daddy, you need to keep it. It could help you decide what to do about this scholarship. Are you actually going to go ahead and apply or not?*

I groan out loud. Maybe that's why I was holding on to my

anger so tightly: If I blame everything on Daddy, I don't have to make any decisions of my own.

I click save. The computer asks me what I want to call this file. I feel a bitter smile creeping onto my face. I type four words:

"Whitney Court Scholarship Essay."

Now—

continued

All that anger has wiped me out. I feel like I've been run over by a truck.

I tell myself I don't have to decide anything tonight—I don't have to do anything. But giving myself permission to be floaty and vague just makes me feel that much worse. I'm like a ghost haunting myself. I need to eat dinner—that's down-to-earth. That should be easy. But I can't even decide between heating up leftover Hamburger Helper or boiling water for spaghetti. I spend fifteen minutes trying to decide if I want to spend fifteen minutes cooking.

I can't decide, so I don't eat anything at all.

I open my calc book to work on homework, but the formulas that made perfect sense in class today have turned into meaningless knots of letters and symbols. My eyes keep blurring them together, tangling them even worse.

I shut the book.

Just go to bed, I tell myself. *Go to bed and do your homework in the morning, when your brain works again.*

But when I lie down, I can't sleep. My brain shifts into high gear, racing in circles.

I'm trapped, I think. *I can't dig too much into finding out for sure if the Court scholarship is Daddy's hoax, because that might get him into even more trouble. And if I prove to myself that it is . . . then I really am a criminal if I take it.*

But what if I'm wrong about everything? What if being Daddy's daughter makes me see hoaxes and scams where there aren't any? What if I act all high and mighty and refuse to even apply for the Court scholarship and miss out on my only chance of being able to pay for a really good college?

I flip over, then over again. I toss and turn, back and forth, side to side. The sheets tangle around my legs.

I haven't stepped foot inside a church in three and a half years, not since the Sunday before Daddy was arrested. But before that I went to church a lot. (Duh—it was the South. That's what people do.) So, whether I like it or not, I have all sorts of Bible stories floating around in my brain, along with Daddy's lies. The story I can't help thinking of now is about Jacob wrestling with the angel. I remember it the way my overcaffeinated third-grade Sunday school teacher Mrs. Grindley told it, with *g*'s dropped from the words "fighting" and "wrestling" and a drawl that got thicker as the story went along. It seemed poor Jacob was alone in the middle of nowhere, and suddenly some other man attacked him. And of course Jacob fought back, even though he didn't know who the man was.

"And then," I could remember Mrs. Grindley saying, her heavily mascaraed eyes growing wider, as if she was surprised by her own words, "the more they fought, the more Jacob started thinking that maybe it wasn't a man he was fighting after all. Maybe it was an angel. Maybe it was a demon. Maybe it was God. Maybe it was the devil. He didn't know, but he just kept fighting. He fought *all night long* without giving up! And he didn't even know who or what he was fighting! He didn't know what he was fighting against, and he didn't know what he was fighting *for*!"

I can't actually remember how it all turned out for Jacob after that—maybe some of the boys in the class started flicking glue sticks at one another, and Mrs. Grindley didn't finish the story. That happened a lot in third grade Sunday school.

But I feel Jacob's story in my bones right now. I don't know what I'm fighting, either. Is it my conscience? Is it my fear? Is it Daddy?

Is it God?

Is this how Daddy felt, on the verge of his first crime? Did he debate and wonder and agonize and stew?

Somehow I don't think so. Somehow I think Daddy just did it without a second thought. He crossed the line, broke the law, fooled his victims, ruined his life—and Mom's and mine— without a single backward glance.

Unless . . . what if setting up the fake scholarship for me *is* his backward glance?

I wake up in the middle of the night with four words floating through my head: *You can find out.*

I smile drowsily. I am calm, even serene. There is a way for me to find out if the Court scholarship is just another one of Daddy's scams without ruining anything.

At least, there's a way for me to find out if it *isn't*.

In the middle of the night, that sounds good enough to me.

Now—

hopeful

I am waiting at Rosa's locker long before school starts the next morning.

"I couldn't figure out that fourth problem in calc, either," she says as soon as she sees me.

"I didn't even try," I admit. All my homework still sits untouched in my backpack. I have never come to school before with undone homework. But I'm holding onto my drifty, calm, middle-of-the-night feeling.

Rosa drops her backpack to the floor and spins her combination lock.

"I wanted to ask you about something else," I say. "Did you check with any other Whitney Court Scholarship winners before Emily Riviera and David Lin?"

This is my theory: If I can confirm that the scholarship was set up before Mom and I moved to Deskins, that will prove Daddy had nothing to do with it.

If David Lin's Court Scholarship two years ago was the first one, that doesn't prove anything one way or another. But I'm trying not to think about that.

Rosa jerks up her locker release and swings the door open.

"Do you *like* making yourself miserable?" she asks. "You want to read every single winning essay that's so good you want to gouge your own eyes out?"

"I'm curious," I say. "I want to know if they've ever repeated a winning topic."

Of course I don't tell her that isn't the *main* reason I'm asking.

Rosa grunts as she starts moving textbooks from her backpack to her locker.

"My Facebook sources only go back so far," she says. "I'll have to check with my sister to see if she knows who won the years before she graduated."

I guess Rosa's sister graduated the same year as David Lin. It's funny to think that Rosa has this whole other person attached to her that I barely know anything about—a whole family, actually. I always steer conversations away from family talk, because I don't want anybody asking about mine.

But now I say, "It won't make your sister feel bad, since she didn't win the scholarship?"

Rosa snorts.

"Lily won't care," she said. "I don't think she even applied. She was majoring in boys her senior year. She thought David Lin was hot—that's why she remembered him winning."

Rosa swings her locker open wider. I've never been the type to hang out at my friends' lockers, so I've never seen the pictures inside her door before. Where other girls might hang pictures of their boyfriends—or hot celebrities they wish were their boyfriends—Rosa has photos of various colleges and universities. The pictures are perfectly matted, precisely labeled: Yale. Stanford. Georgetown. Washington University. Northwestern.

Rosa sees that I'm looking.

"Yeah, that's the wish list," she says with an embarrassed

shrug. "Don't tell me they're out of my league. Stuart already has."

I am suddenly almost as furious with Stuart as I was last night with Whitney Court, her family, and my father.

"I think some of these schools are *beneath* you," I tell Rosa. I touch the Georgetown photo and do a snobby imitation of Stuart: "I mean, Georgetown? It's not even Ivy League!"

Rosa laughs and shuts her locker.

"Don't forget about asking your sister," I say.

"I won't, but I hope you're not in a hurry," she says. "Lily's not too fast about answering messages. Unless there's testosterone involved."

Rosa starts rushing toward her first-period class. I glance at the clock and veer toward the guidance office instead. I *am* in a hurry, and Ms. Stela might be organized enough to remember what year the Whitney Court Scholarship started.

But there's a sign taped to the guidance office door:

ALL GUIDANCE OFFICE STAFF IN MEETINGS THIS MORNING.

WE WILL BE OPEN FOR <u>URGENT BUSINESS ONLY</u> THIS

AFTERNOON.

That's about how the rest of the day goes too. We have a pop quiz in gov that I would have aced if I'd spent three minutes looking at the book last night. (But I didn't.) At lunch Stuart goes on and on and on about needing commitments from everyone who wants to go on his Southern college tour at the end of October. For some reason, he's nagging me most of all.

"I'd like to see Vanderbilt," I admit, and this feels horribly brave, like walking into a room with only a bikini on when everyone else is fully clothed. *Do I still want to see Vanderbilt? Do I still want to go there, or has Daddy ruined it for me?*

I can't think about that right now.

"But Emory?" I say, putting maybe a little too much scorn into my voice. "Ugh. Why not combine Vanderbilt with some-place else instead—Wake Forest, maybe? Duke?"

Stuart bristles.

"Emory is the Harvard of the South!" he says.

"No, *Vanderbilt* is the Harvard of the South!" I correct him.

There's something really ugly between us. I hate Stuart right now because he doesn't have to worry how he's going to pay for college visits or college itself. And because he made fun of Rosa and because he doesn't have to wonder if his father has set up a hoax that could turn him into a criminal too. I don't know why Stuart hates me right now, but it's clear that he does. His eyes are little and squinty, his face is flushed, and his mouth is snapping open.

I can feel the wave of vitriol about to come toward me, and I am not ready for it.

Clarice sticks her phone between us, with its voice app acti-vated: "At least six different universities have been called the Harvard of the South. Shall I list them?"

The bell rings just then, and even though it would probably do us good to sit there listening to a calm computer voice, we all flee in different directions.

In calculus class the last period of the day, I discover that I got a 68 on last week's test.

I sit there staring at the lowest grade I've ever gotten and think, *This is what happens to other people.* It's other people who get bad grades because they're distracted by boyfriend or girl-friend problems, or they party too much, or they just don't care about school as much as other parts of their lives.

And weren't you distracted by the Court scholarship? I ask myself. *Didn't you break your laser focus on getting good grades?*

It's totally unfair that trying to get the money to go to a good college should make me mess up the grades that were supposed to get me *in* to that good college.

It's totally unfair if one of Daddy's schemes has ruined this part of my life too.

"All right, everyone," Mr. Hattimer says from the front of the room, a million miles away. "The world did not just end. *None* of you did well on this test. Neither did my morning class. In fact, the highest grade in either class was a 68."

A 68? I think. *I got the highest grade of anyone?*

"So there'll be a thirty-two-point curve?" Lakshmi asks in a wobbly voice from across the room.

"No, Ms. Patel," Mr. Hattimer says scornfully. "I am not just going to *give* you all better grades. You need to know this material for the AP test at the end of the year. You need to know this material for college. And if any of you are going to become civil engineers or architects someday, you need to know this material so the bridges and buildings you design don't fall apart and kill me or someone I care about. Or anyone! There is no curve in real life!"

He's been on a big kick lately about how calculus isn't just theoretical and that it can have real-life consequences beyond grades. Whatever. With half the girls in the class on the verge of tears—and maybe some guys, too, though they're hiding it better—today his lecture just feels like bullying.

"So we all fail?" three kids wail almost in unison.

Technically, I think 68 is some kind of D, but I don't think I should point that out.

"No," Mr. Hattimer says. If anything, the scorn in his voice has thickened. "Because high school is evidently another name for preschool nowadays, I am going to reteach this material, and then you will be retested. But that pushes everything in the course back a week, so we're going to have to pick up the pace after this. And remember, once you get out of this playpen, you won't get do-overs in real life. If you're a surgeon, you can't kill your patient on the operating table and then say, 'Oops, can't I start that over again?' If you're a pilot, you can't crash your plane and then say, 'Hey! Let me have another chance!' If—"

I've had enough. I raise my hand. Mr. Hattimer looks surprised—he's not used to being interrupted. But he nods at me and says, "Yes, Becca?"

"It's not like we weren't *trying*," I say. My voice is only a little steadier than Lakshmi's was, but I forge ahead. "It doesn't help to hear 'You're not going to get do-overs in real life' when all of us are already stressed out about choosing the right college and getting in and picking the right major and . . . and everything else." No need to mention what's specifically stressing me out. "All of us already feel like every decision we make is do or die, and could maybe ruin the rest of our lives, and . . ."

I realize that everyone in the class is staring at me. This is not like me. I don't talk back to teachers. No one expects me to stand up for myself.

". . . and . . . Mr. Hattimer, could I maybe go to the guidance office right now?" I ask.

I expect him to say, "Of course not. You're going to sit there until I beat calculus into your brain! Even if it kills us both!" But he just looks at me sadly for a moment and then says, "Yes, Becca, you may."

I must sound even more on edge than I actually am.

Or maybe I really am dangerously on edge?

I gather up my books and take the pass Mr. Hattimer hands me. I escape out the door and down the hall.

When I get to the guidance office, I'm relieved to see that the door is open now. I rush in past the secretaries. I sweep right into Ms. Stela's private office. She's hunched over her computer keyboard, surrounded by stacks of papers on either side.

"Ms. Stela, can you tell me, how long ago did the Court scholarship start? How many years has it been going on?" I ask.

Ms. Stela turns and blinks at me.

"Um . . . I don't know, Becca," she says distractedly. "I think it was before I got here."

When did Ms. Stela get here?

I remember: She started my sophomore year.

This proves nothing. Daddy could have been a fast worker, even from prison. He could have set up the fake scholarship my freshman year.

I slump against Ms. Stela's doorway. Ms. Stela starts watching me with more interest than usual.

"Why do you want to know?" she asks.

I ignore her question, and counter with one of my own.

"Who would know when the Court scholarship started?" I ask. "I mean, someone here at school."

"Well, if it's really that important to you, I could ask Mr. Bixby and get back to you," Ms. Stela says.

Mr. Bixby is one of the other counselors. I can just see Ms. Stela forgetting completely.

"That's okay; I'll ask him," I say.

Mr. Bixby's office door is shut, but I am full of boldness—or something—today. I open his door, poke my head in, and say, "Ms. Stela says you're the person to ask about how long ago the Whitney Court Scholarship started."

Mr. Bixby frowns and mutters something under his breath about why Ms. Stela can't handle her own section of the alphabet. But he looks at his computer, types a word or two—or, well, probably three—and then tells me, "Five years ago. This year's will be the sixth one."

Five years ago.

My knees go weak, and I have to clutch Mr. Bixby's door.

Five years ago I was just starting seventh grade at McCormick Middle School back in Georgia. Five years ago everyone thought Daddy was a wildly successful businessman, and nobody knew his secrets. He would have had no reason to start some strange scholarship in a totally different state just in case he ever got caught and sent to prison. Five years ago he would have had no reason to believe he would ever get caught.

So the Court scholarship has nothing to do with Daddy, I realize.

This news should send relief coursing through my body. That should be the reason my knees are weak. I should feel like jumping up and down and cheering—maybe even like kissing the top of Mr. Bixby's very bald head. If the Court scholarship has nothing to do with Daddy, I can enter and win and accept the money without a single pang of conscience. I don't have to worry about it being tainted.

But my body doesn't seem to know I should be deliriously happy. It feels more like I have to hold myself up because I'm unbearably sad. Tears spring to my eyes, and I can barely mumble "thanks," before I have to turn away to keep Mr. Bixby from seeing.

So Daddy didn't make any secret arrangements for me? I wonder. *Doesn't he love me, after all?*

More now

I time my exit from the guidance office badly: I hit DHS's main hallway just as the final bell rings and everyone is dashing out of the classrooms. I walk through the cramped hallway with my head down, giving myself fierce instructions:

Don't let anyone see that you're almost crying. Don't let anyone see that you are crying. Don't cry. Stop it!

I wipe my face across my sleeve at a moment when I hope no one is looking. And then I slam directly into some other person.

"Sorry," I mumble without looking.

Whoever it is doesn't step aside. I feel big hands cupping my shoulders. I have to look up now: It's my friend Oscar holding on to me. He's the one I ran into.

"Hey," he says. "Are you all right?"

I shrug because I don't trust my voice right now.

The truth is, Oscar is built a lot like an overgrown teddy bear, and it would actually be quite pleasant to put my face down against his shoulder and sob and sob and sob.

Right, I think. *And that would be so pleasant for him, too, some psycho girl slobbering all over his shoulder in front of everyone. . . .*

I step back to break Oscar's hold on me. I want him to see I'm not just going to fall down.

"Hey," Oscar says, with a shrug of his own. "*Everyone* got an awful grade on that calc exam. And Mr. Hattimer will have to make it easier next time—you at least are bound to get an A." He pauses. "Did you know Stuart got a forty-two? Doesn't that make you feel better, to know your worst enemy totally failed?"

"Stuart isn't my worst enemy," I say. "Competing with him just forces me to work harder."

"Oh," Oscar says. "My parents really wish somebody would do that for me."

He grins. And there's something so incredibly infectious about Oscar's grin that I stop crying. I don't think I'm even in danger of crying anymore.

I discreetly wipe my hand across my face again. It's time to do a little damage control.

"I'm thinking maybe grades don't matter anyhow," I say. "Maybe I won't even go to college. Maybe I'll just join the Peace Corps."

"I already looked into that," Oscar says. "They won't take you unless you've got a bachelor's degree."

"Oh," I say. "Well, then . . . maybe I'll just work at Riggoli's the rest of my life. I'll dedicate my life to bringing the finest pizzas and pasta to the people of Deskins."

"They'll never give you more than twenty hours a week," Rosa says, stepping up beside me. "And they'll never pay you more than minimum wage."

I look back and forth between Oscar and Rosa—did Oscar send some secret message to her: *Help! Crying girl here! What am I supposed to do?*

It actually wouldn't surprise me if Oscar had an app like that programmed into his phone, that he hit when I wasn't looking.

Rosa puts her arm around my shoulder.

"I know how you feel," she says. "Every time my grades slip even a little, I think, so if I do actually go to one of those big fancy schools I'm killing myself to get into—what if I can't hack it? What if I'm not smart enough to do the work?"

I refrain from telling Rosa that's not why I was crying.

But, great—thanks for giving me something else to stress about, I think.

Oscar puts his arm around me from the other side. It's like they want to turn us into a human chain: smart kids against the world!

"Becca, you of all people—you don't have anything to worry about," he says. "You're so smart, it's like your brain was made for college!"

Rosa rolls her eyes at him and jokes, "Oh, Oscar, I bet you say that to all the girls."

But I barely hear her, and if Oscar delivers a comeback, I miss it completely.

No . . . it's like Daddy shaped my brain to get me ready for Vanderbilt, I think.

I remember him reading books with me before I could read myself; I remember him teaching me the multiplication tables in third grade. I remember him showing me computer tricks the other kids didn't know, so even in elementary school my Power-Point presentations were multimedia extravaganzas. . . .

Tears well in my eyes again.

"Oh, you've got it bad today, don't you?" Rosa asks, patting my back.

"You need . . . ice cream," Oscar blurts.

"Ice cream?" I ask, and my voice makes it sound like I've never heard of such a thing.

"Okay, if you want to be all prissy and health conscious and everything, you can get Froyo instead," Oscar says. "But this is a moment that calls for food."

I am obviously in a weakened condition: That doesn't sound ludicrous. It doesn't even sound impossible. Rosa and Oscar go into full texting and calling mode: I think they contact everyone from both AP calc classes. Some kids, like Stuart, have marching band or sports or some other commitment. But when we arrive at Graeter's in Oscar's beat-up Toyota, ten kids are already there waiting for us.

"Let's call Jala, too," I say impulsively. "She doesn't have class on Wednesday afternoon—let's see if she's available."

That's how I end up at a table with Oscar and Rosa and Jala and a jumbo cup of mint chocolate chip ice cream. After a burst of other kids coming over to tell me, "Good for you, for standing up to Mr. Hattimer!" somehow we stop talking about school. We don't talk about the homework we're ignoring, either, or about our college applications or hopes or fears. I certainly don't say anything about Daddy or the Court scholarship. Instead, Oscar tells how hard it was growing up as the only Chinese-American kid anyone has ever heard of who hates rice. Rosa amuses us with imitations of the best and worst telenovelas from Mexico. Jala and I laugh and laugh and laugh.

Eventually we're the last ones left at Graeter's except for the workers.

"Why didn't we ever do this kind of thing while *I* was still in high school?" Jala asks.

Rosa makes a show of pulling out her empty pockets and repeating a line from one of the telenovelas: *"No dinero, no tiempo."*

No money, no time.

"But we can do it a lot more this year," Jala says. "Just— maybe not four-dollar ice cream cones. Maybe . . . maybe we could just eat jelly beans at the park or something?"

"Jelly beans?" Oscar asks incredulously. *"Jelly beans?"*

"What? It's not rice." Jala defends herself, which makes the rest of us laugh.

By the time I get home, Mom has already left for work. Somehow going out for ice cream has made it so that I'm able to try calling Tiffany and Rachel Congreves again. My luck has changed: Both of them answer their cell phones. And both of them say, yes, they have time and are willing to talk to me about Whitney the babysitter; Whitney the patient neighbor and pseudo big sister; Whitney, their idealized view of what it was like to be a teenager. They talk about how they watched her from afar during her high school years, and how she made them believe that they would be the star of everything when they got to Deskins High School too.

Both of them get strange tones in their voices when we inch toward any mention of Whitney's life after high school, but now I know what that's about. I let them steer the conversation back into safe territory. I am anything but a persistent interviewer. Everything was safe and charming and perfect for Whitney in high school, and if Tiffany and Rachel want to pretend that that's how things stayed in Whitney's life, who am I to object?

After I'm done talking to them, I manage to bang out a decent rough draft of my scholarship application essay. It's about how much Tiffany and Rachel adored Whitney and how sad it was for them when she grew up and left them behind: two peasants in the Land of the Two Seas, longing for their queen to return.

I know I'm not really writing about Tiffany and Rachel and how disillusioned they were by Whitney.

I'm really writing about me and Daddy.

Now—

a few weeks later

It's two days before the Whitney Court Scholarship application is due, and I've decided I'll turn it in tonight. Over the last few weeks I've tweaked my essay so it positively overflows with nostalgia for long-ago happiness; I've edited out any hint of blaming anyone for the way things changed.

I am a model of efficiency putting together the cover letter I'm going to send by e-mail, along with the basic grid of information—name, address, phone number, etc.—that's required. But when I open the essay to read it one last time before sending it off, I can't quite let go.

Maybe I should put it aside for an hour or two, then proofread it one last time with fresh eyes, I tell myself.

I minimize everything and open another application form instead: the Common App. I know I am way behind Stuart and Rosa and even Oscar, who's usually the worst procrastinator in our group. Stuart *loved* getting to explain to me, "No, Becca, you don't have to fill out a different application for every school you apply to. Just about every college takes the Common App—you just fill it in online and then it's done." Stuart finished the Common App back in August and is now working his way through the supplemental forms so many colleges require.

I just haven't been in the right mood to attack any college application.

But tonight, with my Court scholarship essay done except for a final read-through, I can dare to believe everything will turn out okay: I will get to go to college. Regardless of Daddy. Regardless of all the psychological booby traps he left in my mind. Regardless of money.

I download the Common App and begin filling in my legal name, my preferred name, my social security number . . . I'm amused that they ask for an "IM address" as well as e-mail. I don't get to "family information" until page 2. But even this doesn't faze me.

It will work out. It will work out. . . .

I leave everything connected to "Parent 2" blank. Maybe I will end up checking the "Unknown" box. It wouldn't be a lie, exactly. Sure, I lived with Daddy until I was in eighth grade; I talked to him every single day of the first fourteen years of my life. I spent hours and hours and hours with him. But evidently I never knew him at all.

I still don't understand anything about him.

I start getting bogged down in questions I'm going to have to ask Mom about—will I be able to apply for financial aid or not? Before it can depress me, I minimize the Common App as well, lining it up at the bottom of my screen with all the Whitney Court Scholarship documents. I start looking at college websites instead: Vanderbilt and Duke and Georgetown, along with some lesser-known schools like Oberlin, DePauw, Denison . . . Everything I'm looking up is private, and therefore very, very expensive. I decide to keep an open mind and look at public schools, too. I start with the two Ms. Stela mentioned as giving a lot of merit aid, Toledo and Kentucky.

I've just opened the Kentucky site when the handle of the front door rattles. Mom's been at work for the past three hours and nobody else should be trying to get into our apartment. I'm trying to decide between diving behind the couch to hide or looking for a weapon to fend off an attacker, when the door swings all the way open:

It's just Mom.

"You scared me to death!" I say. I actually put my hand to my chest, as if that can slow down my pounding heart.

"I had a headache and things were really slow, so they sent me home," she says, dropping her purse onto the couch. Her eyes are bloodshot and her hair's a mess—she really does look awful.

"You mean, you're finally taking a sick day? Your very first one?" I marvel. This has been a point of pride for her, that she never takes time off. My private theory is that both of us were so miserable that first year here that she could have been very, very ill and not even noticed, because it was no different from how lousy she usually felt.

"No, it's not an official sick day—they just didn't need me tonight," Mom says.

So, you won't get paid? And now we'll have even less money? I think, but don't say.

Mom walks behind me on her way to hang up her coat. She stops abruptly.

"University of Kentucky? Why are you looking up UK?" she asks, staring down at my computer screen. Something in her tone has shifted—it's almost like she's mad.

Or even more scared than usual.

"Ms. Stela said they give big scholarships," I say. "I thought I'd look, anyway."

"But—you can't go to UK!" Mom protests. "We have relatives

there, or used to—my cousin's kids . . . what if somebody recognized you?"

Even before Daddy was arrested, it'd been a long time since we'd visited any of Mom's relatives. I don't think I'd be able to tell Mom's cousin's kids apart from any other UK students.

But I guess they might remember me.

"Don't worry about it," I say, closing the UK website. "I was just looking. I don't really want to go there, anyhow."

The Common App form I'd been filling out pops up to replace the UK site.

Mom leans closer and squints at the screen.

"What's that?" she asks, and there's panic in her voice now.

"The Common App—you know, how I'm applying for college?" I say. "I fill it in online and then—"

"Online?" Mom interrupts. She makes the word sound like "poison" or "genocide" or "murder"—something with a grim, potentially fatal meaning. "Oh, you mean, you just got the form online, and then you'll print it out and send it in, right?"

"Well, I *can* do it that way," I say. I click back to the information page. "But look—they strongly recommend people do the whole process online. And I was thinking . . ."

It strikes me that this is a huge step for me. I sat down and started filling out the Common App and *didn't* think, *Oh, no, where will this information be stored if I hit save? Who has access to it? What if this site gets hacked?* And I really did have it in my mind that I would fill out the information and send it in online, just like Stuart and Rosa and Oscar and Clarice and Lakshmi and every other college-bound kid I know.

I was going to act normal for once, without even thinking I was acting normal.

I point to the "https" at the top of the screen.

"Look, it's safe," I tell Mom. "They ask for social security numbers and everything. "They've got to keep this site secure."

Mom makes a skeptical sound. Or maybe it's gagging.

"Your father hacked sites like that," she says.

"Okay, okay," I say. "I'll mail it! But this is going to cost a fortune in postage, and—"

"How many schools were you planning to apply to?" she asks. She pulls up a chair beside me. She's hovering way too close.

I do my best not to sound annoyed.

"Well, I don't really know what I want to major in, so I want a school with a wide range of good programs," I say. I could be quoting from one of the websites I just looked at. "For my reach schools, I was thinking Georgetown, maybe Duke, maybe . . ."

I am not going to say "Vanderbilt." Not when Mom already has an expression of horror spreading across her face.

"But, Becca, those are schools people *watch*," she says. "Places the national news media go when they do reports, 'What are college students thinking about now?' Georgetown—Georgetown's in Washington, D.C.! Do you know how many reporters there are swarming all over Washington, D.C.?"

She makes them sound like a plague of locusts. And she makes it sound like those reporters would be as interested in swarming all over Daddy's story and us as they were three years ago.

No, actually she sounds even more terrified of that possibility than she was three years ago.

Why? What's wrong with her? Has she totally lost her mind?

I can't face those questions head-on. It's like I can only handle having one defective parent at a time.

"Well, Duke's just in North Carolina," I say defensively.

"Right, and haven't you thought about how many Belpre High kids try to go there?" she asks. She rubs her temples. "What if you ran into someone you knew from Georgia on campus? Don't you think they'd put it on Facebook? 'Guess who I just saw . . .'

And then the word would spread, and the next thing you know, there'd be TV reporters following you around, sticking microphones in your face . . ."

Vanderbilt is also a place a lot of Georgia kids would want to go, I think.

And then I am too mad to think clearly.

"Why would reporters care anymore about me? Or you? Or Daddy?" I ask Mom. "And even if they did, what if I just said, 'Leave me alone! I don't want to talk?' Did you ever think of that? If you'd just done that three years ago, we wouldn't have had to move, wouldn't have had to start over . . ."

I am completely rewriting the past—I wanted to move just as much as she did. But there are rebellious thoughts tumbling in my mind: *What if we'd stayed? Mom was supposed to be the grown-up. What if she'd just said, "Becca, we've got to tough this out. I know it's hard, but we'll survive." Would we maybe have been better off? Would we both be fine now—not always so terrified of our own shadows? What's there to be afraid of if the whole world already knows your secrets?*

"Reporters don't take no for an answer," Mom mutters.

"Well, who cares?" I explode. "It's not like they're going to tie us down and torture us until we talk!"

Mom puts her hand down on a pencil I left lying on the table. She starts rolling it back and forth, back and forth, a nervous tic.

"Becca," she says slowly. "I didn't want to tell you this at the time, but . . . there were death threats. People wanted to kill us. Not just Daddy. Us. To get back at him."

I know this is supposed to horrify me. I know I am supposed to cower beside Mom, to start sobbing, "Oh, thank you, Mommy! Thank you for saving my life!" Maybe I'm even supposed to thank her for acting so insanely fearful on my behalf for the past three years.

But I'm not feeling any of it. There's no room in me for anything but anger right now.

"So what?" I say. "Isn't it kind of like we buried ourselves alive so they didn't have to?"

"Becca . . . ," Mom says.

I lift my chin defiantly.

"That was all three years ago," I say. "It's *over*. How much longer do we have to live like this? How much longer do we have to hide? The rest of our lives?"

I spin my laptop toward her.

"Where do *you* want me to go to college—some Podunk University in the middle of nowhere, with nothing to offer?" I challenge. "Or, no, wait—why bother going to college if I'm just going to have to live in a cave the rest of my life?"

Mom does not reach for the computer. She has tears in her eyes, but that doesn't stop me.

"Deskins actually has hot and cold running water and indoor plumbing and Internet access and everything—I'm surprised you let us live *here*," I say.

"Deskins has . . . very good schools," Mom says faintly. "That's why we moved here."

She might as well have stabbed me in the heart with that pencil.

"Oh, right, so I can get a good education that *I can't ever use*," I shout at her.

"Once your daddy's out of prison," Mom begins. "Then—"

"Then I can have a real life?" I demand. Her reasoning makes no sense. Wouldn't Daddy being around again put me more at risk? Bring back the death threats, maybe? But I'm not calm enough to pick apart the holes in her logic. I settle for screaming, "So I can't do anything until I'm twenty-four? *Seven more years?*"

I jerk the computer back away from Mom's side of the table.

"Leave me alone," I demand. "I've got a scholarship application to work on. Because I don't care what you say. I'm going to college *next year*!"

I pull the Court scholarship e-mail I'd written back to the center of my laptop screen. My hands shake as I attach the information sheet and my essay. One more click of the mouse—it's sent. I guess I'm not going to give that essay one last read-through. I'm living dangerously now.

I guess I've been living dangerously all along.

Now

The next morning, in the near darkness before I go to school, I reread my essay. It's fine. There's not a single word I want to change. So it doesn't matter that I didn't proofread it last night.

Is it going to matter that I fought with Mom? Is it going to matter what either of us said? Is it going to matter that I don't want to stay as terrified as she is?

Except for the dim glow of the computer, I don't turn on any lights. I sneak out and close the door as quietly as possible, so I don't wake Mom.

For the next week or so I avoid her as much as possible. I beg Riggoli's for extra work hours during the afternoon, while Mom's still at home. I do my homework at the library instead of the apartment. I walk everywhere, so I don't have to ask her for the car.

I avoid Stuart, too. I know there's no way I can go visit Vanderbilt and Emory with him and Rosa and whoever else. But I can't bear to say no, to completely shut that door.

I tell everyone I have to skip lunch every day to work on calc. And then, just so it's not a lie, I really do work on calc at lunch.

I get a 98 percent on the makeup exam. But I feel no sense of triumph, no relief, no joy. No matter what Mr. Hattimer says, calc is not real life. What good is calc, anyway, when my own mother seems determined to keep me from going to college?

And then that same afternoon I swing by the apartment after school to pick up my laptop before heading to the library. Mom should still be asleep, and if I tiptoe in and tiptoe out, she'll never know. But as I walk past the row of mailboxes at the end of the building, I see that ours is overflowing; we have so many letters, the mail carrier couldn't even latch the door.

Maybe there's a letter from Daddy, forwarded by the attorney, I think as I reach for the stacks of letters. *Maybe he'll tell us . . .*

What? His letters never sound like him anyhow. They're always typed and too formal and nothing like the fun-loving Daddy I remember. What do I want from him, anyway? The man is in prison. Do I really think he's going to be able to convince Mom, "Let Becca apply to any college she wants. Let her fill out financial aid forms and college apps and anything else she wants to online! It's safe"?

Yeah, right.

I rip one of the envelopes, trying to pull the whole stack out. No, not an envelope—it's the back page of a thick brochure, practically a booklet.

It's a brochure from Harvard.

Harvard? I think. *Harvard wants me? Or, at least, wants me to apply?*

The stack of mail is almost all college related: Besides the Harvard brochure, there are flyers or envelopes or packets from the University of Chicago and Yale and the University of Akron and Transylvania University and Ohio State University and Miami University and University of Michigan and Kent State University . . . All sorts of colleges, large and small, well-known and barely known—*all* of them want me to apply.

Which means—all of them already know about me.

Did they buy some list from Deskins High School? I wonder. *Did they get information from the SAT people or the ACT people because last year I was too nervous, taking those tests, to think about checking boxes to keep my information secret? Or because maybe even back then I had already started caring more about going to college than keeping secrets?*

The stack of mail is *heavy*. I lift it high, my thoughts swirling. I sort of want to stalk in to Mom's bedroom, hold out the stack of mail, and yell at her, "See? I got all this because my name is already in some online prospective-college-student listing somewhere—and nobody has shown up trying to kill us! So stop worrying! Stop ruining everything!"

But I also sort of want to hide all the letters and brochures.

Because what if Mom thinks she has to take all this away from me too? What if she decides I'm not even allowed to see my own mail?

I try to cram the stack of mail into a more compact pile, because I *am* going to hide it in my backpack before I walk into the apartment. I can decide about yelling about it or hiding it for good later on. But Harvard's brochure is too rigid to bend well; the Ohio State and Michigan letters seem to be refusing to lie side by side. A letter that I missed noticing before slides out and starts fluttering toward the ground. I catch it.

Its return address says "Whitney Court Scholarship Fund."

I instantly drop all the other letters. I stand there in a blizzard of Harvard and Yale and Chicago and Michigan and Ohio State and Miami and Akron and Kent State and tiny Transylvania all yelling up at me, "Apply now!" "Come be a student at our school!" And I am terrified to open the letter that might make any of that possible.

Ms. Stela said the Court scholarship winner is announced by the end of December, I remind myself. *This is only October. It's too early for this to be "You won!" or "Sorry, you lost."*

That gives me the courage to slide my finger under the flap of the envelope and pull out the single thin sheet of paper inside. My hands are shaking—I have to brace the letter against the row of mailboxes to hold it still enough to actually read.

Dear Ms. Jones,

Thank you for your application for the Whitney Court Scholarship. As judges for this scholarship, we have decided we would like to meet with a select group of applicants before making our final decision. Could you please e-mail us with a list of times you would be available to meet with us on October 24 or 25 . . .

It's not a "You won!" or a "You lost!" letter. It's a "You're still in the running, but you need to wow us in person" letter. This is a callback.

I am a finalist for the Court scholarship.

Now—

a nerve-racking now

"What if we're missing something?" Rosa asks. "What if there's some reason they're doing interviews this year, when they don't usually have finalists, they usually just announce a winner. . . ."

Rosa and I are sitting on folding chairs outside Room 106. We are both finalists for the Court scholarship. According to the clock on the wall, her interview with the scholarship judges is three minutes away. Mine is eighteen minutes away, but I promised to keep her company ahead of time because otherwise, she said, she might spontaneously combust. I hope it doesn't matter that I'm not exactly listening to her. I think I'm mostly here to give her an excuse to talk and talk and talk without looking crazy or cell-phone obsessed. Both of which could be problems for the scholarship judges.

So should I have refused to sit with Rosa, to sabotage her, so I can win instead? I think.

I decide I'm not that diabolical. I certainly don't want to seem that diabolical, not now, not when there's a full-ride scholarship riding on my behavior over the course of the next half hour.

Rosa elbows me, either because she realizes I'm not paying attention or because she just figured something out.

"Oh, no!" she moans. "Why didn't I think to analyze the size of the scholarships for the years they did or didn't do interviews? *That* could have been useful data!"

"Rosa," I say. "Don't worry about it. Just . . . take a deep breath. Or hold your breath, maybe. I think you're on the verge of hyperventilating."

Rosa starts giggling.

"Thanks for the crystal-clear advice!" she mutters.

I laugh too.

"You want medical advice, next time ask Jala, the future doctor, to sit with you," I tell her. But Rosa looks so off-kilter, I take pity on her. I put my hand on her arm. "Here, try this. Good air in." I inhale. "Bad air out." I exhale.

I work her through a solid minute of breathing in and out. I don't know about her, but *I* feel a little calmer now.

Then the door of Room 106 opens.

"It was such a pleasure to meet with all of you," the voice of the finalist ahead of us wafts out, sounding annoyingly confident. It's Ashley Stevens, surprisingly enough, a girl from the Shannon Daily mean-girls crowd. "Thank you for giving me the opportunity to talk with you in person. It was great being able to tell you face-to-face how much I admire Whitney, since I heard so much about her from my cousin Alex."

Oh, no, I think, my calm vanishing. *Did Ashley write about Whitney too? And she had some relative with inside information?*

Beside me, Rosa pantomimes sticking her finger down her throat and gagging.

Ashley steps out of Room 106 with a man in a dark-gray suit. They're shaking hands. The man has his back to Rosa and me, so I have time to notice that Rosa's bangs are sticking up. I pantomime patting my hair down, and she catches on quickly. She smoothes her hair, then stands up. She gets in a last-minute straightening of her dress before the man turns from Ashley to her.

"Ms. Alvarez?" the man says.

"Yes. Mr. Court?" Rosa says, extending her hand.

Rosa sounds calm and cool and confident now, too. I feel like I've just witnessed a transformation that goes beyond hair. It's like, once she stood up, she was no longer a high school student ready to beg for money for college. She instantly became . . . an investment. A future professional. A future attorney.

Attorneys, I think. *Ugh.*

Rosa and Mr. Court disappear into Room 106, and Mr. Court shuts the door behind them. I'm left with Ashley Stevens.

"Congratulations on being a finalist," I say. I don't know that Ashley and I have ever exchanged a single word before, but I've got fifteen minutes to kill, and I can understand how Rosa felt, wanting someone to talk to.

Ashley turns her head and looks at me as though it's just occurred to her that there's another life form present. Even if the life form is roughly equivalent, socially speaking, to a cockroach.

"Oh, no," she snaps. "Don't think you can get me to tell you all the questions they asked in there! I'm not going to help you! You're on your own!"

Then she turns on her heel and stalks away.

Okay, then.

I'm tempted to shout after her, "You think you can rattle me with *that*? After everything I've been through—even death threats!—you think you can throw me off with just a little random meanness?"

I don't say anything, of course. If I were still the kind of person who prayed, I would also be tempted to pray, *Oh, please, God. Even if I don't win the Court scholarship, please don't let Ashley win either.*

And then I kind of am praying, *Please, please, please, let me win this. Let me get the full ride. Let things work out for Rosa, too—let her get a lot of scholarships and financial aid so she can go wherever she wants. But please let me win this one . . . so there's not even a question of me having to apply for financial aid. So I can go to college without upsetting Mom.*

I remember that Mom got upset just by the thought of me going to any reasonably decent school, or anyplace that someone we knew in Georgia three years ago might possibly go. That knocks out pretty much every school I might want.

And . . . when I win the Court scholarship, please let it help Mom stop being so afraid, and not be so crazy about keeping everything about Daddy secret.

Now I'm sounding crazy. I can't think about this now, right before my big interview.

I remind myself that I'm not the type of person who prays. Not anymore.

I look at the clock: I still have twelve minutes before Rosa comes out and I go in and whatever I say determines my entire future. I can't sit here for twelve whole minutes, panicking at the momentousness of what's going to happen twelve minutes from now.

I stand up and walk down the hall to the drinking fountain outside Room 112. Bending over to get a drink, staring down at somebody's chewed-up gum spit into the drain, I have an odd sense of déjà vu. This is the same drinking fountain I fled to during freshman orientation three years ago, when I fake-coughed to avoid Shannon Daily's question, "Where are you from, Becca?" And Room 106, where the scholarship interviews are taking place—that's where we had freshman orientation. The room I was brave enough to return to only because Jala was beside me.

That doesn't mean anything, I tell myself. *It's just a coincidence. It's not symbolism or foreshadowing or anything like that. This is real life, not AP lit. And, anyhow, it doesn't matter anymore where you're from. It matters where you're going.*

Somehow that thought freaks me out even more.

I start shuffling back down the hall, trying to make it take eleven minutes to walk fifty feet. Someone taps me on the back.

"Tag, you're it!" Oscar's relaxed, comical voice calls out behind me.

I whirl around.

"You could have given me a heart attack, sneaking up on me like that!" I accuse. I don't think my words carry much sting, because I can feel myself beaming at Oscar.

And he's beaming back.

I have to stifle the impulse to wrap my arms around him and cry out, "Thank you for not making me spend the next eleven minutes alone! Thank you for not being another mean person like Ashley Stevens!"

"Are you the next victim after me?" I ask. "The Court scholarship finalist who goes in at three forty-five?"

"Nope," Oscar says, shaking his head and shrugging. "I didn't make the cut. But Rosa said you were keeping her company before her interview, and she was feeling bad that nobody would keep you company before yours, so . . . that's why I'm here."

"I *love* Rosa," I say. I'm about to add, "I love you too"—it's the kind of thing I've jokingly said to Oscar a million times before. But, I don't know, there's something a little odd about the way he's leaning toward me, like he can't wait to hear those words.

I can't handle odd right now.

I lean away and say instead, "Thanks. I mean it. I was about two minutes away from needing a rubber room. This whole scholarship thing is making me crazy."

"College, scholarships . . . it's making everybody crazy," Oscar says glumly.

"Yeah, well, some of us really need the money," I say. I instantly clap my hand over my mouth. "I can't sound that desperate in the interview, can I? I sound like I'm about two *seconds* away from grabbing a gun and holding up a bank."

"You just sound like it's really important to you," Oscar says gently.

I blink. I've barely seen or spoken to Oscar since that day we all went for ice cream. Avoiding Stuart has kind of meant avoiding Oscar by default, because they hang out together so much.

How can he *still* be so nice to me?

"Can you just spend the next ten minutes telling me stupid jokes?" I ask him. "I'm not sure I can take anything serious right now."

"Okay, um . . . ," Oscar says, as we both sit down on the folding chairs outside Room 106. "You know that thing about how you're supposed to handle an interview situation, don't you? Where you imagine interviewers in their underwear? I've always had a problem with that, because what if they can look at you and tell that you're thinking about their underwear? Like, doesn't that make you some kind of a pervert?"

He's actually starting to blush. But he forges on.

"So here's the Oscar Wong solution," he says. "I try to figure out, when those interviewers were little kids, did they wear Superman Underoos? Or were they more of a Spider-Man briefs kind of kid? Or Batman?"

"You mean, by thinking about them in little-kid underwear, that makes you not a pervert?" I ask skeptically. I roll my eyes. "Doesn't that make you *worse*? Like, a child predator wannabe?"

Oscar's blush deepens.

"No, no, no!" he protests, waving his hands like he's trying to erase his own words. "I didn't mean it like that! Not like a child predator thing! More like, just, what superhero did they prefer when they were little? Like it's a clue to their personalities! Not anything, um, sexual?"

Oscar buries his face in his hands, then peeks out sideways between his fingers.

"You know how, sometimes there's nothing you can say to make something better?" he asks.

Oscar is such a nerd. I guess for him, just saying the word "sexual" in a female's presence is humiliating beyond words.

For some reason it's making me blush too.

I laugh, trying to make him feel comfortable again.

"I think you have officially gotten me over thinking about how nervous I am," I say. "Leaving out the underwear connection, what was it for you?"

"Huh?" Oscar says.

"Who was your favorite superhero when you were a little kid?" I ask. "Superman? Batman? Spider-Man?"

"Oh, that's easy," Oscar says. "Spider-Man. Duh. Biggest supernerd of them all."

"But isn't Superman's alter ego pretty nerdy, too?" I ask. "What's his name—Clark Kent?"

And then we're off on a ridiculous comparison between various superheroes and their alter egos. We decide there should be some scholarship based on making up the perfect superhero talent, and I start laughing so hard at the examples Oscar comes up with—mowing a yard with a single glance? Winking to turn school cafeteria slop into something delicious?—that I almost forget that the whole rest of my life will be determined in the next fifteen or twenty minutes.

Then the door of Room 106 opens again.

"Thank you for meeting with me," I hear Rosa say.

"It's been a pleasure," I hear Mr. Court say.

"Don't forget, superhero Underoos," Oscar whispers.

I barely have time to smirk at him and mouth *Thanks a lot,* before Rosa and Mr. Court are coming out of the room and she's moving away from him and I have to step up and shake his hand.

"Hi. I'm Becca Jones," I say.

And already something is off. Mr. Court is a tall, barrel-chested man in an expensive suit; even his thick silver hair seems to gleam with the not-so-hidden message, *I'm prosperous! I'm a success! I'm wealthy enough to give away thousands of dollars to people I don't even know!* But he hesitates a moment too long before he puts out his hand and shakes mine. When he finally says, "Nice to meet you," his voice carries . . . what? Doubt? Worry? Fear?

Because of me? I wonder. *He didn't sound like that when he was talking to Rosa or Ashley. But why would he be afraid of me?*

I push those thoughts aside and concentrate on smiling in a way that I hope looks confident and friendly and relaxed, not terrified and desperate and already in despair.

"Right this way," Mr. Court says, holding the door for me and gesturing toward the room.

I glance over my shoulder for one last jolt of reassuring encouragement from Rosa and Oscar, but they look a little puzzled too. Oscar fumbles to give me a thumbs-up, and Rosa smiles and nods, but I can't tell if she means that her interview went well or if she's wishing me luck with mine.

I step through the door and turn toward a table that's replaced the desks in the center of the room. Two women are sitting on the other side, with a laptop open between them. One of the women looks to be in her fifties or sixties, her hair a tasteful shade of ash blond, her salmon-pink sweater twinset a perfect match to her nail polish. Her appearance is so prissily perfect that she reminds me of certain grandmothers I knew in

Georgia—not mine, but ones belonging to other kids, women who'd tell their grandchildren, "You can bring a friend to swim with you at the club, as long as they're well-behaved." I was often the well-behaved friend of choice. I remember one of those grandmothers oohing and aahing over me, proclaiming, "Well, aren't you just about the cutest thing I've ever seen." But then I sneezed and she was horrified that I wasn't carrying my own handkerchief to deal with the dripping snot.

I couldn't have been more than five or six at the time.

You don't have any snot dripping down your face right now, I tell myself. *You're fine.*

I turn my attention to the other woman, who's just as blond but younger and skinnier—almost painfully thin. She's looking down at her hands, which are strangely rough and chapped. Then she lifts her head and I figure out who she is, and I am not fine anymore.

I am now face-to-face with Whitney Court.

Now—

Fifteen of the most horrifying minutes of my life

Why didn't anybody warn me Whitney would be here? I wonder. *Why didn't I think of it ahead of time so I could brace myself?*

I know I'm staring, but I can't stop. Whitney is still pretty, with her delicate features and long blond hair. But that's not the first thing anyone would notice about her anymore. It's her eyes that get to me, that won't let me look away. They seem haunted and haunting—almost washed out, as though their rightful greenish-blue color has leached away.

It's the drugs, I tell myself. *Can drugs do that?*

There are other, smaller details that just seem wrong. In contrast to her parents—for surely the woman in the pink twinset is her mother?—Whitney isn't dressed up. She's got on jeans and a jarringly orange T-shirt. The T-shirt is sliding off one slim shoulder, revealing a maroon bra strap, and the normal thing for anybody to do would be to hitch her shoulder up and shift the T-shirt slightly to the right, hiding the bra strap. It'd be the normal thing in a high school classroom, I mean—maybe Whitney is so wasted right now that she thinks she's at some sort of club, someplace where everyone else is too spaced out to notice.

There is also a line of drool starting in the corner of Whitney's mouth, slipping slowly down her chin.

Oscar's jokes about superhero Underoos seem pathetically innocent and sad right now. So what if Whitney wore Wonder Woman or Supergirl underwear when she was little? So what if everyone expected her to be wonderful and super and incredible her whole life? She threw all that away.

She ruined her life after high school, I think. *Even with what Daddy did, even with everything Mom's afraid of—I am not going to let anyone ruin mine.*

I realize Mr. Court is introducing me to Mrs. Court and Whitney. Belatedly, I shake hands with both of them and say, "Nice to meet you." I make my handshake firm, even though Whitney's isn't. Her hand feels like a fish out of water, trying to flop away. It's also clammy, which annoys me, because now my hand is moist, and what if Mrs. Court thinks I have sweaty palms?

While I'm shaking hands with Mrs. Court, I notice out of the corner of my eye that Mr. Court is straightening Whitney's shirt and wiping the drool from her chin. Now she looks normal again. Relatively.

Sad, I think, pitying her and feeling superior, all at once. *So, so sad.*

Everyone sits down, the Courts on one side of the table and me facing them with my back to the door. They're all watching me, and it's a struggle not to squirm in my seat, a struggle not to let panic overwhelm me.

Why isn't anyone saying anything? I wonder. *Aren't they supposed to ask questions?*

The silence grows, and I can't stand it anymore.

"Um," I begin, just as Mr. Court says, "Would you mind telling us—"

We both hesitate, and then I say, "I'm sorry. Go ahead—what did you want to know?"

Mr. Court looks over toward his wife and daughter. It's Whitney who speaks up now.

"What have you liked best about your high school years?" she asks in an unnaturally high voice.

Oh, no! Don't ask questions about me! I think.

But would it be any better to talk about the glories of Whitney's high school years when ruined-Whitney is sitting right in front of me?

"Well," I say, even though my mind is blank. I have a quick flash of remembering laughing in the hallway with Oscar, and in contrast to this horrible moment, that seems like the happiest ten minutes of my entire high school career. Maybe my entire life. "I would say the best thing about high school has been the friends I've made. I moved to Deskins right before freshman year, and I wasn't sure what it would be like meeting new people."

When I couldn't be myself, I think. *When I couldn't let anybody get too close.*

I don't say that.

"I got involved in extracurricular activities, just like everybody tells you to—I ran cross-country freshman year, I've done service club and math club and other activities like that," I say. Then I shrug. "Well, you already know that, because it was on my application. But I think the most fun moments have been just ordinary things like going out for ice cream with my friends, or joking around at lunch, or making up silly rhymes with them so we could all remember chemistry or biology formulas . . ."

"That's how I felt too," Whitney says softly.

She's looking right at me, and I feel a jolt of connection. She was the queen of Deskins High School, and I am nobody here; she was drooling a moment ago, and I will never, ever, ever let myself fall that far. But we have something in common.

I remember that I have gone out with my high school friends for ice cream exactly once, and I haven't eaten lunch with my friends in more than a week.

That still doesn't mean my answer was a lie.

Whitney tilts her head, still watching me intently.

"Sometimes your eyes bleed," she says. "You probably think it's just tears, but it's really blood."

Did I hear that right?

I look to Mr. and Mrs. Court as if I expect them to translate.

They're both looking at Whitney, and then past her, toward each other.

"Whitney," Mr. Court says, easing an arm around his daughter's shoulders. "Did you take your medicine this morning?"

Code, I think. *Because he doesn't want me to know it's not really medicine she took.*

Whitney grins and then puts her hand over her mouth, hiding it. Her eyes still glow. She looks like a little kid who's been caught doing something bad but doesn't regret it in the least.

"I wanted to be *alert*," she says emphatically. "I wanted to talk to this one. To tell her—"

"That her eyes are bleeding?" Mrs. Court asks, with heavy skepticism. She and Mr. Court seem to have a good cop/bad cop routine going. She's the bad cop.

Whitney giggles.

"Of course not," she says. "How would I know her eyes were bleeding until I saw her?"

What is she on? I wonder. I think back to freshman-year health class, when we filled in grids about drug side effects. The only drug I can remember causing hallucinations is LSD.

Didn't people pretty much stop taking LSD after the 1960s? I think.

I want to run out of the room and down the hall and find some kid who's hanging around after school to get high and ask, "This isn't how people on drugs usually act, is it? Isn't this really bizarre?"

How could this be happening during *my* interview?

Oh, wait, what if she's just acting? I wonder. *What if this is some kind of test, to see how I'll react to people who are . . .*

I can't even classify Whitney's behavior. But I sit up straight and try to hold a patient, understanding expression on my face.

Even though I completely do not understand.

"Whitney," Mr. Court says as he maneuvers his hand around her arm and begins pulling her up. "I think it would be best if you and your mother take a little walk while I talk to Becca."

"But I want to tell her—"

"I know everything you want to say," Mr. Court assures her. "I'll pass it along."

Whitney crosses her arms and shakes her head no. She's got to be—what? Thirty-two? Thirty-three?—but she's acting like a petulant little kid.

"No, me," she says.

"Whitney," Mrs. Court says. "Think. If this girl's eyes are bleeding, shouldn't we go find bandages for her? Wouldn't that be the kind thing to do?"

I can almost see this idea burrowing into Whitney's fogged mind. She stops shaking her head and her eyes go wide with concern. And then she jumps up and heads for the door.

"Right!" she calls. "We'll be back as soon as we can! Try not to let the blood drip everywhere!"

Mrs. Court trails after her.

I turn and watch them leave. And then they're gone, and the door's shut and I know I need to face Mr. Court again. But what am I supposed to say?

As I'm trying to pull myself together to act normal—though, what is normal in a situation like this?—I hear Mr. Court clearing his throat behind me.

"It's not what you think," he says in such a heavy voice that each word seems weighted down. "She's not a drug addict."

I whirl around.

"I didn't say anything about drugs," I tell him, trying to sound both innocent and sympathetic and still as though I'm reacting "normally," whatever that means. I remind myself I've had plenty of experience trying to hold myself together in bizarre circumstances.

Mr. Court frowns as if he doesn't believe me.

"What you wrote . . . ," he begins. He stops and waves this away, as if he wants to start over. "I know you saw newspaper articles about Whitney. From when she was at Kenyon."

How does he know that? I wonder.

I squint, thinking about my scholarship essay. Of course I didn't write anything about Whitney being arrested. But did I slip up and accidentally hint that I'd seen those articles?

No, I couldn't have. . . .

I want to deny everything, to pretend I don't know anything Whitney did between her high school graduation and today. But Mr. Court is already wading deeper into his story.

"Whitney began acting strange toward the end of her junior year in college," Mr. Court says. He lets out a heavy sigh. "At first the police and the college thought she was on drugs. Marlene and I—her own parents!—we thought she was on drugs too. But she wasn't."

Is he still in denial? I wonder. *Maybe it's like Mom and me, how after Daddy was arrested we were so convinced he was innocent, so certain the prosecutors made a mistake. . . . Nobody wants to believe somebody they love could do such awful things.*

Except Whitney's strange behavior dates back twelve years.

If Mr. Court is still in denial, that would be like Mom and me still believing in Daddy's innocence even after he'd been arrested and convicted and sentenced, and had already served his full term in prison.

Now Mr. Court is looking me straight in the eye.

"Whitney is mentally ill," he says.

I jerk back. I wasn't expecting that.

"What?" I say. I'm having trouble processing this. "But Whitney was so *normal* in high school. No—not normal. Extraordinary. *Incredible.* How does someone go from that to being . . . being . . ."

I barely stop myself from using the word "crazy." I also have to struggle not to say, "I don't believe you." I change tacks.

"She was already twenty, right?" I ask. "How could she be one type of person for twenty years and then suddenly become someone totally different?"

I don't have to say "I don't believe you." The skepticism is thick in my voice. I want to force Mr. Court to admit "Well, it all started because she experimented with psychedelic drugs. . . ." I want there to be a reason.

I want to be able to blame Whitney for what happened to her, just like I blame Daddy for what happened to him.

Mr. Court keeps gazing at me, as steady as an anchor in a storm.

"That's how schizophrenia works," he says. "Average age of onset for females is twenty-five. It's younger for males—eighteen, I think. And it wasn't exactly sudden. There were signs. She stopped wearing shoes—at best, even with snow on the ground, she might wear flip-flops." He laughs halfheartedly. "On a college campus, that didn't stand out as much as you'd think. And anyhow, she'd always been a little quirky, always had such a great imagination—"

"Like how she invented the Land of the Two Seas," I say. I'm struck with horror: *Did I pull out one of the first signs of her insanity as something that made her great?*

Mr. Court looks jolted, as if he'd forgotten I talked to Rachel and Tiffany Congreves.

"Well, yes," he says. "But then in college she started crossing the line from being quirky and creative and imaginative and fun to . . . just being sick. Having delusions and strange hallucinations and thinking they were real."

"Telling people their eyes are bleeding," I say.

Mr. Court nods.

I have yet to do a college visit, but I don't think college is *that* different from high school. If someone started saying crazy things like that in the hallways at DHS, everyone would laugh at first, thinking it was a joke.

And then everybody would start avoiding the person.

How did people treat Whitney, the golden girl, when she went crazy in college?

I can't ask.

"A lot of Whitney's hallucinations have to do with eyes," Mr. Court is saying. "She usually only sees blood like that when she's worried about someone. When she thinks someone's in pain."

I shift uncomfortably in my seat. Should I laugh this off, act as though Mr. Court himself is crazy for taking Whitney's hallucination seriously? It's not like I'm going to confess that I have problems of my own. Or admit that, even now, even as we're talking about Whitney's illness, I'm fighting a tide of rage inside me—ridiculous rage, unreasonable rage, rage no normal person would feel.

Am I supposed to say, "You know, I'm really mad Whitney would say that about me. I'm really mad that she's crazy. And . . . I'm really mad that it's not her fault, not anything she did to make this happen. Because I wanted to be mad at her for ruining her life, like Daddy ruined his. And mine. Don't you know, as long as I could split my anger between her and Daddy, it wasn't so bad?"

I'm not crazy. Not crazy enough to say that aloud to Whitney's father.

Or anyone else.

"Isn't there medicine she can take?" I ask, trying to shift the focus back to Whitney. I suddenly realize I misunderstood Mr. Court's question about medicine—he *was* talking about a prescription, something Whitney needed. Something she'd forgotten to take? I try to sound meek and mild and only concerned about her. "Isn't there something that could . . ."

I want to say "fix her" but I'm afraid that would sound bad. And I'm afraid it would loosen my iron control, send the fury spiraling out of my mouth.

And then who knows what could happen?

Mr. Court frowns and lets out another heavy sigh.

"It's complicated," he says. "Lots of people, with medicine, can lead fairly normal lives. Whitney . . . not so much. And the side effects . . . She hates how foggy her brain gets with certain medications. Some of the meds make her look and act crazier than without them."

The drool, I think. *The shirt falling off her shoulder.*

"She has good days and bad days," Mr. Court says. "Good and bad months, even good and bad years. Sometimes we can't take care of her at home—that's why we moved down to Cincinnati, to be close to the hospital where she stays."

"So—no one in Deskins even knows she's sick?" I ask.

Mr. Court winces.

"No, people here know," he says. "But we've found they have a remarkable degree of . . . well, I know it's meant as loyalty. A lot of the people who remember Whitney growing up, they refuse to talk to outsiders about her problems now. They think they're protecting her."

Mrs. Congreves, I think. *The teachers I interviewed. Maybe even Corey Wisner and the other classmates who set up the reunion page.*

I think about what Ashley Stevens said leaving her scholarship interview, about how her cousin had told her all about Whitney. Of course people like her would have known everything right from the start. They had the advantage. They weren't outsiders like me.

"So why don't you just explain everything in the scholarship handouts?" I ask. "So nobody else has to?"

No matter how much I try, I can't keep the bitterness out of my voice. The sense of being left out and deceived.

Mr. Court shakes his head.

"We were surprised this year to find out that Whitney's mental illness *wasn't* mentioned in the scholarship handouts," he says apologetically. "We had a whole paragraph about it in the information we gave the school way back at the beginning, when we set everything up. Somehow I guess that's been left out every year."

Ms. Stela making yet another mistake? I wonder. Then I remember she hasn't been at DHS that long. *So was it some old Deskins person once again trying to "protect" Whitney?*

Mr. Court is still talking.

"This is the first year we found some students didn't know all about Whitney," he says. "We kind of forgot how much Deskins has changed, that there are so many new people whose parents wouldn't even remember."

Or students who haven't heard gossip about her, I think. Because I'm pretty sure if people like Ashley Stevens know, there was gossip. Would I have known all about Whitney if I hadn't cut myself off from everyone over the last few weeks?

No, my friends didn't know either, I think, remembering the lunch where everybody else, like me, assumed Whitney was dead. All my friends are Deskins transplants like me.

This thought comforts me enough that I can tamp down my anger and sense of betrayal and say, almost graciously, "That's okay. It's not your fault the school didn't tell us everything."

I'm shifting to an almost-normal thought process: *Does this mess up anything about my essay? Could we possibly just go on with the interview like normal now?*

But Mr. Court won't let the subject drop.

"No, it's not okay," he says. "This makes it seem like we were trying to hide Whitney's illness—like we're ashamed or something—and we're not. And anyway, we don't want people to be upset about the early deadlines. We want them to understand."

I squint at him, confused once again. What do deadlines have to do with anything?

"You know how our contest starts and ends earlier than the other local scholarships?" Mr. Court asks. "It's because Whitney usually does really well in the fall, and this way she can help pick the winner."

What I saw was Whitney doing well?

Maybe I telegraph that question with my eyes, because Mr. Court says defensively, "She was perfectly fine during the other interviews. It's just, she was so worried about you . . ."

I'm back to squirming again. I jump in with another question.

"Why do you even do the scholarship program?" I ask. It's the closest I can come to what I really want to know: Why parade your crazy daughter around when she's drooling and half-undressed? Why make it likely that people like me will find old articles about her being stopped by the police and judge her for things that weren't her fault? Why force Whitney's old friends to relive the past and put them on the spot, deciding every year what they should or shouldn't say? Why not be like everyone else in Old Deskins and keep the secret from all outsiders?

"Whitney loves the scholarship program," Mr. Court says, and now he's sitting up straight, as if he's cast off the worries that were weighing him down. It's as if, regardless of Whitney, he's so anchored, nothing can faze him. Or maybe the scholarship program is part of his anchor. "She loves helping kids go to their dream schools. She always felt so lucky that she could go to Kenyon, like she wanted. A lot of her friends were limited financially, and she always felt bad about that, always thought choosing colleges made it way too important whether someone was rich or poor . . ."

"But you didn't ask for financial statements," I say, and I barely manage to sound curious, not surly. I didn't miss something I was supposed to fill out, did I?

"We don't want to duplicate the financial aid kids would get anyway," Mr. Court says. "Sometimes we do ask the counselors which kids are longing to go to a school that's out of their reach."

So it's good I told Ms. Stela I want to go to Vanderbilt, I think. Focusing on Vanderbilt helps me tighten the control on my emotions. They're layered now, worry and anxiety and resentment, and then, down below, the fury that's been there from the start.

I tamp the fury down deeper and try to figure out how to weave Vanderbilt into the conversation, how to make it clear that I'm exactly the kid he's describing.

But Mr. Court is still talking.

"Anyhow, we can usually find everything we want to know from the essays kids write about Whitney's graduating class," Mr. Court says. "It's in who they pick to write about, what they pick out from that person's life. And Whitney loves to read those essays, loves remembering how her friends used to be.

She and her classmates had such a special experience in high school—we wanted other Deskins classes to know what that was like, and get ideas for making their own senior year special. We—and Whitney—want her life to be about more than just the schizophrenia, more than just focusing on herself and her own problems."

I'm back to struggling for control over my fury: *So did I screw up completely by picking Whitney herself as my subject?*

Maybe I did. Mr. Court is grimacing now.

"We probably shouldn't have let her read your essay," Mr. Court says. "I think it was too much for her."

The rage I've been holding at bay surges past my control.

"Just because the whole essay's about her?" I ask, and my voice is stingingly bitter. There's no hiding it now. "Because I didn't know what really happened, or that she would be a scholarship judge, or that it would hurt her to be reminded of how *she* used to be? Why didn't you just say no one's allowed to write about Whitney?"

I want to explode: "It's not fair! I never had a chance at this scholarship, did I? Why'd you say I'm a finalist? I bet I'm not even a real finalist—you probably just wanted to shock me by introducing me to Whitney and then lecture me about what a loser I am for researching Whitney for a whole month and never even knowing she was crazy."

It's not like I'm so disciplined, I can hold all that anger back. It's not my self-control that keeps me from screaming, "That's not fair!" It's the expression on Mr. Court's face.

He's squinting at me, his brow furrowed, his eyes glazed with confusion.

"Your whole essay wasn't about Whitney," he says. He shakes his head. "I mean, sure, you mentioned her, but—"

"Every single word I wrote in that essay was about Whitney!" I insist. I am still drowning in fury, but this is my *scholarship* interview, this is the fifteen minutes that can determine the rest of my life. I can still grasp for something reasonable, something to save me. "You must have confused my essay with somebody else's."

The furrow in Mr. Court's brow deepens, but he reaches down into a briefcase beside his chair and pulls out three stapled-together papers. He drops them in front of me.

"This is what you turned in," he says.

I look down, and those are my words on this paper. But it isn't my essay about Whitney and the Congreves girls, about their magical times in the Land of the Two Seas.

What lies before me—what I turned in, what all the Courts read—is my furious rant about how much I hate Daddy.

Still the horrifying now.
Only, it gets worse

"Nooo," I moan.

In a flash I see what happened. I was so mad at Mom the night I turned in my scholarship application by e-mail. I was half-blinded by rage. And my rant at Daddy, labeled "Whitney Court Scholarship Essay," would have been right below the actual "Whitney Court Scholarship Application Essay" in my computer files. I must have clicked on the wrong label.

I have to fix this.

"I made a stupid mistake," I say, and attempt what should be a tinkling laugh, a charming effort to poke fun at myself.

The laugh comes out sounding like maniacal hysteria.

Mr. Court is watching me much too carefully.

"I can explain," I say. "I attached the wrong file. I'll send you the correct file right away, and you'll see by the date stamp, I did it before the deadline. It's what I *meant* to turn in. And it's really good."

I consider another reassuring laugh, making fun of myself for bragging about my own essay. But I can't afford to have another laugh turn into another epic fail.

This time it would probably sound more like sobbing.

Mr. Court touches the papers in front of me, which practically seethe with my rage at Daddy when I thought he might have made up the whole Court scholarship as a scam to give me money.

"So if this wasn't what you meant to turn in," he begins, "what is it?"

"Oh, I can explain," I say confidently. "It's . . ."

I hesitate, trying to find the best lie. An English-class exercise? An acting-class role-play?

What if Mr. Court checked and found out I'm not even taking an acting class? What if he talked to my lit teacher?

I am lost. I can't make up a good lie fast enough.

"Whitney read this, and she was worried about you," Mr. Court says. "We all were. Marlene and I—we've seen a lot of other mentally ill people besides Whitney over the years. What you wrote seemed so . . . paranoid. We began to fear that you were—"

"What?" I say, and my voice is sharp now, a knife slashing through my own half-planned lies and pretense, through Mr. Court's careful inching forward.

Nothing can protect me now.

"This essay seems like a classic case of paranoid schizophrenia," Mr. Court says. "We were worried about your mental health. That's why we wanted to talk to you."

His eyes hold such gentle concern. And I learned enough in AP psych to see what he means. I do sound delusional in that essay. I do sound like I believe my enemy—my father—holds almost supernatural powers, pulling the puppet strings of dozens of people in Ohio while he's imprisoned thousands of miles away.

I do sound crazy.

"No," I say. "*No*. You don't understand. I'm not crazy. It's my life that's crazy. I'll prove it."

I grab the laptop Mrs. Court and Whitney abandoned. I turn it sideways between Mr. Court and me.

"Let me show you . . . ," I say, typing frantically. I am a whirling dervish, the only thought in my mind, *fix it, fix it, fix it* . . . Lies about English assignments or acting class or role-playing aren't good enough right now.

The only excuse I can save myself with is the truth.

"This is my father," I say. I'm on the Internet now and I've typed in the words "Roger Jones." And it's amazing how desperate I am to reveal the secret that my mother and I have spent three years desperately hiding. Everything's flipped around—suddenly it's backward day. I know Mr. Court will never believe me—will never look at my actual scholarship essay, will never help me go to college—unless I can convince him who I really am.

I click on one of the nine hundred thousand sites that hold information about my daddy.

My father's picture stares out at me, his cockiness glowing from eyes that are shaped and tinted just like mine. The words beside the picture shout, "Infamous criminal bilks millions from victims in multiple layers of scams."

"I know who Roger Jones is," Mr. Court says quietly from across the table. "During his trial—when was that? Four years ago? Five?—he was all over the news. Nobody could stop talking about him. But . . . you didn't list Roger Jones as your father on your scholarship application. Jones is a common name. Maybe you just want to believe that you're related to someone famous? Even if he's famous for awful things?"

I clench my jaw, grinding my teeth.

"Look," I say.

I minimize my father's picture and go to the genealogy website where I searched for proof that Whitney died. I remember all the other records they bragged about having.

"Here's my birth certificate," I say.

I type my name and birthdate and "Fulton County, Georgia." I add my parents' names.

A split second later the site tells me no such person exists.

"I must have typed something wrong," I say. I click the back arrow, and all the information's there, everything that made me me from the very beginning.

Maybe there was just a clerical error, I think. *Something miscategorized . . .*

I start eliminating information, erasing one fact about myself at a time.

Erase my birthplace?

I still don't exist.

Erase my middle name?

I still don't exist.

Erase my mother's name?

I still don't exist.

Erase my father?

Mr. Court puts his hand over mine, stopping me from this search.

"It's okay," he says. "Don't torture yourself. Obviously you're a very troubled person. It's not your fault. There are things you're not going to understand until you get some help. And we *want* to help you."

I jerk my hand back from Mr. Court's.

"I know the guidance counselors are still in their offices," he says. "We'll just go in and talk to Ms. Stela. . . ."

I stare at him—wide-eyed, startled, terrified. There is nothing left for me to do, nothing I can possibly do to rescue this disastrous interview. There is no way I could ever win the Whitney Court Scholarship now.

I turn around and flee.

Now—

Do I exist?

I whip the door open and race out into the hall. Oscar and Rosa are sitting there waiting for me—they're relaxed; Rosa's pressure is off. . . .

I can't bear to look at them.

I jerk away, sprinting in the opposite direction. Their cries follow me, crazily distorted: "Becca, what's wrong? What happened?" The hall's acoustics are weird, creating some eerie form of the Doppler effect. Or maybe my ears are just working the same way they do in nightmares.

I keep running. I was lousy at cross-country, but nobody could catch me now.

I smash out through a side door, across the lawn, across the street, through the apartment complex parking lot. Then I'm at the door of my own apartment, and I shove it open, banging the doorknob against the wall. I know Mom's asleep in her bedroom but I don't care. If the banging door doesn't wake her, then my ragged breathing will. I'm as loud as a steam engine, as a freight train—as any mechanical thing that's loud and primitive and practically impossible to stop.

I slam the door behind me and race into Mom's room. I stand over her bed, grab her by the shoulders, and shake her hard.

"Why don't I have a birth certificate?" I scream. "What happened to it?"

She opens her eyes and blinks, a woman startled from deepest sleep.

"What . . . do you mean?" she mumbles, squinting stupidly up at me. She has a crease across her cheek from her wrinkled pillowcase, and her gray hair is tangled around her face. "Of course you have a birth certificate. You've seen it. It's in the file in my desk, with our other important papers."

"I don't mean *paper*," I say scornfully. "Anyone can fake *paper*. We used a version without Daddy's name to get my driver's license, remember? I mean *online*. It's missing online."

She's still squinting at me—it's like I'm speaking a language she's never heard before. I let out an exasperated snort and run out of the room for my laptop. I left it recharging this morning so it's already on. I yank it away from the cord and run it back to Mom. Even as I sprint down the hall, I'm calling up the search form, I'm typing in my own name.

I thrust the laptop at Mom.

"See, this is me," I say. "Right?"

I click on "search now."

"So where am I?" I ask Mom. "Why doesn't my birth certificate show up?"

Mom's squint intensifies. The furrows in her forehead seem as deep as some unexplored trench out in the ocean.

"I . . . don't know," she says. "I didn't think . . ."

I am not patient enough to listen to thoughts or speculation or theories. I want explanations. I want facts.

"Let's see if yours is there," I say. "What's the name of the county where you were born? Owsley?"

Mom sits up to watch me fill in her information and click the "search now" button.

This website says she doesn't exist either.

"Look for my marriage license," Mom says quietly.

It's missing, too.

"Maybe . . . ," Mom says.

There's a buzzing from the living room—the sound our phone makes when it's set to vibrate and light up rather than ring. It's not loud enough to wake Mom when she's sleeping, but it sounds like a pounding alarm to me right now.

"You can get that," Mom says.

"No," I snap at her. "It's probably Oscar and Rosa, and I can't talk to them. I ruined everything today, because I didn't know my birth certificate vanished—"

I break off, because even though the phone hasn't stopped buzzing, there's now someone knocking at our front door, too. Distantly, I hear, "Becca? Are you all right?"

Of course I'm not all right.

I stride across the room and slam Mom's bedroom door, though this is ridiculous. The doors in this apartment are as thin as cardboard, and the extra layer of closed door doesn't block out the voices or the buzzing phone. If Oscar and Rosa really want to find out how I am, they could break in easily, and the doors would be no protection.

But Oscar and Rosa are law-abiding types. Neither of them would risk acquiring a police record just to make sure I'm okay.

Surely they don't care about me that much.

I turn back to Mom and look at her, really look at her deeply for once. Under the blankets she's got her knees drawn up to her chest in a cowering, terrified position. Her eyes are wide with fear and—what? Confusion? Anguish? Pain?

It still hurts to look at her. Worse than ever, actually. Her hair is still sticking up, and she's been sleeping in a ratty old bluish-green T-shirt. Because of her cowering, I can't read the shirt's front except for the flourish of the top of the letter *F*. But I know this shirt. The *F* is for "Florida"—Daddy bought this T-shirt for Mom on our last family vacation before he was arrested. It was just a quick weekend getaway; Daddy had to get back for "business." But he said the shirt was a promise of fun trips in the future. He said the shirt was the exact same color as the ocean at dawn; he said it was the exact same color as Mom's eyes.

How can Mom stand to still wear that shirt? I wonder. *How can she stand to still wear anything Daddy gave her?*

I know how: We're poor. I can't think of any clothing Mom has bought for herself in the past three years. And when it comes right down to it, all the clothes Mom owned before Daddy was arrested came from him. Why should this shirt be worse than any other?

Maybe the shirt doesn't mean anything to Mom, I think. *Maybe it never did.*

Still, the shirt and Mom's cowering position—and her gray hair—make it seem like she's trapped in the past. She will never escape.

I have to, I think. *I have to have a future.*

But I can't have a future if I keep getting sabotaged by things I don't know from the past.

I cover the distance back to the bed in three long strides.

"I'm going to find out what's going on," I tell Mom as I reach for the computer again. "Do you think Daddy's birth certificate is missing too?"

I've just typed the *R* of "Roger" when Mom shoves my hands away from the keyboard.

"Don't bother," she says in a flat, bitter voice. "Even if it's there, it's not real."

"What are you talking about?" I demand.

She stares up at me. I can name the emotion carried in her eyes right now. It's sorrow, all sorrow.

"Do you really want to know about *another* lie your father told?" she asks.

No, I think.

"Yes," I say.

Now—

and there's more

"This happened before I met your father, and I didn't know about it until after the trial," Mom says. "His attorney managed to get the evidence thrown out, so it never became public, but—"

"*What?*" I ask.

"Your father's real name isn't Roger Jones," Mom says.

For a second I actually feel a flare of joy: *So there! I knew it all along—my daddy* isn't *that evil criminal Roger Jones. This was a case of mistaken identity from the very beginning.*

Then I understand what Mom really means.

"You mean he even lied about his *name,*" I say in a dull, dead voice. "He lied to everyone he met from the first word out of his mouth."

I'm still trying to grasp it all: Mom took his name when she married him and it wasn't his to give. He passed the name down to me, so he made me into a liar before I could even speak.

Mom is frowning at me so, so sadly.

"Your father had a fight with his family when he left home," she said. "He says it was their fault, but who knows? He didn't want them finding him. So he changed his name. He says he did it legally, but the courthouse where it was recorded conveniently burned down . . . and this was before everything would have been online."

Daddy even burned down a courthouse to hide his crimes? I'm thinking.

"Becca? That courthouse was struck by lightning," Mom says, as if she knows how my brain's working. She frowns. "Or, for all I know, maybe your daddy heard about some courthouse burning down and used that detail to make his lie convincing."

What's the difference? When Daddy hid this secret from me too?

I shake my head, trying to clear it.

"What's Daddy's real name?" I ask.

Mom shrugs.

"Robert Catri," she says, spitting out the unfamiliar words. "Not that I care. Not that it matters."

I remember how Daddy always said his whole family was dead. Another lie, probably. I remember way back to the day Mom and I first talked about running away, how Mom said we didn't have to make up fake, anonymous-sounding names to go into hiding because we already had anonymous-sounding names.

Even then my name wasn't real. Daddy made sure my name was a fraud right from the start. He made sure *I* was a fraud.

"Why didn't you tell me?" I ask Mom. Once again, it's Daddy I should be mad at, but Mom's the one sitting in front of me. So she's the one I scream at.

Mom holds up her hands helplessly.

"Remember how . . . destroyed . . . we both were after the trial? Before we moved?" she asks. "Did you really need another reason to believe your father was scum? You were fourteen. You'd always been such a daddy's girl. I thought one more bit of evidence might . . . might . . ."

"What? *Kill* me?" I challenge. I am full of bravado, my face shoved down low so I'm in Mom's face. "Like just a *name* would ruin me forever?"

It could have, I think. I don't want to, but I can remember how I felt three years ago: wobbly and fragile and frail, like my whole body was tissue paper. There had been moments when the gentlest puff of wind could have torn me to shreds.

"Becca . . . ," Mom says. She lifts her hands again, a useless, fluttering motion, going nowhere.

I will not be helpless or useless like my mother.

"Sure, I was fourteen then, but I'm *seventeen* now," I say. "Almost an adult. You had *three years* when you could have told me the truth about Daddy. Why didn't you? What else are you still keeping secret?"

Mom's eyes dart to the side, a familiar movement. There have been dozens of times over the last three years when she's looked away like that. And I've let her. I've looked away myself, or I've buried myself in homework or grabbed my computer or stuffed in earbuds and turned my iPod up loud.

But I just blew any chance I ever had of getting the Court scholarship, and I'm going to have to think up some excuse to give Rosa and Oscar tomorrow for ignoring them. And unless Ms. Stela is even more incompetent than I think, I'm going to have to figure out some way to convince her I am not a paranoid schizophrenic or psychologically deranged or anything but a good student stressed out by the pressures of senior year.

I can't get tripped up again by something unexpected like a missing birth certificate.

And . . . I actually told the truth today. I told the whole truth and nothing but the truth for the first time in three years, and even though it didn't go well, somehow speaking the truth just once made me even more disgusted with the past three years of secrets and lies.

No—my whole life of secrets and lies.

"There *is* something else, isn't there?" I hiss at Mom. "Something else you've been keeping from me, something else you've lied about—"

"I was just trying to protect you," she wails back at me. "Why frighten you even more?"

I grab her by the arm.

"Tell me," I insist. "Tell me, or else I'll, I'll . . . I'll tell everyone in Deskins who we are."

The color drains from Mom's face. She wrenches her arm from my grasp and grabs me by the shoulders.

"No!" she shrieks. "Weren't you listening to me before? There are people who would *kill* us if they knew!"

I pull away easily.

"Oh, right," I scoff. "The death threats. You're just paranoid. All those months after Daddy was arrested, all those weeks the trial went on—everybody in Atlanta knew where we lived then. Anybody in the world could have found us. If someone was going to kill us, wouldn't they have done it when we still lived in Georgia?"

"We had special protection through the FBI," Mom says. "Twenty-four hours a day."

Okay, I didn't know that. I try not to let my reaction show on my face.

"Anyhow," I say. "That was a long time ago. Anyone who hated Daddy that much—they've got to know he's in *prison* now. He's already being punished. He'll be punished for another seven years! Whatever danger we were in three years ago—it's *over*!"

"Keep your voice down," Mom says.

I realize the buzzing of the phone and the pounding at the front door stopped a long time ago. My friends gave up on me, just like I expected. Just like I wanted.

Mom is still white faced and cowering. And she's glancing

around as though there might be spies and enemies anywhere around us.

"The danger isn't over," Mom says. "None of this is over. It's worse than ever. Your father and his attorney are trying to work out a deal to get him out of prison early. All he has to do is betray some former clients. And they'd do anything to stop him."

I want to say, "You're exaggerating! They wouldn't actually *kill* us! What good would that do?" I want to say it in the same sarcastic, scoffing tone I'd used before. But I'd sat through hours of testimony at Daddy's trial. I heard the type of person he really was, the type of people he did business with. I can imagine some of them deciding to kill Mom to warn Daddy about what they'd do to me if he talked, or vice versa. I could see them kidnapping us or torturing us or . . .

"Becca?" Mom says gently. "This is why I didn't tell you."

I realize I am standing stock still, frozen with fear.

"It's all right," Mom says, still in that same cautious, easy tone. "This is the real reason we ran away. We're perfectly safe here. Nobody knows anything about us. I swear, I didn't know about the missing birth and marriage certificates online, but that must have been some other protection the attorney set up. Like extra insurance."

She's smiling at me—hopefully, reassuringly, kindly. She looks calmer, too, as if she feels better now that she's spilled the last secret she was keeping from me.

It really does seem like this was her last big secret.

And maybe I would have felt reassured—maybe I would have trusted her and felt completely safe—if only she'd told me this yesterday or the day before or practically any other day over the past three years.

Why did she wait to tell me on the very day I just revealed our biggest secret?

Now—

too much now

If there's such a thing as "un-cowering," that's what Mom is doing. She stretches out her legs and un-hunches her shoulder. Even her face smoothes out, the furrows gone.

"Wow," she marvels. "I never realized how relieved I'd feel, finally telling you that."

I want to punch her right in her smooth, happy, relieved face. I want to put my fist through the wall. I want to kick the door off its hinges. I want to grab Mom by the shoulders and shake her until she screams—until she's back to being as miserable and terrified as I am.

I don't want to tell her what I did.

"How could you have kept this from me?" I scream. "How could you have believed that I wouldn't accidentally let something slip—and get us both killed?"

Mom's face turns solemn again.

"I never worried about that," she says. "You were so . . . pathologically mortified. Fourteen is kind of the worst age to be embarrassed by anything, and you had the whole world knowing what you were ashamed of. I knew you wouldn't slip up."

"Didn't you think I'd ever outgrow being fourteen?" I want to shout at her. But I can't, not without confessing what I told Mr. Court.

Mom is staring me straight in the eye. How is it that over the past three years I never noticed that she avoided looking directly at me as much as I avoided looking directly at her?

I force myself to gaze right back at her. My face feels stiff as stone, as if I've dared to peer at Medusa.

"Honestly?" Mom says. "When we first moved here, what frightened me the most was the psychological damage I thought this might do to you. You were always such an open, loving child. You had such a gift for making friends. I should have been urging you to trust people again—select people, anyway. Instead, I had to keep telling you, 'Hide! Keep secrets! Don't get over any of this!'"

"And, 'Don't even think about going to college,'" I snarl.

Mom winces.

"The danger, the secrecy, the hiding . . . it was only supposed to last a few months," she says. "A year, tops. We were already talking about moving, anyway, when I found out about the deal your daddy and the attorney were making. It's under something called Rule Thirty-five, where a prisoner gives prosecutors information about a crime somebody else did. Once the prosecutors checked it out and arrested the Excellerand officials, then—"

"Excellerand?" I say. "*That's* what this is about?"

Excellerand is like Apple or Microsoft or Google—one of those companies that everyone knows about and wishes they'd bought stock in ten years ago. It's *huge*.

"Remember how proud your daddy was when he did that contract work for Excellerand seven or eight years ago?" Mom asks. "Evidently, he found proof they were double-dipping on government contracts, charging millions for computer work they never actually did."

"Why didn't he turn them in then?" I ask.

I think about how different my life would have been if he had: I would have been the hero's daughter, the one whose father nobly sacrificed his own business to blow the whistle on cheats and scoundrels.

Mom shoots me a disdainful look.

"That would have put the spotlight on him," Mom says. "His own crimes would have come out too."

"They came out anyway," I grumble.

Mom nods.

"But this way, with the whole Rule Thirty-five deal, there's *some* chance your daddy can make up for what he did," she says. "At least a little."

Redemption, I think. If—when?—this news comes out, I won't exactly be the daughter of a hero, but at least I'll be the daughter of someone who tried to make up for his crimes. Someone who isn't all bad.

No, just someone trying to get out of prison early, I tell myself.

"So, why wasn't this Rule Thirty-five thing over in a year?" I ask. "Why are we still waiting?"

Mom sighs.

"Every time I talk to the attorney, there's some new complication," she says. "Excellerand is rotten to the core, and the prosecutors keep finding new evidence they want to nail down before they go public with any charges. Everything's taking longer than expected."

How long will it take the secret I told Mr. Court to travel to Excellerand? I wonder. *How much time do Mom and I have?*

"Can't the attorney get them to hurry?" I ask. "Don't they know we're in limbo here?"

"Mr. Trumbull knows you want to go to college next year," Mom says.

That's not a close-enough deadline. I sink down onto the bed. I rub my temples.

I'm going to have to tell her what I did, I think.

I try another approach instead.

"College applications are due by the end of December," I tell Mom. "That's just two months away. I have to turn in financial aid forms in February. And I'll *have* to get financial aid. We'll have to reveal—"

"Excellerand holds some computer service contracts for administering the FAFSA," Mom says. She lets this sink in for a moment, then she adds, "Mr. Trumbull says they know your father's trying to betray them. They know he has proof that can sink them. And he's pretty sure they have searches looking for us on *every* site they have access to. On the entire Internet."

Fear shoots through me. What if they find us because I started filling out the Common App? Because I sent in my Court scholarship by e-mail? Because it's practically impossible to do anything online without leaving footprints that lead right back to you?

Isn't that how Daddy succeeded at a lot of his crimes?

Isn't that what tripped him up in the end?

Mom starts wrapping and unwrapping the edge of the sheet around her fingers.

"I didn't take this as seriously as I should have when your daddy and Mr. Trumbull first told me about it," she says. "I was so . . . shellshocked by the trial and the whole media circus. And anyway, I thought, who in their right mind would believe anything your father said? I just wanted to get away. Get you and me both to a place where nobody was watching us, nobody was screaming questions at us, nobody was going through our trash looking for their next big story."

"Me too," I mutter.

Mom stops for a minute in the midst of unspooling the sheet.

"You were right, what you said the other night," she said. "All those reporters would have lost interest in us by now, even if we'd stayed in Georgia. But Excellerand wouldn't. They're more desperate than ever to find us. They know there's a ticking clock here."

I squirm. How many ticking clocks did I set off with what I told Mr. Court? He said he was going to talk to Ms. Stela about me. Would he call or e-mail? Who else would he tell? Would he post anything on Facebook? Would Ms. Stela? How many times would my name and Daddy's and Deskins, Ohio, be linked out there in cyberspace? Because of Daddy's scams, I know how easy it is for a talented computer expert to find even one link, even one gleaming bit of golden information that anyone else would consider a needle in a haystack.

And how many thousands of talented computer experts work for Excellerand?

"Even if they find us," I say weakly. "What do you really think they'd do?"

Mom squares her shoulders, bracing her back against the wall. The expression on her face makes me think of a doctor preparing to tell a patient his illness is fatal.

"Some of the new information the prosecutors found," she begins, "was about two men who worked for Excellerand, who got fed up and wanted to go to the authorities and tell them everything. One of those men died in a car crash. The other—his house burned to the ground. With his two-year-old son inside. Then he vanished. I guess . . . I guess he still had another son he wanted to protect."

Mom lifts her face to me, her eyes shiny with unshed tears. She gives a bitter laugh.

"The irony is, being in prison means your daddy's safe. Excellerand can't do anything to him directly," she says. "We're the only ones they can use to get him to retract his story, to get him to refuse to testify."

I see now why she's acted so terrified the past three years. Ever since the drive to Ohio, ever since the radio report about where we were supposedly going. Ever since we would have been exposed if Daddy's attorney hadn't planned ahead and switched the U-Haul trailers.

I don't want the burden of all that terror myself.

"Everything *might* come out within the next couple months," Mom says. "And then Excellerand couldn't do anything to us. They'd have no reason to, because everything would be out in the open. We'd be safe again. We could tell anyone anything we felt like telling. You could apply to any college you wanted, try for all the financial aid and scholarships you need . . ."

I flash back to that stupid note Mom left the day I talked to Mrs. Congreves, when Mom said she'd work lots of overtime or take a second job to pay for my college. This is what was behind that note. Mom knows I can't afford college without help. She was just trapped: She didn't want to tell me about Excellerand, but she wanted me to keep believing college is possible.

Only, it actually isn't. Not right now.

"You don't think everything's going to work that way," I say, because I know that's coming. I can hear it in her voice. "You don't think the charges against Excellerand will be revealed that fast. We'll have to wait—how much longer?"

Longer than it would take for what I told Mr. Court to find its way to Excellerand?

Mom shakes her head.

"It wouldn't be the end of the world if you had to wait an extra year before college, would it?" Mom asks. She's trying so hard. "After everything else you've been through, what's another year? Lots of kids *want* a gap year after high school. By next year surely everything will be taken care of and you'll be able to apply to college then."

I can see by Mom's face how much she wants to believe this fantasy. How much she wants me to agree, "Oh, yes, Mommy, what a wonderful idea. Another year of limbo wouldn't matter at all. You're right—we can be sure everything will end after another year. Thank you for keeping me safe."

But this scenario is just as much of an illusion as the past three years. I've *never* been safe. I just thought I was.

"Oh, right, so I don't have to wait until I'm twenty-four to start my life," I say sarcastically. "Just until I'm nineteen. And then—who knows?—maybe things could stretch out another year and I'd 'just' have to wait until I was twenty. Or twenty-one. Or twenty-two. And by then, who am I? Someone who's been buried alive for seven or eight years instead of three. I might as well be in prison *with* Daddy!"

"Becca, please . . . ," Mom murmurs.

I jump up, too twitchy to keep sitting on the same bed with Mom. To have anything in common with someone who's so ineffectual and helpless and willing to sit around and wait. I tower over her now.

"It's too late for 'please,'" I hiss. 'Because, guess what? I already ruined everything. I *already* applied for my first college scholarship. I had the interview today. And I blew it. You want to know why? Because I didn't know all your secrets. Because I thought I could save myself by admitting who I am!"

Mom stares at me. I can pinpoint the exact moment when she understands. She falls back against the wall. Her face seems to dissolve—who knows if it's because of her despair or the tears gathering in my own eyes? There is only one other time I've seen her so instantly gray skinned and dead eyed and desolate, and that time it was Daddy's fault, when he was arrested.

I am back to being unable to look at her.

I spin on my heel and run away.

Now—

a terrible now

There's nowhere to go.

I have been hiding in Deskins for three years now, and it's never occurred to me how open all my hiding places are. I hide at the school and the library and Riggoli's, and all those places are crawling with people. I'm out the front door of our apartment in a flash, but even as I jerk the door shut behind me, I can see kids in the school parking lot across the street. Marching band practice is ending, the sunshine glinting from a tuba here, the rim of a bass drum there. Any minute now someone I know will spot me and shout a greeting or a question—maybe Stuart asking how my Court scholarship interview went, maybe Clarice asking what I'm doing for my next AP lit essay . . .

I sprint around the side of the apartment building and run deeper into the complex.

There's a narrow swath of trees at the back of the property—two or three spindly pines, a few oaks and maples in their last gasp of autumn glory before cold, deadly winter.

Probably all the other trees were cut down to make Whispering

Pines Apartments, I think, because, oh, am I ever cynical now; oh, am I ever certain there's nothing but deception and destruction and despair in the world.

Still, I'm grateful for what few trees there are, and I crash into their midst. My eyes are too blurred to see straight, and I slip in some mud—no, actually a tiny stream trickling through the dead leaves. Who knew this was back here?

I sniff, bringing a sickly sweet odor to my nose. I hold my breath for an instant and listen—yes, there are voices coming from a clump of trees just upstream from me.

Pot smokers' paradise, I think. *I guess a lot of people know about this place.*

I think I recognize some of the voices: Tyler Marco from lit class, maybe, and isn't that Ashley Stevens, who was so mean to me at the Court scholarship interviews?

That's just great, Ashley, I think. *You go from telling the Courts how much you deserve a scholarship to crouching in mud a half hour later smoking pot? I should turn you in!*

But I know I won't. I'm not my father. I don't believe I can make up for my own mistakes by busting anyone else.

Also, if Ashley and Tyler are smoking pot together, then they're not alone, like I am. And I don't want anyone to see how I have nobody left. I've lost or left behind my father, my mother, my friends in Georgia, my friends here . . .

I follow the little trickle of water downstream, and I'm hoping for thicker and thicker woods, more trees to hide in. Somehow I end up in downtown Deskins instead. I creep under a bridge I've never noticed before on Main Street; I press my back flat against mossy, crumbling stones.

Rundown old Deskins, I think. *Hiding under glitzy new Deskins.*

What if everything that's shiny and gleaming and beautiful

has something nasty and disgusting and evil at its core?

Like Daddy's wealth, like Excellerand's success, like Stuart said—cheating is the only way to win?

That's not exactly what Stuart said, but I'm not thinking clearly enough to dissect it.

Sometimes things start out great and then turn rotten, I think. *Like how Whitney Court's life went, like how mine used to be so happy . . .*

If Daddy was a lying crook before I was even born, what was my happiness ever worth? Was there ever any truth in it?

It's too awful to think these thoughts alone. I want somebody to talk to, Rosa or Oscar or Jala or Clarice, but they're all such good people, and I would be the rot that contaminates them. Even Stuart . . . Stuart talks tough, but compared to the evil I'm facing—people wanting to kill me—Stuart is a Sunday school choirboy.

None of this is my fault, either, I tell myself. *I'm just the innocent victim. Like how Whitney Court didn't do anything wrong. It's not her fault she went crazy. It just happened.*

There's something wrong with this comparison, but I can't figure it out. Not when my back is pressed against filthy, mossy stone. Not when the bridge above me rattles every time a car drives over it, which is approximately every other second, because this is rush hour and everyone in glitzy new Deskins is going home to their safe, happy homes.

Not me, I think.

At least nobody could find me under this bridge. Not my mother, not my friends, not any Excellerand-hired assassins. I'm not like Mom—*I* wouldn't sit cowering indecisively in the apartment until somebody showed up to kill me.

But Mom actually might.

This thought sears me. It makes me jump so violently, I scrape my back on the stone.

This is the difference between me and Whitney Court, I think. She's limited, but she still seems to be trying to do the best she can with what she has. She wanted to help me. But I left my own mother behind in danger . . . danger that I made worse. . . .

I jump up and start scrambling back along the stream, back toward Whispering Pines. It's not like I think Excellerand would already have found out what I told Mr. Court and instantly dispatched assassins who were conveniently located right outside Deskins. But I run as though I believe that.

I crash through the streambed, throwing up clumps of mud with every step. When I get the first whiff of sickly sweet pot, I veer to the right and stumble into the Whispering Pines parking lot. I zigzag around the buildings and am paranoid enough to press my back against the wall of my own apartment building before turning the last corner. I peek around toward my own door: The sidewalk out front is deserted. Mine is just one vacant, blank door in a row of many. I listen: There are no screams or dying gasps.

But I do hear a car engine in the parking lot, speeding out toward the street. I turn my head and peek out farther. I catch a glimpse of gray metal in the dying sunlight.

It's my mother's car, driving away.

Now—

and things can get worse

Is she running away and leaving me behind? I wonder. *Or going out to search for me?*

I flip back and forth between these two possibilities a dozen times in an instant. My feet make their own decision: I dash after the car.

"Mom!" I scream. "Mom! I'm sorry!"

Even if I could run well, I'd be no match for a speeding car. I run and run and run, and still the car disappears into the distance.

I guess for once Mom isn't glancing at her rearview mirror. She isn't looking behind her.

Or she is, and doesn't care.

Those thoughts—and the possibility of assassins—make it impossible for me to go back to our apartment to wait for her to come back (if she's coming back). Somehow I can't even bear to go see if she's packed up and taken her things from the apartment.

I keep running. There's nowhere to go, but I keep running anyway.

Is this how Daddy felt all those years ago? I wonder. *He fought with his family, he ran away, he just wanted to be somebody else? With a different life?*

I pace my thoughts to the pounding of my feet against the sidewalk. And for a moment I can imagine doing this myself: disappearing, going somewhere new, taking on a new identity . . .

It wouldn't be that different from what I've done in Deskins, except that I would be completely alone this time.

Like Daddy was.

But it'd be harder for me than it was for Daddy twenty-five, thirty years ago, I think. *Back then everything wasn't online, they didn't have safeguards to keep people from using fake identities to get jobs . . . look how much trouble Mom and I have had, even with the attorney helping us, even keeping our own names.*

And everybody knows what happens to teenage girls who run away. Everybody knows what is left for them when they can't support themselves legally.

I haven't been paying attention, but somehow I've ended up in another part of Deskins I didn't know existed: a dark alley. A door opens and raucous laughter spills out—it's some ratty bar with a bunch of motorcycles parked out front.

So here's the kind of irony my English teachers would love, I think. *I'm running away from assassins I think want to kill me specifically because of who I am. And so I've run to a place where I might get killed just randomly, because I'm in the wrong place at the wrong time.*

I'm being melodramatic. The same sociology teacher who told us about free lunch percentages at Deskins High also talked about how the murder rate in Deskins is practically nil, just one homicide every fifteen or twenty years.

"You live in one of the safest places on earth," he told us.

Crime in Deskins is pretty much limited to stupid high school kids smoking pot behind Whispering Pines, and probably people doing the same kind of white-collar offenses that Daddy did, except not so audaciously as to get caught, and not very often. It's people thinking that lying and cheating and taking a little more money than they deserve isn't actually *crime*—there's not really a victim when you're just shifting a column of numbers from one place to another.

Except I was a victim of Daddy's crime, I think. *Me and Mom and all those other people. Daddy didn't take anybody's life; he just ruined people's lives and tortured them by leaving them to go on and on in pain. Leaving Mom and me to go on and on in pain. . . .*

Would it be better to be dead?

My feet evidently don't think so, because I veer away from this dark, dangerous alley.

I turn corners blindly, because it is dark everywhere now, not just in old alleyways. I am hungry and thirsty and cold, and the only reason I'm not crying anymore is because it seems as useless as everything else.

Then I turn a corner and there's light ahead of me, crazy-colored light: purple and green and blue and orange and red. . . .

It's stained glass.

I blink and realize I know exactly where I am: I'm standing outside the church Mom goes to, the one I've resolutely refused to enter for the past three years.

And there's Mom's car in the parking lot, not ten feet away from me.

I remember: It's Tuesday night. And on most Tuesday nights, if Mom doesn't have to work, she goes to this church program where they have a soup supper and a service for all their members.

I'm torn between relief, because she wasn't running away from me, after all, and disgust: How could she *not* be searching for me? Isn't she worried? Doesn't she care? How could she just sit in church, wasting time, when we should be planning what to do to keep the news I told Mr. Court from traveling all the way to Excellerand?

But is what I've done any better? I wonder.

A soft drone of voices comes from inside the church, and I recognize it as some kind of responsive reading. Then that ends. It's replaced by organ chords, the start of a song I also recognize.

It's "Amazing Grace."

I haven't stepped foot in any sort of religious service in three years, but I remember what grace is. It's being saved—and forgiven for everything, even when you don't deserve it. *Especially* when you don't deserve it.

And I want grace. I want to be forgiven for messing up and telling Mr. Court our secret, for running away from Mom, for yelling at her, for hating Daddy so much, for turning away from him when he wished me happy birthday that day in the courtroom all those years ago. And for never, ever, ever writing back to him over the past three years.

But if I get grace and forgiveness, does that mean Daddy gets it too? Daddy, with all the horrible things he did? The horrible things that could even lead to someone killing Mom and me?

"I once was lost, but now am found, was blind, but now I see," the people in the church sing.

And I know I am still lost and I can't see anything clearly, but I stand there listening, because I've got nowhere else to run to. I can remember singing this song myself when I was a little girl in a beautiful frilly dress, sitting in church knowing I was pretty and good, and my life was pretty and good, and God and everybody else loved me. Once something bad has happened to you and you've done bad things yourself, how do you ever get that feeling back?

The song ends, and now the people in the church start reciting something together again. I catch the words "who art in heaven . . ." so it must be the Lord's Prayer.

I slump against the side of the church, my scraped, sore back cooled by a metal doorframe. I don't know what I should do next, but at least I've got some time before I have to decide. Nobody will come out of the church until the Lord's Prayer is over, until the rest of the service is over.

Just as I think that, the door behind me swings open, knocking me out of the way. The person in the doorway grabs me before I fall, and I see who it is.

It's Mom.

Now—

and it's better

She gasps, but doesn't say anything. She just throws her arms around my shoulders and hugs me tight. And I hold on to her just as hard. We both clutch each other and sob into each other's shoulders. And there are so many things we need to talk about that I can't sort them out. I just say the first thing that pops into my mind.

"Why were you walking out in the middle of the Lord's Prayer?" I ask. "You would have killed me if I'd done that when I was a little kid."

Mom is still holding on to me, but she pulls back enough that she's staring me straight in the eye. Is there laughter mixed in with her sobs? A glint of humor in her eyes, along with the tears?

No, I decide. *It's all tears.*

"I haven't been able to get through the whole Lord's Prayer since your father was arrested," she says.

I stare back at her. Even with all her fear, I'd thought my mom was so smug and holy and self-righteous. But she can't even pray right anymore? She's that much like me?

"But . . . you go to church," I say numbly. "All the time."

"I'm *trying,*" Mom says. "I'm trying to get things right, to trust God again. . . . Usually I just sit there in silence during the Lord's Prayer. But tonight I was having more trouble than usual. There's one line I can never bring myself to say."

I study her face, tinted by the red and blue and purple light from the stained glass. It looks like a bruise. I know exactly which line she means.

"'Forgive us our trespasses,'" I quote. "'As we forgive those who trespass against us.' You haven't forgiven Daddy either!"

Why does this make me happy?

Mom nods, her face a study in shame.

"Sometimes that's the reason," she says. "Sometimes it's more like . . . I don't *want* to be forgiven. Because I can't forgive myself."

"Yourself?" I squint at her. "Why?"

She shifts to having only one arm around my shoulder, and we start walking together toward the car.

"I'm a grown-up," she says. "A *mother.* I should have understood what was going on. I should have stopped him. I never should have let him ruin our lives . . . especially not *your* life."

These are things I've thought, but I didn't know she felt that way too. Her voice practically throbs with guilt. It hurts to listen.

"No, Mom, it's not your fault," I say, and for once I feel the truth of this; for once I don't blame her at all. I snort disgustedly. "You could say it's more my fault. Remember what Daddy said? 'How else would someone like me ever be able to send his own kid to college?' He told *everyone* he was stealing that money for me!"

Mom stops so abruptly in the middle of the parking lot that her arm around my shoulder jerks me up short. She turns to face me directly. We are standing under a light pole, so the two of us are bathed in light.

"Becca, you don't actually believe that, do you?" she asks.

I don't answer. Mom lets go of me to clutch her head in her hands.

"I thought I was protecting you, not telling you everything," she murmurs. "But I was hurting you worse."

"Wait—is there something *else* you didn't want me to know because then I might think my father was a scumbag?" I ask.

How could there be anything else? How could my father's crimes be such a bottomless pit?

Mom pushes her hands back into her hair. It's a despairing gesture, and there's nothing but anguish on her face.

"If your father had *really* been stealing any of that money for you for college," she says, "he would have put it in some designated fund—a five twenty-nine, a Coverdell . . . I thought he *was* doing that with his legal earnings. I thought he *had*. I was so happy when the attorney told me one of the things the government wouldn't seize—one of the things we were allowed to keep along with the house and the car—was college savings. Except . . . there weren't any. He hadn't saved anything for you."

I wait for the anger to surge over me again—anger at Daddy for yet another lie, yet another failing, anger at Mom for yet another secret. And anger because this is just one more reminder that I don't have the slightest idea how I'm going to pay for college, if I ever get to go. This is another door slammed in my face.

But somehow, this time, the anger doesn't come. I don't know if I found some tiny crumb of forgiveness as I stood under the glow of the stained glass, listening to "Amazing Grace." Or maybe I'm just tired of being angry all the time.

"If it helps, I know your father thought none of this would be a problem," Mom says. "He thought he could go on making—

stealing—money hand over fist, so he wouldn't have any trouble paying for your college or anything else. I don't think he ever expected to get caught."

It doesn't even make me mad that Mom is still making excuses for Daddy.

"Is there anything else you're waiting to spring on me?" I ask dejectedly. "Anything else you think you're protecting me from, that's really just another booby trap to destroy me?"

Mom studies my face. I can tell it's on the tip of her tongue to say, "No, honey, that's the last secret I was keeping from you. You know everything important now. Honest."

But that isn't what she says.

"I don't know," she admits. "That's everything I can think of right now, but it's been three years and I'm still figuring things out. I'm stumbling around in the dark here, too."

There's something different about how she says this—the pain she lets into her voice? The agony splayed across her face? The helplessness she openly reveals? It's like she's been unmasked.

She isn't trying to protect me anymore, I think. *She isn't trying to hide anything from me. She isn't pretending she has all the answers just because she's the mother, the grown-up.*

And that's when I understand: In that one instant, she switched over to treating me like a grown-up, too.

This time it's me who puts my arm around her shoulder.

"Come on," I say. "Let's go home."

And it's not that I think we will truly be safe there; it's not that I think we've solved anything.

But neither one of us is alone in looking for answers anymore.

Now—

it all comes out

We talk all the way home. We take a short break only to tip-toe into the apartment and check behind all the furniture and double-check and triple-check the locks. We're being foolish and superstitious and paranoid—surely we've got some time before Excellerand could find us because of what I told Mr. Court. And anyhow, what difference would any of our precautions make if there were assassins nearby? It'd be so easy to break in through a window; it'd be so easy to put a silencer on a gun and take two quick shots at shadows that can't be hidden by our flimsy blinds.

Still, I feel like we're being bold and fearless just turning on the lights, just sitting down to eat leftover chili at our kitchen table.

Maybe the past three years when all I saw was Mom acting terrified, she felt like she was being bold and fearless just letting me go to school every day, just heading to work herself, just barely managing not to fall apart completely?

We go back to talking endlessly. I tell Mom everything about the Court scholarship, from the very beginning. I tell her how I thought Whitney was dead and how I found out that she wasn't. I tell her about the conclusion I jumped to about the scholarship, and how much I wanted to believe that Daddy, from prison, had brilliantly worked out a scam to funnel money to me for college. I tell her about the mistakes I made: writing that furious screed to Daddy, accidentally turning it in as my scholarship essay, then trying to use truth as my defense when the Courts assumed my problem was the same as Whitney's.

Mom sighs a lot during my story. More than once, tears well up in her eyes. But she doesn't interrupt except for a few questions now and then, and these are minor, inconsequential, just to get me to explain more clearly.

When I finish, we sit in silence for a moment, our empty chili bowls in front of us. I can hear the tick of Mom's alarm clock from her bedroom. Gently I tap Mom's hand.

"Your turn," I say.

Mom startles.

"I . . . I don't have any answers," she says. "I'm sorry, but I don't know what we can do to be sure what you said won't get back to Excellerand. I don't know how we can stay safe until your daddy's accusations against them come out. . . ."

I feel a pang of guilt, answered by a defensive, *Well, how was I supposed to know this was a matter of life and death, when Mom never told me* . . . The cycle of anger and accusation is starting again.

No, it just wants to start again, I think. *I can stop it.*

I put on a rueful smile for Mom. And it's not fake, not hiding anything. It just holds kindness, too. And understanding.

"I just meant, can we figure things out together?" I ask. It's strange how shy I feel even saying this, suggesting we might actually function as a team. Or . . . a family. "Just tell me what you're thinking."

Mom makes a wry face, wrinkling up her nose.

"Honestly? I'm thinking this is why I like the jobs everyone else hates at the hospital," she says. "When a patient vomits, or someone's adult diaper leaks—I know how to deal with that. This? Where do we even start?"

"Ugh, Mom, that's disgusting," I say, pretending to gag.

But I can understand. Maybe part of the reason I've studied so hard the past three years was that it was such a relief to know *some* right answers. Give me a fill-in-the-blank Spanish quiz, give me a multiple-choice chemistry test, give me an AP lit essay exam, even, if you have to. But don't expect me to know how to deal with real life.

"What if we called the attorney and asked him what to do?" I suggest.

Mom grits her teeth.

"I hate calling Mr. Trumbull," she says. "I hate that man. I have been fighting with him for weeks about how you could go to college without getting us both killed. Every time I talk to him, there's this undercurrent: 'Well, Mrs. Jones, if only you'd married someone else, none of this would be a problem, now, would it? Seeing as how you and your husband screwed up big time, shouldn't you do everything you can to keep your daughter safe?' So many times I think I've worked out a way to get us a little more freedom, a little more possibility . . . and every time he makes me feel that much more trapped. That much more certain that Excellerand has eyes and ears everywhere. Because they *do*."

I think about how Mom hacked off and dyed her hair, how she used fake work records to get her job at the hospital, how we've never once written Daddy's name on any school form, how I can't even have my picture in the yearbook. I realize belatedly that none of that was because Mom was scared of the news media. It was because she was afraid of Excellerand.

"I know we never would have managed without Mr. Trumbull," Mom says. "And I know he's just trying to keep us safe, always telling me how Excellerand is trying harder and harder to find us. The last time I called him, he insisted we use only code language, because he said it was possible Excellerand had tapped his phone. He said I had to get off the phone quickly, before Excellerand could trace the call. He said we could only communicate by mail from then on—and not anything like Express Mail or UPS or FedEx, where the letters could be tracked online. . . ."

So, nothing that would work quickly, I think, my stomach twisting.

"I guess we should be glad Excellerand doesn't have contracts for regular mail service," Mom says ruefully. "But I was so upset when Mr. Trumbull told me all that, I had to come home sick from work . . ."

The night I turned in the Court scholarship application, I think. *When I messed up everything because I was so mad at Mom.*

"It goes on and on, doesn't it?" I ask. "What Daddy started . . ."

Mom doesn't ask what I mean. She puts the palms of her hands against her cheeks and presses hard.

"I just want it to *end,*" she says, letting go with a violent slash of her hands through the air. "If the government would just finish investigating Excellerand—whether they arrest anybody or not, whether Roger gets out of prison early or not—it would be *over.* We could move on. You could apply to college and go wherever you want. I could apologize to my family and actually go visit them while my parents are still alive. . . ."

"Wait a minute—*apologize?*" I ask. "Apologize for what?"

Mom gives me a sidelong look.

"Eight years ago Roger stole money from Grammy and Papaw," Mom says. "He denied it, and I believed him . . . and that's why we stopped going to visit anyone in Kentucky."

This is something else I didn't know, but somehow it doesn't surprise me.

"So . . . that's why we didn't go hide there," I say.

"No, we didn't hide there because it might have endangered my entire family," Mom says grimly. "It was bad enough having you and me in danger, but everyone?"

Mom doesn't say, "And that's why we can't go hide there now, either." She doesn't have to.

"If we had the FBI protecting us during the trial, why can't we get their protection now?" I ask. "Especially if it's the government making this take so long?"

"They don't think it's 'warranted,'" Mom says bitterly. "They think we're safe enough as it is. Mr. Trumbull says it's a matter of time and money. The trial was just a couple weeks, and this could be months or years . . ."

Years, I think. It seems like that's more honest than Mom saying I might have to wait an extra year for college, and don't lots of kids want a gap year, anyway? It's like I can see Vanderbilt fading off into the distance, all my dreams dying.

Why should Excellerand bother killing me if all my dreams are already dead?

"It's like we're being held hostage," Mom says bitterly. "We're trapped. I couldn't even divorce Roger, because that would require official documents and leave a paper trail. And maybe we'd have to get into that whole mess about his name. . . ."

"You—you wanted to divorce Daddy?" I ask. I gulp. "Do you still want to?"

And this is ridiculous—my father's in prison, I haven't seen him in three years, and I myself have refused to even write to him. But I still feel a jolt at the thought that my parents might get divorced.

"*I* don't know, Becca," Mom says, spreading her arms, another helpless gesture. "I don't know what to think. During the trial, when I heard everything the prosecution said about Roger, I started thinking, no question about it, the instant I could carry it off without destroying you, yeah, I'd cut all ties. Make it official. Declare to the world that I want no part of being connected to Roger Jones. But . . . I am connected, no matter what, and it's been three years now and . . ."

"You still love him," I whisper.

Mom stares back at me without saying anything for a moment.

"Maybe," she finally admits, grimacing. "I'm capable of feeling sorry for him now, anyway. It's like he's broken, or there's something missing in him . . . that's the only way I can come close to understanding what he did. So I feel sorry for him but I'm still mad, and I can't forgive him but I worry about what his life is like in prison, and I hate that we can only communicate back and forth through letters through the attorney's office. . . ."

And that's another precaution because of Excellerand, not the media, I realize. *And Excellerand is the real reason we don't call.*

"And nothing ever changes," Mom complains. "We can't really forgive or heal from any of this because we're still stuck in it. Nothing can change until Roger's accusations against Excellerand come out."

She slumps back against her chair, a gray-haired woman trapped in despair. The dirty dishes in front of her might as well be prison bars.

I shove away the dishes in front of me.

"But something did change today," I tell Mom. I lean forward. "Because of what I said to Mr. Court, because . . ." I can't quite bring myself to say everything I'm thinking: *Because you and I stood under the glow of the stained glass together, because you finally trusted me enough to tell me my life is in danger, because you're treating me like an adult now.* What if Mom doesn't feel any of that is such a dramatic change? I decide to push for action, not explanation.

"Maybe now we have to try something . . . riskier," I say. "What if we went to see Mr. Trumbull in person? Or the prosecutors? We could demand—"

Mom is already shaking her head.

"Mr. Trumbull says the prosecutors have asked that I never contact them," she says. "It would be seen as tampering with the case, or something like that. And . . . Becca, are you sure you want to hear the rest of this? It might really frighten you."

Oh, because nothing else she's told me today has been scary in the least?

"Tell," I demand.

"You know what facial recognition software is, right?" Mom says.

"Sure," I say.

Mom swallows hard.

"A few weeks ago Mr. Trumbull's firm discovered suspicious cameras outside their offices," she says. "*And* his home. They did a little searching, traced back the work orders . . . it looks like a subsidiary of Excellerand put them up. He's pretty sure they're there to watch for us, because they haven't been able to find us otherwise, and he's certain they're using facial recognition software there and probably other places in Atlanta as well. Mr. Trumbull says we're playing in the big leagues here. These are horrible people who don't care who they kill or what lengths they have to go to, as long as they can protect their billions. . . ."

I get chills just listening to Mom. I was feeling so good that neither of us was alone in this anymore. So we're two people together now—so what? We're two people against a corporation that owns the entire world.

No, God owns the world, I think, a stubborn, ridiculous remnant of my childhood of going to church every Sunday.

This is as useless as thinking about that story of Jacob fighting the angel when I believed Daddy might have set up the entire Court scholarship. Before I made a complete and utter fool of myself and ruined everything. I might as well tell myself fairy tales, like Daddy's version of the Gingerbread Man or . . .

Somehow my scorn and thinking about Daddy have jarred something loose in my brain. For the first time I remember what Jacob got at the end of his night of fighting the angel. It's the same thing Daddy took for himself when he left home: a new name.

I sit up straight.

"Mom, what if . . ."

Just then the phone rings, a jarring sound that makes us both jump. Mom must have turned the ringer back on when I ran away. Neither of us even glanced at the phone when we walked in, but I see now that there are eight messages waiting for us on the answering machine.

Mom goes over and scoops up the phone.

"Hello?" she says. There's a pause, and then I hear her say, "Yes, Ms. Stela, Becca did tell me everything that happened this afternoon, and believe me, she deeply regrets it. She was just so desperate to win that scholarship that she went a little crazy . . . no, I don't mean literally crazy, though, yes, she could take a psychological profile test to reassure everyone. . . . No, there's no reason for you to worry that we really are related to Roger Jones. . . ."

Mom sounds so calm that I'm sure Ms. Stela is falling for it. But then there's a long spell where Mom is silent, and I can see the horror growing on her face.

"I'm going to have to ask you to take that down immediately," she says. Though her voice is still steady, I can see her knuckles turning white because she's clutching the phone so hard. "I understand you didn't use Becca's name, but I still consider this a terrible invasion of my daughter's privacy. If you don't take that down this instant, you'll be hearing from my attorney."

A moment later Mom hangs up and sinks into the couch. She drops her head and presses her forehead against her fists.

"What happened?" I demand.

Mom looks up.

"Ms. Stela was so worried about you that she posted a description of the whole situation on some guidance-counselor listserv," Mom says faintly. "Asking for advice. She promised me she'd take it down right away, but . . ."

But it's too late. Even if something like, "teenager in Deskins, Ohio, claiming to be Roger Jones's daughter" was up on that listserv for only five minutes, that could leave all sorts of traces.

Ms. Stela might as well have sent a map directly to Excellerand telling them where to find me.

"What can we possibly do now?" Mom asks hopelessly.

I remember the plan I'd been about to tell Mom before Ms. Stela called. If I had any doubts before, they're gone now. I just have to see if it's possible.

"Let me check something," I tell Mom.

I pick up the phone and dial quickly, even though this is a number I rarely call.

"Hey, Stuart?" I say. "Are you still looking for people to go to Emory and Vanderbilt with you this weekend?"

"You mean, the day after tomorrow?" he asks. "Uh, we still have room in the SUV, but . . ." I hear the clicking of laptop keys. "Whoa, that's a surprise. Registration is still open for the overnights at both schools. But they might count it against you down the line, if it looks like you're some big procrastinator or—"

"I'll take my chances," I say. "Count me in!"

And then, before he can ask why I changed my mind or how my Court scholarship interview went or anything like that, I hang up.

Mom's looking at me like I'm certifiable.

"What was that about?" she demands. "Don't you understand anything? Emory—Emory's in Atlanta, and Excellerand has the whole city staked out watching for us—"

"No, Mom," I say. "They have the whole city staked out watching for *you*. I've grown four inches in the past three years, and I'm sure my face size and shape has changed, too. I don't look anything like my old pictures anymore. So that software *wouldn't* recognize me. Neither would anybody watching for me."

Mom only looks more skeptical.

"But . . . why risk everything for a college visit?" She sounds horrified. "Especially somewhere you could run into people we used to know?"

"The college visit is just a way to get to Atlanta," I say. "What I'm really going to do is go see Mr. Trumbull. Since you can't call him anymore, and we don't have time for letters."

"But why . . . ?" Mom's still not getting it.

"I'll tell him I ruined everything, and there's no way we can stay in Deskins," I say. There's a lump in my throat, but I ignore it. "And then I'll get him to give us new identities. So we won't be trapped anymore."

Now—

two days later, the start of fall break

The scariest thing about my plan is that Mom actually agrees
to it.

She and I talk through a million possibilities, and each time
we think of another problem I decide, *Well, that's it. This isn't
going to work. I don't even have to try.* And I'm not sure whether
to be relieved beyond words or upset all over again when we
work through the complications and go back to the original idea
again and again.

I skip school the next day because we stay up so late talking—
and, anyhow, would it be safe to go back to school? We spend
the next night in the cheapest hotel we can find near Deskins,
and that pretty much blows any budget we have for hiding on
our own, without Mr. Trumbull's help.

He *has* to help us.

And then suddenly it's Thursday morning, barely thirty-six
hours later, and Mom and I are on the long, winding driveway
up to Stuart's house. Ahead of us, I can see Rosa moving a sleeping bag from her beat-up old car to a gleaming black SUV that
belongs to Stuart's mom.

This is really happening. I'm really going back to Atlanta.

Oscar appears around the side of the SUV and drops a sleeping bag onto the blacktop. He makes a lazy wave of his arm, obviously telling Rosa, *No hurry. I'll put my stuff in after you.*

Rosa and Oscar think I avoided them Tuesday afternoon—and then skipped school Wednesday—just because I was upset about the Court scholarship. They know my interview went badly, but they don't know why. When I called Rosa to "explain," I said I didn't want to talk about it; I just wanted to focus on the college visits.

Rosa thinks this trip is compensation, something I'm seizing for myself because I won't get the Court scholarship. I feel like I lied to her just because I didn't tell everything.

And now I'm going to sit in a car with her—and Oscar and Stuart—for the next nine hours?

Mom parks next to Rosa's car.

"Got to keep the trashy vehicles together," she mutters under her breath. "It's surprising they don't have a moat around the whole neighborhood to keep out riffraff like us."

I give her a startled glance, and she sighs.

"I'm sorry," she says. "I know Stuart's your friend. I know you were used to being well-off the whole time we lived in Atlanta. But honestly, I felt like I was pretending as much back then as now. Maybe that's why I didn't see that your father was faking everything, because I always felt like an impostor anyhow."

And once again, Mom has flipped around my whole outlook. Her new I'm-going-to-treat-you-like-a-grown-up attitude is really disorienting.

But I can see it. I can see how Mom's speech about being "poor but honest," the way she'd grown up, was almost meant as a declaration of independence on the way to Ohio three years ago. I can see now how her Ann Taylor clothes and perfectly coiffed hair in Atlanta seemed like a costume to her, when it seemed like her true self to me.

"Mom," I say. "Class warfare? Not what I need to think about right now."

"Oh, right," she says. She slides over and gives me a huge hug. "Be careful. If anything happens, if you start feeling unsafe, then . . ."

"Then what?" I ask. "Pray? Go to the police, who wouldn't believe me?"

Mom pulls back a little to study my face.

"Praying's good," she says. "Depending on the problem, maybe the police would be good too. But what I was going to say was, come home. Don't do anything desperate. Just come home, and we'll figure out something else to try."

Something we haven't been able to figure out despite thinking about it constantly the past day and a half? I think but don't say. *Something we probably wouldn't be able to afford, anyway?*

Maybe the skepticism shows on my face, because Mom tightens her arms around me again, pulling me into a second hug.

"The thing is, even if this were just an innocent trip to look at a faraway college, I'd be scared and worried and nostalgic and sad," she mutters. "It's like I don't even get the chance to feel normal emotions. . . ."

She breaks off because someone is opening the door beside me.

I squint in the near darkness—it's Jala.

"You came to see us off?" I ask.

"No, I'm going, too!" she says. "I decided maybe I'd want to transfer—it's not like I even looked around at which college I wanted to go to. I just went to Ohio State because my parents told me to go to Ohio State."

She's practically dancing with excitement.

"That's great!" I say. I pull away from my mom to climb out and hug Jala, too. Jala is five foot one and probably barely weighs a hundred pounds, so it's not like she would be much use as a bodyguard. But I'm so happy she's going to be along for this trip.

Though, when I break away to go see Mr. Trumbull, I'll be totally alone. . . .

I push that thought aside and concentrate on moving my sleeping bag and backpack into the SUV. Mom introduces herself to the two grown-ups standing beside the SUV—Stuart's parents, I guess.

You don't think we could talk them out of it, do you?" Mrs. Collins says plaintively to Mom. "Convince them to only look at schools close to home?"

"Mom, *stop* it," Stuart commands. "You promised we could do this!"

I look closely at Mrs. Collins. Even though it's barely six a.m., she's already wearing makeup and her dark hair is shaped into the same kind of perfect hair-helmet so many of my friends' mothers had back in Atlanta. Because of what Mom said in the car, I wonder, *Does this come naturally to Mrs. Collins? Or is she faking too, pretending to be someone she really isn't?*

Mrs. Collins flinches at Stuart's words. Naturally rich and perfect or not, she still has feelings.

"Eventually I guess we have to let them grow up," Mom says softly.

And then my friends and I are saying final good-byes and scrambling into the SUV. Stuart starts to put it in gear, but before he can start driving, his mom raps on the window.

"You all have your cell phones, right?" she asks. "To stay in touch in Atlanta and Nashville?"

Everybody else dutifully nods yes. I shrug and give my head

the most minimal shake no. I'm hoping Mrs. Collins won't notice, but she zeros in on me.

"It's not going to matter," I say. "I can borrow somebody else's to call home, and if we break up into different groups, we'll have meeting places planned ahead of time or—"

"Oh, no," Mrs. Collins says. "That won't work. Take mine for the next three days."

She rushes into the house and comes back with a phone in a turquoise case, which she hands in through the window. She's thought of everything: She gives me a charger, too.

I do a double take.

"Mrs. Collins, this looks like a brand-new iPhone," I say.

"It's my personal cell," she says. "I'll just use my work cell until you're back, so forward any text messages; Stuart can tell you the number. I already changed the voice-mail message, so ignore any calls that aren't for you. And, Stuart, you *will* call my work cell twice a day, but never while you're driving—"

"Sure, Mom," Stuart groans. "Now, can we go already, so we don't get stuck in traffic?"

Stuart rolls up the window and hits the accelerator. He keeps his eyes on the rearview mirror.

"I don't believe it," he says. "They're letting us go. For real. They're not chasing after us."

Mom and the two Collinses are standing at the top of the driveway, looking forlorn and cast-off and left behind. I glance around and see that Oscar, Rosa, and Jala all seem to be holding their breath, as if they're incredulous too. I go back to staring down at the iPhone.

"Why would your mom trust me with her brand-new iPhone?" I ask.

"Oh, my parents think you walk on water," Stuart says. He rolls his eyes. "You coming on this trip was the only reason they agreed to let me go without some adult present. You know, since the original plan was for Mom to drive us, before she had that emergency at work."

"You totally saved this trip!" Rosa raves.

Stuart's mom had called mine back right away Tuesday night, double-checking to make sure Mom understood that a last-minute change in plans meant we wouldn't be "chaperoned." But I hadn't realized that anyone else's plans depended on me.

So . . . was that why Stuart nagged me to go? I wonder. *Why would it matter?*

It bothers me that I evidently missed some undercurrents connected to this trip. And that I still don't understand them.

What if Mom and I also missed something big in our plans for dealing with Mr. Trumbull?

I'm glad Stuart's not looking toward me in the rearview mirror anymore. He's focused on making the turn out of his neighborhood.

"Stuart's parents probably thought Becca wouldn't really go," Oscar says, spinning around jubilantly in his seat. "And my parents thought they were safe saying I could go if his parents said yes—because there was no way his parents would say yes!"

"Helicopter parents," Stuart mutters under his breath. He makes it sound like a curse.

"At least I don't have that problem," Rosa announces. "Lily got into so much trouble her senior year, my parents gave up. But Jala"—she turns sideways, to look at Jala sitting between us—"I thought your parents were crazy-overprotective. How did you convince them?"

Jala looks down at her hands.

"They don't know I'm here," she says quietly. "They think I'm on a three-day biology class field trip for OSU."

We all stare at her, even Stuart, who should be keeping his eyes on the road.

"What?" Jala says defensively. "Stuart knows what it's like. Sometimes you just need to tell your parents, 'This is *my* life. I need to decide some things for myself.'"

"But you didn't tell them that," Rosa points out. "Not if they don't know you're here."

"Sometimes you need some space away, so you can figure out *what* you want to tell them," Jala explains. "What if I don't want to be a doctor, after all? What if I don't want to speed through college and med school as fast as I can? What if I actually want to have some fun with my friends before I'm suddenly thirty-five and married with three or four little kids and working seventy hours a week in the ER?"

It's unsettling to hear normally sweet, easygoing Jala sound so fierce.

"Didn't you get the memo that 'fun' is supposed to be spring break in Florida?" Oscar asks. "Or wild parties or . . . really, anything but driving twenty hours round trip to go to two stuck-up colleges where they tell you, 'You should have studied harder in high school, and, oh, yeah, already invented the next Facebook, if you want in to *our* school.'"

"If I'm trying to figure out who I am, can't I rebel in my own way?" Jala asks him, just as fiercely as before.

"Okay by me," Stuart says, steering the car onto I-270, our first freeway of the trip.

Rosa and Oscar nod agreement. Oscar even dredges up some outdated "Power to the people!" fist pump. But I'm jolted that even Jala—*Jala!*—has ulterior motives for this trip. I thought having her along would make me feel safe and secure—I never thought she might have serious issues of her own.

Not to mention, her confession makes me feel like I should confess too.

But I can't tell my friends why I'm really going to Atlanta, I remind myself. *And it's not like it's going to affect them. I'm not endangering them or anything.*

I hope.

Jala is turning toward me, like she's about to ask how my sup-posedly most-overprotective-of-all mom would let me go in an SUV full of teenagers all the way to Atlanta. It's time to dodge. And I'm still curious about something, anyway.

"Hold on, let's back up," I say. I lean forward, so I'm sure Stuart can hear me. "Your mom giving me the iPhone, your par-ents saying you could go on this trip if I go along—why? Your parents don't even know me!"

"They know you kept him on the straight and narrow," Oscar answers for Stuart.

I squint at them both in confusion.

"The cheating scandal in calc?" Oscar says.

I can feel my expression becoming blanker.

"What cheating scandal?" I ask.

"Have you been living under a rock?" Rosa asks.

"Um, yeah, pretty much," I say. "Studying calc myself, you know?"

Rosa rolls her eyes.

"Didn't you hear that Caden, Riley, Sam Chase, and Dillon Arterfuss all got suspended for cheating on the last exam?" she asks.

"Didn't gossip queen Rosa tell you?" Stuart asks sarcastically.

Rosa glares at him.

"Even *I* heard about it," Jala chimes in.

Had Rosa said something to me about kids cheating? I'm not sure. And it's not like I can explain why I've been so distracted lately.

"Okay, so four kids got suspended," I say. "What's that got to do with Stuart's parents?"

"All four of those kids are in marching band with Stuart," Oscar tells me. "They had what they thought was the answer key—"

"Only it wasn't," Rosa says. "It was, like, a decoy test Mr. Hattimer set up because he was suspicious—"

"And Stuart's friends offered him the answer key too, but he refused to use it," Jala finishes the story.

I can picture Mr. Hattimer setting up a trap. What I can't picture is Stuart refusing to cheat. From where I'm sitting in the backseat, I can see Stuart is clutching the steering wheel way too tightly.

"Tell her," Oscar commands Stuart.

Stuart keeps his eyes trained on the windshield.

"Everybody knows I'm friends with you, Becca," he says. "So when Dillon offered me that answer key, he wanted me to check the answers with you, just to be sure they were right. Since you'd had the highest score on the first test and all. He thought you'd do it, so you could get a good grade too. But I knew you wouldn't cheat. And then all I could hear in my head was what you said at lunch that one day: 'Cheaters get caught. They lose.'"

He makes me sound like some Old Testament prophet or something, speaking with the voice of God. Hadn't he noticed that day how close I was to crying?

"So . . ." I'm still trying to piece everything together. "Your parents think I'm the reason you didn't cheat?"

"You were," Stuart says quietly. "I almost did it. I almost threw away everything."

Everyone falls silent. We all know how badly Stuart wants to go to some impressive school next year. We all know that being caught cheating senior year would have ruined that.

"But why did you even tell your parents Dillon offered you the answers?" I ask.

Stuart's gaze could drill holes in the bumper of the car in front of him.

"They forced it out of me," he says. "They heard about the other kids getting suspended and . . . they thought I cheated too. They were afraid I'd get caught the next time."

Ouch, I think. *Even Stuart's own parents think of him as a cheater?*

"Maybe this whole story should be your college essay, Becca," Rosa says mockingly. "'How I made the world a better place by making sure Stuart Collins can get in to an Ivy League school.'"

"Hey, Stuart made his own decision," I say, trying to match her light tone. "So it's his essay topic, not mine."

But I'm thinking, *Stuart actually paid attention to me? Even when I was really talking about my dad, not him?*

"I did try writing about this," Stuart says. "For the Chicago essay, 'Describe a time you went against the crowd.' But I just sounded terrible for considering cheating. Or like a freak, for not doing it."

"Doing the right thing is freakish?" Jala asks.

"Didn't you see what most people were doing during your time at DHS?" Oscar asks her.

"Not really," Jala admits. "I always had to study or babysit."

"DHS is a hotbed of drug users, the morally bereft, and kids who won't have a future because they won't work at their education now," Oscar says in a pompous tone. He's clearly quoting somebody—his parents, maybe? "Once we're in college, we will look back and see what a waste of time high school really was."

Jala giggles. She looks sympathetically toward me.

"Are you having trouble writing your college essays?" she asks.

I shrug, because I can't say, "I haven't even started, because I'm more worried right now about one of the largest corporations in America directing all its resources to finding and destroying my mother and me. I don't know—do you think I have my priorities messed up? Isn't it more important to make sure I survive until graduation than to focus on what I'll do next?"

"I know what would really make you look good," Jala tells me. "Tell what happened with that sub, Mr. Vickers."

"You mean, when he got fired?" Stuart asks. "I thought that was because of you, Jala."

"What? You don't know the whole story?" Jala asks.

She launches into it, and I only half listen, because I'm remembering it from my perspective.

It was early freshman year, when I was still lost in the morass of missing and hating Daddy, and being terrified of being discovered, and facing the nuclear winter of Mom and me both being miserable. I was sitting in social studies class, barely paying attention because we had a sub and he'd already made it clear we weren't going to do anything important. Also, Mr. Vickers seemed to think he'd missed his calling as a stand-up comedian, because he kept cracking stupid jokes. None of them sounded funny to me, but I wasn't the best judge of humor that year. The guys sprawling at the back of the room kept laughing. But maybe that was just to keep Mr. Vickers from talking about social studies.

Somebody knocked at the classroom door, and Mr. Vickers joked, "Who could that be? Think it's a terrorist? Think we should all hide?"

Mr. Vickers opened the door, and there was Jala in her hijab, holding a late pass from orchestra.

"It *is* a terrorist!" Mr. Vickers proclaimed, beaming like it was his best punch line ever.

A few guys at the back of the room laughed, as usual. But everyone else seemed to go into a shocked, frozen silence. Jala looked frozen too, for an instant, and then she muttered something like, "Sorry. Wrong class," even though it wasn't. She belonged in that class as much as I did. But she turned and walked away.

And, somehow, that was too much for me. The triumphant cruelty on Mr. Vickers's face balanced against the stunned horror on Jala's—it was the last straw for me, the tipping point. At that exact moment I had suddenly had enough of cruelty and horror and people hurting other people. I couldn't stand another second of the world being so filled with pain; I couldn't just sit there, shocked and frozen and silent like almost everyone else. I had to *do* something.

I raised my hand.

"Mr. Vickers, I have to go to the bathroom," I said.

I didn't wait for permission. I just fled the room, scurrying after Jala. I caught up with her easily. She barely glanced at me from under her hijab.

"If you think we're such good friends that you're going to come cry with me in the bathroom, don't bother," she said flatly.

Her hijab blocked so much of her face that I couldn't tell if she was crying or not.

"No," I said. "No. That's not what we're going to do. We're going to go down to the office and we're going to tell the principal or the vice principal—or somebody!—exactly what Mr. Vickers said. And we'll say he has to be fired. People like him shouldn't be teachers."

Jala turned so I could finally see her whole face.

"Okay," she said. "That sounds like a better plan."

And then it was like Jala turned into Rosa Parks, because when we got down to the office, she did the talking. She even said, quite calmly, that she was sure DHS didn't want a reputation as a bigoted school, and it'd be better if the administration could handle this quietly, without any sort of lawsuit or national media coming in. . . .

I almost choked over that, but it didn't matter. Mr. Vickers was out of the building before the end of the day. And he's never been back.

"I wouldn't have had the nerve to tell, if it hadn't been for Becca," Jala says now, finishing up her version of the story. "I wouldn't have even told my parents. But after that—well, that's when Becca and I really became friends."

It's strange she remembers it that way. Because the whole way down to the office that day, I'd been thinking, *It's not like Jala and I can ever be friends, because I can't tell her about my daddy. But at least I can help her with this.*

"Whoa, Becca, you are a saint," Oscar says, and it's humiliating how much admiration glows in his eyes.

"Stop," I protest. "I was just doing what anybody would do."

"But you were the only one who did it," Jala says quietly.

And it's awful that I can't tell them why I'd followed Jala, or why I'd been so anticheating with Stuart. I want so badly to say, "I'm not a saint. Kind of the opposite—I've lied to all of you for the past three years. And it's not like I'm innately good or anything. It's that my daddy got caught and sent to prison and that changed everything."

Is it possible that I'm actually a better person because of what Daddy did?

I sort of want to tell my friends everything and ask them this question. But of course I can't.

How is it that I can care so much about these people and their opinions when they don't know me at all?

Now—

the drive south

We change drivers every hour or two, sticking to some schedule
Stuart's parents came up with to make sure we do this as safely
as possible. I get the second leg of the trip, from Cincinnati to
just south of Lexington. I'm glad Cincinnati traffic is so bad that
I have to concentrate on driving, rather than obsessing, *This is
where the Courts live now. What if I turn my head and look out the
window and see one of them driving beside me?*

Lexington traffic is not so extreme, so I have time to wonder,
*Do I really have cousins here, going to UK? Will Mom ever get to
see her family again?* I also start thinking about how Mom said
it's safe for me to have a driver's license only because Excellerand has no contracts with Ohio. If I were to get stopped
in Kentucky for, say, speeding, would that kick my name into
some database Excellerand could see? I drive very carefully,
and try not to worry. Fortunately, everyone else in the car is
talking a lot, so I can mostly tune out my own thoughts and
listen instead. My friends argue over whether it's better to
listen to satellite radio or to hook up somebody's iPod. They
make up ridiculous college-essay spoofs for various people

from our senior class: Shannon Daily's as a Miss America–style "I just want world peace" discussion; the football captain's as a diatribe about how elections should be decided by sporting events. They debate endlessly about the best place to stop for lunch—until I'm so disgusted that I pull into a McDonald's.

"Fine, because you can't make up your mind, you get the most ubiquitous food in America," I tell them.

But once we get out of the car, we somehow are suddenly in exact agreement: We'll leave the car right where it is but walk over to the Burger King next door.

Oh, yeah. We are such a band of rebels.

After lunch it's Rosa's turn to drive, and Stuart and Oscar fall asleep: Stuart with the front passenger seat leaned back against Jala's knees, Oscar hunched over awkwardly in the middle back-seat between me and Jala.

"You know they're faking," Rosa says. "Thinking we'll start talking about them and they can eavesdrop."

"Rosa," Jala says, "you *are* talking about them."

"Only because I'm hoping guys in college will be more mature," Rosa says. She reaches over and flicks Stuart's arm. He doesn't even flinch. "I do *not* know how my sister could have wanted anything to do with high school guys."

"Maybe because they're kind of cute to look at?" I say, glancing toward Oscar. In his sleep—or, I guess, pretend sleep—he eases into a soft grin. I know he expects me to bust him for it, to call out, "You are such a faker!" or hit him, like Rosa just did with Stuart. But I don't. I just keep watching his face.

"Yeah, but underneath the pretty packaging, they're like five-year-olds," Rosa snorts. "Psychologically, emotionally, *mentally . . .*"

Jala yawns.

"They do have the right idea about taking a nap," she says. "I think I'm going to need one before it's my turn to drive. Rosa, are you okay if all the rest of us go to sleep?"

"Why do you think I got the jumbo Diet Coke?" Rosa says with a laugh.

Jala huddles against the door and seems to be out in about three seconds.

"I guess her conscience isn't bothering her about lying to her parents," I whisper to Rosa.

"I think that's a very forgivable lie," Rosa whispers back.

So many lies, I think.

On impulse, I lean forward so I can talk practically right in Rosa's ear. There is one thing I might be able to make right with her.

"Did the Courts tell you what really happened to Whitney after high school?" I ask.

Rosa shoots me a startled look, as if to say, *Oh, so now you're willing to talk?*

"Yes," she says. "Because they said somebody else's essay made them realize not all DHS students knew the whole story. It was yours, wasn't it? I would have warned you before you went in, if I could have, but—"

"There wasn't time," I say, shrugging. "I just wanted to make sure you didn't think I knew all along that Whitney was mentally ill, and I kept it secret to mess you up."

"I wouldn't think that!" Rosa says hotly. "But is that what messed you up?"

"I messed myself up," I say. For a moment I feel like someone from Old Deskins—I don't want to tell Rosa about Whitney's strange behavior. Or am I just protecting myself? Am I scared that if I start describing my interview, I'll end up telling Rosa all my secrets?

"None of that matters now, anyhow," I say.

It hits me that this is entirely true. Even if I won the Court scholarship, I'd never be able to claim it. Not if I get what I'm asking for in Atlanta.

And then I can't keep talking to Rosa one-on-one anymore. She's smart. She'll figure out that something is really, really wrong. She'll *make* me tell her.

I mutter something about being afraid of waking the others, and I settle back in my seat. But I'm too jittery to sleep myself. I think about making another attempt at college essays, but it's impossible to write an essay when I don't know who or where I'll be when I send it in.

I pull out Mrs. Collins's iPhone instead. I dropped out of the whole cell-phone scene before everyone started getting smart-phones, so it's amazing to me that I have the entire Internet at my fingertips while I'm sitting in an SUV speeding across south-eastern Kentucky.

And I can look up anything without having it traced back to me, because this isn't my phone. . . .

I type the name, "Robert Catri" and "Tennessee" into a search engine. I couldn't do this at home, not if there was any chance Mom would see what I was looking for. I'm a little sloppy on the unfamiliar keyboard—I forget to put quotation marks around the name. So I pull up information about all sorts of Catris and unrelated Roberts, all across Tennessee. I'm about to go back and start over when I see "fourth conviction for breaking and entering." I slow down and scan the articles I pulled up.

It looks like, in the corner of Tennessee where Daddy grew up, the Catris are some big crime family. They're not necessarily talented; they don't seem to have ever made off with more than a couple hundred dollars from any of their crimes. But they are amazing in their persistence and their dedication to breaking the law.

My eyes well up with tears.

What if Daddy didn't take his fake identity because he wanted a life of crime? I wonder. *What if he was actually trying to get away from it? What if 'Roger Jones' was supposed to be a clean slate for him, a chance to start over and be good? And, then—he couldn't stick with it?*

Do normal teenagers get this constant sense of seeing their parents redefined?

I don't know if my new version of Daddy's life is right or not. I can't think about it anymore, not when I'm in a car with four other people. Not when I look up and see Rosa waving her hand at me over the back of her seat, then frantically pointing toward the window.

It's the WELCOME TO TENNESSEE sign just ahead that she's pointing at.

I lean forward, nod, smile, and flash a double thumbs-up at the rearview mirror so she can see how happy I am to be entering the next state. But I'm quelling panic as I settle back again.

Tennessee, I think. *Where Daddy grew up. Where I might go to Vanderbilt someday. Or not. Where we'll at least visit Vanderbilt on our way home, after Emory. Where this is the last state before Georgia, before I have to make the plea that will affect the rest of my life. . . .*

I'm so flustered, I accidentally hit the contacts icon on Mrs. Collins's phone. The screen floods with names.

Do normal people really have that many people they stay in touch with? I wonder.

Of course they do. Back when I had a cell phone, I had hundreds of friends available to me anytime I wanted to call or text.

And then, after Daddy was arrested, I had no one.

That just proves none of them were true friends, I remind myself. *Mom's wrong to worry about me running into any of them. They wouldn't recognize me. I wouldn't recognize them.*

But it strikes me that there's an easy way to find out what my old friends look like now, so I can at least see them coming, if they're by Emory or Mr. Trumbull's office. Jala did give me permission to log on to her Facebook anytime I wanted, and now I have a legitimate reason.

I have spent the past three years trying not to think at all about any of my friends from Georgia, but the names come flooding back: Brittany Connors, Alicia Giovanni, Savannah Hayes, Hailey Korshaski, Dustin Ivers, who was technically my first boyfriend, back in sixth grade when everyone started "going with" guys, but never actually went anywhere . . . I log into Jala's Facebook account on Mrs. Collins's phone and start looking up everyone. My old friends evidently didn't learn much from hearing about my father stealing from Facebook: Very few of them have good privacy settings. So I can see pictures of Savannah and Hailey where they're clearly drunk; I can read every word of Brittany's explanation of how God saved her from committing suicide. Some of my old friends have become partyers; some have become devoutly religious; some are fixated on activities like soccer or ballet or Habitat for Humanity. I scan certain Timelines and discover that a few of my old friends have passed through several of these phases over the past three years. And I wouldn't have been able to predict any of it—sometimes it's the ones I thought had the world at their feet who seem to have messed up their lives the worst, while some of the ones I'm almost afraid to look up seem to be doing fine.

I'm like a glutton devouring all this information—I can't stop myself. I'm obsessed.

Oh, wait, what about Annemarie Fenn? I think belatedly, remembering the friend I was with when I was exposed on Facebook, when I found out I couldn't go on with normal life after Daddy's arrest.

I'm a little worried calling up her Facebook page because, until that last day, I always felt like I needed to protect Annemarie. She'd always seemed like someone meant for a kinder, gentler world.

Annemarie hasn't made a picture available to the general public, but she's posted a status update for anyone to see:

> Thanks to everyone who sent flowers or came to Mom's funeral. Her fight against the breast cancer was long and hard, and she appreciated each and every one of you who supported our family through that struggle.

And below that it says, "RIP Jocelyn Carter Fenn" with her birth and death dates.

The death date was only last week.

Annemarie's mother just died of cancer? I think. *She had to deal with all that, and I didn't even know?*

I haven't seen or talked to Annemarie in more than three years, but I feel a strange emotion burrowing into my gut: guilt.

I should have been there for Annemarie, I think. *Who did she have to take care of her?*

I search back through Annemarie's page. I find a link to a newspaper article about Annemarie and Mrs. Fenn participating together in a breast cancer benefit race, at a time when Mrs. Fenn could barely walk, let alone run.

It looks like Mrs. Fenn found out about her cancer the week before my father's trial.

And then I remember something I hadn't thought about in three years. One day, shortly before the trial, I was hiding away in our house, feeling sorry for myself. The doorbell rang and rang and rang, and even though we'd stopped answering the door long before that, I peeked out and saw Annemarie. And I *almost* opened the door to her, *almost* rushed out and threw my arms around her and clung to her like she was my last hope.

I didn't, of course. I told myself she'd be like everyone else; I told myself she would only want to gossip or make fun of me, or smash me down into the shame so hard that I could never get back up.

I can't place that day exactly in time, but what if that was the very day Annemarie found out about her mother's cancer? What if *she* was coming to *me* for comfort?

I try for balance: I make myself remember how mad I was at Annemarie when I was outed on Facebook. But now even her question that hurt me so much sounds different in my memory: *Why didn't you tell me?* What if Annemarie was just stunned and bewildered and a little hurt herself? What if there wasn't any malice behind her words?

What if she has felt for the past three years that I abandoned her, instead of the other way around?

I have been sitting sideways to look at Mrs. Collins's phone so no one else will see it, even if Oscar suddenly opens his eyes. But now it's my face I need to hide: Suddenly tears are streaming down it. I turn my face to the window, to the riotous explosion of yellows and oranges and reds of the trees around us. It's autumn in all its glory, and this makes me cry harder. Autumn is about endings, and it was a huge ending when I abandoned all my friends in Georgia three years ago. And now, if everything works out with Mr. Trumbull, I will abandon my Deskins friends just as completely. Getting a new identity doesn't just mean being safe from Excellerand. It also means leaving Deskins and never seeing or speaking to Rosa or Oscar or Jala or Stuart or anyone else from high school again. And even though I've told myself they're only school friends, only people I've held at arm's length for the past three years, somehow they became more than that.

I can't do this, I think. *I can't, I can't, I can't.*

But I have to.

I sniff, making a disaster of my attempts to keep my crying silent. A second later I feel Oscar's warm hand patting mine and then, wrapping around mine.

He's holding my hand.

And it feels wonderful.

It doesn't mean a thing, I tell myself. *He's still asleep and just flailing around, or . . . it's more of his joking around. . . .*

But I know lies, and I know truth, and there is no way I can make myself believe this.

I glance quickly toward Oscar, and he is so completely *Oscar.* Of course all that flirting that was supposed to be fake was actually real—it was Oscar being awkward and scared that I wouldn't like him back, and me being awkward and scared about letting anyone get too close. A normal guy, acting interested straight out, would have sent me running. But Oscar was slow and steady and goofing around, and just so *kind* every time I needed him to be that way.

And now here we are and he's holding my hand.

And I'm holding his right back.

Without even opening his eyes, Oscar slides his other arm around my shoulder and pulls me close and whispers in my ear, "Will you go to homecoming with me next week?"

And I can't. I can't be that girl, the kind who gets to go to dances and have a boyfriend and squeals when he gives her flowers. Daddy stole all that from me when he stole everything else. And anyhow, I probably won't even be in Deskins by next week. It won't be safe. I don't know how fast Mr. Trumbull will be able to get new identities for Mom and me, but I could be in a new school by then, I could be an entirely different person.

I snuggle against Oscar anyhow. I snuggle against him and I whisper back: "Yes."

Now—

Georgia

I am an emotional wreck by the time we get to Atlanta. Or, I should say: I am *still* an emotional wreck; I am even more of an emotional wreck than before. I am keeping layers of secrets now. Oscar has to let go of my hand before anybody else notices and take his turn behind the steering wheel. And it's like Oscar and I have silently agreed not to announce, "Hey! We're going to homecoming!" That's too delicate a secret, too fragile to hold up for everyone else's examination. But he keeps shooting me meaningful glances that our friends would have to be blind not to see.

Or do they notice, and they think it's no different from the way he looked at me yesterday or the day before? I think. *Has he been looking at me like this for weeks or months or years, and I never noticed?*

What does it matter if I'm going to change my name and vanish from Deskins and never see Oscar again?

Stuart is driving again as we hit the crazy traffic of Atlanta.

"Speed up and go around that car in front of you," Oscar advises him from the passenger's seat.

"I can't," Stuart snarls. "My parents can tell if I speed, because of the GPS."

"I bet that just shows your average speed, not one burst of going seventy-five," Oscar scoffs. "But here, if you're so scared, I'll disable that function. . . ."

He starts fiddling with the GPS, and suddenly the whole screen goes black.

"Now I don't know where to go!" Stuart screams, instantly soaring into full-fledged panic as cars zoom around us.

"Take the exit for I-85 north," I tell Stuart from the backseat.

Everyone turns and stares at me except Stuart, who seems more focused on returning his breathing rate from "hyperventilate" to "normal."

"You know your way around Atlanta?" Oscar asks me curiously. "Have you been here before?"

The way he's looking at me, I am so close to answering honestly. I am so close to telling everything.

"I heard the GPS voice say it a minute ago," I tell him instead. "Weren't you listening?"

How can I lie like that, even now? I am a terrible person. I deserve to lose my friends. I deserve to live the rest of my life in exile.

It's a good thing I deserve that, I think. *Because that's the only future I can have.*

Oscar restores the GPS, and we get to Emory. We park and lug our bags into a huge auditorium, then the beaming admissions officials direct us to dinner in a huge dining hall. I look around and try to decide if any of the students look like fifth-year seniors or grad students.

Were any of them here four or five years ago when my father stole laptops? I wonder. *Did he scam any of their parents or grandparents into sending him money?*

I can hardly stand to be on Emory's campus, thinking that. But Rosa is looking around like she's reached the promised land,

and Oscar and Stuart are drooling over food choices in the serving lines: "Pizza and cheeseburgers and pasta and soft-serve ice cream and vegan choices and sushi and . . ." Stuart lists.

"They have dining halls like this at Ohio State, too," Jala snaps, rolling her eyes. "For students who live on campus, anyway."

I have no idea what I end up eating. I can't pay attention at the info sessions afterward either.

Tomorrow, I think. *Tomorrow, tomorrow, tomorrow . . .*

We're matched with current Emory students to spend the night in a typical dorm room. I forget my host student's name five seconds after hearing it. I'm sure she thinks I'm a total idiot because I ask nothing about college. I put my sleeping bag on the floor of her room, and then I sit down, staring at the wall.

"Want me to show you where the best parties are?" she asks eagerly.

"I just want to sleep," I say.

But of course I can't. I lie on the floor and pretend to as unknown-name-girl and unknown-name-girl's roommate head out to party without me; I'm still wide-awake hours later when they tiptoe back in. I hear them whispering a little too loudly about what a lousy student guest they got. Then I listen as their breathing slides into the soft steadiness of sleep.

I wish Mom could be here to do this with me tomorrow, I think. *That would be okay, if we could do this together. I wish I could call her or text her right now to tell her how scared I am.*

But it's three a.m. by now, and of course Mom doesn't have a cell phone. And I can't call our home phone, because Mom is still staying away. Tonight she's at another nurse's house—it wouldn't be right to call and wake up the woman who took Mom in even though Mom's excuse was that Whispering Pines Apartments had to fumigate for bedbugs.

I guess we actually both found good friends in Deskins, I think.

This makes me want to cry again, but I don't let myself. I just lie there, staring into darkness. And then, though this seems like the longest night in history, somehow it gets to be morning, and I'm padding down the hall to the strangeness of a communal bathroom.

I meet my Deskins friends for breakfast back at the dining hall, and they chatter about how nice their host students were and what they did and how excited they are about sitting in on classes this morning. They've all pored over the list of possible classes, and I wait until everyone else has revealed a choice before I tell mine.

"I'm going to Religion and Contemporary Experience," I say, picking the class least likely to attract anyone else. "It gets out the latest, so I'll just meet you all back here for lunch."

I'm hoping that gives me enough time for what I actually plan to do.

But Oscar chimes in, "Oh, that sounds better than Computer Science Fundamentals! I'll go with you!"

Panic floods over me.

"No, no, no offense but . . . if you're there, I won't be able to concentrate," I say. "It'll feel like it's still high school and—"

"And back off, lover boy," Stuart says, snickering.

I look back and forth between the two of them. I'm pretty sure Oscar must have told Stuart I said yes to homecoming, and now Stuart is making fun of him for it, and—

And why can't I do this without hurting Oscar's feelings? I wonder.

"Just for today," I say quickly. "At Vanderbilt tomorrow, I'll go to every session with you, I'll, I'll . . ."

"It does make sense to get an idea of what college is like by yourself," Jala says, nodding sagely. "It can feel kind of lonely."

And now I feel bad for Jala, too. But all I can do is back away from my friends and pretend I urgently need to find Smith Hall.

In reality, as soon as I'm out of sight, I rush toward the bus stop at Clifton Road and Gambrell Drive.

Atlanta does not have the best public transportation. If I took Stuart's SUV, or if I could afford a cab, I could get to Mr. Trumbull's office off Peachtree Road in fifteen minutes. But the combination of bus and metro and walking will take me more than an hour. Mom and I were paranoid enough to map it all out on a computer at Deskins Public Library, not on my laptop. The route looked daunting enough then, when I had Mom beside me.

It feels unbearable now that I'm alone. I look around, and it seems like any of my fellow bus passengers might be spies for Excellerand. That man in a suit, scratching his ear—is that a signal? That woman with the little girl beside her—is she trying to trick me into thinking a spy wouldn't have a kid with her?

Now you're totally losing it, I tell myself. *Stop it. Nobody knew you'd be on this bus. Except Mom.*

I edge Mrs. Collins's iPhone out of my pocket and summon up the number Mom gave me to contact her at her friend's house. I don't call it, because what would I say, here on the bus where anyone could hear? But it makes me feel better just to have the number in front of me.

I finally get to Mr. Trumbull's office building, and it's as huge and overwhelming as I remember. It's all metal and glass, probably some architect's vision of the cruel heartlessness of justice.

This is a stupid plan, I think as I step into the elevator and it lurches up. *Why couldn't Mom and I have come up with something better?*

I know why: Because there isn't anything better, not for either of us. Daddy's crimes and his bargain with the government and Excellerand's evil ruthlessness shoved us into a tiny, tiny box, and this is the only way out.

I get off the elevator and walk down the hall to the receptionist's desk. The elderly receptionist I remember from three years ago has evidently been replaced—this one doesn't seem any older than me. She has long dark hair like I do, and she looks as uncomfortable in her stiff blue blazer as I would feel.

Is this the kind of job I'd have to take if I don't get to go to college? I wonder.

I don't know much about it, but being a receptionist in a law firm would probably require some training beyond high school, and that would mean financial aid, too.

I'm ranked fourth in my class, but being a receptionist is beyond me if I can't change my identity, I think.

"Can I help you?" the receptionist asks. She may be young, but she's already mastered the snooty law-office tone that seems to say beneath the words, *My time is worth so much more than yours—how dare you bother me!*

Maybe they teach that in receptionist-training classes.

I clear my throat.

"I'm here to see Mr. Trumbull," I tell her. "I don't have an appointment, but I know Mr. Trumbull will want to talk to me."

This is the wording Mom and I agreed on. She thought that, given how difficult Mr. Trumbull has been lately, I should show up unannounced and take him by surprise. But we did call on Wednesday to make sure he'd be in the office today.

We called from a pay phone in Deskins, just to be safe. Do you know how hard it is to find a working pay phone nowadays?

The receptionist looks unimpressed. She looks like someone who has just discovered crumbs on an otherwise perfect white tablecloth—like she's annoyed that she will have to exert the effort to brush me away.

"I'm . . . ," I try again. It's strange. I've said my name dozens of times over the past three years, always savoring the protective anonymity of "Jones." But here in this office I have to throw all that away. Even though I now know everything I'm risking, I have to identify myself fully. "I'm Becca Jones. Roger Jones's daughter."

My heart pounds, but no alarms go off. No horde of camera-toting TV crews appear out of nowhere to scream at me, "How did you feel when your father was arrested? Did you know where all the money was coming from? Did your mom?" No Excellerand assassins swing in through the windows, guns blazing.

The only thing that happens is that the receptionist's eyes widen, and she gasps, "Ohhh . . ." Then she stares at me, as though I've suddenly become fascinating. Or horrifying.

She may be new here, but of course she knows who Daddy is.

You're back in Atlanta, I remind myself. *Everybody remembers here. What did you expect?*

At least the receptionist doesn't start peppering me with questions. But she stares long enough to make me feel I have to stare back, with a little defiance: *Yeah, that Roger Jones. Want to make something of it?*

What if I'd acted like that three years ago, when everybody stared at me all the time?

I couldn't, back then, I think. I'm barely managing to hold the stare now. At least the receptionist looks away first. She gives a little jump, as if remembering she's supposed to act professional.

"I'll see if Mr. Trumbull is available," she says. She trots off to Mr. Trumbull's office on heels that seem too high for her. She reminds me of a little girl playing dress up. I think she was probably supposed to stay at her desk and just buzz Mr. Trumbull, but what do I know? It's hard enough figuring out what I'm supposed to do, let alone anyone else. I feel weak and dizzy just from three seconds of staring down the underage receptionist— how am I going to deal with Mr. Trumbull?

I step over to a display of framed magazine articles on the wall, because reading might calm me down. Big mistake: Most of the articles seem to be about how brilliantly Mr. Trumbull handled Daddy's case—"the biggest case any defense attorney could hope for," as *Atlanta* magazine put it. Apparently it was actually a miracle that Daddy didn't get *more* than ten years in prison; apparently Daddy was pretty much the poster child for how defendants *aren't* supposed to behave. The articles all have titles like, "What to Do When Your Client Becomes a Loose Cannon" and "Loose Lips: When a Client Sabotages His Own Case."

Who has ever used the term "loose lips" since World War II? I think disgustedly, because it's easier to hate the headline writer than to think about what Daddy really said and did.

Still, I can't help myself: I keep reading. I'm surprised the articles focus more on Daddy's impersonal crimes—the computer hacking, the money laundering, the Ponzi scheme—instead of the ones where he scared parents and grandparents into giving him money because they thought their children or grandchildren were in trouble. Those were the crimes I thought were the worst.

But it's all about the money, I think. *The bigger the money, the bigger the crime.*

It's coming back to me, everything Mr. Trumbull told us three years ago about the law. Money is easier to measure than pain and suffering, so that's what the justice system looks at.

I hear the receptionist's heels click-clacking toward me, and I quickly move away from the wall. I go back to standing by her desk.

"He will be able to see you," she says. "Briefly. But it will be a few more minutes. Have a seat."

She sounds like she's had to practice saying things like that in front of a mirror. She points toward a leather couch that also seems new. I sit down and sink into it. I struggle back up into a standing position. I don't want Mr. Trumbull's first view of me to be as I flounder around just trying to escape his couch.

Receptionist girl watches me while pretending not to.

"Nervous energy," I tell her. "Can't sit still."

I'm pretty sure this makes me sound like a drug addict or something, but I don't know how to fix that. Not when my head is going all spinny on me again. Maybe this is what it feels like to be a drug addict. Or crazy.

I pull out Mrs. Collins's iPhone. Isn't that a normal thing to do, waiting? But I've lost my skill at goofing around on a cell phone. I could text my friends something like "Wow, Relig and Contemp Exp is great! How's ur class?" But I can't stomach yet another lie right now. Instead, I pretend to be absorbed in flipping through apps. I accidentally turn on the recording function, then scramble to turn it off.

This is going to be hard enough, without knowing every word I say is recorded, and then I have to make sure it's erased completely from the phone, I think.

I glance up, and Mr. Trumbull is turning the corner. I stuff the phone back into my jeans pocket.

"Becca!" he says. "Good to see you! Well, haven't you grown up!"

The way he's looking at me makes me almost wish I hadn't developed breasts and hips. It also makes me think there's something kind of wrong about him having such a young receptionist. Like he didn't hire her for her job qualifications.

"Nice to see you again," I say automatically, shaking his outstretched hand.

"Tria, hold my calls," Mr. Trumbull tells the receptionist.

"Oh, yes, sir!" the receptionist says immediately. The way she sounds, she might as well snap her arm into a salute.

Mr. Trumbull puts his hand on my back, steering me toward his office. This is something else I remember about Mr. Trumbull: how he always took control. I remember feeling relieved by that three years ago, when my daddy had turned into a criminal stranger, and my mother seemed thoroughly lost.

But today I kind of want to step away, to tell Mr. Trumbull, "I know where your office is."

I let him guide me anyway.

We go into his office and he shuts the door. He indicates a chair for me to sit on. Then he settles in behind his massive mahogany desk. He looks the same as he did three years ago: a rich man in a rich man's suit, his glossy brown hair improbably thick for a man in his fifties. He could play a defense attorney on TV—he kind of already did, as a star of my father's trial.

But somehow his demeanor has changed. He no longer has that defense-attorney air of confidence that seems to say, *Of course my client's innocent. Of course I could convince any jury that any defendant's innocent.* It's like a mask slipped, revealing the pool of anxiety below.

I correct my own impression: It's not that Mr. Trumbull lost that confident aura over the past three years. He still had it out in the lobby, in front of the receptionist. The angst didn't come out until he was alone with me.

He leans urgently toward me.

"Where's your mother?" he asks. "Why are you here?"

I hesitate. Could his office be bugged? I try to guess from Mr. Trumbull's expression, but it's hard to tell. The lines around his eyes telegraph extreme worry, but is that because he's concerned about Mom? Or because he thinks I'm in danger, just sitting in his office? Wouldn't he give some signal if it wasn't safe for me to speak?

I opt for caution, regardless.

"Mom's still back home," I say, and I am oh so careful not to say, "in Ohio" or "in Deskins." "She's fine. We just thought it would be . . . safer if I came without her."

The worry lines around his eyes turn into disapproving trenches.

"It's not safe for you either," he says.

I feel a jolt of irritation: Is he trying to make me feel even *more* terrified?

He probably thinks it's for my own good, I tell myself. *So I don't do anything stupid.*

Too late for that.

"I had to come here," I say. "Because . . . I made a mistake."

Shouldn't Mr. Trumbull be impressed that I'm admitting fault?

I remember suddenly that Mr. Trumbull never asked Daddy if he did his crimes or not. Defense attorneys aren't that interested in actual guilt or innocence.

Mr. Trumbull just lifts an eyebrow and waits.

"I told someone," I say quickly, getting it over with. "I told someone who I was."

Mr. Trumbull grabs a yellow legal pad from his desk and begins taking notes.

"Any possibility that that person was connected to Excellerand?" he asks.

I stare at him and fight back the panic that threatens to overwhelm me.

"Um, no?" I say uncertainly. "I mean, I don't think so, but . . ."

But I had wondered if the Court scholarship was a hoax. What if it wasn't concocted as a misguided way for my father to help me, but as an evil snare for Excellerand to trap me?

That's truly paranoid, I tell myself. *And illogical.*

I remember that the Court scholarship was set up two years before Mom and I moved to Deskins. I remember that Whitney

Court has problems of her own, and that the Courts *still* want to help other kids. I remember that Mr. Court was worried about me.

"The person I told was innocent," I say, and I sound sure of myself now. "But I know he told my guidance counselor, and—"

"And so the secret is out," Mr. Trumbull says, frowning. "You've ruined the extreme efforts your mother and I went to, to protect you."

Doesn't he think I know that?

"That's why I'm here," I say. I swallow hard. "My mother and I need your help to move somewhere safer. We need completely new identities. And documentation that . . . that lets me go to college."

Mr. Trumbull puts down his pen and stares at me for a moment.

"What you're asking for is huge," he finally says. "You'd need new names, new social security numbers, a fake high school transcript, fake SAT scores . . ."

"I could retake the SAT," I say, though my reluctance comes through in my voice. I clench my teeth and ask the question that terrifies me most. "But it's possible, isn't it? To get new identities?"

Mr. Trumbull absentmindedly picks up his pen again. He taps it against his jaw.

"Anything's possible for the right price," he says.

"Price?" I squeak. Mom and I didn't talk about this. She didn't pay extra for his help when we moved to Deskins. Wasn't that just part of Mr. Trumbull representing Daddy? Now that Mom has told me everything, I now know that what we paid Mr. Trumbull three years ago pretty much used up all the money she made from selling our furniture and her car. She had to max out credit cards to survive after that, before she got her job. And then she made so little selling the house that every penny went to settling debts.

I edge Mrs. Collins's phone out of my pocket, below the level of the desk, so Mr. Trumbull can't see. I can't stop in the middle of talking to Mr. Trumbull in order to call and ask Mom for advice about what to do or say next. But holding on to the phone is the next best thing.

Mr. Trumbull shakes his head at me.

"What you're asking for—that would cost thousands of dollars," he says. "Maybe even hundreds of thousands of dollars."

"Mom and I don't have that kind of money," I say. "We're barely holding on, as it is."

Mr. Trumbull shrugs.

"You can't expect me to work for free," he says.

"Couldn't the government help?" I ask tentatively. "I mean, this is their case, and they're the ones who have taken so long getting their case together. Don't they want to protect people like me? Innocent bystanders?"

Mr. Trumbull snorts.

"What kind of idealistic pablum are they teaching you at that school in Ohio?" he asks, and it seems as if he's said "Ohio" deliberately. As if he's trying to tell me, "You want to be difficult? Then I can be reckless with your safety too."

I flinch. Mr. Trumbull leans across the desk toward me.

"You're the daughter of a convicted felon," he says. "The government doesn't care about people like you."

Three years ago the words "daughter of a convicted felon," spoken in that brusque tone, would have reduced me to a weeping puddle on the floor. I would have been like a swatted fly: broken and fatally wounded and buzzing helplessly through my last moments of life.

But I've had three years to adjust to who I am, to being the person my father's crimes turned me into. Those three years didn't kill me. They just made me see things differently.

I see Mr. Trumbull differently now too.

The way he acted in court, cross-examining a witness whose testimony he wanted to destroy . . . that's how he's treating me, I think. *Why?*

I don't know the answer to that question so I mentally set it aside, like a calculus problem I might be able to figure out later on. I decide it wouldn't hurt to act a little more injured than I actually am. I look down as if I'm struggling to recompose myself. Mrs. Collins's iPhone is lying there in my lap, its screen offering me a dozen choices, and links to dozens more.

A lot of good that does me, I think. *When there's no one I could call for help, no one I could text, nothing I could look up . . . all I can do is record things I don't want to remember. . . .*

But hasn't remembering Daddy's crimes helped in some ways? It's the reason I convinced Stuart not to cheat; it's the reason I was brave enough to help Jala stand up for herself.

Isn't there something in those bad memories that can help me now?

Suddenly I have an idea. And I'm so proud of it—so convinced it will work—that I surreptitiously press the iPhone screen to start recording. I'm going to want Mom to hear how brilliantly I handle this. Retelling won't do it justice.

I tuck the phone back into my pocket and then I look up at Mr. Trumbull. I pretend to blink back tears as I scoot forward in my seat, as if I'm ready to stand up.

"Well," I say. "Maybe I'll just have to *make* the government care about me. I'll go talk to the prosecution team myself."

A bland, bored look settles over Mr. Trumbull's face. I don't know if he's refusing to take my bait, or if he just wants me to believe that he is.

"Surely your mother explained why that isn't possible," Mr. Trumbull says. Three years of watching the DHS mean-girls clique from afar makes me think I can tell: He's working hard to get that careless tone into his voice.

I slide a little farther out, to the edge of my seat.

"Ah, but you're thinking I'm as timid and easily frightened as my mother," I say. Oops—maybe I won't want Mom to hear the recording of this conversation. But there's not time to glance down and turn it off. I keep my gaze drilled on Mr. Trumbull's eyes. "Remember, half my DNA comes from my father. The 'loose cannon'—isn't that what you called him in *Atlanta* magazine?"

Maybe it was useful, after all, to read the articles on Mr. Trumbull's reception-area wall.

Mr. Trumbull shifts slightly in his own chair.

"What exactly are you proposing to do?" he asks. "What could you do, that wouldn't endanger you and your parents more than ever?"

I fight to keep from letting him see me wince.

"I could tell the government that if they won't protect me, I'll make the whole story public," I say. "I could ruin their case completely. I'd give an exclusive interview to . . . I don't know, Nancy Grace."

I've picked the most obnoxious TV personality I can think of. Three years ago she devoted hours of her show to ranting about how despicable my father was.

Maybe some of my disgust shows, because Mr. Trumbull just waves this away.

"You wouldn't do that," he says quietly.

"I want to go to college," I say. "I want to have a life. A real life, not one where I'm hiding and terrified all the time. I wouldn't have to actually talk to the media. Just threaten to. The prosecutors wouldn't know I was bluffing."

Mr. Trumbull watches me, one eyebrow cocked.

"I suppose that is one route you could take to achieve your

dreams," he says, and the sarcasm in his voice surprises me.

"It is?" I say, momentarily thrown off.

"Well, *possibly*," he amends himself. "With all the budget-cutting lately, I'm not sure how many prisons still offer college classes to their inmates."

"Prisons?" I repeat numbly. "Inmates?"

Mr. Trumbull stands and strolls toward his office window. He looks out for a moment toward the Atlanta skyline, then turns to face me.

"Prison is where you're headed if you start trying to *black-mail* the government," he says. "You do understand that what you're proposing would be considered blackmail, under the circumstances? Believe me, the government would have no inclination to give you the benefit of the doubt."

Could what I'm talking about be called blackmail?

"American citizens have rights," I say, and I'm proud I can stand up to him. I'm not proud of the waver in my voice. "We have the right to go to the news media when we're not happy with the government. There . . . there's a free press. First amendment rights."

Now I'm rambling. Mr. Trumbull shoots me a look that makes me feel about three years old.

"Ordinary American citizens have rights," Mr. Trumbull concedes. "An underage teenager whose father is a notorious criminal all the prosecutors hate . . . someone like that has to be careful. Especially if she and her mother have been breaking the law for the past three years."

"My mother and I haven't broken any laws!" I protest.

Mr. Trumbull leans back against the windowsill. The look he's giving me now doesn't just make me feel young and foolish. It makes me feel subhuman. Maybe I'm an amoeba. Maybe a paramecium. To him, I'm just some insignificant creature flailing about in a waterdrop.

"Falsifying documents," Mr. Trumbull says, ticking off my mother's supposed crimes on his fingers. "Faking a work history. Using fictional social security numbers. And those are just the infractions I know about. Who can say how many other frauds you've perpetrated?"

"Those were all things you helped Mom with!" I shout. "Things you told her to do!"

Mr. Trumbull strokes his chin.

"Surprisingly, there would be no paper trail leading back to me," he says. "It would just be the word of a felon's wife against mine. Who do you think the rest of the world's going to believe?"

Something slams against my spine—the stiff wooden back of my chair. I wasn't conscious of slumping or sliding backward. It feels more as though I was thrown backward by the force of Mr. Trumbull's words.

"You . . . you're blackmailing *me*," I manage to say. "You're just threatening me and Mom with prison to get me to do what you want. To stay silent."

Mr. Trumbull lets a half smile play over his lips. I saw him look exactly this way in court, when he knew he'd beaten a witness down to a pulp. I never knew how terrible it'd feel to be on the receiving end of that smile.

"You are a perceptive child," he says. "I can see why your grades are so high."

"So shouldn't I get to go to college?" I almost wail. "Why are you treating me like the enemy? Why do you want to ruin my life?"

Mr. Trumbull takes two steps. Now he's standing over me.

"*I'm* not the one who ruined your life," he says. "It's your father's fault. And your mother's. They're the reason you're stuck in that rathole in the middle of nowhere—"

"I'm not in a rathole!" I protest, and it strikes me as funny that, after hating so much of my time in Deskins, I still feel obligated to defend it. Laughter starts burbling out of me.

Except, maybe it isn't laughter. Maybe Mr. Trumbull has goaded me into crying for real.

"The next place you'll have to go would be a rathole," he says grimly. "You'll have to hide in worse and worse places every time you or your mom slip up."

He paces back toward the window.

"Your parents have caused me no end of aggravation," he says. "Your father—forcing the speedy trial even when I told him we needed more time to prepare, refusing any plea agreement, not revealing the evidence he had against Excellerand until *after* the trial—"

"That's not my fault," I say. "Or my mom's."

Mr. Trumbull ignores me.

"And your mother . . . do you know how much money she could have made on book deals, movie deals, interview deals three years ago?" he asks. "My firm was ready and willing to negotiate all that. She could have set all of us up for life. *I* could have retired on that money."

I stare at Mr. Trumbull.

"But . . . Excellerand," I say. "Wouldn't that have ruined the case the government's trying to build? Wouldn't it have meant that everyone saw us, that we could never hide . . ."

Mr. Trumbull shrugs.

"She could have done the interviews with her face hidden," he said. "She wouldn't have had to say anything about Excellerand. Just . . . what it was like all those years living with your father, the serial liar? Did she suspect him of marital infidelities, too? Was anything about him true?"

I wince at "marital infidelities" and am practically slaughtered by "Was anything about him true?" How did Mr. Trumbull know to ask the exact question that has plagued me for the past three years?

I channel my fury into my answer.

"So you and your firm wanted my mom to open a vein and bleed on national television?" I ask. "For money? You wanted her to sell her shame?"

I remember how I felt three years ago. Mom telling our story on TV—that would have destroyed me.

"It's what everyone does nowadays," Mr. Trumbull says, with another careless shrug. "She could have supported you that way. In the lifestyle you were accustomed to."

"My mom has supported me just fine," I snarl. I spring to my feet. I'm done. I can't stand another second with this evil man.

I'm whirling around, headed for the door, when I feel Mr. Trumbull's hand on my shoulder.

"You came here with a request," he says softly. "I just had to see how serious you were. How badly you want it."

I freeze.

"You already told me there's nothing you can do," I say.

"I never actually said that," Mr. Trumbull tells me, and I can hear the change in his voice. He really should not use his lawyer techniques on someone who sat and watched him disembowel witness after witness during the longest three weeks of my life. I recognize this shift: This is his buddy-buddy voice, with the undercurrent of *What? You thought I was being mean? How could you misunderstand so badly?*

"Oh, so now you're going to help, after all?" I ask. I don't sit back down.

"I'm going to tell you your choices," Mr. Trumbull says. "You can appeal to your mother—the asking price has gone down immensely, but she could still get a book deal or an interview deal. Maybe leading up to the five-year anniversary of the trial—something like that."

"You want me to ask my mother to sell her soul?" I ask incredulously. "And mine?"

Mr. Trumbull holds up a cautionary finger.

"Or you can write a letter to your father," he says. "Ask for his help."

"Have you of all people forgotten he's in prison?" I ask. I'm still poised to flee. "How can he help me from there? By dropping all his accusations against Excellerand? Signing something that guarantees he'll never testify against them? Ensuring he'll be in prison seven more years?"

I can't keep the bitterness out of my voice.

Do you think my father loves me enough to spend even an extra second in prison? I want to ask. *When he didn't even love me enough to avoid doing the crimes that sent him to prison in the first place?*

"No, no," Mr. Trumbull says impatiently. "He'd give you *money*. Or access to it, anyway. I'm sure you heard the rumors about your father's funds in the Cayman Islands? Surely, if you just ask . . ."

I stare at Mr. Trumbull in amazement.

"Is it even legal for you to tell me to use that money?" I begin. I have to stop and try again. "If that money really exists . . . if my father really loved me . . . don't you think he would have found a way to give it to me already?"

Now—

Despair

I jerk away from Mr. Trumbull's hand and stalk toward the door.

He lets me go.

Revelatory bombs are going off in my brain.

This is why I stopped believing in the Cayman Islands money, I think. *Because Daddy would want to share it with Mom and me. He does love me. And us. He does!*

Maybe these aren't revelations. Maybe it's just desperation, hope against hope because there's nothing else for me to believe in.

I can't think like this without crying, and I can't let myself cry until I get out of Mr. Trumbull's office, past the receptionist, out of the building. I concentrate especially hard on turning the door handle, propelling myself into the hallway outside.

Step one—done, I think.

I keep my head down passing the receptionist. She seems to be totally focused on her computer screen, anyhow.

Step two, I think.

I'm at the elevator bank now, and I stab at the down button with a shaking hand. It takes me three tries to actually hit it.

Never mind, I tell myself. *No one's watching.*

"Oh, wait—Ms. Jones?" the receptionist calls from her desk.

What—does she think it's part of her job to critique clients' elevator-button-pushing abilities? I wonder.

I turn back, ready to mumble some excuse or apology—anything to get away. I can hear the elevator dinging closer, floor by floor. Why does Mr. Trumbull's office have to be so high up? I don't think the elevator's going to be here in time for me to slip away.

The receptionist—Tria?—is actually rushing toward me. It's a race: Tria vs. the elevator.

Tria wins. She's right beside me now.

And she's holding out an envelope as though she expects me to take it.

"It's my first week on the job," she says. "There's so much I don't know yet. This letter came yesterday for you and your mom, and I kept meaning to ask Mr. Trumbull what I was supposed to do with it. But I guess I can just give this to you, and then I won't have to ask Mr. Trumbull another stupid question . . ."

I'm thinking Mr. Trumbull would be a pretty intimidating boss. He probably treats Tria like she's on the witness stand all the time.

"Thanks," I say, taking the envelope.

The elevator arrives at that exact moment. I brush past Tria and hit the button for the first floor and then, quickly, the one to close the doors. But the doors are just starting to ease together when I turn around. Tria is still standing there, as if she's doubting herself now. I can almost see her thinking, *What if Mr. Trumbull wouldn't have wanted me to give that letter to this girl? But it's addressed to her—who else would it go to? Shouldn't Mr. Trumbull be happy I've taken care of it without bugging him?*

The shiny silver doors close, blocking my last view of Tria. I sag against the wall.

Awful, awful, awful, I think. *Is there any way that could have gone worse?*

I bend forward, the closest I can come to curling into a fetal position while still standing. I can't let myself go completely, not while I'm on the elevator and we could stop on any floor. It turns out, I still have some pride left. But bending forward means the iPhone in my pocket stabs into my stomach. I yank it out. It's still faithfully recording the soft thrum of the elevator gliding down.

At least I can stop that, I think, tapping the screen. *That's one thing I can accomplish.*

I will never again want to listen to what Mr. Trumbull said, or what I said back to him. I will never want to let anyone else hear it. I might as well erase it right now.

But I'm still shaking. As I look down at the phone, ready to erase everything, I'm apparently incapable of holding on to anything else at the same time: I drop the letter Tria gave me to the floor of the elevator. I bend down to pick it back up, and the address is screaming up at me: "Susan and Becca Jones, c/o Burton Trumbull . . ."

Just the sight of that address is enough to bring tears to my eyes, because it's in my father's scrawling handwriting. Every other letter we've gotten from him over the past three years has been typed.

What changed? I wonder.

But of course, maybe the letter inside *is* typed. Maybe it's just the envelope that Daddy wrote by hand this time.

Why? I wonder.

My brain is donkey-stubborn. It won't let me pick up the letter, cram it in my pocket, and turn my attention back to the iPhone. But I'm also somehow reluctant to actually open the letter and see my father's routine comments about the prison food or his prison buddies who got there by doing who knows what themselves or, his usual question, "How are the two of you?"

I drink in the sight of my father's actual writing and mentally review the whole process. Sending our letters through Mr. Trumbull's office has always been just one more way to protect us. It kept anyone in Deskins from finding out that we're connected to Daddy, that we're connected to a prisoner. Always before, every time a letter from Daddy arrived in Mr. Trumbull's office, I guess the old receptionist would have put Daddy's envelope in a second envelope, addressed that envelope to Mom and me from Mr. Trumbull, and then dropped that envelope in the outgoing mail.

There wouldn't be any reason anyone in Mr. Trumbull's office would take Daddy's letter out of the original handwritten envelope and then put it in two *layers of typed envelopes instead,* I think. *Would there?*

A reason springs to mind immediately: That way Mr. Trumbull could hide that fact that he's been reading our mail.

I gasp a little and jerk my head back, as an even more puzzling reason presents itself to me: That way Mom and I would never see the actual return address on Daddy's letters.

I think this, because now I'm looking at the return address on this letter, written in Daddy's own hand, and it doesn't say what I expect. It doesn't give his location as "Federal Correctional Institution, Herlong, California."

Instead, it says, "United States Penitentiary, Atlanta, Georgia."

Now—

Stunned

Daddy's here? I think. *In Atlanta? Same as me? Where I could see him if I just took another short bus ride?*

I can't take my eyes off those words: "Atlanta, Georgia." It's as if I think that looking away even for an instant will cause the letters to rearrange and change into "Herlong, California."

The elevator dings and I jump—I'm back on the ground floor. I stumble out of the elevator through a lobby full of adults in suits, where a teenage girl in jeans stands out and looks odd. I hadn't thought about that going up to Mr. Trumbull's office. If Excellerand has cameras trained on this lobby, they'd notice me right away. And if I stop to read a letter with a return address that even a fairly low-res camera could read as being from "Roger Jones" . . . what then?

I press the letter from Daddy against my chest, the blank side of the envelope facing out. I put my head down and barrel toward the door.

The sidewalks out front are empty, but that just makes me feel more exposed. I walk a block, then two. The envelope is practically burning against my hand, but it doesn't seem safe to glance at it again in such an open space let alone actually read the letter.

There, I think. *There.*

Beside a low brick wall around a Starbucks patio, I see a cluster of bushes. I wait until I'm sure no one is looking, and then I slide down between the wall and the bushes. Branches snag my hair and the bricks scrape my arm, but I'm out of sight.

I squat down in the mud, brace myself against the wall, and dare to look at the envelope again.

It still says "Atlanta."

I flip the envelope over and slide a trembling finger under the flap. I pull out a thin sheet.

It's more of Daddy's handwriting. Nothing in this letter is typed.

I file that under "Interesting, but who knows what it means?" I blink a few times because my eyes seem determined to go blurry on me. And then I read:

> My dear, dear Susan and Becca,
>
> I know you probably get sick of hearing me say how much I miss you, but it's still true. I know you are busy, and I know I deserve you still being mad at me, but your letters seem to come slower and slower. Becca, I enjoyed reading the two essays you sent from your schoolwork—the one about the girl who went to your school 15 years ago, and the one about <u>Moby Dick</u>—but what I really want to hear about is your life.

What? I never sent Daddy any of my essays! Would Mom have actually . . .

288

I remember Mom's reaction when I told her about my Court scholarship application—she never read that essay. There's no reason she would have snooped on my computer and sent my schoolwork to Daddy.

Then who did? How could Daddy have seen those essays?

I shiver but force myself to go back to reading Daddy's letter. He talks about how I got a lot more out of *Moby Dick* than he ever did in high school, and about how the food at the penitentiary is getting monotonous after three years of the same thing week after week, the same scorched grits, the same overcooked okra . . .

Wait a minute—three years of grits and okra? That means he's been in Atlanta for three years, doesn't it? Why would grits and okra be on the menu in California?

I finish the letter and immediately start reading it again. But what I'm looking for isn't there—there's no paragraph I accidentally skipped over the first time explaining, "This is why I'm in Georgia when you thought I was in California" or "This is why I thought you've been sending me your school essays, when you really haven't." I also don't find the answers I want the most: "And this is how you can go to college without tipping off Excellerand—and without having to cut off and abandon all your Deskins friends. . . ."

But if Daddy actually told me what to do, would I trust his advice? I wonder.

I put my head back against the brick wall and ease Mrs. Collins's phone out of my pocket. I dial the home number for Mom's friend.

It only rings once before Mom's voice rushes at me: "Becca, I'm so glad you called! I was just telling Denise that it's killing me, not knowing how you're doing!"

This is code. I know Mom is trying to tell me, *Denise is sitting right here with me, so if you're going to tell me something I need to hear privately, let me know so I can work it out.*

I don't want Mom to hear about Daddy's letter or my time with Mr. Trumbull while she's sitting beside someone who can't know the truth about us.

But I'm also having trouble figuring out what I would feel safe telling Mom by phone, in any location, when even my school essays were sent places I never expected. Have hordes of spies been watching us all along? Could there be listening devices on the brick wall behind me? In the bushes around me? What's really going on?

"Um, I'm okay," I say, even though it's a lie. "I just met with the, um, college advisor. It didn't go very well, but I'm looking into other possibilities. Don't worry."

Mom is not stupid. She can probably tell from my trembling voice just how badly everything went with Mr. Trumbull, just how baffled and scared and helpless I feel.

"Can I do anything to help?" she asks, and I can hear the strain in her voice—and the need to sound like a normal mom with normal worries for the sake of her friend beside her.

I'm back in the South, and sometimes old habits come back in a familiar place.

"Pray for me," I tell Mom, without the slightest trace of irony. "I've got to go."

I hang up.

The "I've got to go" was a lie, because I don't actually know what to do next. Do I really think I'm protecting Mom by not telling her everything? Or am I just protecting myself from having to relive it all?

A bus rattles past on the street outside my hiding place, and I think longingly of just going back to Emory and joining my Deskins friends for lunch and pretending that none of this ever happened. I think I could almost do it. I could go back to Deskins and live out my senior year and throw caution to the wind and apply for college in spite of the Excellerand threat. It almost seems inevitable that Excellerand is going to get Mom and me in the end—we might as well enjoy ourselves before that happens.

Mom would never go along with that plan, I think.

Or the two of us could go into hiding without Mr. Trumbull's help. We'd be refugees on the lam, maybe living in abandoned houses, eating in soup kitchens, moving to the next place whenever we get the slightest hint of danger . . . We'd fall further and further out of the scope of normal life, further and further from any chance of finding out what's really going on. . . .

No, I think. *No.*

It's bad enough that I was so ignorant the past three years.

I look down at the envelope from Daddy's letter. I stare at the words "Atlanta, Georgia" like I'm going to develop x-ray vision and see straight through to what that actually means.

What does anything about this messed-up day mean?

Maybe I could study that in college, I think sarcastically. *Not that I'm ever going to get to go to college now.*

Tears sting at my eyes over everything I'll miss. Maybe I was listening to more of the presentations last night than I thought. I remember the Emory admissions people saying that college isn't just about going to frat parties or getting to brag about what a great college you got into or getting a better job than you could have straight out of high school. What college is mostly for, they said, is seeking knowledge, and finding out things you've always wanted to know. Or things you never dreamed anyone could know.

"There's more than one way to get knowledge," I mutter under my breath.

I pull out Mrs. Collins's iPhone. I type a few words into a

search engine, click through screenfuls of information, and study the phone number I eventually find.

Am I brave enough for this? I wonder. *Is this really what I want?*

I am. It is.

I tap the phone number and bring the iPhone to my ear. As soon as someone answers, I ask, "Can I visit one of your inmates today?"

Now—

logistics and hopes . . . and revelations

"No," the woman on the other end of the line says in a flat voice.

She goes on talking, something about the appointment slots at the penitentiary already being full for today, something about having to sign up in advance and needing to be an approved visitor. But I barely hear her, because I'm plunged into despair. Of course this won't work. Of course this is another door slammed in my face.

"—tomorrow?" the woman says, and this word actually breaks through my fog.

"E-excuse me?" I stammer.

"I said, we do have openings tomorrow," the woman says. "Saturday morning?"

She's speaking slowly now, enunciating each syllable as if she's decided I'm a nearly brainless creature.

And maybe I am, because it seems to take me forever to process this. Tomorrow? I'm supposed to tour Vanderbilt tomorrow. My friends believe that's the whole reason I came on this trip. I'm not supposed to spend another night here in Atlanta, let alone another day. I'm supposed to be in Stuart's car by three o'clock this afternoon, headed toward Nashville.

"Want to sign up for a visit tomorrow?" the woman asks.

Impossible, I think.

"Yes," I say.

The woman begins telling me I need to bring two forms of ID and, yes, a driver's license and school ID will work fine.

I have my school ID because I thought I might need to show it at Emory, and of course I needed the license to drive. But suddenly it hits me that I've been reckless carrying either of them with me in Atlanta.

And now I'm going to march up to Daddy's prison and show both IDs right at the gate? I agonize. *With my name and "Deskins, Ohio" right on both cards?*

My brain tells me to hang up right now—to give up completely—but I don't. I let the woman keep talking, warning me that I will be turned away if I wear anything too "provocative," and . . .

And what am I going to tell my friends? I wonder. *What lie can I make up to explain wanting to stay in Atlanta an extra day— when everybody knows I'm more interested in Vanderbilt than Emory? And how am I going to get back to Ohio if I stay here when everybody else goes on to Nashville?*

The woman asks for my name and the name of the inmate I want to visit, and I'm so rattled that I just give both, straight out. She doesn't react, but maybe there's some special training that prison workers go through, so they don't make a big deal about inmates' crimes, no matter how infamous they are.

As soon as I hang up, I remember that I was scared a moment ago about listening devices on the wall behind me or in the bushes around me. That's silly, but cell-phone transmissions can be intercepted. I don't know all the technology Excellerand has at its disposal.

I scramble out of my bushes and scurry down the block,

because if Excellerand was listening in, maybe they could pinpoint the exact spot where I spoke my name and my father's name. I don't want them to catch me until after I've visited Daddy.

I really don't want them to catch me at all, but that's another issue.

I smooth down my hair and force myself to slow my stride to a normal pace, not a desperate dash. I can't stand out. But of course I do. Kids my age aren't supposed to be out wandering the streets of Atlanta this time of day.

So, back to Emory's campus, where I blend in?

This thought comes as a relief. I glance at the time on the iPhone's screen—it's only 10:35. It feels like I've lived a lifetime since I got on the bus back at Emory, but it's only been a few hours. I've got enough time that, if the bus and metro schedules work in my favor, I can meet my friends back at the Emory dining hall at noon, right on schedule.

And then could I just "accidentally" get separated from them and not make it back to Stuart's SUV when it's time to drive to Nashville? Would they leave without me?

No, not even Stuart would be that heartless. And the others wouldn't let him—Rosa and Oscar and Jala would put out an all-points bulletin; they'd alert the national media; they'd tell anyone who would listen that someone as responsible as me wouldn't just disappear.

Even after this miserable morning I feel a burst of joy, because I have friends who would be that loyal. Who would do everything they could to take care of me if they thought I was in danger.

So I have to come up with a bulletproof lie, so they don't know I really am in danger.

One thing at a time, I tell myself.

I find my way back to the metro stop, buy my ticket, plan my route. I'll get back to Emory by 11:49. Perfect. On the bus I check the price of a plane ticket tomorrow from Atlanta to Columbus, Ohio: hundreds of dollars. Ouch. Going by Greyhound bus would be less than half that, but it's still about what I would make in two shifts at Riggoli's.

This is worth it, I tell myself.

The phone gives the little ping that means I have a text. I look, thinking it's something for Mrs. Collins that I should forward. But there are actually four messages waiting that I must have missed before, and they're all for me.

From Jala: **Is this crazy? Emory seems too small after OSU. Keep wanting to ask: Where's the rest of campus? Where's the rest of students?**

From Stuart: **U right. Emory can't be Harvard of South. People too friendly. I hate that.**

From Rosa: **I'm in love with this prof! Why aren't h.s. teachers like this?**

I'm not sure if she means she loves how brilliant the guy is or that she thinks he's hot. With Rosa, it could be either. Or both.

Then I get to Oscar's text: **Have u had enuf of college alone? Please say you'll go to afternoon class w/me. B/c that's how college will be for u. Not lonely. Everyone will want to be around u.**

From Oscar, this is practically a declaration of love. It's as bold as someone else sending roses or proposing a moonlight stroll or leaning in for a first kiss. I can imagine him spending the whole Computer Science Fundamentals class struggling to write this text. Maybe because I've just been working so hard to find hidden messages in my father's letter, I believe I can see what Oscar really wants to say: *I miss you. I don't want to be apart from you. I think you're wonderful.*

Under the circumstances, this should feel like a burden. It

should feel like something I have to push away, nip in the bud. But I can't do that to Oscar. Or—I'll be honest—to myself. Not when reading his text feels like safety, like coming in from a storm, like that moment in the church parking lot when Mom and I stood bathed in light, facing truth together. And it's not just Oscar. The texts from all my friends steady me. They tether me, at a time when I really need it.

I couldn't tell Mom the mess I'm in, because she's in it with me, and telling would have only sent us both further into paralyzing despair. But my friends are different. I need them. They help.

I'm not even going to try to make up a good lie about why I'm staying in Atlanta.

I'm finally going to tell them the truth.

Now—

the moment of truth
(Well, several moments, actually)

"—and that's why I'm not going to Vanderbilt with the rest of you," I finish up.

I'm sitting with my four friends in a secluded part of Emory's campus, sheltered by trees. I've just told them my entire story, beginning with Daddy's arrest and running through my move to Deskins, the Court scholarship fiasco, and the story-behind-the-story I heard from Mom only last week. Then I told them how my morning went when they thought I was at the Religion and Contemporary Experience class, and why I decided to stay in Atlanta another day to visit Daddy.

I'm not sure exactly where I was in the story when Oscar moved over beside me and put his arm around my shoulder. I'm not sure what I was saying when Jala's eyes began to glisten with tears, and she also moved close, to pat my arm every time my voice broke and I had to struggle to keep talking.

But now I'm done, and everyone's silent.

"Well?" I say tentatively. "Did any of that make sense?"

Stuart clears his throat. He's sitting the farthest away from me.

I'm not sure he's met my eyes even once since I started talking.

"You know what this means, don't you?" he asks. "When you bring down Excellerand, you're so going to have the best college essay, ever. Every school in the country is going to want you!"

Rosa shoves him so hard he falls over.

"Would you just shut up?" she hisses. "That's not what this is about! This is *real.*"

Stuart puts out an arm and props himself back up. But he doesn't retaliate against Rosa.

"I was trying for comic relief," he says. Then, uncharacteristically, he adds, "Sorry. I'm not good at this kind of thing."

I snort.

"Who is?" I ask. "It's not exactly covered in SAT prep classes. Or *life* prep classes. But, Stuart, I don't have any hope of bringing down Excellerand. My father's been working on that for three years, and it's not exactly going well. I'm just trying to get out of this alive."

"No, you're not," Rosa says.

And then it's Stuart shoving her and hissing, "And *that's* being supportive? At least I was trying to make her laugh!"

Rosa puts out her hand to hold Stuart at bay.

"I *am* being supportive," she says. "Becca, I think you're doing the right thing. But you're not just trying to stay alive. If that was your only goal, you'd go hide somewhere else with your mom, totally off the grid. But that would be like letting the bad guys win. Letting the bullies win, because you're scared to go visit your own father."

I'm surprised Rosa has sorted through my choices so quickly and figured out my reasoning. This is one of those times it's really good to be hanging out with the smart kids.

"And we're talking about your *daddy,*" Jala chimes in. "I can tell you still love him and miss him, no matter what. And that's okay. That's how it should be. You have to go visit him."

I knew what I was doing when I pegged Jala as one of the nicest kids in Deskins, all those years ago at freshman orientation. She still sees Daddy as human when everybody else in the world wrote him off as a monster. She can actually understand why I still love him.

I blink back tears.

"Thanks, guys," I say. "I wasn't really asking for permission or approval, or anything like that. It's just . . . I wanted you to know. So if I do have to disappear . . ."

Oscar tightens his arm around my shoulder.

"You won't have to do that!" he says fiercely. I'm surprised to see tears in his eyes too. "We're going to help you solve this. Even if I have to hack into Excellerand's files myself!"

I pull away from him slightly.

"I don't want to make anybody else into a criminal," I say. "Really, you guys can just go on to Nashville like you planned. I already checked the Greyhound site, and I have enough money with me to take a bus home, so—"

"You think we'd leave you here to go visit a prison all by yourself?" Oscar asks incredulously. "And then ride home alone?"

Oscar glances around the whole circle, narrowing his eyes ever so slightly at Stuart.

"I don't know about the rest of you," Oscar says. "But I'm staying here with Becca."

"Me too," Jala says quickly. She gives me a shy smile, which would have been a smirk on anyone else's face. "My parents already don't know where I am. What does it matter if I'm in Nashville without their permission, or Atlanta without their permission?"

I gulp. It'd be great not to have to go through the next twenty-four hours alone. I hadn't even thought about anybody else skipping Vanderbilt. But I have to answer Jala's question.

"It could be dangerous staying with me," I say. "I don't want to risk anybody else's life."

"Oh, who cares?" Rosa says. "It was risky coming down here, especially with Stuart driving. It'll be risky going off to college next year. Some risks are worth taking, and this is one of them! I'm in too!"

We all turn to look at Stuart.

"Does everyone have to stay with Becca?" he asks weakly. "Can't it just be one person, or maybe two? It's not that I don't care, but . . . do you know how mad my parents are going to be if we don't follow the original plan?"

"You are such a coward!" Rosa says disgustedly. "And a hypocrite! You didn't even want to visit Vanderbilt in the first place! You told me you hated country music and Vanderbilt was full of rich Southern kids with twangs and their own polo ponies!"

"But—my parents," Stuart says, and at least he has the grace to sound apologetic. "If we don't go on to Vanderbilt, I'd have to get permission. I'd have to tell them . . ."

"No, you wouldn't." Of all people, it's Jala who takes up the argument now. "You're eighteen. You're going to be in college in less than a year, making all sorts of decisions without them. Think of this as a test run. Figure out what's right, not what you think Mommy and Daddy want you to do."

Stuart is staring way too intently at the dead leaves in the grass before him.

"I think I will tell them . . . *after*," he says. He looks up, calm now that he's apparently made a decision. He's back in confident mode, back to acting like he's the smartest kid in the class, so naturally his answer is right. "Of course I can't tell them now, because Excellerand might be able to intercept cell-phone calls. But afterward—they'll be proud of me."

"So we're all staying with Becca?" Rosa asks. "We'll all just drive home Saturday afternoon, all the way from Atlanta, not Nashville?"

Stuart nods. Rosa throws her arms around him and cries, "Well, that's good, because I *didn't* have the money for the bus ride home! Not if I want to eat tomorrow!"

The others start making all sorts of plans. Rosa puts herself in charge of locating a cheap but safe hotel for the night. Stuart sends an e-mail to Vanderbilt saying that "unavoidable circumstances" will prevent us from making it to their overnight. Oscar speculates about where to look for a list of Excellerand's government contracts, so he can see if they have any connection to the federal prison system's computers. I listen to their chatter, and it feels a little suffocating. Is this just another adventure for them? Are my pain and agony just sources of excitement—like Rosa and me watching the mean-girls clique at school?

Rosa and the two boys are already starting to head back toward the car, but Jala hangs back with me. She gives me a hug.

"You're following your own advice," she says.

"What?" I ask.

"Freshman year?" she says. "When Mr. Vickers was mean and bigoted? You said I had to tell. And I had to tell the right people. That's what you just did."

I hug her back.

"You guys were the right people," I say.

A gust of wind blows across campus just then, momentarily lifting the leaves from the grass, revealing everything that lies beneath. Then a new torrent of leaves comes down, covering everything that much more thoroughly.

I don't have the slightest idea what tomorrow will bring. But with my friends buoying me up, I think I'm ready for it.

Now—

Saturday morning at prison

I glance back over my shoulder. Razor wire, guard towers, a taxi-cab driving away . . . my friends wave at me from the back window of the taxi. Last night in the hotel room Oscar scoured the penitentiary's online visitors guide, hoping to find some loophole that would allow all four of them to come in with me. He failed—I'm standing here alone, after all.

But they'll be waiting for me afterward . . . just not in the prison parking lot.

Stuart freaked out when Rosa went online and discovered that Excellerand does have a contract with the federal prison system for "perimeter security technology"; he didn't want his mom's SUV or license plate showing up on any prison cameras. At least he was the one who thought of calling a cab, so my friends could deliver me directly to the visitors' entrance of the penitentiary.

And he paid for the cab himself.

See, even Stuart cares, I tell myself. *So it's like I have my friends with me, even though I'm walking through this door alone. . . .*

Check-in is a blur of questions. The heavyset African-American woman at the counter squints for a long time at my driver's license and school ID. She looks at me hard. Then she frowns.

"Let's see, your birthday's in July, so you're . . . don't tell me, let me do the math here, keep my brain nimble . . . you're eighteen, right?" she asks. "That's a relief, because if you were younger, we'd have to have permission forms signed by your mother or guardian."

I'm so dazed I almost correct her, "No, I'm seventeen." Then I catch on and realize she's helping me.

She winks at me.

"Let me guess, your mama never wanted you to come visit your daddy, the three years he's been here, but now that you're old enough, you're going to visit him on your own," she says. She looks me right in the eye. "Nothing sadder than a prisoner whose family never visits."

I know she's trying to praise me for coming now, but her words still hurt.

Don't you know what Daddy did? I want to ask. *Don't you know he's still torturing us?*

But she works in a prison. She's probably heard it all.

And did she just say, "three years"? I wonder. *Did she just confirm that Daddy's been here in Atlanta the whole time?*

The woman pats my hand even as she tells me I have to leave my cell phone and other valuables behind in a locker. I appreciate the kindness. I am fragile here. I think I would feel fragile visiting Daddy in prison no matter what—even if I weren't worried about Excellerand killing Mom or me, even if I wasn't so puzzled by Daddy's last letter.

My new best friend—Gloria, I see by her name tag—guides me through the rest of the procedure. I have to go through a metal detector; I have to have my hand stamped with invisible ink; I have to be buzzed through the doors, each conspicuously guarded by both humans and cameras.

Cameras probably monitored by Excellerand, I think, but it's too late to worry about that. Do I really think Excellerand could swoop in and kidnap me from the middle of a federal prison? If I'm afraid of that, I might as well be afraid of air.

And after? After I leave the prison, if Excellerand knows I'm in Atlanta, if they have all my information now . . .

I can't let myself worry about that either.

A silent, stone-faced guard walks me down a long corridor that seems to be partly underground. I feel buried. Trapped. From down here I can't see the guard towers or the high prison walls that surround this building, but I'm still acutely aware that they're out there. My heart pounds. I've lost count—how many fences and walls and locked doors and guards and high-powered guns stand between me and freedom?

This is prison.

My parents never let me visit Daddy when he was locked up before and during the trial. Daddy kept saying, "I don't want Becca to see me like this, and it's all a mistake, so I'll be out soon." And then we left Atlanta in such a rush; I didn't visit him in prison then either. But I've seen enough movies and TV; I thought I could imagine it.

TV and movies can't show what it's really like, knowing you can't just turn around and run, knowing you're at the guards' mercy . . .

And I've been here only a few minutes. How must Daddy have felt, walking in here, knowing he was supposed to stay ten years?

We climb a flight of stairs, and then there's another set of barred doors for us to be buzzed through, along with a window where I have to show the stamp on my hand again. I haven't been out of the guard's sight, but it's like no one trusts me to be the same person I was when I got the stamp only a few minutes ago, before the doors and the corridor and the stairs.

Am I the same person? I wonder. They're making me doubt it myself.

The last door clicks shut behind me as I step into the official visiting room.

If seeing Daddy is too much for me, I really won't be able to get away, I think.

Stone-faced guard glides away. Maybe he said something to me before he left; maybe I just didn't hear. Another guard behind a desk says impatiently, "Sit. Your inmate will be here soon," and that's the first time I see that there are chairs. I slide into one.

The guard behind the desk watches me suspiciously, as if he's certain that if I'm related to someone in prison, I must be scum, too. Crazily, I want to tell him, "I have straight A's. I'm going to Vanderbilt." Is this how Daddy felt, too, with his criminal family? Is that why he started lying and telling people he had gone to Vanderbilt?

I will probably never go to Vanderbilt. My chances of going to college at all aren't looking good right now. And those are the least of my worries.

I keep my head down and clutch the metal sides of my chair. I don't dare to even look around, to see how other visitors cope with the guard's suspicious glare.

Then there's the buzzing sound of a door being unlocked and opened on the other side of the room. I look up. A man in a khaki uniform steps into the doorway, and it kind of looks like Daddy. But the Daddy I remember was always confident and grinning, and this man is shattered and seems to be trying to hold back sobs. I tilt my head, staring. The man stumbles into the room and stops; his gaze skips over me, falters, and comes back. But then he just stands there, trembling. No—shaking. Shaking with sobs.

This is Daddy. Daddy now.

Mom was not his picture of Dorian Gray, I think.

Daddy looks even more destroyed, even more distraught and

devastated. His beard is stubble and his hair is buzzed off in an unflattering burr, and he appears decades older than the last time I saw him.

I stand up, and it's like I'm giving him permission: He careens toward me. He throws his arms around me and sobs against my shoulders. I'm sobbing now too.

"You came!" he wails. "I thought you and your mother never would. I thought I'd never see you again. And, oh, you're so grown up now, so beautiful. . . ."

"I missed you," I whisper.

We both collapse into chairs, and I can see how hard Daddy is trying to get control of himself. He starts to reach for my hand, then stops.

"They have rules," he says, glancing nervously toward the guard behind the desk. "You can't hug too long, you can't hold on . . . Not that I've had any visitors I wanted to hug the past three years. Why . . . why didn't you or Susan come before?"

I stare at him. I pull my hand back, so it's not even close to Daddy's.

"*You* know," I say. And I can't help it: My voice comes out harsh and judgmental. "Because of Excellerand? Because you're still being selfish, trying to get out early and not pay for your crimes, by turning in Excellerand instead? And so Mom and me, we have to hide, we have to live in fear, because *we* don't have prison walls protecting us . . ."

Daddy jerks his hand back too, and puts it over his mouth. But he can't hold it there. His fingers slide down, pulling at the loose skin of his cheeks.

"I don't understand," he says. "That ended. Two and a half years ago. There wasn't enough evidence. Excellerand never knew I had anything on them. Why would you think you and your mom are in danger?"

Now—

confusion

Daddy didn't used to be this stupid.

"Don't you ever think about consequences?" I ask, and three years of fury go into that question. "Don't you see how this affects Mom and me? I can't even go to college! Just yesterday Mr. Trumbull told me . . . Mr. Trumbull said . . ."

My brain catches up with Daddy's words: ". . . ended. Two and a half years ago . . ."

"Mr. Trumbull?" Daddy repeats.

Mr. Trumbull is always in the middle, every time Mom and Daddy send letters back and forth. Mr. Trumbull is the one who told Mom it wasn't safe to call. Mr. Trumbull was the one who told us Daddy was in California, too far away to visit. Mr. Trumbull is the one who said I couldn't apply for financial aid. Mr. Trumbull is the one who helped us hide.

Mr. Trumbull is the one who wants even more money, so we can go even deeper into hiding. So no one would ever be able to find us again.

Maybe not even Daddy.

"But . . . but . . . ," I sputter. I'm almost too confused to come up with a question that makes sense. Then I find one. "Why didn't you tell us before?"

"I *did*!" Daddy erupts. "In my letters . . . I told you and Susan we could write each other directly now, without going through Mr. Trumbull. I said we could call each other; you could move back to Atlanta and visit any time. . . ."

He's back to struggling to hold himself together.

"We never saw those letters," I say numbly.

Daddy gapes at me.

"Susan wrote back," he insists. "She said she still didn't want to do any of that. She . . . she wouldn't even tell me where you were! I thought . . . if the letters stopped . . . I could lose you forever!"

Daddy starts sobbing again, but I'm too stunned to react. I *saw* the letters Mom wrote Daddy. Not all of them, but a lot, especially freshman year, when she'd leave them on the counter "just in case" I wanted to add a note before she mailed them. I saw the Deskins return address on the outside; I read her descriptions of the town and my school and her job. She said it was safe; she said the news media wouldn't see Daddy's private mail in prison.

Mom wouldn't have pretended she was going to send those letters and then thrown them away.

Mr. Trumbull. . . , I think.

Did he censor my parents' mail back and forth? Was he concerned about Excellerand having some security contracts for inside the prison, not just outside?

But then, why didn't he tell Mom or Daddy that? Why did he make up fake letters instead? Isn't that what he must have done?

I remember something else that was evidently faked. It takes courage to tell Daddy, but I do it anyway.

"I never sent you a single letter," I say. "Not in three years. I was too mad."

If I think this will bring more tears, I'm wrong. Daddy stares at me for a long moment, as if he just doesn't understand.

"I *got* letters from you," he says. "They were never very personal, and never really sounded like you . . ."

I think about how Daddy's letters never quite sounded like him either. He's still talking.

"But . . . I thought all this had to have changed you," he says. "It was mostly just your school essays you sent me. Or— somebody did. That one you wrote a year or two ago about secret crimes and *The Scarlet Letter . . . that* was a stab in the heart. But it felt like you were inching toward forgiving me, even if I didn't deserve it."

Daddy bows his head. I did write an essay about *The Scarlet Letter* sophomore year, and every word I wrote condemning Arthur Dimmesdale was actually about Daddy. And when I came around to some forgiveness for Arthur Dimmesdale in the end, that was for Daddy, too. But I never meant for Daddy to read it. I never sent it to him, any more than I sent the Whitney Court essay or the one about *Moby Dick*.

I start telling Daddy everything Mom has believed for the past three years. I tell him she did write letters telling him where we were. I tell him how I decided to risk coming to Atlanta, and how Mr. Trumbull's inexperienced receptionist gave me the handwritten letter yesterday, when every other letter I'd ever seen from Daddy was typed. I tell him how the letter tipped me off to where Daddy was really imprisoned, and to the fact that Daddy *thought* I'd been sending him letters.

"Do you think Mom . . . ," I begin doubtfully.

At the same time Daddy says, "Would you know how to tell if somebody put a keystroke tracker on your laptop? Can you think of a time your computer just started running a lot slower?"

Now it's my turn to gape at Daddy.

"When Mr. Trumbull sent my laptop back," I say. "Three years ago, after it wasn't evidence anymore. It's been slow ever since, but I just thought . . ."

I just thought my laptop was like me, dragged down by everything that had happened. Dragged down and slow and sad.

"Do you think the FBI was monitoring my keystrokes?" I ask. "So I didn't do anything to ruin the case against Excellerand, back when there was a case against Excellerand?"

"The FBI wouldn't care what you wrote," Daddy says, shaking his head almost violently. "You didn't know anything about Excellerand, so you couldn't ruin anything. But Mr. Trumbull . . ."

"Why would he care?" I ask. I am suddenly so, so grateful that I never trusted my laptop over the past three years, that I haven't been a typical teenager pouring her heart and soul into her Facebook page and posts and messages to friends.

But maybe I did pour my heart and soul into things like my *Scarlet Letter* essay.

Daddy's got a look on his face that makes him look more familiar than ever—for a second I feel like I'm back in sixth or seventh grade, and Daddy's waiting for me to figure out some complicated math problem he's working with me.

"You think Mr. Trumbull stole my essays to send to you, don't you?" I ask. "But why? What's in it for him? And why would he still be telling Mom and me that we have to watch out for Excellerand? Why wouldn't he just tell us the truth?"

"Money," Daddy says. "With Trumbull, it's always about the money."

Wasn't that what Mr. Trumbull told us justice was about?

"Mom and I don't *have* any money!" I practically scream at Daddy.

I've forgotten about the suspicious guard at the desk or the other people around me, visiting their own prisoners. But my near scream barely earns me a glance from anybody. I guess this is the type of thing people yell here all the time.

"Think hard," Daddy says. "You just talked to Mr. Trumbull. I haven't seen him in two and a half years. Maybe . . ."

I remember what Mr. Trumbull said yesterday: how he was trying to force Mom and me into selling our story to the media, even though it wouldn't be worth as much now as it was three years ago. I remember how he said I was supposed to write and beg Daddy for access to his mythical Cayman Islands fund.

So that's why Mr. Trumbull wanted Daddy to think I was writing him constantly, I think. *To set him up to give me his money.*

I laugh bitterly.

"Oh, wait, this goes back to you," I accuse. "That secret Cayman Islands fund you have to have had? Mr. Trumbull wants you to give it to me, so we can give him a huge chunk."

Daddy groans.

"God's honest truth," he says. "I don't have any secret stash of money. Not in the Caymans or Switzerland or anywhere. I was too confident . . . too foolish . . . to do that. I didn't think anyone in law enforcement was smart enough to catch me. So why mess with offshore accounts? Why save anything for the future, when I could always make more money then?"

I guess that went for college savings, too.

Daddy's looking me straight in the eye, and he doesn't bother lowering his voice for the sake of the guard behind the desk. And I believe he's telling the truth. Or what he thinks is the truth. My father is a liar, and I no longer trust and hang onto every word he ever uttered. But in my three years apart from him, I think I have developed . . . discernment. I think that's the right word: I can see what I can trust and what I have to hold at arm's length. What I can still love, and what I can condemn without having it ruin me.

Is that really so different from Stuart realizing that sometimes he has to go against his parents' expectations? Or Jala deciding that to be true to herself, she has to discover whether she agrees with her parents' plans or not? Maybe all teenagers have to make some kind of break with their parents, to figure out who they are on their own.

I just got the extreme version of this transformation. My parents just presented me with the most outlandish choices.

"I guess Mr. Trumbull still thinks you've got a lot of money," I say sarcastically. "Enough to be worth this huge scam, faking letters, keeping Mom and me hidden, terrifying us constantly . . ."

Daddy frowns at me.

"That's not enough of a payoff," he says. "All that work just for the *chance* that I have a secret stash? There's got to be something else. Some bigger prize he's after."

In the next moment Daddy's face turns about three shades lighter. He's already got a bad case of prison pallor, so now he could almost be a ghost.

"What?" I say.

Daddy hits his hand against his head.

"He's blackmailing Excellerand," Daddy says. His voice is hushed again, but it seems to be more from horror than from any conscious effort. "I'm sure of it. That's the only explanation. He's telling them they have to pay him . . . oh, millions, probably . . . or else his client will reveal their crimes. He's using *me* as his bait. He's telling them I've got the goods, but Trumbull will keep me quiet as long as they pay up."

I'm not quite following him.

"What do Mom and I have to do with any of this?" I ask.

"If you're hiding—that shows I'm involved," Daddy says. "If Trumbull can show Excellerand proof that you two have disappeared . . ."

"My birth certificate vanished from the online records," I say. "So did Mom's. And your marriage license."

Daddy's nodding, frantic and horrified.

"Trumbull might even be showing them your mom's letters," he says. "The real ones, not the doctored ones I get. Does he ratchet up the fear every now and then, to terrify you two even more?"

I remember how Mr. Trumbull told Mom his office phones might be bugged, how he said the cameras with facial recognition software went up near his office. It was all lies. How far back did they go? Mr. Trumbull could have even been the one who leaked the news about our U-Haul rental three years ago. It would have fit: Mr. Trumbull needed Mom and me to be scared and vulnerable and gullible enough to believe whatever he told us. And we were. We were both so lost and broken and distraught that it seemed he was the only one we could trust.

Only, because Mom was protecting me, I didn't have quite as long as she did to fall for Mr. Trumbull's lies. And when I did find out about them, I still believed there could be a way out.

"This is like one of your scams," I tell Daddy. "Innocent people got hurt."

Daddy flinches, but then he grits his teeth and nods.

"I deserve that," he says quietly. "I deserve all the worst things you could say to me."

He sounds so humble that I realize: Daddy has changed. But then, so have Mom and I. We've healed some; we've toughened up. I even dared to come see Daddy despite the Excellerand danger.

Then I remember: There actually isn't any Excellerand danger. That's what's at the heart of this. It's over. The threat of Excellerand hasn't been anything but a bogeyman for the past two and a half years.

"Daddy," I say excitedly. "Daddy, it's okay. Because, don't you see? This means we can just walk away. Mom and me, anyway. You don't have to worry about us. We don't have to live in fear. I can go to college, after all!"

I'm practically bouncing up and down in my seat, as excited as a lottery winner. I think about sending out college applications, filling out forms for financial aid . . . I'd still have to admit who I really am. I'd still have to run the risk of someone finding out—not necessarily the news media anymore, but nosy, gossipy people in general.

That's not life or death, I remind myself. *Compared with thinking Excellerand is going to kill me, having my identity revealed is nothing. And—it's like the risks Rosa was talking about yesterday. College is worth it.*

Daddy doesn't seem to share my joy. He slumps in his chair.

"Becca," he says, clutching his head. "It's not that simple. Burton Trumbull is a vindictive man. You do anything to threaten his payoff from Excellerand . . . then *he'd* be the one endangering you. And your mom. You have to be careful!"

I stop bouncing.

"So what are we supposed to do?" I ask. "Are we trapped forever? As long as you're in prison? As long as you're *alive*?"

A crafty smile starts breaking over Daddy's face.

"No, no . . . you can beat him at his own game," he says. Now he's leaning toward me, sharing secret advice just between the two of us. "He's blackmailing Excellerand? You blackmail him."

I recoil so violently I almost fall off my chair. Daddy *hasn't* changed. Not enough, anyway.

"I don't want to be a criminal like you," I whisper.

Daddy freezes.

"I didn't want to be a criminal like my father, either," he mumbles back.

And there's such sorrow in his face. I realize that everything

I guessed about Daddy running away from home and taking on a new name must be true. He was trying to escape his family's criminal history, but he fell right back into it, just on a grander scale. Maybe that was the only way he knew how to live; maybe he really did think he was doing it all for me. Maybe it's like it says in the Bible: The sins of the fathers are visited on their sons.

What if there's no way to break that chain? What if daughters have to inherit their father's sins too?

"Maybe . . . maybe this is how you and Susan should play it," Daddy says.

And as he begins telling me his slightly revised plan, my heart sinks. Because—what he's describing? No matter how much I hate it, no matter how much it terrifies me, it's what I have to do.

It's my only choice.

Now—

Friday, six days later

Mom and I walk into the Panera Bread together. We're in a place called Smyrna, one of the northeast Atlanta suburbs, and that alone frightens Mom. She's glancing around like she still believes Excellerand has spy cameras watching for her all around the city. She has a scarf wrapped around her head, hiding her hair just like Jala. Except Jala in her hijab is always beautiful; with her hollow cheeks and terrified eyes, Mom looks like she has cancer or some other potentially fatal disease.

"He's not here yet," she whispers to me.

"We're *supposed* to arrive first, remember?" I remind Mom.

We go to the counter. Mom orders coffee and I get a chai tea latte. I sip it, and it's too sweet and cloying, but I pretend to like it. I've had a lot of practice pretending over the past three years; it's going to be even more important in the near future.

I wait for Mom to add cream and sugar to her coffee, then by silent agreement we sit down at a four-person table in the most remote part of the restaurant, in a sea of empty tables.

Mom keeps toying with her scarf, tugging it forward, then back.

"Act natural," I whisper.

"If he's got someone watching us, don't you think they'd expect us to act nervous?" Mom whispers back.

I glance around. That bearded twentysomething guy hunched over his laptop at the back of the room—is he a true midafternoon Panera customer? Or is it deliberate, how he won't glance my way as long as I'm looking at him? The two suburban-mom types over to the side—do their workout clothes actually look like disguises? Are they trying too hard to make it seem like they just came from a yoga class?

It's funny: A week ago on the bus going to Mr. Trumbull's, I felt like everyone around me might work for Excellerand. Now I'm watching for different spies.

"That's him!" Mom hisses through clenched teeth.

I see Mr. Trumbull walk in through the front door. I see him seeing us. He lifts his hand to wave.

Mom waves back.

"Don't!" I scold under my breath.

"Wouldn't it be weird *not* to wave at someone who's meeting us?" she whispers back.

She's right. We're so on edge, it's like we're taking turns not thinking straight.

We've both got to be sharp when he sits down, I tell myself. *We can't make a single mistake.*

Mr. Trumbull is ordering; now he's at the coffee dispenser; now he's walking toward us, steaming cup in hand. He's carrying a briefcase in his other hand, and I have to force myself not to stare at it. Has he brought everything he's supposed to?

Mr. Trumbull puts his coffee cup down on the table across from Mom.

"Hello, Mrs. Smith," he says, a slightly bitter twist to his words. He turns to me. "And Sarah."

I have to grit my teeth to hold back hysterical giggles, to hold back even the thought of hysterical giggles. It wasn't a good idea, after all, to choose those fake names for the new identities Mr. Trumbull is bringing us. I'd thought I'd get courage from using the same name I'd made up on Facebook when I was researching Whitney Court. I'd liked the irony of it, my little inside joke.

I hadn't expected it to panic me this much.

Mr. Trumbull doesn't notice. He's sitting down, then bending over to pull a thick manila envelope from his briefcase. He drops the envelope on the table.

"It's all there," he says.

Mom and Mr. Trumbull both stare down at the envelope like it's a ticking time bomb. But I notice out of the corner of my eye that a couple in business attire have started putting down trays on the table behind Mr. Trumbull. I'm jealous of the very concept of this couple: people whose lives are so leisurely they're eating cinnamon rolls at three o'clock in the afternoon.

Can Mom and I ever live that peacefully, once we carry this off? Will we ever be able to stop glancing over our shoulders all the time?

Maybe I flick my eyes to the right a little too obviously; maybe the couple is too loud scraping out their chairs. Mr. Trumbull spins around and looks at them, then he turns back to glare at Mom and me. It's like the three of us are having an argument with our eyes. From Mom and me: *Hey, we followed the instructions! It's not our fault that couple chose to sit so close when they had thirty other tables to choose from!*

From Mr. Trumbull: *Well, this is not acceptable! We have to move to another table! And we have to make it seem natural, not forced!*

I'm about to say, loudly, "Is anybody else having a problem with the sun being in their eyes?" when the woman in the couple behind Mr. Trumbull complains, "Oh, no! Didn't you see how dirty this table is? We can't sit here!"

They move one table back, and Mr. Trumbull looks satisfied. Mom picks up the envelope.

"I have to check to be sure," she says, not even pretending she trusts him.

"Everything's in order. You'll see," Mr. Trumbull says confidently. "I even gave you passports this time, like you asked. Though the pictures I had to use . . . you're not really the looker you used to be, are you?"

He's actually saying this to Mom. The man is just mean.

Mom blinks rapidly, as if the jab hit its target.

"I didn't mind losing my looks so much," she says softly. She gazes pointedly at Mr. Trumbull. "That's not as bad as someone throwing away his morals."

You go, Mom! Way to fight back!

Mr. Trumbull just rolls his eyes.

"Oh, please," he says. "Spare me the sanctimonious bullcrap. You lived with a criminal for twenty years."

"I didn't know," Mom whispers.

"And what you're doing now?" Mr. Trumbull asks. "Blackmail is a crime, you know."

"Shouldn't you have thought of that before you started blackmailing Excellerand?" I ask. My voice rings out a little too loudly. It makes Mr. Trumbull glance back toward the couple two tables behind him. They seem oblivious, hunched over something on an iPad. It could be baby pictures or a business report or architectural designs—ordinary things for people with ordinary lives. Unlike Mom and me.

Or Mr. Trumbull.

"What I want to know," I tell him, "is how you could have done this to us. We trusted you! Did you ever think about how we'd feel when we found out? Did you even think of us as human beings? Or were we just pawns to you?"

Mr. Trumbull glances at me in a way that makes my skin crawl. Something in my bra itches, but there's no way I'm touching my breast to scratch it. Not in front of Mr. Trumbull.

"I saw you both for what you were three years ago," he says. He points at me. "You were a spoiled brat, whose daddy had always given you everything you wanted. He never told you the bill always comes due."

"I found out," I mutter. "Just like you're finding out now."

"Touché," Mr. Trumbull says, and he laughs as if I've truly amused him. He turns to Mom. "And you . . . you were stuck in that small-town mentality of being ashamed of what the neighbors would think. You were so pretty back then—you were magazine-cover ready! You stole millions from my firm, not letting us negotiate media deals for your story."

"It was *my* story, not yours," Mom says, with more feistiness than I've seen her show in three years. "Mine and Becca's. I had to protect my daughter."

Mr. Trumbull smirks.

"You're going to have to remember to start calling her Sarah," he reminds her. He spreads his hands wide, a courtroom gesture I remember him making whenever he pretended to be conciliatory. "Anyhow, didn't I give you exactly what you wanted three years ago? You wanted to run away and hide. It was win-win. I got the evidence I needed to convince Excellerand; you got to skulk away into exile."

Mr. Trumbull reaches out and touches Mom's scarf.

"Look at you. Three years down the road, fifteen, twenty miles outside of downtown Atlanta—and you're still hiding," he says. "You're still cowering in fear."

Mom shoves his hand away.

"Three years isn't long enough for people to forget," Mom says. "I could still be recognized."

"But three years was long enough for us to change what we wanted," I say. "*I* stopped caring about the secrets so much. I really did start feeling ready to tell people we could trust."

In spite of everything, Mr. Court actually did fit in that category, I think. *And of course Oscar, Jala, Rosa, and Stuart . . .*

I'm hit with a pang of missing my friends. They all drove back to Ohio last weekend. In the end, they did go without me. It seemed like an eternity that I was here alone, waiting for Mom to drive down to meet me, to set Daddy's plan in motion.

"Three years was long enough for us to be ready to heal," Mom says softly.

Mr. Trumbull narrows his eyes at us.

"You think you're going to be happier as Evelyn and Sarah Smith?" he asks. "When you have to keep even more secrets? You can't tell a soul now. You know that, don't you?"

We've talked ourselves into a trap. If Mr. Trumbull pursues this, our whole story could unravel. I've got to think of some sort of distraction, some . . .

"Lying on a beach in the Caymans *could* make up for that," Mom says with a teasing grin.

Mr. Trumbull was starting to turn toward me, but now he jerks his attention back to Mom.

"What?" he erupts. "You mean, that husband of yours really does have an offshore account? And all this time he's been lying to me . . ."

He's incoherent in his rage at not being able to get his hands on any last remnant of Daddy's stolen funds.

Mom smiles angelically and says, "Gotcha."

Wow, Mom, I marvel. *Didn't know you had that in you. Well played!*

But it's my turn now. I have to strike while Mr. Trumbull is still thrown off, still looking back and forth between us like he's not sure what to believe.

"What I want to know," I say, "is why it even mattered to you what we did or where we went. Maybe I'm too stupid to see how it all fit together, but . . . you had all the evidence from Daddy. You had him believing you'd taken it to the FBI. That FBI 'agent' he met with three years ago—who was that, *really*?"

Mr. Trumbull grins at me, and I realize I've struck the perfect tone. He's an egomaniac, and I've just invited him to brag.

"Oh, so you figured out that part of it?" Mr. Trumbull says. "Harlan is an actor friend of mine. I hire him every now and then. He thinks of it as improv."

I squint the same way I do in calculus when the problems on the board seem unsolvable.

"But why didn't you just do what Daddy expected?" I ask. "Why didn't you bring in real FBI agents, do everything honest and aboveboard?"

Am I laying it on too thick?

"There would have been no advantage in that," Mr. Trumbull says carelessly. "Your father's evidence wasn't enough. The FBI would have just patted him on the head and said, 'Yeah, right. Come back when you have something real.'"

"Excellerand must have thought the evidence was enough," I say, the puzzled squint still on my face. "If they were willing to pay to keep it secret."

"Excellerand thought it was *almost* enough," Mr. Trumbull says. He's leaning in close, and I can tell he wants us to understand how a lesser strategist would have just given up at that point. But not him. Oh, no. Not him.

"I took the information to Excellerand in secret," he says. "And I could tell they worried about it, but they were already calculating who they could fire to make it seem like it'd just been an isolated incident, something that appalled the upstanding, morally righteous executives. Before I was halfway into my presentation, I could tell they'd already planned their damage control and their spin, and they thought they'd still come out smelling like roses. They'd look like the good guys for cracking down on government fraud."

"So you changed your story," Mom says.

Mr. Trumbull glances her way appreciatively.

"Oh, so you *did* learn something from living with Roger all those years," he says. "Of course I changed my story. I made it up on the spot. I told Excellerand those were just some of the documents Roger had. I said there were more—more papers, more computer files, more incriminating evidence—but his wife was holding it hostage until he gave her access to his offshore accounts. There's nothing like the wrath of a trophy wife scorned and humiliated and cut off from any chance of ever buying another BMW—"

"I was never a trophy wife!" Mom protests. "Roger and I are the same age!"

I kick her under the table. How could she interrupt Mr. Trumbull now?

Mr. Trumbull doesn't seem to care. You can tell he's having a lot of fun telling his story. And, really, we're the only ones he can tell it to.

"All the Excellerand executives have trophy wives," he says. "Very high-maintenance trophy wives. So they fell for my story hook, line, and sinker."

I frown, like a serious student just wanting all the puzzle pieces to match up. I've had three years of experience plastering that expression on my face, so I'm sure it's convincing.

"I don't understand," I say. "Did Excellerand think they were

paying you to keep Daddy quiet? Or to keep Mom from revealing the evidence she supposedly had, which would have set
Daddy free?"

Mr. Trumbull positively beams.

"That's the beauty of it," he says. "It was an all-of-the-above
situation right from the start. They were paying me to keep your
mother furious at your father, so she wouldn't just give in and
help get his sentence reduced. They were paying me to convince
your father his case was hopeless, and so he should keep all the
money for himself, for ten years down the road when—once he's
out of prison and living it up in the Caymans—why should he
care about turning in Excellerand? And, to prevent your parents
from ever comparing the stories I'd told them, Excellerand was
indirectly paying me to keep you and your mother from visiting
him, because your mother was too poor and terrified to come to
Atlanta, er—California, should I say?"

His smirk is infuriating.

"But . . . you had no proof of any of that," Mom stammers.

"Of course I did," Mr. Trumbull says. "Your *letters*, back and
forth. Let's just say that I did some judicious editing, but . . .
Excellerand loved it that you were so terrified of them, that I
had you so convinced that they were out to get you. They loved
it that Roger was so forlorn, begging you to come visit him in
Atlanta, begging you to tell him where you really were."

Excellerand actually saw some of the real letters, I realize,
the handwritten ones that truly did sound like Daddy. And, of
course, just as Mr. Trumbull kept Mom and me from knowing
where Daddy really was, Daddy never saw the parts of Mom's
letters describing where we were.

Even when Daddy got out of prison, he would have had no
way of finding us.

"You are a thoroughly evil man," I say.

I decide that Mr. Trumbull has finally answered one of my original questions: He didn't see us as human. We never were anything but pawns to him.

"Oh, and you and your mother are saints?" he asks sarcastically. "You're not even eighteen yet, and your father's already taught you so well, you're trying to manipulate one of the top lawyers in Atlanta!"

Should Mom and I worry about that one word, "trying"?

"You wouldn't have known anything if my receptionist hadn't screwed up," Mr. Trumbull continues.

"You didn't fire her over this, did you?" I ask. I'm partly just trying to buy some time. But it strikes me that poor Tria was a pawn in all this too.

Mr. Trumbull ignores my question. I take that as proof that he did fire Tria, and he hasn't given her a single thought since.

This does not surprise me.

"You know," Mr. Trumbull says, "when you called Monday and said you and your mother were both in Atlanta, I was almost afraid that you'd gone to the authorities. I should have remembered I was dealing with a criminal family. I should have known your first thought would be blackmail, and you'd try to turn the situation to your own advantage no matter what."

He's right, I think. *That is where Daddy's brain went first.*

But there's that word, "trying," again.

Mom's face has gone pale.

"You really think we'd be able to withstand *another* media firestorm, if all this came out?" she says.

"And what proof did we have?" I ask. "It would have been our word against yours. It's not like anybody else knew you'd told us Daddy was in California. It's not like Mom kept copies of the letters she sent Daddy, that you intercepted. And who'd believe Daddy, anyway?"

"So it actually is win-win, this time around," Mom says. "You get to keep blackmailing Excellerand. We get to escape with new identities. And Becca—I mean, Sarah—gets to apply for college."

I keep my eyes down, so Mr. Trumbull doesn't see any emotion in my eyes about abandoning my Deskins friends. I reach across the table and pull out one of the smaller papers from the envelope in front of Mom. It's a bank check, a special kind that Mr. Trumbull couldn't double-cross us by canceling.

Special or not, I've never seen any kind of check with so many digits after the dollar sign, before the decimal.

"And I get everything I need to pay for college, all the way through a PhD, if I want," I say. I make myself grin. "Or just a lot of really good spring breaks."

"And you two moralists don't feel any guilt about engaging in blackmail yourselves?" Mr. Trumbull asks.

"Of course not," I make myself say. "I've learned a lot from you *and* Daddy. This is how the world works. We're just getting what we deserve."

Mom holds out her hand to me, and I give her the check. She tucks it back into the manila envelope along with all the paperwork "proving" our new identities: two new birth certificates, two new social security cards, an entirely fictional high school transcript, and a copy of SAT scores that are even better than the ones I really got. (Hey, if you're going to cheat, why not go whole hog?)

Mom puts the envelope in a messenger bag she's been carrying and pulls out a thinner envelope to hand to Mr. Trumbull. I know there are twenty letters in there, which I've watched her write out by hand over the course of the past week. The last one in the pile tells Daddy she's never going to communicate with him again.

Mr. Trumbull tucks this envelope into his briefcase without opening it.

"You're not even going to make sure I did what you wanted?" Mom asks.

Mr. Trumbull shrugs.

"This is only insurance," he says. He grins wickedly. "I've gotten Excellerand to trust me over the past three years. They're not looking that carefully anymore. But, if need be, I can always forge your handwriting. I've done it before. Even *Roger* was fooled."

I hate this man. For a moment I can't even see straight.

"Wh-what if . . . ," I sputter. "What if someday we decide to tell? What's to stop us?"

Mr. Trumbull keeps grinning.

"Oh, I've got insurance against that too," he says. He begins fiddling with his tie clasp. "Amazing, isn't it, how technology can make cameras that fit into such a thin strip of metal? And that it's so easy to edit raw video? So *I* don't look guilty? Believe me, I'll keep this video of you two confessing to blackmail for a very, very long time."

I've been so engrossed in watching Mr. Trumbull that I haven't been paying attention to any of the other people around us. But I suddenly realize that the two yoga moms from the side table are standing beside us now.

"FBI—you're under arrest," one of the women says. She flashes a gold badge in a leather case. Even from across the table I can read the words "Federal Bureau of Investigation."

A split second later the cinnamon-roll couple from behind Mr. Trumbull pull out FBI badges, too, and a pack of men in FBI jackets swarm in through the front and back doors shouting, "FBI! Don't make a move!"

We're surrounded.

Mom and I freeze. Mr. Trumbull looks startled for only an instant, then his face smooths out and he's as calm as ever.

"Oh, yes," he says loudly, with just as much confidence as he always showed in court. "I'm glad you're here. These two women are trying to blackmail me. All the evidence is right here."

He taps his tie clasp.

"Nice try," the woman says. "And we will be using that evidence. But *you're* the one we're arresting."

And then both women grab Mr. Trumbull.

Now—

relief

Beside me, Mom starts tugging at her bra. She digs down and pulls out a wire.

"Okay, if this is standard procedure for the FBI in sting operations, why haven't they come up with listening devices to put in women's bras that *don't itch*?" she asks.

"Good point, ma'am," one of the "yoga moms" says. "I totally agree. Allison and I will bring that up with our superiors."

The "yoga moms" are actually Special Agents Allison Moritz and Toni Bitters, members of the FBI team Mom and I started working with after Daddy told me to go talk to the federal prosecutor who'd sent him to prison. (This is where Oscar's computer skills really helped: He's the one who found the prosecutor's home address last Saturday. And my taping Mr. Trumbull in his office helped, too, to prove I wasn't lying. It's just a shame it wasn't enough evidence to arrest him.) The FBI team rehearsed and rehearsed and rehearsed with Mom and me, all week long, so we'd know exactly how to get Mr. Trumbull to reveal everything—or as I thought of it, to set him up, then bring him down.

Mr. Trumbull struggles against Allison and Toni's grip, even as other agents grab on to him too.

"You don't understand," he protests. "You have it backward! I was just making up a story to get these two criminals to confess! They're the ones you should arrest!"

"You have the right to remain silent," Allison says, rolling her eyes ever so slightly, as though she really wishes he would. She goes on with rest of the Miranda warning. Mr. Trumbull keeps struggling, but it's useless. I think it would be useless even if the only ones holding him were still just Allison and Toni—they really do work out. A lot. They're stronger than they look.

So are Mom and I.

Behind Mr. Trumbull and the FBI agents, I see a Panera worker coming from behind the counter. He's pulled out his iPhone and appears to be videotaping the entire scene. I can imagine that video rolling on TV or going viral online.

I don't care. Mom's right—the listening device in my own bra is insanely itchy, so I pull mine out too. And then I look Mr. Trumbull in the eye and say what I've been longing to all along.

"One thing you said is true," I tell him. "This is a win-win. Only, it's really win-win-win. You go to prison like you deserve. Since Daddy had the idea for this sting operation, he gets to make up for some of the awful things he did. And Mom and me—we get to live the rest of our lives the way we want to, from here on out. We don't have to be afraid ever again. And . . . I get to go to college."

I could actually go on listing wins—this moment seems full of them. I *am* still a little afraid of that iPhone videotaping behind me, but unlike three years ago, I can just ignore it. Because this time Mom and I are going to be known for something we actually did ourselves.

And—it was good.

Mom and I throw our arms around each other and hug and

hug and hug. I knock Mom's scarf back a little, revealing a strand of dark blond hair. The two of us have mostly been on lockdown all week, hiding out in a hotel room in a remote location. But I sneaked out last night to pick up a box of Clairol Nice 'n Easy for Mom. We're both going to see Daddy before we head back to Ohio. I have no idea what's going to happen with my parents' marriage—I have no idea what *should* happen—but I don't think Mom should look like she's aged a hundred years the first time she sees him in prison. Mom pulls the scarf off entirely and grins at me. I don't think the hair color actually matters—I think it's just that she's so relieved and happy at the moment—but here's something else that Mr. Trumbull was wrong about.

Mom is still absolutely beautiful.

I have to admit: I was wrong about her too.

"Do you think it's okay now?" I ask.

Mom nods, and I pull out the iPhone that Mrs. Collins generously let me keep for an extra week. I'm probably going to be "poor but honest" for the rest of my life, and I'm okay with that. But I am never living without a cell phone again.

I begin a text to Oscar, Rosa, Jala, and Stuart:

It's over, I write. **Everything went perfectly.**

There's a huge party when I get back to Deskins. Okay, it was previously scheduled, and it's for all of DHS, not just me. But no other school event could be so well-named: It's homecoming.

I never had time to buy a dress for the dance. And because Mom and I didn't keep that bank check from Mr. Trumbull, it's not like I could easily afford one, regardless. But Rosa assures me that her older sister, Lily, has a closetful of possibilities she's willing to loan me. Lily doesn't just have dresses from her high school dances—she also has several more sophisticated (or, depending on your perspective, sluttier) ones she bought for

clubbing now that she's at Columbus State. So I head over to
Rosa's as soon as Mom and I arrive back in Deskins Saturday
afternoon. I end up in the tiny bedroom that Rosa and her sister share, and Jala and Rosa and Lily work together to pull out
dresses for me to try on.

It's a little overwhelming: The room is so small, and there are
so many dresses, and Lily talks every bit as fast as Rosa. And the
two sisters have so many posters on the walls showcasing their
differing interests in hot actors and famous lawyers—Mario
Lopez faces off against Alan Dershowitz; Ryan Gosling faces off
against Sonia Sotomayor . . .

Then I realize that's not what's overwhelming me.

*This is the first time I've been over to a friend's house since the
day Daddy was arrested,* I think. *Since Annemarie Fenn's.*

Do I deserve this kind of thing again? Am I worthy now?

It wasn't that I was unworthy before, I remind myself. *I was
just scared.*

Jala tosses a dress at me and it lands on my head. She jokes,
"Really, there's not enough material in that dress to be a scarf."
All four of us laugh.

I do deserve this. I think. *I deserved it all along.*

I end up choosing the dress that fits the best, even though it's
fire-engine red and covered in ruffles. After three years of picking clothes based on not wanting to be noticed, this is about as
far as I could go in the opposite direction.

I look at myself in the mirror and think, *A defense attorney
would definitely* not *want a girl wearing this to court. And there's
no way I would be allowed to visit my daddy in this outfit.*

But I'm not going to court or visiting prison tonight. I'm not
just the daughter of a criminal. Those aren't the only things that
define me.

"Oscar is going to love that on you," Rosa says, grinning in a way that makes fun of her sister's taste and gives me an out if I want to refuse this dress.

Even if Daddy weren't a criminal, even if he hadn't been caught, this dress never would have been my style. I start to think, *It's awful being too poor to even buy my own dress for home-coming.* But that's instantly swept away by another thought: *I'm so lucky someone cares enough to loan me a dress.*

It strikes me that those two thoughts are about a lot more than dresses. Whether I feel pathetic and despairing or lucky and blessed—it's all up to me.

"Ignore my sister, who has no fashion sense," Lily says. It's funny how much she sounds like Rosa, even as she's making fun of her. They look alike, too, except that Lily clearly spends a lot more time on her hair and clothes. "How do *you* feel about it?"

I realize that I've never once worn a dress in my past three years in Deskins. I've never had a reason to.

"I feel . . . ," I begin. "I feel like a little girl sitting in church in a frilly dress, thinking about how much God and everybody else loves her."

"Oh, no!" Lily cries in dismay. "It's not sexy enough? We can fix that!"

She tugs the top part of the dress downward. I pull it back up.

"No, no," I say. "I mean, it's good."

There's so much else I could say, about deeper topics than dresses, but Rosa is the one who's distracted now.

"Can you believe this?" she says. She's bent over the laptop open on her desk. "Stuart's supposed to pick me up for home-coming in just an hour, and—"

"What?" I say in astonishment. "You didn't tell me you were going too!"

"Yeah, yeah," Rosa said, shrugging. "I just thought you should get the first pick of the dresses, after the week you've had. After what you've been living with the past three years."

She really is a great friend. But she's not going to manage to distract me.

"Hold on," I say. "You—and Stuart—and . . ."

Rosa rolls her eyes.

"We're going as *friends,*" she says. "Just for fun. Like you and Oscar, right? I won't have time to think about romance until I'm thirty. High school relationships—who needs the drama?"

"My sister is an idiot," Lily says. She glances hopefully at me, as if expecting me to force Rosa to reveal some deep, long-simmering desire for Stuart. Or maybe to declare that I, at least, am passionately in love, and my high school boyfriend is "4Ever."

I don't say anything. I'm not doing that to Rosa. Not in front of Lily and Jala, anyway. And I'm not sure what Oscar and I are, except that he's kind and I trust him. And that seems incredibly romantic to me after three years of trusting no one.

Oscar and I are . . . a possibility, I think. *One of the many possibilities I didn't have before.*

"Anyway," Rosa says, pointing at the laptop in front of her. "When he *should* have been getting ready, Stuart just sent me another draft of his Common App essay. That boy is crazy!"

Jala sits down by the computer too, and watches Rosa open the essay.

"Whoa," Jala says. "He wrote this one about last week, and why he decided to stay in Atlanta with the rest of us instead of going on to Nashville like his parents expected."

I lean in to read the essay too.

"It's actually . . . humble," Rosa marvels. "Self-deprecating. Mature. This is *good.*"

Jala drapes her arm over my shoulder.

"When he gets in to Harvard, it really is going to be thanks to you," she says.

"Girls," Lily says strictly. "Worry about the fancy college plans another time. I've only got an hour left to do your hair and makeup. Put that computer away and let me get to work!"

Within the next hour Lily arranges my hair so it towers over the rest of my head. She also plasters way too much makeup onto my face, and then, at my request, removes about 99 percent of it. And then Oscar and Stuart arrive, and our friends Lakshmi and Clarice with their dates, and we all go to the park, where Mom and the other parents take pictures of our whole gang.

This is so high school, I tell myself, smiling broadly. *Daddy didn't steal it from me, after all.*

Oscar drives us to the dance, where I discover there's a big difference between middle school and high school dancing. Or maybe "dance" means something completely different in Georgia and Ohio.

It doesn't actually matter, because Oscar doesn't know how to dance either.

"Let's just make it up as we go along," I suggest.

I'm sure we look ridiculous, but who cares?

It's almost time to leave when Ms. Stela, who's one of the chaperones, comes up to me.

"There are reporters out front," she tells me. "I'm sorry— somehow they found out you were here. We wouldn't let them in. We had rules that everyone had to go out the front door, but . . . if you want, I can get the janitor to open a back door, and you and Oscar can sneak out that way."

I square my shoulders.

"No," I say. "They're not going to make me sneak around. I'm done with that. But, Oscar, *you* could go out ahead or behind me if you want. You shouldn't have to deal with this."

Oscar looks offended.

"What?" he says. "And miss my chance to let the whole world

see that I have the prettiest, best date at the whole dance?"

We walk out together.

There are indeed adults with microphones and TV cameras and recorders standing on the front sidewalk. They're talking to Shannon Daily, who's somehow managing to live down the shame of breaking her family tradition of always being voted homecoming queen.

"Oh, yes," Shannon's saying. "I met Becca at freshman orientation three years ago. I always thought there was something so sad about her, so I've always tried to be nice."

Try, you always ignored me, as long as you thought I wasn't any help to you, I think.

Then Shannon's friend Ashley Stevens shoves her way into the spotlight.

"Yeah, Becca and I were both finalists for a big scholarship," Ashley says. "It must have been hard for her, since the rest of us were *honest* about who we are and what we're really like."

Yeah, right, Ashley, I think.

"Are you going to tell everyone what liars those two are?" Oscar whispers in my ear.

"Not worth my time," I say.

And . . . maybe I feel a little sorry for them. I know what it's like to feel small and desperate and worthless. I know what it's like to think you can never show your true self.

Someone in the crowd of reporters recognizes me, and they surge in my direction, abandoning Shannon and Ashley. My eyes blur for a moment: In the glare of the cameras and facing the darkness beyond, it's hard for me to tell if there are just four or five of them or fifty.

Either way, I know anything I say could potentially be seen and heard by the entire world.

"Miss Jones! Becca! Over here!" the reporters are screaming.

And then they're all spitting questions at me at once: "How did you come to suspect your father's defense attorney?" "How did you and your mother set up the sting?" "How much did the FBI help?" "What do you think should happen to Burton Trumbull now?"

I lift my hand for silence.

"I can't comment on anything connected to the charges against Mr. Trumbull," I say. "That information would have to come from the FBI or the U.S. Attorney's office in Atlanta. I wouldn't want to say or do anything to hurt the case."

I have learned many things from my father's mistakes. And this is exactly what the FBI told us to say if anyone asked.

But the reporters aren't satisfied.

"How did you get through the stress of the past week?" they ask. "Were you this calm all along?" "How many people here in Deskins knew the truth about you and your mother?"

I glance at Oscar. There's actually a question in there that I want to answer.

"Look, my mom and I were in this together, so that helped," I say. "And I told four of my very closest friends about a week ago. I had a Catholic, a Muslim, and a Presbyterian all praying for me. I even had an agnostic praying for me, just in case!"

That makes the reporters laugh. For a moment it seems like that should satisfy them and I can just go on with my life.

No—that was too much to hope for.

"Are you very religious?" one of the reporters calls out. "Did that help carry you through the past three years?"

Yes . . . no . . . maybe? Maybe in ways I didn't even know?

"I don't know what I am," I say. "But I intend to find out."

Nobody seems to know what to make of that answer.

"Have you forgiven your father?" someone else asks.

There is silence now, because apparently everyone is curious about this. I can imagine my answer to this question traveling farther out into the world than anything else. I can picture the kids I knew back in Georgia seeing it online; I can imagine Mom watching it in our Deskins apartment; Daddy watching it in prison.

"Yes," I say softly, looking directly into the cameras. "I have forgiven my father."

Some idiot follows up with the question, "Does that mean you think everything your father did was okay?"

I glare at him.

"That's *not* what forgiving means," I say. I point back toward the DHS entrance. "Do you need to come back to school for some remedial vocabulary help? I know several English teachers who would love to help you be more precise with your words."

The rest of the reporters laugh at this.

They actually like me, I think. For the first time I can see how someone could enjoy this kind of attention.

But it's not something I plan to seek ever again.

"Where do you want to go to college?" someone asks.

Stuart would tell me this is the time to deliver the killer line: "Vanderbilt. I've dreamed my entire life of going to Vanderbilt." But I've never even been there. What if it's not actually a good place for me? What if it is just a bunch of rich Southern kids with their own polo ponies? All the reasons I had for wanting to go there seem to have disappeared. I don't need to go to Vanderbilt to prove anything to anyone.

"I don't know," I say honestly. "I'm still figuring that out. I know someone who really loved Kenyon. I have a friend who's at Ohio State, and if I went there, maybe we could room together someday."

I bet Jala would like OSU a lot better if she lived on campus, I think.

"Really," I add, "I'll probably be like most of my classmates and end up choosing based on where I can get the best scholar-ships and financial aid."

At least now I'll be able to apply for financial aid. Using my real name.

"Are you going to write your college essay about your father and Mr. Trumbull?" someone else asks.

Oscar squeezes my hand.

"Too complicated," I say. "That's too much to cover in five-hundred words, don't you think?"

Stuart could do it because he had such a small part of the whole story. But not me. Anyway, it's not what I want to get me into college. Though . . . I do actually see now why colleges would want kids who have faced serious problems.

Because, kids like me, we've learned how to survive, I think. *We already know that the world is not always going to treat us with kid gloves. And we can thrive in spite of that.*

Or—maybe even . . . because of it?

"What do you want to study?" another reporter asks.

"Maybe . . . ," I say. An idea occurs to me for the first time. "Maybe I could learn how to help other kids like me, who have a parent in prison."

"Like a social worker?" someone asks. "A counselor?"

Ms. Stela steps forward just then, and I forget that I ever con-sidered her a failure as a guidance counselor.

"Please, can't you just let Becca go?" she asks. "She's been so patient with you, but this *is* her homecoming. Let her enjoy herself."

"One last question," someone shouts. "What do you think the future will bring?"

That is a ridiculous question. Who knows? Three and a half years ago, the day my father was arrested, I had no idea what lay ahead. I'm actually glad I had no idea.

The funny thing is, I can kind of see how the future will take shape now.

Odds are, tomorrow I will see some coverage of this interview that will be utterly awful and cringe worthy—maybe some newspaper will use a stupid phrase like referring to Oscar as my "tall, silent, Asian date." Or they'll try to describe this crazy dress I'm wearing.

But it can't hurt me, whatever they write or show video of. I will still be myself, and Oscar will still be himself, and it won't matter how anyone else defines us.

And anyhow, I'll have too much else to worry about, with a week's worth of homework to catch up on and colleges to decide on and applications to fill out. And after that? I'm pretty sure Rosa will get the Whitney Court Scholarship—just in case it helps, I'm going to write the Court family a letter telling them I think she should win. I'm also going to thank the Court family for their part in making college possible for me, even without giving me a dime.

And I'll write Annemarie Fenn, too, and tell her how sorry I am about her mother dying. I'll offer to be her friend again. Maybe I'll get back in touch with some of my other old friends, too. There are a few others I probably wrote off too quickly, just because they didn't know how to handle my father's arrest any better than I did.

And my parents and I will keep working with the FBI. I'm not telling the reporters this because it's not for sure, but it looks like Daddy might be able to transfer to a prison that's closer than Atlanta, maybe even one that's just a couple hours from Deskins.

And based on the evidence Daddy had against Excellerand—combined with his helping Mom and me with evidence against Mr. Trumbull—it does look like Daddy could get out of prison before the full ten years.

"Don't expect him to be there for your high school graduation," the federal prosecutor told me. "But your college graduation? I think maybe that could be arranged."

Daddy just wants to make sure that nothing he does now would endanger Mom or me. The prosecutor assured us that, with a *real* investigation under Rule 35, that wouldn't happen.

And the real investigation will happen quickly.

Mom and I believed way too many of Mr. Trumbull's lies.

I'm taking too long, thinking about all this. Oscar steps up and answers the question for me.

"You really want to know the future?" he asks. All the reporters lean close. "In the future . . . a minute from now . . . Becca and I are going out for ice cream with our friends."

I was actually thinking about saying, "I'm going to have the best rest of a senior year anybody ever had at DHS, while also filling out college apps and scholarship apps and keeping my grades up." But Oscar's answer works as well.

None of the bad times in my past can be erased. They'll always be there: scars in my memories, shame buried deep. There'll always be someone new finding out about Daddy, and judging me because of him. I wish my father had always stayed on the straight and narrow. I wish I could have finished my eighth-grade year without a single jolt or evil surprise, right up through that sweet, innocent eighth-grade dance. But I can't bring myself to wish I'd never moved to Deskins. That would mean giving up Oscar and Rosa and my other friends; that would have left Jala to deal with bigoted Mr. Vickers all by herself freshman year; maybe it would have left Stuart to be a disgraced cheater this year. Three years ago all I could see were the bad things piling up around me. Now I can see how good things and kindnesses piled up and multiplied even more: Mom wanting to keep me safe; Jala coming to find me at the drinking fountain; Stuart challenging me to get good grades; Oscar always taking my side; the Courts building on their daughter's problems to help other kids; all of old Deskins refusing to gossip about Whitney; Mrs. Collins loaning me her cell phone; Mr. Trumbull's receptionist giving me Daddy's letter; Gloria the prison guard letting me in to see Daddy; Rosa's sister loaning me this dress . . .

A lot of the people trying to do good things were misguided or made mistakes, so sometimes it was a little hard to see. But I made mistakes too: I was totally wrong about what I needed to protect me.

For a moment I am so overcome with happiness at being me, right in this moment, standing beside Oscar, holding his hand— even in front of all the cameras and reporters—that I want to rise up on my tiptoes and kiss him for the very first time.

But I know Oscar too well and I like him too much for that. There is no way I'm embarrassing him by forcing him into a first-kiss situation in front of the whole world. That will be something else to look forward to in the future.

Everyone is still watching, waiting for me to speak.

"Oh, ice cream?" I say, and I pretend to treat this like a profound question. "Now that would be a good start to exactly the kind of future I want."

ACKNOWLEDGMENTS

Several people were extremely helpful to me in planning and writing this book.

First, I am grateful to kids I met at the Central Ohio Youth Center in Marysville, Ohio. I was invited to speak to them about one of my earlier books, *Among the Hidden,* and at the end of our conversation, they begged me to write about a topic that was very much on their minds: imprisonment.

I don't know that this is quite the book they were thinking of, but it is what I felt called to write.

I had a great deal of help in my efforts to make the legal information in this book as accurate as possible. I owe a huge debt of gratitude to Douglas W. Squires, a federal prosecutor and adjunct professor of law at the Ohio State University Moritz School of Law. When I was plotting the book, he gave me lots of advice about what would and would not be plausible, and several times when he told me an idea wouldn't work, he offered very useful alternate suggestions. He also volunteered to read the book when it was finished, and caught some legal inaccuracies that I didn't even know enough to ask about. (Of course, as with any of my books, any mistakes that might remain are entirely my fault, not anyone else's.)

My friend Jodi Andes, who has worked as a newspaper reporter and an analyst and investigator with the Ohio Attorney General's office, gave me good advice about resources to turn to and told me stories that made me even more interested in writing about a criminal and his family. Jonathan Blanton, who is principal attorney in the Economic Crimes Division of the Ohio Attorney General's office, gave me information about how criminals carry out and get caught doing various scams, including the "grandparent scams" Becca's father perpetrates in this book. Craig Gillen, an attorney in the Atlanta area, was kind enough to give me detailed descriptions of the federal courtrooms in Atlanta and the visiting procedure and visiting room at the Atlanta Penitentiary.

For other aspects of the book, my husband, Doug Haddix, provided information about in-depth computer searches. And for help with the most obscure question I had for this book, I have to thank Lyle Lankford, senior officer in University History and Protocol at the public affairs office at Vanderbilt University. He was able to give me names of Vanderbilt dormitories that a freshman male could have lived in twenty-five to thirty years ago, that are still in use today.

I should probably thank my kids, Meredith and Connor, for giving me experience with the college search over the course of three years straight (since my daughter began looking seriously during her junior year of high school). Appropriately enough, I went on a campus visit with my son the day before I wrote about Becca and her friends visiting Emory. My daughter also served as an early reader of the book and did some research for it for me. My friends Linda Gerber, Erin MacLellan, Jenny Patton, Nancy Roe Pimm, Amjed Qamar, and Linda Stanek also read early versions of certain sections and had helpful advice.

And, as always, I am grateful to my agent, Tracey Adams, and to my editor, David Gale, and everyone else at Simon & Schuster for their help.